CUSTOM BAKED MURDER

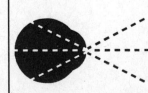

A PAWSITIVELY ORGANIC MYSTERY

CUSTOM BAKED MURDER

LIZ MUGAVERO

THORNDIKE PRESS
A part of Gale, Cengage Learning

GALE
CENGAGE Learning·

Farmington Hills, Mich • San Francisco • New York • Waterville, Maine
Meriden, Conn • Mason, Ohio • Chicago

GALE
CENGAGE Learning®

LIBRARY OF CONGRESS CATALOGING-IN-PUBLICATION DATA

Names: Mugavero, Liz, author.
Title: Custom baked murder / by Liz Mugavero.
Description: Large print edition. | Waterville, Maine : Thorndike Press, 2017. |
    Series: A pawsitively organic mystery | Series: Thorndike Press large print clean
    reads
Identifiers: LCCN 2017003997| ISBN 9781410499851 (hardcover) | ISBN 1410499855
    (hardcover)
Subjects: LCSH: Large type books. | GSAFD: Mystery fiction.
Classification: LCC PS3613.U3773 C87 2017 | DDC 813/.6—dc23
LC record available at https://lccn.loc.gov/2017003997

Published in 2017 by arrangement with Kensington Books, an imprint
of Kensington Publishing Corp.

Printed in the United States of America
1 2 3 4 5 6 7 21 20 19 18 17

In memory of Michael Lourie,
our favorite chef, always.

CHAPTER 1

Stan Connor peered anxiously through her oven window, watching her first peanut butter and pumpkin Pup-Pie bake, hoping it hadn't fallen flat, and breathed a sigh of relief. So far, so good. It actually looked good enough for a person to eat — which technically, it was. That was part of her dog and cat food's appeal. The ingredients were all human-grade, organic and as local as possible. The dogs and cats could taste the difference, and their humans felt good about the menu. A win-win.

"What do you think, guys?" she asked the four dogs sitting at attention in a perfect semicircle, eyes glued to her. They could clearly smell the golden pumpkin aroma floating through the house. Stan understood. She drooled for pumpkin herself.

Scruffy's stubby schnoodle tail vibrated with excitement, the only part of her moving. Stan's first rescue dog behaved perfectly when it came to food. Usually. Unless she came across something tempting with no one around to catch her. Henry, her brown and white pit bull, never made a big fuss about anything, but he'd be the first to inhale the entire pie if given the chance. The other two dogs, Duncan the Weimaraner and Gaston the Australian cattle dog mix, technically belonged to her boyfriend, Jake McGee — and by extension, her, even before Jake moved in. Duncan, the least patient of the four-legged crew, danced in place, exercising a great deal of control by not tackling her. Gaston, a new rescue still adjusting to his surroundings, hung back, taking a wait-and-see approach.

When food was in the oven, they could be counted on to strike these very poses. She and Brenna, her assistant and Jake's younger sister, called them "The Review Crew." Luckily, they were easy-to-please critics, but Stan knew enough not to sit back on her laurels and take their adoration for granted. Even though her treats and pet pastries had over a year of good reputation, appearance would be everything when the doors to her Pawsitively Organic Pet Patisserie and Café opened in December, less than three short months away. She'd chosen the date to coincide with the town Christmas tree lighting, planning to take full advantage of the already-festive mood that would have surely overcome the Frog Ledge townspeople by then.

Her doggie customers would be ecstatic over anything in her cases, but their parents wanted to buy pretty things for their precious pets. She had time to perfect her new recipes, but the sooner she nailed the winning grand-opening combinations, the better.

And she was perfectly content to spend her time until opening day locked in her cozy yellow kitchen, jazz music playing and delightful smells emanating from the oven. And since she'd just gotten a big client — a new pet supply store down by the shore that wanted freshly baked doggie goods twice a week — she had even more reason to be in the kitchen. Alas, real life would inevitably intrude. She could sense her happy creating time coming to an end even now, as footsteps approached.

"Babe?" Jake appeared in the kitchen doorway, eyebrows raised. "You wearing that tonight?"

Stan glanced down at her ratty T-shirt from a 5K she'd run three years ago and yoga shorts that had seen better days. Her long blond hair fell out of its loose ponytail, and she felt the dusty coating of flour on her face where she'd likely scratched an itch with coated hands. She had a sudden, giddy urge to take Jake's comment to heart and go to the party in this outfit, just to see her mother's reaction.

By contrast, Jake already wore his suit. Or as close to a suit as he'd be caught dead in — black dress pants, a white button-down shirt, purple tie shot through with silver threads, and a leather jacket he'd slung over his shoulder. He looked like he was heading out for a photo shoot in *GQ*. The combination fit his rugged good looks and slightly rebellious dark blond, shoulder-length hair to a tee. Then again, most outfits suited him. He was just that sexy.

She felt a happy warmth spreading through her belly simply seeing him standing there, in "their" house. Jake had moved in a few weeks ago, and already the cozy Victorian overlooking the Frog Ledge town green felt even more like home.

"I may," she said, answering his question. "You think my mother would approve?" She giggled, imagining the reaction. Patricia wouldn't wear an outfit like this to clean the house — not that she ever did *that* — never mind to a hoity-toity engagement party.

"Kristan," she would say in that haughty tone she'd perfected probably before she could walk. "*Whatever* are you thinking? Moving to this tiny town has affected you terribly."

It wouldn't be a particularly good argument, since Patricia lived here most of the time too with her beau, the mayor, Tony Falco. Hence the reason for the fancy party tonight. Patricia and Tony wanted the entire town — or the most influential people, anyway — to be part of their big engagement celebration. Which meant Stan had to show up and smile, or hear about it forevermore.

"You always look gorgeous to me, you know that. Which works out to your advantage, because" — Jake glanced at his watch — "you really don't have time to shower."

"Eh." She shrugged. "Too bad it's not a costume party. I could go as the gardener. My mother wouldn't even notice me. Wait, yes she would," she corrected herself. "She'd expect the gardener to wear pantyhose." She let out a loud, long-suffering sigh. "I wish I could call in sick."

"Good luck with that," Jake said dryly.

"When did you get back from the pub? I didn't even hear you come in."

Jake owned McSwigg's, Frog Ledge's

legendary Irish pub. Saturdays were the busiest night of the week and since he wouldn't be working, he'd gone over to help his staff set up.

"About an hour ago. The mixer was going, so I didn't want to disturb you." He kissed her, then ran a finger down her nose. "You have flour on your nose."

She scrubbed at it self-consciously. "I know. So much for the dogs warning me about someone coming in," she said. "I should stop letting them taste test if they're going to ignore the fact that another human walked through the front door and spent an hour here without me knowing."

"Then there'd definitely be mutiny. So are you going to get ready? Want me to let your mother know we'll be a few minutes late?"

Stan wrinkled her nose. "I wouldn't bother. We'll get there when we get there." She hesitated. "Unless there's some emergency that would keep us from going?"

"Nice try," he said. "You know you'll never get away with it."

"Tell me about it," she grumbled. "When did I become such an introvert? All I want to do is stay home and snuggle with you and the dogs and cats."

He pretended to consider this. "I don't think you're an introvert. I think I'm irresistible."

"You may be right." She groaned. "I guess I'd better get going."

Jake slipped his arms around her, hugging her tight. "It'll be fine," he said. "We'll go for a few hours, then slip out. No problem. The worst that can happen is that we're bored to death, right?"

She hugged him back, resting her head against his chest. "You never know, with my mother," she said. "But you're right. I have to change my attitude. This will be fun." She stepped back and squared her shoulders, readying for battle. "We'll have a fabulous time."

"Practice that in the shower," Jake advised. "Stop gritting your teeth and try it with a smile."

"Ugh. Going now." She tried not to think about how she'd rather poke herself in the eye with a fork.

"I'm going to let the dogs out before we leave," he said. "Come on, guys." He headed for the back door. All the dogs immediately followed except Henry, who stayed sitting in front of the oven, eyes still glued to the treat inside.

"Oh, shoot! My pie." Stan raced to the oven and yanked it out, cursing as she inspected the edges. "I burned it." She set it on the counter, out of reach of the dogs.

Jake came back and peered over her shoulder. "Where?"

"Right there." She pointed to the tiniest bit of dark brown around the outside of the pie.

"You're a perfectionist. Bet you the dogs would eat that in one gulp."

"Yeah, but that's not the point."

"I know, I know. Go." He pointed to the stairs. "Come on, Henry."

Henry sent Stan one last, pitiful glance.

She smiled. "You can have some after it cools, Henry."

She swore he sighed, but he got up and lumbered to the back door behind the others. Such a gentle soul, the antithesis of what pit bull haters would have you believe. Stan had rescued him from the local shelter after he saved her life last year during a sticky situation after she moved to town.

She watched them all troop outside, then poured herself some iced tea. Her two cats, Nutty and Benedict, sauntered in, having waited for the dogs to exit. Nutty, her Maine coon, leaped gracefully onto the counter, his regal tail pluming like a peacock's. He went over to sniff the pie. Benedict, a round orange guy, did not attempt to make the jump. Instead, he sat beneath Nutty and mewed plaintively.

"I know, you're starving. You guys are always starving." She opened their cat cookie jar and took out two fresh blueberry bites. Breaking them into pieces, she left the cats to their treats and started upstairs to make herself presentable. She'd made it up two steps before the doorbell rang.

Grumbling, she retraced her steps to the front door and pulled it open. Her eyes widened in surprise.

"Caitlyn?"

CHAPTER 2

Her younger sister smiled — nervously, Stan thought — and tucked her perfectly high-lighted blond hair behind her ear. Caitlyn looked stunning in a short gold minidress with matching five-inch heels. "Hey, Krissie. I'm here for the party."

Stan ignored the nickname she hated — her mother and sister both refused to call her by her preferred nickname — as her gaze strayed to the little girl standing next to her sister. Caitlin's six-year-old daughter, Evangeline. Stan hadn't seen her in more than a year. She looked adorable in her party dress, a miniature version of her mother's, and a tiny tiara in her ebony hair. But even more noticeable were the two suitcases on the porch, one adult-sized, one child.

Eva waved at her. "Hi Auntie Krissie!"

Stan knelt and opened her arms to her niece. "Hi sweetie! Look at you all dressed up. You look gorgeous."

Beaming, Eva allowed Stan to hug and kiss her.

Greetings complete, Stan stood and faced her sister, forcing a smile to her lips. She was sure she wasn't able to mask the question in her eyes. "Come in," she said. "I don't want the cats to get out."

Evangeline looked at her mother and burst into a grin from ear to ear. "I love cats!"

"Yes, Eva. I know you love cats." Caitlyn nudged her daughter inside and grabbed the suitcases, which she dropped just inside the door. "I knew she'd love this," she said to Stan. Then she did a double take. "Aren't you going to the party? Tell me you're not going like that."

Stan touched her messy hair self-consciously. "I was on my way to the shower. I've been baking. Testing new recipes for the shop."

"Shop? The pet bakery?" Caitlyn propped her sunglasses on top of her head. "You still doing that? I thought you kicked that slimeball Sheldon Allyn to the curb."

"I did." Stan and her sister reconnected over the summer when she'd gone to a chefs' retreat in Newport with the famous Allyn, who'd been intent on investing in her pet patisserie. Unfortunately, that partner-

17

ship faced some challenges and ultimately didn't work out. "Jake's investing. And Mom. Didn't you know?"

"Mom?" Caitlyn's mouth dropped open, then she hurriedly closed it. "Oh, yeah, I did know. I just forgot."

Stan raised an eyebrow but let it go. "So what's with the suitcases? You staying with Mom overnight?"

"Actually, I hoped Eva and I could stay with you for a while." Caitlyn met her sister's eyes, unflinching. "Things have been unbearable at home, with all the divorce nonsense. Michael is really being a jerk and milking this for all it's worth. I don't get a moment's peace, and he refuses to leave until all the legal stuff is worked out." She waved a hand in the air dismissively, as if she could blink all her troubles — and her soon-to-be-ex-husband — away as easily as Samantha on the TV show *Bewitched.*

Well, you got caught cheating, Stan thought, but kept her mouth shut and focused on the really disturbing part of that statement. The part where Caitlyn wanted to stay with her. "You . . . you want to stay here? With me?"

"Why not?" Caitlyn shrugged. "It's actually kind of cute here. The town, I mean. I wasn't sure what to expect. I was prepared for cows and, you know, smelly stuff." She wrinkled her nose. "But I didn't smell a thing. And your house is adorable." She looked around, nodding approvingly at the shiny hardwood floors, the lavender walls in the foyer, the staircase leading upstairs accented by beach scenes on the wall. "Homey."

Stan looked around, trying to see through her sister's eyes. She thought her home was simple but happy. Much like her life had become over the past year. Caitlyn's tastes were more aligned with their mother's. Which meant big and fancy. Between family money and her almost-ex's successful banking career, Caitlyn had more money than she'd ever be able to spend, although she certainly gave it her best effort.

By contrast, Stan took credit for her own comfortable lifestyle, bypassing her trust fund and forging her own path instead. Her former corporate job paid her well, and she'd made excellent investment choices over the years. When she'd been liberated from her job last year, she was in a position to take her time figuring out what was next. That exercise led her here, to her mint-green Victorian house in this small farming town. Which would definitely not be Caitlyn's cup of tea.

She cast around for a good way to say that without sounding like she wanted her sister to leave. "There are cows down the street," she hastened to point out. "A whole dairy farm. When the wind blows . . ." She shook her head.

"Cows!" Eva screeched and clapped her hands.

"Plus I thought we could, you know, bond." Caitlyn folded her arms and narrowed her eyes. "Are you saying you don't want us here?"

"No, of course not," Stan rushed to assure her. "I mean, of course I do. I'm just . . . surprised. What about school?" She nodded at Eva.

"I let them know she'd be out for a week. After that, her father and the nanny can bring her to school during the week, then she can come back on weekends. We both needed a vacation," Caitlyn added.

"Babe? You almost ready?" The back door slammed and doggie feet stampeded down the hall preceding Jake, who stopped short when he saw Stan still covered in flour, now entertaining guests. Scruffy and Duncan catapulted themselves at Caitlyn and Eva. Horrified, Caitlyn took a step back, shielding herself from whatever attack she expected. Eva gasped in delight. Henry and

Gaston hung back, observing, tails wagging in sync.

"Duncan! Down," Jake commanded.

A sheepish Duncan dropped to the floor in front of Caitlyn, tail still furiously waving back and forth. Scruffy, meanwhile, was in her glory, sitting still while Eva carefully petted her head and kissed her nose.

"Sorry," Jake said, eyes sliding to Stan, then back to Caitlyn. "I didn't know we had company."

"Jake McGee, my sister, Caitlyn, and my niece, Evangeline," Stan made the introductions. She watched her sister's eyes widen appreciatively at the sight of Jake, and wondered what he would think of all this. He didn't know much about her sister aside from Stan's stories, and the most recent one — her affair with a chef wanted for murder — didn't portray her in the best light.

"Hi." Jake stepped for ward and, in that perfect welcoming way he had, gave Caitlyn a hug. "We didn't get to meet in Rhode Island."

"So you're the perfect guy," Caitlyn said, but she hugged him back. "It's great to meet you. I've heard so much about you."

Jake's eyebrows shot up. "That's quite a description," he said to Stan. "I think you're misleading your sister."

"That's actually from our mother," Caitlyn said, as Jake knelt and offered his hand solemnly to Eva, who giggled and shook it. "I think she has a little crush on you."

Now Jake burst out laughing. Stan turned crimson.

"Caitlyn's, um, coming to the party," Stan said, hoping to change the subject.

"Great," Jake said.

"And she might stay for a few days."

To his credit, Jake's face didn't change. "Yeah?"

"Yeah." Stan blew out a breath. "I need to get in the shower."

As she raced up the stairs, she heard Caitlyn say, "So is there a spa in town? I need to get my nails done."

CHAPTER 3

An hour later the four of them drove up to Tony's house at the top of a long, winding, private road where only two other houses sat. The stately design oozed old Connecticut money, but it looked like it had been overhauled to achieve new-money glamour. Stretching far and wide across lush acres of grass, it looked big enough to fit Stan's entire house along with Jake's pub inside it. This was not the norm for Frog Ledge.

They got out of Stan's car and stood in front of Tony Falco's wraparound front porch, staring up at the grand, white house before them. Lights blazed from every window. Women wearing beautiful gowns and men in tuxes were visible though the open curtains. Dusk settled on this still-warm, late September night, that perfect time between light and dark when everything seemed a little magical. The scene in front of them could've been from a movie.

Stan had no idea how her mother did it. They were in a town where the average person existed in overalls, work boots, and flannel shirts, and the fanciest party to date was the annual library fundraiser. Yet somehow Patricia Connor created a setting that would rival any party in her elite Jamestown, Rhode Island, neighborhood.

"I didn't know he was rich," Caitlyn remarked.

Stan looked at Jake. "I didn't either." Truthfully, she'd never given Tony's house, or his finances, a second thought. She'd certainly never visited.

Jake shrugged. "This house has been here for decades. Belonged to the Trumbull family. Last time I saw it, it didn't look quite like this. I never put two and two together that Tony lived here, but now that I think about it I haven't seen old man Trumbull around in a long time. Guess he sold it."

"We going in?" Caitlyn asked. "You know we're already late."

"We're only an hour late. And that doesn't even mean we're *late,*" Stan reasoned. "These parties don't start and end on time."

"You don't need to convince me, sweetheart," Jake said, squeezing her hand as she pressed the doorbell. "If she asks me, I'll

24

tell her it was worth the wait. You look amazing."

Stan blushed, smoothing her simple black dress. Definitely not the glamour-girl look her sister had gone for, but presentable just the same. She hoped her mother wouldn't notice her still-wet hair. Behind them, Eva chattered incessantly to Caitlyn about how many kisses she'd gotten from the dogs and cats, and can she please just live at Auntie Krissie's house forever?

The door swung open, revealing a woman in a maid uniform complete with black tights, hair in a bun, and soft-soled shoes. Stan pressed her lips together, afraid she'd burst into nervous laughter. A maid. All she was missing was the feather duster from days of yore.

"Good evening," the woman said, holding the door wide. "Please come in."

"Are they kidding me?" she muttered to Jake before she followed the woman inside. "A maid?"

Jake's lips twitched. "The mayor's a very important man."

"I guess so." Stan paused in the foyer to look around as the woman took Jake's jacket. Before they even made it all the way inside, though, her mother swooped over, heels clicking on the marble tiles. She conferred briefly with the maid, then stepped over to them.

"Kristan. Caitlyn. Where have you been?" A smile hid the bite behind her words. "You're quite late!"

"Sorry, Mom," Stan said. "My fault. I was working on something for the shop. You want to get a good bang for your buck, don't you?" She offered a hopeful smile.

Her mother's flat stare could've withered the exotic-looking houseplants decorating the hall table. Once she could safely assume Stan got the message that she was not amused, Patricia turned to Jake and smiled a real smile. "Jake. How are you, dear? Thank you for coming." She air-kissed his cheeks.

Stan met her sister's eyes behind their mother's back. Caitlyn made a gagging motion. Stan bit back a laugh. As usual, Patricia looked like royalty, with her champagne-colored skirt and jacket combination — Dior? Givenchy? Stan couldn't tell — and elegant heels in the same hue. Her frosted blond hair framed her chin in a stylish bob. But her green eyes flamed with something more than her daughters' tardiness.

Patricia let go of Jake and turned to her granddaughter. "Evangeline! Come here,

26

darling." She opened her arms to the little girl, who approached her cautiously and let herself be kissed. Nothing like the big, sloppy hugs she'd given the dogs before they left Stan's house.

Once the greetings and scoldings were complete, Patricia adjusted her skirt, smoothed her hair, and waved them into the main party area. "Go get some food. Have a drink. There's a full bar and buffet tables in the great room" — she pointed behind them to the main, open area of the first floor — "the second dining room and farther down the hall. There's also a bar out on the patio. Please make sure you sign the guest book." She pointed to a podium discreetly positioned in the hallway with an elaborate gold book and matching pen. It reminded Stan of a wedding. Or a funeral.

She opened her mouth. Jake squeezed her hand, a warning. She closed it again. Patricia didn't notice. She grabbed one of the servers and lectured something about stuffed mushrooms and cold tomatoes.

"What? I was just going to ask where Tony was. It's weird that they aren't greeting people together, no?" Stan asked in a low voice as they walked away.

Jake shrugged. "Probably not the best time to ask. And I wouldn't have the first clue

27

about the correct protocol for something like this. The fanciest my family got was a corned beef and cabbage bash on St. Paddy's Day."

"Thank God. That's more my speed." Stan took a breath and slipped her arm through Jake's. They stepped into the party area.

Guests dressed in impeccable gowns and suits flitted around, holding flutes of glittery champagne. Caitlyn snagged one from a server gliding by. Classical music played softly in the background, perfect ambience to complement the tinkles of laughter and lilting conversational tones. It took Stan a moment to realize a real, live harpist stood in the corner of the living room working some musical magic.

This is so *not Frog Ledge. Leave it to my mother.*

Jake whistled softly under his breath. Despite herself, Stan started to laugh. "I know. It's ridiculous. Where'd she say the bar was? I need something a lot stronger than champagne."

"This way." Jake pointed to another room crowded with people. He was obviously the better listener.

"Stan! Jake! Helllooooo, my honey-bunches!" Char Mackey rushed through the

28

crowd, nearly upending an entire tray of champagne with her bulk, dragging her husband, Ray, behind her. She wore a sparkly red dress that clashed with her bright orange hair, and five-inch silver platform heels to help her tower over most people in the room. Stan's mood immediately improved. The New Orleanian in Char made sure everyone had fun at a party. Stan sent up a prayer of thanks that her mother and Char had become friends, even though how it happened remained a mystery.

Char engulfed her in a bone-crushing hug. Stan smelled her fruity perfume mixed with the hair spray inspiring her hair to its great heights. "Gotta work on that smile, baby girl," Char whispered loudly in her ear. "It's not that bad!" She let her go and gave the same welcome to Jake. "Don't y'all look gorgeous! Best-looking couple here. Don't you think, Raymond? Well, aside from the bride- and groom-to-be, of course. And us." She winked at Stan.

"Lovely," Ray declared after he'd offered his own hug. He'd abandoned his normal jeans and suspenders for a dapper pinstriped suit, no doubt chosen by Char.

"And who are these lovelies?" Char asked, turning to Caitlyn and Eva.

"My sister, Caitlyn, and my niece, Eva,"

Stan said. "This is Char and Ray. They own the bed-and-breakfast with the alpacas. Eva would love to meet them," she added, but Caitlyn didn't catch the hint.

Caitlyn offered her hand, but Char hugged her, too. "No handshakes for Stan's family," Char declared. "We're so delighted to meet you. Aren't we, Raymond?"

Ray stepped forward. "Certainly are," he said, winking at Caitlyn before bending down and offering his hand to Eva. Eva shook it shyly. "You're the prettiest girl here," he said.

Eva looked down and scuffed her toe. "Thanks," she mumbled.

"And you're a close second, Trooper," Ray added, returning to a standing position and waving over Stan's shoulder.

Stan turned. Jessie Pasquale, Jake's other sister and the Frog Ledge Resident State Trooper First Class, stood behind them with her boyfriend, Marty Thompson. Jessie's simple, green sheath dress complemented her long red hair, which she'd left loose — something Frog Ledge residents rarely saw. More notable was the hint of blush and eye shadow she'd applied. Jessie rarely used makeup. Which worked for her, since she didn't need a stitch of it to look gorgeous.

But she looked absolutely out of her element without a gun at her hip. Marty, however, wore a grin the size of New York. Probably his first fancy party. He owned a local moving company, a job that didn't typically require appearances at such events. His dress pants and shirt could've come from the local Target, a sharp contrast to most of the men there, but he didn't seem to mind a whit.

Jessie smiled at Ray. "Thank you."

Marty slipped an arm around her waist and squeezed. "Best-looking cop in the state, isn't she?"

Jessie rolled her eyes.

"I agree with Ray. You clean up good, Jess," Jake said.

"See?" Marty said to her.

"Hush," she muttered. "The two of you make it sound like I don't shower before I go to work."

"We were just about to hit the bar," Jake said to his sister. "Want to join us? Although you look like you got a head start." He nodded at the drink in her hand.

Jessie bared her teeth. "It's ginger ale." Jessie didn't drink. Everyone in Frog Ledge knew that. As a cop, she swore the majority of problems started with alcohol. For a while it bothered her that her brother ran a pub, but Jake ran a classy establishment and she'd relaxed her views over time. "We'll walk out with you," she said with another skeptical look around the house.

"We can all surely have another drink or two," Ray assured Jake. "There's a backyard bar, and the big one's right through there." He pointed into the next room.

"Let's go outside. I already need some air," Stan said.

Char led the way, the rest of them trailing behind her like an entourage as she stopped to squeeze, hug and gush over every person they passed. Ray watched her with affection. "She's in her element," he said. "She'll be talking about this for years."

Stan laughed. "So you've seen Tony, then? Char said he and my mother looked lovely."

Ray frowned. He lowered his voice and leaned closer to Stan. "We haven't, actually. I said to Char that it seemed odd."

"He's not here?" Stan asked.

Ray put a finger to his lips. "Your mother mentioned to Char something about an earlier engagement. But I don't think she wants to call attention to it."

No wonder Patricia seemed so agitated, greeting people alone. Stan turned to whisper to Jake, but he and Marty were engaged in a lively discussion about some sporting event.

After what seemed to be a never-ending trek through the house, they finally stepped through a set of French doors onto the elegant deck encircling the entire house. The party spilled outside onto the lawn below. People stood around the in-ground pool, already covered for the season. As promised, a full bar beckoned from the patio. People stood chatting on the deck, and below more groups congregated around various tables. Stan saw former mayor Mona Galveston and her husband chatting with another couple. Betty Meany, minus her cranky husband, Bert, held court below in front of a group of Frog Ledgers as only the town librarian could.

"What're you having? Pomegranate or sour apple?" Jake asked. He knew her well enough to know a night like this would require martinis.

"Anything strong."

Jake grinned. "I'll be right back." He descended the deck stairs with Ray.

Stan glanced around. Char huddled a few feet away with a woman Stan didn't recognize. They'd lost Caitlyn and Eva, too. Jessie and Marty stood in the corner of the deck whispering to each other. Jessie's face softened in a rarely seen relaxed smile. Stan moved to an empty spot against the deck railing and took the opportunity to enjoy the moment of silence, soaking in the environment and mentally prepping herself for the night of meaningless conversation. Then she heard her name.

"Stan Connor! My Lord, is that really you?"

CHAPTER 4

That voice. Stan couldn't place it immediately, but something about it . . . She spun around, her mouth forming an impolite O of surprise when her eyes landed on the woman standing directly in front of her. Eleanor Chang. Her former colleague hadn't changed a bit since the last time Stan had seen her more than a year ago. What on earth was she doing at her mother's engagement party?

"Eleanor," she managed, trying to force some enthusiasm into her voice. "What a surprise! What brings you here?"

Eleanor's rail-thin frame screamed *salad, no dressing.* She looked ghostly in her expensive dress, an off-white, beaded affair. A filmy white scarf hung trendily over one shoulder. She'd smoothed her straight black hair into a low ponytail tossed over her other shoulder. A young woman with a trace of Eleanor in her nose and eyes stood beside her, also small-framed, but so thin she looked unwell. She wore an ill-fitting pink dress that threatened to swallow her up in its sea of ruffles. Her fingers clasped and unclasped themselves in front of her and her eyes darted around the room, reminding Stan of trapped shelter animals desperately imagining a way out of their cages.

"Tony, of course!" Eleanor laughed. "Don't tell me you didn't know."

"Know what?" A sinking feeling bloomed in the pit of Stan's stomach.

"I'm working for Tony. As part of my consulting business. I'm his executive coach." She smiled triumphantly. "I've branched out. Since I'm full-time now at Warner, I can be more choosy about the kinds of consulting I do, especially given my hours. Media relations can be a round-the-clock endeavor. Well, you know that." She chuckled, but her hawk eyes watched Stan for a reaction. "After all, you did that job."

And lost it. The unspoken words hung in the air between them. Eleanor insinuated she'd taken over Stan's old job. Stan expected it to feel like a sucker punch in the gut, but to her surprise, she felt nothing.

Which seemed to confuse Eleanor. Her gloating smile stumbled a bit when Stan failed to react, but she recovered quickly and continued. "So there's extra time to focus on my interest in politics. And Tony is a wonderful candidate to start with. Of course my work has always been, at its core, about coaching. As you well know."

Stan tried to find a rescuer out of the corner of her eye, but everyone she knew was otherwise occupied. So she applied the tactic that had gotten her through a decade in corporate America. She faked it, with a little help from her old coping mechanism. Theme songs. Billy Joel's "Big Shot" immediately jumped to mind as she readied herself for the verbal spar. Song lyrics soothed her, especially when they had special meaning.

"Executive coaching for political campaigns? Tell me more. Although Tony just won his election last year. I guess you're getting an early start?" Stan pasted on her best interested expression, but she was curious. Why was Tony already campaigning again for a small-town mayor gig three years away? Unless he really thought his brand was in need of an added boost.

"Well, just you wait." Eleanor leaned in, as if about to drop a huge secret. "I can't talk about it now, but you'll hear soon enough."

Oh, boy. This didn't sound good at all. Stan

managed to not cringe and kept her smile pasted on.

Eleanor straightened. "Anyway, I can't believe your mother didn't tell you. She sought me out over the winter through some of our mutual friends. Tony needed some assistance. She mentioned that you didn't have the time. Understandable, since that's also not your area of expertise." She patted Stan's arm. Stan fought the urge to recoil. "I hear you have a new business? Dog food, was it?" The words carried a typical Eleanor inflection: condescending amusement combined with false interest.

Stan bared her teeth and opened her mouth to respond when Jake appeared, handing her a pink martini. *Thank God.* "It's actually gourmet pet food," she said, letting go of any pretense of polite. "Fancy enough for the Food Channel." True story. Sheldon Allyn's botched summer retreat could've secured them a contract with the national network, if someone hadn't been murdered during their big pitch to investors.

The TV angle caught Eleanor's attention. Stan saw all the possibilities running across her face as she pondered the pros and cons of rekindling this relationship. "How interesting," she exclaimed. "I never would've guessed there was such a market. You'll have to tell me all about it." Her gaze shifted to Jake, who was silently listening to the exchange. Immediately forgetting about Stan, she turned on the charm. "Eleanor Chang," she said, offering a hand. "Stan and I are former colleagues."

"Is that right?" Jake shook Eleanor's hand. "Good to meet you."

"You as well." Eleanor's piercing black eyes scanned Jake's face. Then she seemed to remember the pathetic-looking girl standing next to her, desperately trying to disappear inside that ridiculous dress. "And this is my daughter Monica. I'm sorry, I neglected to make the introductions." She shoved the girl forward. Monica's foot slipped and she stumbled. Jake reached out a hand to steady her before she fell on her face. Red-faced, Monica fixed her gaze on the floor, missing the nasty look her mother sent her.

"Monica is learning the business," Eleanor said. "She loves politics and will make a fabulous coach once she's got some experience under her belt. She graduated from college this past spring. Magna cum laude from Princeton with a double major in politics and economics." She beamed, but Stan got the sense it was less a proud mother moment and more personal bragging. "Monica, Stan Connor and Jake . . ."

"McGee," Jake supplied.

"Nice to meet you," Monica said in a voice barely above a whisper. When she shook Stan's hand, her grip was limp and damp. Stan felt sorry for her. Her mother would eat her alive if she presented this way to clients.

"Eleanor! So lovely to see you." A man in a pinstriped suit with a pink pocket hankie appeared at Eleanor's elbow.

"Harold! You as well." Eleanor turned back to Stan and slipped a card into her hand. Stan hadn't even seen her pull it out of her evening bag. "In case you don't have my contact information any longer. Please be in touch. I'd love to understand more about your business. And perhaps even work together again!" With one last bright smile at both of them, she turned to Harold and promptly forgot all about them.

Stan steered Jake away. "Wow," Jake said once they were out of earshot. "And you think your mother's bad. That poor kid." He glanced at Stan. "You didn't look happy to see her."

"Was it that obvious? Darn." Stan sipped her martini. Nice and strong.

"Frenemy?" he asked with a small smile.

Stan gave up trying to be polite and made

a face. "She's horrid. And she's got my old job."

"How do you feel about that?" Jake asked.

Stan spread her arms wide. "I couldn't care less. It feels great."

Jake laughed. "I'm glad. So what's she doing here?"

"Apparently, my darling mother hired her to coach Tony after I turned down her oh-so-generous offer over the winter." Stan made a face. What was her mother thinking? And why hadn't she told her? She took a larger swig of her martini.

"Easy," Jake said. "Pace yourself."

"Easy for you to say." As much as she didn't care what Eleanor did, she didn't want to know about it. And she definitely didn't want her old life invading her new one. Seeing Eleanor here in Frog Ledge felt . . . wrong.

"Come on." Jake slid an arm around her waist. "Let's go find some food. You must be starving. Don't worry about her. After tonight you won't have to see her again. Let's just have a good time, okay? I see Izzy over there."

Stan let him lead her through the crowd. He was right. She didn't *own* Frog Ledge. It was a free country. A free town. Eleanor and anyone else could hang out here all they

41

wanted. But really, she wished Eleanor would find another small town to terrorize.

CHAPTER 5

Izzy Sweet stood near a baby grand piano in a silver-spattered dress, looking for all the world like a cocktail lounge singer about to slink on top of it and belt out a tune. The glittery outfit set off her caramel-colored skin and dark, intricately braided hair. Izzy took Frog Ledge by storm a few years ago when she dropped in on a whim with a vision of a gourmet chocolate and coffee shop, which soon became reality. Stan adored her, both for her personality and because she offered the best coffee, home-made pastries, and chocolates Stan'd ever had.

"Did you find the food yet?" Izzy muttered when they walked over. "I'm absolutely starving."

"We were heading that way," Jake said. "Alcohol first."

"Ha! I like the way you think." Izzy high-fived him.

Stan smiled at their easy banter. Jake and Izzy had a rocky history that culminated in an unlikely real-estate partnership earlier this year. They still didn't always see eye to eye, so it was nice to see them on good terms.

A waiter stopped, brandishing his tray to offer samples of bruschetta crowned with fresh mozzarella, slivers of tomato, and wisps of fresh basil on top. Izzy plucked two of them off the silver tray and inhaled them.

"Thank goodness. I was about to pass out. I worked all day at the bookstore and barely had five minutes to eat." Izzy's new bookstore, the product of the realestate partnership with Jake, was opening around the same time as Stan's shop. She looked curiously at Stan. "Did you just get here?"

"I did. Long story," Stan said.

A look of panic crossed Izzy's face. She grabbed Stan's arm as they drifted back toward the great room. "Then you haven't . . . seen a lot of people?"

Stan looked at her strangely. "No. I was busy getting lectured by my mother. I saw Char, Ray, Jessie, and Marty. And this awful woman I used to work with. Why?"

Izzy opened her mouth to answer, but Char's bright orange hair appeared behind her. She waved frantically at Stan.

"Stan! There you are. I've been meaning to introduce you to someone." Beaming, Char reached behind her ample body and pulled a red-faced woman into view. She looked somewhere in her mid-fifties, although Stan's ability to judge ages was poor. Her black hair was shot through with gray and hung in loose curls framing her face. She wore an apologetic smile. Her simple black dress looked well worn, likely to less fancy events.

"I'll catch you in a few," Izzy said. "Meet us over there." She grabbed Jake's arm and steered him away.

Stan watched them go, wondering why her friend was acting so oddly, but turned her attention back to Char when Char loudly cleared her throat. "Sorry."

"This is Francie Tucker," Char announced. "I believe you met at the fundraising dinner for the theater over the summer?"

"Yes, of course," Stan said, mortified that she didn't remember. Her name sounded familiar, though.

Francie shook her hand enthusiastically. "I'm so happy to meet you. My dog loves your treats. I buy him some every week from the general store when I do my shopping.

45

He knows the routine now and waits for them."

"Oh, I love that." Stan beamed. "Thank you so much. What's your dog's name?"

"Cooper. He's a golden."

"Francie does personal training, too," Char said. "It's exercise with mindfulness and meditation built in. She's been helping me get in shape." She picked up her skirt and did a slow twirl to show off her figure, which didn't look any different to Stan than it had a few months ago. She doubted that was Francie's fault, knowing Char's loyal and long-term relationship with Southern food.

"That's wonderful," Stan said. "Maybe you can help me, too."

"I'm so glad you said that, honey!" Char beamed. "That's the point. I think you two can help each other! You remember what we talked about with your mother a few weeks ago. About getting your new staff squared away early?"

Stan had a vague recollection of her mother yammering on about how she needed to hire people and have them in place before the café opened. "Yes," she said.

"Well, here you go." Char pointed at Francie. "Your new employee."

Francie's face turned an even brighter shade of red and she poked Char. "You're so blunt!"

"Hey. You have to ask for what you want. Otherwise things happen slower than molasses running uphill in the winter. Well, Stan? You're hiring, right? You'll need all kinds of help when you open. And Jake just told me about your new client. Congratulations!"

"Thank you," Stan said, thinking fast. Brenna worked full-time for her now, and they had an efficient baking routine down. But she'd need to staff the store once it opened, and keeping her pastry cases full would take a lot of extra baking. Getting people in place early would definitely not hurt. "And yes. I need to figure out my plan, but I do need help."

"Problem solved. Francie is perfect. She can bake, man the counter, play with the dogs, whatever you need. Right, Francie?"

Francie nodded. "Right."

"I'm flattered," Stan said. "And grateful. I'm not opening until December, though."

Francie looked at Char, who nodded encouragingly. "I know," Francie said. "But I can help before then, too. With recipes, or setting up the shop, or baking things in advance. I'm just looking for a couple of days a week. Like Char said, I have my

47

personal training business and I still work as the receptionist at the Unitarian Church. I'm looking to further supplement my income, though."

"That's right!" Stan snapped her fingers as she realized why she recognized the name. "The church. You're helping with my mother's wedding. She's spoken very highly of you." Which was weird. Patricia usually found something to complain about.

"I am." Francie smiled. "She needed a little extra nudge before she felt ours was the right church, but she's happy now. She's lovely."

Stan didn't know if *that* were true, but she let it go. "Let's talk Monday, okay? Give me a call. Or stop by my house. I live —"

"Across the green," Francie finished. "Yes, I know. Your mother pointed it out to me. I always loved that house. And you've made it so inviting."

"Thank you," Stan said. "Yes, do come by. We'll talk."

Francie clasped her hand. "Thank you so much."

Char winked and led her away. Stan heard her say, "See now? She wasn't that scary!"

Chuckling, Stan waved at Izzy and Jake, beckoning them over. They still needed to find food. As they approached, Izzy almost bumped into a woman with a head of big, blond, bouncy curls. As she touched the woman's shoulder in apology, Stan noticed the curls looked familiar . . . but it couldn't be. Could it?

As the blond turned to acknowledge Izzy, Stan saw her in profile. That pit she'd felt in her stomach when she saw Eleanor deepened as she recognized another former colleague, Michelle Mansfield. The last time she'd seen Michelle she'd been with Stan's ex, Richard Ruse, before they were ex. What was this, a Warner Financial reunion disguised as an engagement party? If so, she wished her invitation had gotten lost in the mail.

Eleanor's presence was one thing, but how did Michelle know Tony? And if Michelle was here, did that mean . . .

"Stan?"

So perfect it could've been scripted. Stan cringed. She turned in slow motion and came face to face with her ex.

Richard Ruse looked mostly the same: preppy sweep of thick, wavy, brown hair grazing his baby blue eyes; that charming dimple; the anal-retentive crease in his pants and spit-shined shoes. She'd always thought Richard was handsome. Charming, too. Typical salesman, with a gift for easy camaraderie and a golden tongue. What she hadn't realized for most of the years they were together was his lack of substance. He was still handsome, but . . . different. He looked tired. Thinner. More edgy.

She regarded him coolly. "Richard," she said. "This is a surprise." She felt Jake's eyes on her as he approached, watching the scene with interest. He'd met Richard once, right after Stan moved to Frog Ledge when they went to McSwigg's for a drink. Brenna spilled a drink on Richard. Accidentally, of course.

Richard shrugged, his eyes cutting left before returning to Stan's. "Eleanor and your mother must've coordinated invites." He stepped closer. She could smell alcohol on his breath. "S'good to see you, though. How you doing? You look great." He looked her up and down.

Surprised, she took a step back. Richard didn't typically act so crass. Maybe he'd been drinking to get through the night, too. "I'm fine. I have to go. Enjoy your evening." She spun on her heel to walk away, but Richard grabbed her arm.

"Wait, Stan."

Jake grabbed Richard's arm so fast, Stan didn't even see it happen.

CHAPTER 6

Jake removed Richard's hand from her arm, holding it in the air between them. "Don't," he said, his voice low and pleasant, but Stan heard anger lurking underneath.

Michelle, who'd watched the whole scene, glided over. "What's going on?" she asked, a puzzled smile on her face as she looked from Jake to Stan to Richard. "Hi there, Stan."

Richard's jaw twitched with unspoken words as he regarded his opponent, completely ignoring Michelle. Eyes flashing, he opened his mouth to respond, then closed it again and snatched his arm away.

Michelle reached for him. "Richard?"

"Forget it," he snapped, pulling away from her, too. He melted away into the crowd, heading straight for the front door, shoving past a small crowd to get out. Stan watched the maid catch the door before it slammed.

Michelle watched him go, chewing on her

lower lip. She clearly wasn't going after him. When she turned back to Stan, her smile was gone. "What happened?"

"Just giving him advice to keep his hands to himself," Jake said.

Michelle sized him up. Her allegiance to Richard seemed to falter in the face of Jake's good looks, and she offered her hand. "I'm sorry, we haven't met. Michelle Mansfield. Stan and I used to work together," she added. "Before she was let go." She enunciated the words, wanting to make sure Jake heard them loud and clear.

"Jake McGee," he said, unenthusiastically shaking her hand.

Michelle offered her best big-hair toss. "It's lovely to meet you," she purred. "Who knew little towns like this had residents who looked like movie stars! And here we were feeling badly for Stan, losing her job and moving way out here."

Stan could see the glint in Jake's eye. "Believe me, you don't need to feel bad for Stan," he said. "She got the better end of the deal, in every aspect. Come on, babe."

He led her away, leaving Michelle standing there with her mouth open. They fell into step beside Izzy, who'd been watching from the wings. She grabbed Stan's hand. "I'm so sorry. I wanted to tell you when I realized you didn't know, but we got inter-rupted."

"No worries," Stan said. "It wouldn't have made much of a difference anyway."

Izzy still looked pained, but she turned to Jake. "What'd you say to Richie? He ran away like a little boy. Nice work, McGee."

Jake didn't look amused. "Maybe I should call him a cab," he said. "Since he's clearly had his share of booze." He slipped an arm around Stan's shoulders. "If you want to go home, we'll go," he said. "And you don't need to feel guilty about it. Did you know he'd be here?"

"Nope," Stan said. "You think I'd have come?"

Jake's tight jaw and narrowed eyes signaled his unhappiness with this evening. Stan knew the feeling. They'd given up a night in their cozy house where they could turn on some jazz, cuddle on the couch, and watch their pets sleep, for this?

"You know," she said, about to take him up on his offer, "I think you're —"

Someone grabbed her arm from behind, causing her martini to slosh over the rim of the glass. If it was Richard, Jake would lose it. She turned, but found her mother in-stead. Patricia held her sister's arm with her other hand. "Kristan, a moment," she said.

Stan glanced at Jake and Izzy. Izzy raised an eyebrow, turned, and headed for the food. Stan could hear her: *You're on your own with this one, girlfriend.*

"Actually," Jake started, but Stan cut him off. Getting into it with her mother would only result in a suboptimal experience for everyone.

She stepped in front of him. "What's up?"

Resigned, Jake let go of her. "I'll make you a plate," he said, backing away. "And grab you another martini." Blowing her a kiss, he followed Izzy.

She watched him vanish into the crowd, then turned to her mother.

"Girls, I need your help with something immediately," Patricia said, her tone leaving no room for argument.

Stan gave her mother her best ice-queen stare. "I wish you'd have asked for help with the guest list," she said.

Patricia rolled her eyes. "Another time, dear. You're a big girl. Come with me."

The dismissal of her feelings stung. She should pull her arm away, go grab Jake, and march right out the door like she'd been about to. But Patricia's hand was like a vise around her wrist, and fighting it wouldn't benefit anyone.

"I'd like for you girls to be part of the

engagement ring ceremony," Patricia said.

"Engagement ring ceremony?" Stan asked. "What's that?"

Patricia's scathing look was invisible to most innocent onlookers, but Stan knew it well. A miniscule narrowing of the eyelids, the tiniest clench of her jaw, eyes like flint. "It's when Tony presents the engagement ring officially, of course," she said. "That is, if he ever shows up. Anyway, Pastor Ellis is going to make the announcement and bless us. Francie will get everything ready for him — do you have the ring pillow, Francie?" She turned, and for the first time Stan realized Francie Tucker stood behind her.

"Absolutely, Ms. Connor," Francie said, offering Stan an apologetic smile.

Poor thing, Stan thought. *Maybe I should offer her full-time work so she can quit the church and not have to deal with this wedding.*

"Excellent. It would be lovely if my daughters were part of this."

"I thought you were already engaged," Stan said.

"We are, of course. This is making it *official,*" Patricia said.

Stan glanced at her mother's hand. The ginormous rock she'd been wearing was conspicuously absent. "So you got the ring, wore it, and gave it back so he can present it to you again?"

"Yes," Patricia said, her teeth now clenching. "That's exactly right. Are you going to be difficult, Kristan, or are you going to be helpful?"

Do I have a choice? "What do you need us to do, Mother?" Stan asked, hoping her impatience didn't shine through. "And do you have any idea when Tony's arriving?"

From her mother's expression, he'd be better off staying away. "He'll be here any minute. That's why I want to be prepared. We're quite behind schedule as it is. Once he arrives, we'll do this outside." She waved toward the French doors. "The downstairs patio is lovely. One of you girls will offer the toast, then he'll present the ring. You should be next to me when he does so. Then we'll have cake. Please stay close so we can be ready." Patricia walked away without waiting for them to agree.

Francie clasped her hands in front of her. "I'm sorry you were put on the spot like that." She glanced behind her. "I would've warned — er, mentioned it if I'd known. But you're lovely for helping your mother." Then she dashed off to complete her tasks.

Stan looked at Caitlyn. "Did you volunteer me?"

"Of course not," Caitlyn said. "You know how she is."

Stan cocked her head. "Everything okay with you and Mom?" she asked, dropping her voice a little.

Caitlyn shrugged, attempting blasé. "She's being difficult about . . . my situation."

"With Michael?"

Caitlyn nodded. "She blames me. Doesn't want to hear anything about Michael's part in it. She's just focused on how I'm the one who got caught cheating." The mask of indifference fell, and Stan could see it bothered her. She knew the feeling. She was usually the one on the receiving end of her mother's criticism.

"I'm sorry. That's hard. At the moment I want to wring her neck myself. She invited a ton of my old coworkers to this shindig. Including my ex."

Caitlyn snorted. "Typical. Oh well. She is who she is." She squared her shoulders as Eva ran up, her little gold straps sliding off her shoulders as she rubbed at her eyes. The little girl looked exhausted. A late and boring night for a little kid.

"I wanna go back and play with the animals," she demanded.

"I have your snacks in my bag. We're going to go upstairs and lie down for a bit,

57

and you can have some. Come on." Caitlyn hoisted her up. "Tony's not here anyway. I want to let Eva take a nap. You think Mom'll blow a gasket if I put her in one of the bedrooms?" she asked Stan.

"I wouldn't worry about it. I'll go up with you." Ignoring her mother's mandate to stay nearby in favor of getting out of this crowd for a minute, Stan drained her martini glass, deposited it on a passing tray, and started toward the grand staircase at the back of the great room.

Caitlyn followed Stan, Eva's head nestled on her shoulder. "Really I just need a minute alone. And a bathroom," she said, then bumped into Stan, who stopped short at the velvet rope strung across the steps, the kind you see at trendy clubs.

"Guess they don't want guests upstairs," Stan said, unhooking the rope. Caitlyn followed her, and Stan reattached the clip so the stairs were once again blocked. Once they were up top, she reached for her niece. "I'll find a room. And I won't tell Mom you used the bathroom up here." She winked and headed down the hall with Eva while Caitlyn started opening doors to find the bathroom.

She'd just found a bedroom when she heard a strangled scream coming from where she'd left her sister. Alarmed, she turned. "Caitlyn?"

No answer. She deposited Eva on the bed. "Wait here. I'll be right back," she promised.

She went back down the hall, nudging open the bathroom door. Caitlyn stood still as a statue, staring in horrified silence. Stan followed her gaze to the floor and gasped.

Eleanor Chang lay sprawled on her back, eyes wide open and cloudy. Her elegant, filmy scarf, once a decoration for her bare shoulder, was now wrapped around her neck. And protruding from between slightly parted red lips, a massive, familiar-looking diamond ring.

CHAPTER 7

"Oh. My. God." Stan stood frozen, not sure whether to scream or run away.

"Is she . . . *dead*?" Caitlyn gasped, holding on to the counter for support.

Stan didn't bother answering. She snapped into action, shuttering her mind to the horrific sight in front of her. And since Caitlyn seemed about to have an hysterical breakdown, someone needed to keep it together. She grabbed her sister and pulled her out of the room, yanking the door shut behind her. "I need to find Jessie. Go to Eva."

Caitlyn's eyes widened. "Eva! What if there's a murderer hiding up here?" Her voice rose, on its way to hysteria. "Someone . . . *strangled* her!"

Stan grabbed her sister's shoulders. "Listen to me. Go to that room" — she pointed to where she'd left her niece — "make sure you're alone, then lock the door. And stay calm. Understand?" She waited until her sister nodded, eyes still bulging with fear, errant mascara and tears streaming down her cheeks. "Good. I'll be right back."

Caitlyn grabbed her arm before she turned to walk away. "Who did this?" she whispered.

Stan shook her head grimly. "I don't know." She raced down the stairs despite her heels, nearly twisting her ankle in her haste. This turn of events had already caused her martini to wear off. Her brain ping-ponged between random thoughts: *Who-when-why-how?* to a shameful version of *She crossed the wrong person this time.* Shoving that one away, Stan braced herself against the sick feeling, as well as the *oh-dear-God-not-again* feeling.

An unfamiliar woman paused at the bottom of the stairs as Stan clattered down. "Is there an extra powder room up there?" she asked, her hand hovering near the clip holding the velvet rope to a stand.

Stan froze. "No. Upstairs is off limits," she said, giving the woman an unladylike shove away from the staircase. Ignoring the woman's huff of displeasure, she cast about the room frantically looking for Jessie's red hair, usually a crowd standout. Stan finally caught sight of her out on the deck, miserably adjusting her dress while Marty chatted with someone, their words punctuated by loud bursts of laughter and hand-waving.

She wound her way through the guests until she could lean over and whisper into Jessie's ear. "We need you."

Jessie turned and arched an eyebrow. "Who's 'we' and what do you need?"

"There's a situation." Stan stared at her, trying to telepathically convey what she refused to say out loud.

Jessie's face fell. "Don't even joke about it."

"Just come with me." Stan turned and threaded her way back through the crowd. Jessie said something to Marty and followed her. On the way back, Stan met Jake's eyes across the great room. He held up her drink, an inquisitive look on his face. She shook her head and kept going.

They hopped over the velvet ropes and made their way upstairs. When they reached the landing and the lull of the crowd dropped below them, Stan turned to her. "My sister went to use the ladies' room. You need to see what's in there."

"That's never a good opening." Jessie's lips set in a grim line.

Stan led her to the door. Jessie pushed it open slowly, eyes hardening when they landed on Eleanor's still body. She observed the scene, her gaze slowly roaming over the spacious bathroom.

Stan tried to talk herself out of throwing up now that someone else could take charge. Looking anywhere else but at Eleanor helped. The rest of the room looked like a normal bathroom, aside from the affluence. A deep, bowl-type sink made out of expensive-looking stone rested on top of the vanity. The surface was clear save for a gold soap dispenser, a matching bottle of hand lotion, and a half-full martini glass. Eleanor's? Or had someone else — like her murderer — left it?

Jessie moved into the room and knelt next to the dead woman. When she looked up, her face was in cop mode. "I need a phone," she said. "I don't have mine because there are no pockets in this godforsaken dress. And I need your help keeping people away — and keeping this quiet — until my backup arrives. Can you do that?"

Stan nodded and handed her the cell phone out of her sparkly evening bag. Jessie glanced at the bag with the same curiosity one would reserve for a two-headed animal walking down Main Street. Definitely not a girly girl.

"Did you see anything?" Jessie asked. "Or

anyone? Was anyone else up here?"

"No. I was already down the hall when Caitlyn . . . alerted me."

"Did you touch anything?"

"No. Of course not."

"Did Caitlyn?"

"No." At least she hoped not.

"Where is Caitlyn now?"

Stan pointed to the bedroom across the hall. "There. With Eva."

"Terrific. Did the kid see this?"

Stan shook her head. "I had her with me."

"What's with the ring?" Jessie asked, leaning in for a better look.

Stan said nothing. She didn't want to tell Jessie she suspected the ring was her mother's. But if it was, how on earth had it ended up . . . there?

Jessie sighed. She stood and pushed Stan out of the room, shutting the bathroom door behind them. She took Stan's phone and walked away, turning her back and speaking softly. Stan slumped against the wall, her mind alternating between the Eleanor she'd conversed with less than an hour ago and the dead Eleanor on the floor. This would be a strange place for a random killing, so that meant someone had been really, really angry with her.

Jessie finished her phone call and returned, handing the phone back to Stan. "Bring your niece downstairs before the troops show up. I need to speak with Caitlyn. And while you're at it, tell Marty not to worry but that I'm on duty for the foreseeable future. Good thing Lily is with her dad this weekend," she muttered. Jessie's five-year-old daughter spent every other weekend with her dad.

"What happens next?" Stan asked.

"First, I need to make sure no one leaves. Can you have Jake or Marty cover the back door until back up arrives? And tell them to be discreet about it. The team is on their way. Given the amount of people here — talk about a massive headache — I had to call out the troops. They're sending Major Crimes." She made a face. "So I'll have lots of company during this investigation. We're going to need to do some preliminary questioning of everyone in this house." Her face set into a grim line. "Which means a hell of a long night ahead. And get this. They're sending the team in a bus instead of the van. Because it's the *mayor's* house."

Since Frog Ledge was too small to have its own police force, it was state police territory. As the resident state trooper, Jessie worked out of an office in town hall. Trooper Lou Sturgis was her official partner/backup, although he only worked in town three days a week. When she needed to do more traditional police work, like arrest someone, they traveled to the barracks twenty minutes and two towns away. Jessie'd led the investigations for the town's recent murders entirely on her own, so the Major Crimes unit involvement seemed odd.

Stan frowned. "Who made that call?"

"My boss," Jessie said. "Which makes me think Tony has some special pull. Last I checked, being the mayor of Frog Ledge didn't get you that many perks."

CHAPTER 8

Stan grabbed Eva and took her downstairs. Her niece, sensing something was wrong, had started to cry softly on Stan's shoulder. Stan hugged her tighter as she moved through the crowd.

"Don't worry, honey," she murmured. "Everything's fine. But you have to wait with Auntie Char for a little bit, okay?"

"We can't go to your h-house?" Eva hiccuped.

"In a little bit," Stan promised. Where the heck was Char? For once in her life, she was nowhere in sight. Usually she was drawn to the site of gossip like a moth to a flame. If there was any to be found, she'd be waiting. But not tonight. Stan felt like crying herself.

"Need some help?" Jake asked from behind her.

She turned, knees almost buckling with relief. "Thank goodness. Yes. I need Char to watch Eva for a bit."

Jake glanced at the crying little girl. "Caitlyn okay?" Then his sharp eyes scanned her face. "Are *you* okay? You look really pale."

"I'm fine. Caitlyn's . . . tied up right now," Stan said, then cringed when she thought of the scarf. "Have you seen Char?"

Jake shook his head. "Want me to take Eva?"

"If you want to," Stan said, uncertain. Jake reached for the little girl. Immediately, she quieted and rested her head on his shoulder, still sniffling and hiccuping. Stan leaned into his other ear and whispered, "There's a situation upstairs."

He frowned. "What's going on? What do you mean, a situation?"

"I'll explain later. The police are on their way. Jessie needs someone to watch the back door and make sure no one leaves. Can you and Eva do that? Please?" She sent him a pleading look, hoping he wouldn't push the issue.

He searched her face, then nodded. "I'll be right outside," he said, leaning down and brushing her lips with his. "Come on, sweetie. In a few minutes we'll go home and see the dogs and cats," he murmured to Eva. She nodded and buried her face in his shoulder.

Stan watched him slip through the kitchen to the back door, wishing for all the world she could just take them home. But she couldn't, so she focused on the tasks at hand. Next, she had to find her mother. The thought of telling Patricia — if she hadn't heard already — made her want to crawl into a hole. Her mother would be livid that someone had dared to die during her engagement party. Even if they tried to keep this quiet, something would leak. Tony's position would boost this to headline news. She hadn't seen Cyril Pierce here, which made sense. Her mother wouldn't have bothered with the quirky local journalist. But this was Frog Ledge. He'd hear about it in no time. The larger papers would grab his report and blast it all over state channels. Her former coworkers would report back to their corporate inner circles in no time, and Stan's name would once again be linked to murder. It brought back bad memories of her experience soon after she moved to Frog Ledge, even though the circumstances were completely different.

And, there was a murderer in the house. Unless he or she had already slipped out the door. That reality had finally set in, sending waves of cold fear shooting through her nerve endings. She hoped she hadn't sent Jake into danger by stationing him at the door, but chances were good that the culprit was already gone.

As she rejoined the crowd, a couple holding champagne flutes glanced curiously at her. She probably looked green, on the verge of throwing up. She was. Suddenly, Marty was at her side. "Hey," he said, worry clouding his usually bright eyes. "What's going on?"

"Marty. I was just about to come find you. Jessie . . . is on duty. There's been an incident." She raised her eyebrows, trying to convey the seriousness of the situation.

"Is she okay?"

"Jessie's fine. But she's going to be busy for a while."

"What happened?"

Stan shook her head. "I can't say."

"Is there anything I can do?" he asked anxiously.

"Yes. Can you make sure no one takes off out the front door? And if you see my mother, please tell her to come find me. It's very important."

Marty nodded, wide-eyed. Stan patted his arm, then moved on, continuing her search.

Partygoers blissfully unaware of the drama unfolding directly above them floated around with their drinks and tiny plates of appetizers, talking and laughing about their important minutia. Stan moved through them robotically, hoping to catch a glimpse of her mother. No sign of Patricia throughout the entire first-floor party area. She resisted the urge to pound on the wall in frustration. Her head ached and tears filled her eyes. She slipped through the nearest door, finding herself in the back hallway near the kitchen. Taking advantage of the quiet, she leaned against the wall and closed her eyes.

"Hey," a voice said in her ear.

She gasped, nearly jumping out of her shoes. Trooper Lou Sturgis stood there shaking his head, a resigned look on his face. He looked older these days. Or maybe it was maturity. Either way, he'd lost the pudgy, eager look she remembered from the first time she'd met him, and gained that cop look. Probably because he'd become well versed in murder investigations over the past year.

"Trooper Lou. Hey. I was just . . . taking a minute."

He nodded. "I don't blame you. I heard it's getting messy in there. And I guess we're keeping this one quiet." His disdainful tone said he felt the same way as Jessie about that.

Stan nodded. "Did you see Jake when you came in?"

"I did. I sent him home with your niece."

"You did?" Stan felt a rush of relief. "Thank you."

"No problem. I know where to find him if he turns out to be the culprit." Trooper Lou winked at her. "Am I heading upstairs?"

"Yep. Bathroom. But I don't know how to get up there without going through the party."

The maid appeared as if she'd conjured her. "This way, please," she said to Sturgis. With a look of mild horror, he followed her to what Stan presumed was a back staircase just as Patricia burst through the kitchen door, a tall, thin, balding man at her side.

"Why is there a bus full of police parked in my driveway?" she asked. "I thought it was a joke, but . . ." She trailed off as another cop appeared in the back hall.

"Upstairs?" he asked.

"What on earth is going on here?" Patricia demanded.

The trooper looked at her, unimpressed, then turned to Stan. "Upstairs?" he repeated.

Wordlessly, Stan pointed down the hall where the maid and Sturgis had gone. The trooper grabbed his radio and barked instructions into it. A minute later, another group of cops swarmed in through the back as Patricia watched in horror.

"Mom, Jessie needs to talk to you," Stan said.

"Patricia, I'll go with you," her companion said anxiously.

Her mother's eyes narrowed into slits.

But from somewhere out in the main room, the noise level rose. People started to catch wind of *something* happening. And then, clear as day, a woman's voice rose and crested over the crowd like a tsunami. "Murdered?" she screeched. "Someone was *murdered*?"

CHAPTER 9

Stan covered her eyes with her hands so she didn't have to see the blood drain from her mother's face.

"What. Is. Happening," Patricia said through clenched teeth.

She grabbed her mother's arm and pulled her away from her companion. "Eleanor Chang is dead," she hissed. "Someone killed her upstairs in the bathroom. Jessie needs you ASAP."

Patricia gaped at her, the righteous anger draining away. "What?"

Stan gave her a shove. "Go."

For once in her life, Patricia listened. She grabbed her friend's arm. "Roger. I need your help."

He nodded. "I'll go with you." Turning to Stan, he said, "I'm Pastor Roger Ellis. From the Unitarian Church. I'd like to help, if I can."

"Please," Stan said, relieved. A pastor

seemed like a good idea right about now. Before her mother could walk away, Stan called her back. "Mom. Where's your engagement ring?"

Her mother turned and gave her an odd look. "In my jewelry box. Why?"

"You probably need to check on that," Stan advised. Before her mother could ask her to elaborate, Trooper Lou appeared at the bottom of the back staircase. "Is there a quiet place away from the party where we can talk?" he asked.

Patricia nodded. "Upstairs in the —"

"No," he interrupted. "Not upstairs."

Patricia sent him a filthy look. "We can talk in Tony's study," she said tightly.

Stan thought about trying to slip out, but Trooper Lou caught her eye. Like he knew what she was thinking, he shook his head once. Patricia led them down the hall, bypassing the secret stairway, and pushed open a door next to it.

Jessie emerged from the secret stairway, looking around. Stan pointed to the door. She'd shoved it open, about to step inside, when one of the other troopers approached her.

"Trooper. If you need help with interviews, happy to jump in," he said.

Jessie cocked her head, sizing him up.

"Who are you again?"

He flushed. "Garrett Colby. I'm the new K9 handler. You remember, right? Part-time allocation to Frog Ledge?"

"Right. Thanks for the offer. What I really need is someone who can let the guests know we need their contact information and that officers will be talking to everyone momentarily. If we don't get started soon they're going to be here for a long time."

"What do you mean?" Patricia's voice floated out of the room. "You're planning to harass my guests?"

Stan wanted to crawl into a hole and hide.

Jessie glanced through the door at Patricia with barely disguised contempt. "Ms. Connor. Someone is dead." She took a deep breath. "We'll need the medical examiner to confirm, but it appears to be foul play. Of course people can't leave until we've made sure we at least know who was here." She stepped into the room and closed the door behind her, cutting off Patricia's objections.

Pastor Ellis, still standing in the hall like a deer in headlights, looked at Colby. His face was ashen. "So this was . . . foul play? You're certain?" Ellis asked.

"Unconfirmed as of yet," Colby said.

Pastor Ellis blew out a breath and looked at Stan. He appeared to be about to ask her something, but Trooper Lou emerged from the study, his face grim. "Talk about a party crasher," he muttered to Stan, then turned to Colby. "I'll make the announcement." He moved past Stan, heading back toward the main party. She followed.

Trooper Lou entered the great room and whistled, stopping most of the conversation in its tracks.

"I need everyone's attention," he said. "There's been a situation, and we're asking that no one leave the premises until we've spoken with you and gotten your contact information. The faster we have everyone's cooperation, the quicker we can let you go." With that, he turned and headed back to the makeshift interview room. "Stick around," he murmured to Stan as he passed. "See what the reaction is."

Stan watched as more police worked their way through the crowd with notebooks and pens. She could hear snippets floating through the air: "Someone's dead . . . murdered?" "No, couldn't be, I heard heart attack." "Do you really think someone died?" "I'm telling you . . . strangled."

Stan sent up a silent prayer that most of them were too old to be snapping photos of the situation and uploading them to their Instagram accounts — or worse, Snapchatting them. Although, there were a few young people here, so one could only imagine what they were recording.

Young people. Her head snapped up. "Oh God," she said out loud. She raced into the back hall past a startled Pastor Ellis. Skidding to a stop in front of the study door, she pounded on it.

Trooper Lou yanked it open, glaring. "What?"

Stan motioned him to step into the hallway. He did. "This better be good."

"Monica. Eleanor's daughter," Stan said, frantic. "I totally forgot she was here. Someone needs to get to her before she hears about this!"

"Crap." Trooper Lou chewed on his lip. "Okay. You know what she looks like? Where she might be?"

Stan nodded. "I know what she looks like. I met her a little while ago."

"Good. So you can ID her. Can you get her? I'll ask Jessie to talk to her."

Jessie would love that. Sometimes Stan thought she liked dealing more with dead people then living people, especially when in uncomfortable situations. "Yeah. I'll go look for her. Where should I bring her?"

Trooper Lou looked around, uncertain, his gaze landing on Ellis. "Bring her here, I guess. We'll have to find another room to take her."

Stan turned to go, then paused. "What should I tell her?"

He rubbed his hand over his hair. "I don't know. Tell her . . . you need to talk to her in private." He shrugged helplessly.

"You're a big help," Stan sighed. She turned just as the police radio erupted with activity.

"Suspect out front," she heard from Trooper Lou's radio behind her. "In custody."

Lou moved faster than she'd ever seen, heading toward the great room. Stan followed, pushing through the crowd to get outside. She made it to the front door in time to see a cruiser pull up out front. Two cops escorted a man to the car, and in that pause while they opened the door, Stan realized who their suspect was.

"Richard?" she gasped.

Richard's jacket was missing, and what was left of his impeccable outfit was rumpled, his tie skewed to the left. He argued with the cop, but she couldn't hear what he said. Trooper Lou joined the fray, blocking him from Stan's view.

Stan raced out the door and over to the group of cops, grabbing Lou's arm. "What are you doing? You can't arrest Richard!"

"Stan." Lou grabbed her and dragged her away from the other cops, none of whom looked friendly. "Stop. You don't want to mess around here."

"But he didn't —"

She was stopped in her tracks by another, louder voice that suddenly cut through the chaos. They turned to see Tony Falco running into the front yard. A cop went to grab him, and he wrenched his arm away.

"This is my house," he roared. "What the blazes is going on here?"

CHAPTER 10

Tony didn't look like his normal mayoral self. Nor did he look like he was going to his own fancy engagement party. Dirty jeans and a torn sweatshirt replaced his typical custom-made, elegant suit, giving him the look of a misplaced farmer. Everyone stared. As he burst through the front door, no one seemed to realize who he was. Then as it sunk in, the whispers started up again full force.

"Mayor Falco. Please come with me. I'll explain everything," Trooper Lou said. With a warning look at Stan, he motioned her back into the house behind Tony and followed.

Tony kept his gaze straight ahead despite the guests who tried to reach out. Stan watched them go, biting back all the questions — *What were they doing with Richard? What happened to him outside? Did they really think he killed Eleanor?* — and tried to

81

refocus on finding Monica. The now-motherless daughter. She swallowed against the sick feeling rising up her throat.

Following a hunch, Stan went out to the deck and followed it halfway around the house. Monica hadn't struck her as the type who wanted to be in this mix, so it made sense she would've sought out one of the places not congested with people.

Her hunch paid off. Monica Chang was one of only three people still out on the deck. The ruffled dress was hard to miss. The other two, a man and woman, huddled together whispering. Monica was slumped over one of the only tables. At first Stan thought she was asleep. Her head rested on one fist. Her other hand clutched a cell phone.

Stan cleared her throat. "Monica?" she asked.

No response.

"Monica?" she asked, louder. The remaining couple on the deck paused in their conversation and watched, curious.

Monica's head snapped up and unfocused eyes searched for Stan's face. Her hair stuck to her cheek on the side where she'd rested. "What?" she asked, her words slightly slurred.

Either she'd been asleep, or she was

drunk. Or maybe both. Excellent. "I'm Stan. I met you earlier. Can you come with me, please?"

Monica's brows knitted in confusion. "I guess." She glanced around, maybe looking for her mother, but rose unsteadily and followed Stan inside. She tripped over the doorframe and grabbed for Stan to steady herself.

"Are you feeling all right?" Stan asked, wrapping an arm around the girl's waist.

Monica nodded. "Fine."

"Were you drinking?"

Monica's head snapped up and she glared at Stan. "No!"

Stan let it go and led her inside, trying to usher her past the uniformed officers talking to partygoers. But Monica balked. "What's going on?" she whispered.

Stan's hesitation must've tipped her off that something wasn't right — Monica twisted away from her and tried to take off, but her movements were slow and sloppy and she lost her balance. Stan grabbed her before she fell. Luckily, she weighed so little Stan could easily hold her up.

"It's okay," Stan tried to soothe her, keeping her voice low so eavesdroppers couldn't overhear. "We need to talk to you about your mother."

"My mother," she whispered, her body going limp. "What's my mother doing? Is . . . is she having me arrested?"

Startled, Stan shook her head. "What? No, of course not."

Monica sagged against her and started to cry. Stan looked around helplessly, but the people paying attention to them looked horrified. The rest were caught up in the drama of the night, or complaining about how they were stuck here. Cursing her mother, Trooper Lou, Tony, Eleanor and the Universe, she half dragged, half carried Monica out to the back hall. She'd given up on trying to make this less of a spectacle. That horse had left the barn long ago.

Pastor Ellis stood in the hall, head bowed in some kind of prayer. He raised his eyes at their approach. His gaze locked on Monica, who averted her eyes, then met Stan's, a silent question. She shook her head and pushed Monica past him, pausing only to rap on the closed study door. She turned the corner, pushing doors open as she went. A laundry room. A closet. Then, to her relief, a small guest bedroom. She led Monica in and deposited her on the bed. The girl immediately curled into a miserable ball, her face pale and green at the same time, while Stan caught her breath. She peered out into the hall and waved at Jessie when she saw her doing the same guess-which-door routine.

Jessie appeared in the doorway seconds later. She took in Monica's still figure on the bed, then looked at Stan. Stan recognized the look. It said, *I'd rather deal with a madman than this.* She approached the bed. "Monica. I'm Trooper Jessie Pasquale."

Monica didn't move, but Stan saw one eye fixed on Jessie.

"Do you think you can sit up and talk to me?" Jessie asked.

Monica clearly didn't want to, but she forced herself up and swung her legs over the side of the bed, still clutching her phone. She'd spilled food, something orange, on her ruffled dress.

"When was the last time you saw your mother this evening?" Jessie asked.

Monica shook her head. "I . . . don't know," she whispered. "A little while ago."

"How long? It's really important."

With shaking hands, Monica brought her phone into focus and looked at the clock, then looked helplessly at Jessie. "Half an hour? An hour?"

"Was she upset about anything?" Jessie asked.

"N-no. I don't think so. Why?"

"Monica. Listen to me. This is very important. Did you see her arguing with anyone?" Jessie asked. "Or anyone bothering her?"

Another head shake. This time, she winced at the aftermath of the movement.

Jessie frowned, looked at Stan. Stan pantomimed taking a drink. She could almost see the cartoon word bubble above Jessie's head: *Great. Just what I needed.*

"Monica," Jessie said, more firmly this time. "How much did you have to drink?"

No reply. Jessie closed her eyes briefly, then crouched next to the bed so they were at eye level. "I'm very sorry to have to tell you this, but your mother passed away."

That got her to raise her head. Monica's gaze slowly moved to Jessie's face, then she lurched to her feet. "I need to go to the bathroom," she whispered, and made a beeline out of the room.

Stan reached for her, but before she could grab her, Monica passed out cold at her feet.

CHAPTER 11

What's going on over there? Are you okay?

The text from Jake dinged as Stan raced down the hall looking for the nearest bathroom not containing a dead body. She needed a cold towel for Monica. She also needed a drink. Jake must be frantic by now, but she didn't have time to talk to him. When she found the right door, she ducked inside and texted back:

I'm fine. Call you in a few . . . love you

She grabbed a towel, soaked it in cold water, and wrung it out. Searching through the cabinets, she found a stash of paper cups, filled one with water, then raced back.

Jessie stood in front of Monica's door fiddling with a cell phone when Stan got back to the room. "What a cluster. Your mother is having a meltdown, just so you know."

"Great," Stan said. "And Monica's having

a breakdown, and Richard is arrested. What on earth is going on with that? Why did they —"

"Stan." Jessie held up a hand. "Please. Don't." She looked around, then lowered her voice. "I can't talk about that."

Stan eyed her suspiciously. Jessie's expression warned her not to push. "Meanwhile" — Jessie held up the phone — "any idea what Monica would use as a password?"

"Where'd you get that?"

"She dropped it when she passed out. I want to see if there were any texts with her mother. Or photos."

Stan shook her head. "I have no idea what the password would be."

A trooper came down the hall, a man and woman following him. "Rivers and Menoso are here," he said to Jessie.

"Medical examiner's office," Jessie said to Stan.

"Some place," the woman said, looking around. She had thick black hair and a lilting Spanish accent. "This had to put a damper on the party."

Jessie inclined her head in agreement. "Long time, Menoso," she said.

Menoso grinned. "I would think that's a good thing, no?"

"Where are we headed?" Rivers asked. He

didn't seem impressed with Tony's house.

Jessie pointed to the hidden stairway door. "Upstairs, take a left. In the bathroom."

Rivers sighed. "Always in the bathroom."

"Hey," Menoso said. "From the looks of the house, at least it's probably a nice bathroom." The two snapped on gloves and disappeared through the door.

"I have water for Monica," Stan said, turning back to Jessie. "I can sit with her for a bit."

"Good. Yes. Perfect. Can you ask her for the passcode? And find out if there's anyone to call for her?"

Stan nodded and went into the room, closing the door behind her. She approached the bed, setting the water on the nightstand. Monica lay on her side in a boneless heap, her arm flung over her eyes. Stan sat on the edge of the bed. "Monica?"

Monica moved her arm an inch, revealing red-rimmed eyes, and peered at Stan.

"How are you doing?"

Monica didn't answer.

"I can call someone for you," Stan offered, feeling woefully inadequate. "Your dad?"

That got Monica's attention. She sat up, feeling around for her phone. Her nose dripped and her bloodshot eyes were still unfocused, but she tried to pull herself together. "No. I can call someone else. Have you seen my phone?"

"Actually," Stan said, "Trooper Pasquale picked it up. You dropped it when you fainted. She wants to hold on to it for a bit and wondered if you could give her the passcode."

Monica looked confused. And scared. "Why?"

How was she supposed to answer *that*? Jessie hadn't actually told Monica what happened to her mother, just that she'd passed away.

But Monica didn't need her to answer. She spoke so softly Stan almost missed it. "Someone killed my mom, didn't they? That's why that officer asked me if people were mad at her."

Stan swallowed, resisting the urge to run from the room. She met Monica's eyes, unflinching. "Yes. I'm so sorry."

Monica sank back against the pillow, closing her eyes. Then, in a monotone, she recited four numbers. The passcode, Stan realized.

She repeated them back to her as she tapped them into a note on her phone, then cleared her throat. "So who do you want me to call? Your dad really should know what's going on."

"Only if you want to make his day," she said, but there was no humor in her words. She opened her eyes and looked at Stan. "My parents are divorced," she said, sounding more lucid than she had so far that night. "They don't talk."

"Still," Stan said gently. "He has a right to know. And you don't want to be alone right now. Who else can we call? Do you have siblings?"

She nodded. "Shannon is back at college in New York. Presley is at boarding school up in Massachusetts. She's the youngest," Monica added. "She's . . . only sixteen." She looked away and wiped her nose with her ruffled sleeve. "God. My grandma. My . . . mom's mom. She lives with us. Someone has to tell her." Her eyes filled up again and she looked at Stan. "I can't."

Stan wanted to hug her, this poor kid who'd probably had a tough life with a demanding, ambitious, perfectionist mother, who now had to live without that mother. She thought of Patricia. Despite their ongoing struggles, she'd feel pretty terrible if someone killed her. "I'll have Trooper Pasquale call her. Can you give me her number?"

Monica recited the number. Stan added it into the note on her phone, then stood up.

"Be right back." She was almost out the door when Monica called to her.

"Can I use your phone to call my friend?"

Stan hesitated. "Sure, but you'll have to get cleared from Trooper Pasquale before you leave."

Monica nodded. "It would take a while to get here anyway. I just need to. . . ." Her sentence trailed off into nothing.

Stan handed the phone over, then stood outside the door to give her some privacy.

Less than a minute later, Monica opened the door and handed the phone back to Stan.

"Thank you."

Stan nodded and turned to go, but Monica spoke again.

"Do they know who did it?"

Still holding on to the doorknob, Stan looked back at her. "They're working on it."

Monica studied her shoe. "Do you think you can find my purse for me?" she asked, her voice completely flat. "It's black with a rhinestone flower on the front. It has a broken snap. Guess," she said, and it took Stan a minute to realize she was stating the brand name, not telling her to guess where it was. "I . . . don't remember where I left it."

"I'll look," Stan said. She slipped out the door, closing it behind her. As she did, it struck her that even though Monica had been understandably upset by the news, she hadn't seemed all that shocked.

CHAPTER 12

With Jessie once again behind a closed door, the passcode and Monica's grandmother would have to wait. Stan went in search of Monica's missing purse.

She started on the patio where she'd found Monica. As luck would have it, a small group of her former colleagues were clustered, surrounding a teary-eyed Michelle Mansfield.

"How could they think Richard was involved in this?" Stan heard Michelle wail while a couple of her entourage attempted to comfort her. "He would never! Did you see them *roughhousing* him?"

Stan tried to block out their voices as she moved around the patio willing the purse to appear so she could get away from this crew.

"Honey, I'm sure they'll figure it out quickly. Once they find out who he is," another one said. "Besides, they haven't even said what happened!"

"Someone killed Eleanor, obviously," a third voice scoffed. "Upstairs, right in the bathroom. And since Richard took off in a snit, he looks guilty. Where did he run off to, anyway?"

Michelle sniffled even louder and ignored the question. "They have nerve, making us stay here," she continued. "I mean, there's a *murderer* on the loose! He could be out here right now, watching us. *Plotting.* And they're wasting their time with *Richard*?"

Her entourage tittered their similar concerns.

Stan rolled her eyes as she searched in vain for the aptly brand-named purse, hoping not to make eye contact with Michelle. But of course, since this night was destined to go completely off the rails, Michelle noticed her and made a beeline.

"Stan. What on earth is going on?" Michelle glared at her like she'd been the one to haul Richard away in cuffs. "What are those police officers *thinking*?"

Stan straightened from searching under a table, trying to keep her face blank. "Someone got murdered and there's a whole pool of suspects to eliminate," she said. "Don't worry, Michelle. They'll get it sorted out."

Michelle huffed out a breath, then lowered her voice. "What did your boyfriend do to

Richard, anyway? Why'd he take off like that?"

Stan felt the heat rising up her neck, reddening her cheeks with anger. "Jake didn't do anything to Richard except ask him to take his hand off me," Stan said.

Michelle scoffed. "I don't think you have to worry about his *hand* on you. He's not interested, believe me."

Stan laughed. "Is that the best you can do?" She hated engaging with her, but she couldn't seem to stop herself. "Why *are* you here, Michelle? I wasn't aware you and Tony Falco were tight."

By now Michelle's posse surrounded them, listening unabashedly to the exchange. Some of them looked expectantly at Michelle, but her bravado faltered. After a moment of uncomfortable silence, she tried a different tactic. "Look. I don't want to argue with you, Stan. You seem to know these" — she waved her hand around, looking for the word — "*people. Can't you tell them they have the wrong guy?"

She'd already told them that. It had to be a big misunderstanding. Richard had many faults, but he was far from a killer. But Jessie couldn't talk about it, and Stan had no idea what to say to Michelle now.

Trooper Lou saved her from answering.

He strode onto the patio and locked eyes with Stan. "Scuse me," he said, breaking the formation gathered around her and motioning for her to follow him.

She tried to hide her gratitude until she was away from Michelle and gang. "What's up?" she asked when they were out of earshot.

"The victim's daughter's gone."

"Gone? What are you talking about? She's down the hall from your interrogation room. The guest bedroom."

Trooper Lou shook his head slowly. "She's not."

Stan's heart plummeted, remembering the phone call. She'd promised she wouldn't leave, though. "What? Are you sure? Maybe she went to the bathroom." *Hopefully not the one her mother was killed in.*

"That's what I said, too." Lou looked grim. "But no one can find her anywhere." He hesitated. "I went back in to talk to her but she was gone."

Stan shook her head. "You guys have people at every door. How would she get out? Jessie would never let that happen."

Something crossed Trooper Lou's face, but he didn't respond.

Stan followed him inside, guilt clenching her shoulder blades together. She should never have given Monica the phone. But she didn't seem to be in any shape to go anywhere.

"Maybe she just went to look for her purse," Stan said as she followed him into the back hall. "She asked me about it. That's what I was doing out on the porch. But I couldn't find it."

Trooper Lou shook his head. "Hate to tell you, but she's gone." He pointed toward the open guest room door.

Stan headed in, needing to see for herself. Maybe Monica would materialize out of the blue. Maybe she'd hid from him because she was afraid of cops. Or because she'd been drinking. But she was over twenty-one, so why would she bother?

But she wasn't in the room. Stan checked the other doors nearby, but it was a futile exercise. Monica wasn't hiding in the laundry room, or the linen closet. So where could she be? She couldn't have just left. Cops were at every exit.

Weren't they?

She looked for Trooper Lou, but he was no longer in the hall. She threaded her way back down the hall and slipped into the foyer. No cop, inside at least. She pushed the back door open and stuck her head out, expecting to see a gun pointed in her face.

Nothing.

What was up with that? Unless . . . she swallowed against the dread welling up in her chest. Had they pulled everyone off high alert now that they had Richard in custody?

She stepped out onto the porch. And nearly jumped when a cop stepped out of the shadows. "Ma'am? Can I help you?"

"No. I mean, maybe," Stan said, flustered. "Did you see a young woman come out this door?"

"Only the caterers are permitted to leave by this door," he said.

As if on cue, a man brushed by her carrying a tray piled with appetizers. The cop nodded at him. Stan watched the exchange and sighed. So Monica hadn't been in as bad shape as she'd appeared. She'd been astute enough to grab a tray and pretend to be part of the catering staff to get out of the house.

"Trooper Pasquale asked me to come out here and grab one of the catering folks," Stan said, the lie slipping off her tongue.

The cop frowned. "Who?"

"Jessie Pasquale. Frog Ledge Resident State Trooper."

The cop pulled out his radio and summoned Pasquale. Stan groaned inwardly. She didn't want Jessie to know about this until she was certain Monica was gone.

Too late. Jessie appeared seconds later. "What?" She looked at Stan. "What's going on?"

"Did you send this woman out here?" the cop asked.

Stan sent her a pleading look with her eyes.

"I did," Jessie said. "Is there a problem?"

"No. Just checking."

Jessie grabbed Stan's arm and pulled her outside. They followed the path down to the driveway. "What are you doing?" she muttered once they were out of the cop's earshot.

"Monica slipped out. Pretending to be part of the catering staff, who your boy back there is keeping an eye on."

Jessie muttered a curse. "Let's see if she's out here."

They approached the caterer's van. Tony's baseball-stadium strength flood lights blazed their way in the rapidly darkening evening. The van doors stood wide open. Stan peeked in and saw no one. She stopped and looked around. Only woods behind the house. Woods where Richard ventured, for some reason. Would Monica wander in there? Stan went to the street where people's cars stretched along the winding road leading to Tony's house. She looked in both directions. Nothing.

"Here." Jessie's voice was low but strong, and Stan followed it around the van. A tray of food lay in the grass, overturned. Jessie cursed again. "Stupid. I let her out of my sight."

"She could still be out here," Stan said, then whirled around when she saw lights bouncing up the road. Running back to the end of the driveway, she crouched in the shadow of a large SUV and watched as a car pulled up, deftly maneuvering a three-point turn so it faced down the street again. A red sedan idled, illuminated in the glow from the streetlight. Stan saw some sort of black sticker on the back window. She made out only one of three words — *something something rock.* Then she saw a flash of pink racing across the lawn. Seconds later Monica passed under the same streetlight, giving Stan a side view of her face.

"Monica!" she yelled. She heard Jessie racing up behind her and knew she'd be cursing her outfit, her shoes, her lack of any kind of equipment.

Monica didn't even register that she'd heard. She yanked the door open and jumped in the car. The door slammed and the car coasted away. She strained to see the license plate but could only make out the last three letters — *BDR* — before the car disappeared around a bend in the road, and then they were out of sight.

CHAPTER 13

Stan slunk back inside behind Jessie, but let her storm off down the back hall. She slipped into the kitchen, catching a whiff of the remaining food before the caterers whisked it away. A veritable mountain of goodies. Glazed shrimp and bacon, tiny plates of brie with crackers, cherry tomatoes stuffed with something that normally would've looked delightful, but now made Stan feel sick. And those were only the appetizers. Uneaten prime rib, maple-glazed salmon, baby red potatoes, and rich desserts lined the tables. Stan hoped they'd at least bring what they didn't use to a homeless shelter so it wouldn't go to waste. She'd long since lost her appetite, and now it was exacerbated by Monica's exit. Jessie'd looked like her head was about to blow off.

She stepped back into the party and scanned the living room. The state troopers in charge of gathering contact info had the

103

crowd sorted into more manageable groups from which they pulled people aside individually. Other officers canvassed the floor, making sure they'd accounted for everyone. Stan wondered if anyone besides Monica — like the murderer — had slipped out despite their efforts. She saw a small group of her mother's charity friends from Rhode Island and ducked back through the kitchen to the hallway of doom.

Jessie conferred with Trooper Lou and Colby. Stan caught the words *freakin' incompetence,* but the man who emerged from the stairwell at that moment drew her attention from the conversation. He caught the troopers' attention, too.

"Is there an issue, Troopers?" he asked. His voice, buttery smooth, held a hint of steel in it despite the matter-of-fact tone.

Stan hadn't seen him before. He had a different presence. A tall, commanding African-American man with *no nonsense* practically tattooed on his forehead. Even Jessie stood a little straighter. Stan slipped back into the kitchen, but peered around the corner so she could still hear the conversation.

"Captain Quigley," she said. "I wasn't aware you'd been called in."

He nodded, then cocked his head at her

outfit. "I appreciate your willingness to jump in on your night off."

"It's my job, sir."

"You're correct. Now, is there a problem I should be aware of?"

Stan cringed and ducked out of view, not wanting to witness what came next. But Jessie stood up to the problem like a champ.

"The victim's daughter, sir," Stan heard her say. "She slipped out the back with the caterers and the man on the door didn't notice."

Quigley's voice went lower. "Has she been questioned?"

"We started to question her, then she became ill. We let her lie down for a few minutes."

"Unguarded?"

Stan held her breath and risked a quick peek. Colby and Trooper Lou were frozen.

"We were in the hall most of the time," Jessie said.

"Most of the time," Quigley repeated. "Well, that clearly wasn't enough. I trust we at least have her contact information?"

"I have her cell phone, actually."

That appeased him somewhat. "Noted. We'll discuss this later."

Stan remained pressed against the wall until she heard his footsteps fade, then peered around the corner again. Troopers Lou and Colby still looked shell-shocked. Jessie looked angry. Stan walked over to them. Jessie opened her mouth, but Lou shushed her.

"Not now," he warned. "You know he can hear through walls."

Jessie ignored him and turned to Stan. "Did you get the license plate of that car?"

Stan shook her head. "Just the last three letters. *BDR.* I didn't see the driver."

"So they may have been from the party, too. Great." Jessie bared her teeth. "What do we know about this girl? She hate her mother?"

"I have no idea if she — the passcode." Suddenly remembering, she pulled her phone out of her dress, ignoring Trooper Lou's raised eyebrow, and scrolled through her notes to find the number. "Four-eight-three-nine."

Jessie jabbed the numbers into the phone a lot harder than necessary, then held it up to Stan. "Wrong code."

Stan read them again, then took the phone from Jessie and tried it herself. The iPhone refused to allow access.

"She duped you," Jessie said. "Which really makes me wonder." She stalked around the small space, then paused, hands on hips. "I'll send your sister down," she told Stan. "I'm done with her. I have to call the victim's mother. Sturgis, come on."

Shoving open the hall door, she stomped up the stairs as best she could in her girly shoes. Trooper Lou followed in silence.

Caitlyn appeared a few minutes later, eyes glazed as a zombie's. "Now I know how you felt," she murmured when she saw Stan. "In Newport."

Stan didn't want to think about the parallels of her recent trip to Newport. Seemed like every time she went to a social gathering lately, the unthinkable happened. Maybe people would start leaving her off their guest lists. It wouldn't be such a bad thing.

She squeezed Caitlyn's hand. "Are you okay?"

Caitlyn jerked her shoulder in a shrug. "I guess." Then her head snapped up. "Where's Eva?"

"Jake took her home. She's fine."

"Thank God." She closed her eyes in relief. "He's a sweet guy," she said. "You're really lucky." Her tone held a hint of wistfulness.

"He is. Listen, let's go home. I think we can leave now. I'll see if Izzy's still here. She'll give us a ride."

"Did they catch the murderer?" Caitlyn

asked hopefully.

Stan had no idea how to answer that. "They have a suspect," she said shortly. "I'm not sure what's happening." She whipped out her phone and texted Izzy.

You still here? Are you clear to go? Can you give me a ride home?

The return text came almost immediately:

Yeah. Can't wait to get the heck out of here.

Meet me in the kitchen, Stan replied, then called Jake.

He answered on the first ring, speaking softly. "What's happening? Are you okay?"

"We're fine. Izzy's driving me and Caitlyn home," she said. "How's Eva?"

"Sleeping with Scruffy, Duncan, and Benedict," he replied. "I'm sitting up here with her in case she wakes up looking for her mom."

This guy never ceased to make her heart melt. "Thank you," she whispered, trying to stop the tears from choking her voice. "See you soon."

She hung up before he could ask her anything else and stood. "Let's go," she said to her sister.

"What about Mom?"

"I think they're still talking to her." Stan hesitated. "Do you think she needs somewhere to stay? They won't let her stay here."

"I don't know," Caitlyn said. "Doesn't she have any other friends here?"

Stan grimaced. "I'll see if Char can take care of her."

Caitlyn hesitated as Stan got up to go. "I don't want to see all those people," she whispered.

"I'll text her. She'll come here. Don't worry." She squeezed her sister's hand. Caitlyn squeezed back, and they stood like that for a minute. Stan wondered if Caitlyn realized the last time they'd held hands they were probably ten and seven years old.

Char and Ray burst into the kitchen moments later.

"I was already planning on taking your mama home," Char said before Stan could say anything. "Is she all right? Have you seen her?"

"I haven't. They still have her locked away. I'm sorry, Char, but would you mind waiting for her? I have to get Caitlyn home. Jake brought Eva and if she wakes up, she'll want her mom."

"Of course, sweetie." Char hugged Stan,

then turned and wrapped Caitlyn in a fierce hug, too. "I'm so sorry you had to be part of this," she said to her.

Caitlyn started to cry again. Ray patted her back. "Don't you worry, m'dear. Jessie will get this all straightened out."

I'm not so sure she can. The thought flitted through Stan's mind before she could block it out. Izzy rushed in, carrying her shoes in one hand.

"You ready?" she asked. "Let's go before they lock us down again."

Izzy looked almost more freaked out than Caitlyn. Stan thanked Char and Ray again, promising to call them first thing in the morning — only a few hours away at this point — then led Izzy and Caitlyn out the back way.

None of them spoke until they were safely in Izzy's car. As she shot down the street Stan held on to the armrest and closed her eyes. Once they reached the main road, Izzy let up on the gas and blew out a breath.

"Damn," she said, trying for humor but unable to mask her shaking voice. "Stan, what *is* it with you and dead people?"

CHAPTER 14

Jake waited at the front door, his relief apparent. "I was worried," he said into Stan's hair as he hugged her. He reached for Caitlyn's hand and squeezed. "Eva's sleeping upstairs in the guest room. She cuddled up with the dogs and cats and hasn't woken up at all."

"Thank you for taking care of her," Caitlyn said, then fled upstairs.

Jake turned to Stan. "Marty texted me," he said. "I got some of the story. That woman you knew. Eleanor. She's dead, but he didn't know more than that. Tell me the rest. But first, is your sister okay?"

Stan shook her head. "I doubt it. She found the body. I know from experience how that messes with your head." She moved past him. "I need to sit."

"I put water on for tea," he said, locking the front door behind her and following her to the kitchen.

"Thank you. You read my mind." Stan dropped her evening bag and phone on the table and twisted her hair into a knot. She opened her tea cabinet and pursued her selection. Izzy had given Stan first dibs to sample her new line of herbal teas. She picked lavender honey for stress relief, then leaned against the counter, rubbing her temples. Nutty appeared, as if sensing she needed some comfort, and head-butted her. She picked him up and buried her face in his soft Maine coon fur, listening to him purr. She hoped she came back as a cat in her next life. Cats didn't have to deal with things like crazy families, murder, and arrested ex-boyfriends.

Jake took out two mugs as the kettle started whistling. Reluctantly, Stan let go of Nutty. "What kind do you want?" she asked.

He came over and put his arms around her. "I don't care about the tea," he said. "I care about what happened and if you're really okay. Because I don't think you are."

She leaned against him, feeling the weight of some of her burden lift simply by his being there. "I have no idea why this keeps happening," she said, hearing her voice crack. "But this . . . something's not right about this. Jake, they arrested Richard."

That surprised him. He leaned back so he

could see her face. "Your ex?"

She nodded. "Not Jessie. They sent a whole contingency of cops. Major Crimes, even the captain. They grabbed Richard outside. He went out after . . . the altercation we had. He was a mess, too. But it was a different kind of mess. He was dirty. Like he'd fallen or something." She pulled away and grabbed the teakettle. Her hands shook so much the water splashed all over the counter when she tried to pour it.

Jake nudged her out of the way and took the kettle from her hand. He poured, then wiped the counter with a paper towel and carried the mugs to the table. Stan wrapped her cold hands gratefully around the mug, letting the warmth seep into her skin.

"Someone strangled Eleanor," she said. "With her own scarf. At least that's what it looked like. And shoved a diamond ring in her mouth." She raised her eyes to meet Jake's. "It looked like my mother's ring. She wasn't wearing it. There was supposed to be this blessing-of-the-ring ceremony and Tony was going to give it to her. But he didn't show up until after they took Richard."

Jake slowly lowered himself into his own chair. "Your mother's ring? How would it have ended up . . ." He trailed off, letting the question drift in the air between them.

113

"I have no idea what was going on at that house. I can't even wrap my head around it. Between Tony's being missing, half my old company in attendance —" She broke off and sipped her tea. "I don't know. You know how I feel about Richard Ruse. Trust me, there's no love lost there. But a killer?" She shook her head. "Every cell in my body says no way." Granted, she hadn't seen him in a year and a half. People changed, after all. Did they change *that* much? Had pressures in the financial world gotten so high that killing someone was an option? The thought gave her the chills. How many times had she and her team said jokingly about Eleanor, "I could kill her"? Too many to count.

But who would actually do it?

"So why *were* all those people from your old job there?"

"That's the question of the day," Stan said. "Most of them probably never heard of Frog Ledge before tonight."

Jake was quiet. Stan knew he probably had a million questions, but he wouldn't want to overwhelm her when she was already having a hard time. He wasn't the only one with a million questions, though.

"And then there's Tony. Where was he all night? He walks in right as the police are thinking they got their man, and they just

114

take him away and give him some privacy? Something's not right. Plus, they called in a ton of cops, including Major Crimes. And they had them come in the back to try to limit the disruption. Like Tony was getting special treatment or something."

"Mayor of Frog Ledge?" Jake asked skeptically. "It's not like he's the governor of Connecticut or something."

"Exactly what Jessie said." Stan put her mug down. "I don't think they even questioned him. As soon as Richard presented as an option they ran with it and let everyone else off the hook."

"Richard was pretty drunk," Jake said carefully. "When he tried to talk to you."

"I know that," Stan said. "Which wasn't his typical behavior anyway. But just because he had a few drinks . . ." She trailed off, realizing how she sounded. Of course alcohol could have that effect on someone. Especially someone who normally didn't drink. Richard *had* been acting funny. Drinking a lot and physically grabbing someone to get her attention at a party filled with his coworkers . . . not his typical behavior.

Jake slid his hand across the table and entwined his fingers with hers. "I know it's crazy to think someone you dated could do something like that. But you don't know if

115

something was going on with Richard and Eleanor."

"No, I don't. You're right. But honestly? I could see Eleanor killing someone more than I could see Richard. And I'm not saying that because I dated him, or disliked her."

"I don't think you're defending him because you dated him, Stan. Look. It's not hard to tell this woman wasn't well liked. You told me yourself your old work environment was dysfunctional. Anything could've happened tonight." He squeezed her hand to get her to look at him. "Anything."

He was right, of course. About all of it. As usual. Her constant voice of reason.

"I know," she said. "And of course, *anything* turned into murder. Someone *always* gets murdered around me, or by extension, now my family." She heard her voice crack at that statement and cleared her throat.

"I don't think it's accurate to say people *get murdered around you,*" Jake said. "Just because the crime rate's gone up doesn't mean it's your fault. I'm kidding," he said, as her face fell.

Stan snorted. "That makes me feel a lot better." She got up to put her mug in the sink and tossed her tea bag into the trash. "The elephant in the room is Tony. No one wanted to address where he was for half the night. I don't know, Jake. There's a lot more to this story than anyone's saying. And someone's sitting in jail right now who probably shouldn't be."

CHAPTER 15

Jake finally convinced her to go to bed around four a.m. Stan obliged after a quick peek in on Caitlyn. Her sister was asleep, Eva cuddled up next to her, one arm wrapped around Scruffy, Gaston curled at her feet. Seeing Caitlyn snuggling with her dogs made her smile. She closed the door quietly.

Henry slept in his bed in their room, and Duncan sprawled on the floor. Nutty and Benedict, enjoying this rare treat of no dogs on the bed, abandoned Caitlyn and Eva and claimed their spots. Nutty kept her pillow warm and Benny curled up at the foot of the bed. Stan put on her pajamas and crawled in next to them, then spent the next hour staring at the ceiling as the rest of the house slept around her. She couldn't erase the troubling images of the night from her mind. Eleanor's body, Monica crumbling to a heap on the floor, Richard in custody,

Tony's dramatic arrival all played on a continuous loop in her brain until she was too exhausted to fight it anymore.

It seemed like minutes later when she awoke to bright sun streaming in through her window. Blinking, she rolled over to look at the clock. Eight-fifteen. Jake still slept soundly next to her, but she could hear voices downstairs. Caitlyn? Stan had a hard time imagining her sister full of energy after last night. Her impending divorce had left her reeling, never mind finding a dead body. The images crowded into her brain again, and she considered pulling the shades and putting her pillow over her head.

But she needed to get up and face the world. Or at least what was going on downstairs. She sat up and glanced around the room. Henry slept in his bed, as oblivious to the activity as Jake. Duncan and the cats were gone. With a sigh, she threw the covers off and slipped out of bed, closing the door behind her as she left. She washed her face, brushed her teeth, and swept her hair into a ponytail, squinting at her face in the mirror. Her skin looked blotchy. The bags under her eyes were first-class-ticket worthy. She made a face and turned away. If Caitlyn was up, she hoped her sister had figured out how to make coffee, but didn't have high hopes.

She had a staff for those things at home.

But it certainly smelled like coffee as she made her way down the stairs. Her sleep-fogged brain encouraged her to move faster, get some fuel. When she reached the kitchen, she stopped in surprise. Brenna stood at the counter with Eva. They mixed dough together, Eva's hands deep in the bowl, guided by Brenna. Benedict watched from his perch on top of the refrigerator. The three dogs and Nutty waited anxiously on the floor in a semicircle, hoping for castoffs. A pot of coffee brewed merrily next to their operation, a thoughtful gesture given the to-go cup from Izzy's on the counter next to her.

"Did I miss a day? Is it Monday? And what are you doing here so early?" Stan asked, grabbing the mug Brenna had already set out for her and filling it with coffee before the machine even finished brewing. "And I mean that in a completely grateful way, of course."

"Auntie Krissie! I'm helping you bake," Eva announced. "We're making peanut butter cookies."

"I see that!" Stan said. "Thank you."

Brenna glanced up and smiled. The youngest of the McGee clan, Brenna liked to say she had only the good traits from her older brother and sister. Her hair alternated between blondish brown in the summer and darker in the winter like Jake, and they shared the same brilliant smile. She also had Jessie's intense green eyes and quick temper. The three of them were perfect Irish siblings, straight out of a Nora Roberts trilogy.

"You didn't miss anything. It's still Sunday," Brenna said. "We have a bunch of orders on the docket, and I didn't want you to worry about them. I would've started them at the pub, but the Irish stew cook-off is today and I'll never get near the stoves. I heard what happened last night," she said, her voice dropping an octave, mindful of the child in front of her waving dough-encrusted fingers around.

That wave of nausea passed over Stan again. She paused, her mug halfway to her mouth. "What'd you hear?"

Brenna cut her eyes to Eva, then back to Stan. "Cyril reported a murder at the mayor's house on his website early this morning. One suspect in custody." She spelled out the word "murder" for Eva's benefit. "A couple of guys were out on the green this morning when Scott and I were running and they said the victim was some fancy city woman. Scott was horrified. He figured spending less time in Hartford

121

would mean hearing about fewer murders."

Brenna's new boyfriend, Scott Grayson, divided his time between Frog Ledge and Hartford since they'd gotten together. One could almost argue Hartford was a safer bet these days.

Stan set down her mug as her stomach roiled again, Eleanor's still face flashing in front of her eyes. "So much for keeping it quiet. I wonder who tipped him off."

"He listens to that scanner all day and night," Brenna said.

"Yeah, but it didn't go out over the radio," Stan said.

Brenna looked at her quizzically. "Who was the woman?"

"Her name was Eleanor. I used to work with her." She changed the subject before Brenna could ask. "So the Irish stew cook-off is today. I totally forgot about it."

The annual event Jake hosted drew local closet chefs, people who pulled out their aprons once each year to compete for one of the coveted awards. Categories included best overall stew, most creative use of spices, and best vegetarian option, among others. A local panel of judges tested the stews and awarded the prizes. Then Jake usually had a live Irish band or other form of entertainment after the contest, to round out the day.

"Yeah, the pub will be packed all day," Brenna said. "I'm going to go help out this afternoon. Another reason why I wanted to get here early. I hope I didn't wake you."

"No. I'm glad you're here. You're reminding me how much I need to get done."

"Did you look at the outline I emailed you for the website?" Brenna wanted to know. "No, Eva, we have to keep that in the bowl. Now we're going to make broccoli and cheese treats."

"Ewww." Eva wrinkled her nose. "We should make chocolate instead."

"Kitties and puppies can't eat chocolate. Vegetables it is," Brenna said, opening the fridge and pulling items out.

"I didn't look at the website outline. I'm sorry. I was working on menus yesterday, and doing some baking," Stan said. "Then I had to leave for the . . . party."

"I want to get working on it. The more hype we can get before you open, the more successful you'll be." Brenna hesitated. "Have you figured out who's making the pastry cases yet?"

She hadn't. She'd been putting it off ever since her mother "suggested" she contact a friend of hers to make the specialized dog- and cat-shaped pastry cases she wanted for the store. Which meant her mother expected her to contact this friend, no questions asked. A price she'd pay for her mother's investment in her business.

When her deal with Sheldon Allyn fell apart last month, Jake scrambled to make it right, understanding how much she wanted a brick-and-mortar shop, perhaps even more than she did. Her mother, either in a rare moment of thoughtfulness for her older daughter or anticipating her upcoming marriage to the mayor and doing her part to improve the town's appeal, offered to partner with him. Jake knew how Stan would feel about that and negotiated a sixty-forty split. Stan loved him for it, but sometimes her mother still acted like she had the final say. Stan didn't want some fancy person her mother knew making the cases. But she didn't know if she could get what she wanted elsewhere, either. "I didn't," she answered Brenna's question. "It's on my list."

Brenna wagged a finger at her. "They'll never be ready for your opening!"

"I know, I know." Scruffy came over and stood up against Stan's leg, stubby tail wagging, eyes hopeful as she waited for a kiss. "Hi, baby." Stan kissed the dog's nose. Scruffy licked hers, then ran back over to where Duncan and Gaston waited for falling snacks. "I'll work on it today." At least it was probably the last thing on her mother's mind after last night.

Footsteps clattered down the stairs, then Caitlyn appeared, still in her pajamas and a pair of fuzzy slippers, smoothing her hair with her fingers. She surveyed the scene in front of her. "Good morning. Why are we all up so early? We just went to bed. What on earth are you doing, Eva?"

"Baking!" Eva said, in a tone that suggested her mother was not very smart if she couldn't see that.

"Caitlyn, this is Brenna. Jake's sister. She works with me," Stan said. "Bren, my sister, Caitlyn."

Brenna waved a floury hand. "Hi. Your daughter's adorable."

"She's a character," Caitlyn said. She looked at Stan. "How'd you sleep?"

Great, if you considered two hours of half-asleep-ness "getting sleep." "As well as can be expected, I guess. You?"

Caitlyn shrugged. "Fine. I need coffee."

"Pour me more, too, will you?" Stan held out her mug.

"I think we can cut this batch now," Brenna announced. "Which cookie cutters should we use?" she asked Eva, pointing toward the offering she'd laid out and hoist-

125

ing Eva up so she could see. "We have cats, bears, different puppies. . . ."

Eva pondered the selection carefully before she chose one of Stan's most recent purchases, a schnauzer. They didn't have a schnoodle shape, so that was the best she could do. "That one. It looks like Scruffy."

Scruffy perked up at the sound of her name and went to Eva, licking her leg. Henry finally lumbered down the stairs and into the room. Eva rushed to him, throwing her arms around his neck.

"Easy, Eva!" Caitlyn commanded.

"She's fine," Stan said automatically.

Caitlyn shrugged and poured herself some coffee. "So what happens now?"

"With what?"

Caitlyn shot her a dirty look. "With the *m-u-r-d-e-r,*" she spelled.

Stan sighed. "You too with the spelling? I don't know. Maybe you should ask Jessie."

The phone rang. Stan moved to the counter to answer it.

"Your mother might be on her way over," Char said without preamble when she answered.

Stan walked out of the kitchen and into her favorite room, the small den at the front of the house. She sank down on the couch and rested her head against a throw pillow.

She hadn't gotten nearly enough sleep for this. "Might be?" she asked.

"Well. Tony never came to the B&B and she couldn't reach him. I stayed up with her until five. What a terribly long night that was! Anyway, I got up a little while ago and made breakfast like I always do — routine is everything, and I had guests checking out today — but your mother seemed very agitated and didn't want anything." Char sounded stymied by this. She loved to eat and didn't understand people who weren't as fixated on the activity.

Stan had to laugh. The lack of sleep hadn't affected Char's energy level too much.

"Anyway, if she can't track him down, I figure she'll come to you." Char dropped her voice. "His phone was off and he never did connect with her after he arrived at the party. They had her locked away, then they took him somewhere."

Stan remembered seeing Tony disappearing down the back stairwell with Captain Quigley and her stomach twisted into a knot. "Great," she said, trying to force cheer into her voice. "We have a full house this morning. Brenna's here baking."

"Want me to bring some food over? I made lots of quiche, and I even whipped up some beignets. I can bring chicory coffee."

Char's New Orleans roots made her meals the most coveted commodity in Frog Ledge, with some going so far as to stay overnight at her B and B to get a meal. Others set up town potluck events in hopes Char would bring gumbo or fried catfish she'd ordered from home. "Sure," she said. "If you're looking for a way to get rid of all the food. And you know how much I love chicory coffee." She hoped her stomach would settle enough to enjoy some of the goodies.

It would be good to get some time with Char, anyway. Maybe she could give Stan a rundown of everything that happened at the party before she arrived. Char was the queen of gossip — she had to know something.

CHAPTER 16

Stan went upstairs to rouse Jake and warn him about the full house, but he was already in the shower. Probably getting ready to go oversee his Irish stew competition. While she waited for him to emerge from the bathroom, she sat down with her laptop and pulled up the *Frog Ledge Holler* website. As Brenna promised, the lead story focused on the murder.

MURDER AT THE MAYOR'S, the headline read, and Stan cringed. She read the first paragraph.

An executive moonlighting as Frog Ledge mayor Tony Falco's "executive coach" was murdered Saturday night while attending Falco's engagement party at his home. Eleanor Chang, 48, was found dead in an upstairs bathroom by a party guest. Falco was not at the home when the murder occurred.

Nutty jumped onto her lap, nuzzling her chin. Cyril went on to say the police had a suspect in custody. The suspect wasn't named. No mention of a diamond engagement ring in an odd place, thank goodness. Stan clicked off the website.

The shower stopped and the doorbell rang simultaneously. The dogs did their usual barking and stampeding routine. Either Char with all the food, or her mother. God, she hoped it wasn't her mother. Maybe if she just hid up here no one would notice. She could sneak out the back door and go judge the Irish stew competition. Although she didn't eat meat, so that could be tough if the only offering she could taste was the vegetarian one.

Jake came out of the bathroom wearing jeans, no shirt, his hair still damp. His eyes lit up when he saw her. "Hey, beautiful." He came over to give her a kiss. She lingered, breathing in his clean scent. "How come you're up? You hardly got any sleep."

"You're up," she pointed out.

He smiled. "I'm used to it. I run a bar."

"True. I'm exhausted, but we've got lots of company. Brenna's here baking. I think Char just arrived with breakfast. Can you stay for a bit?" she asked hopefully.

"For a quick bite. I have the —"

"Irish stew. I know," Stan said. "Do you need help?"

"If it's from you I wouldn't turn it down," he said. "I don't know what's going to happen, since Tony's supposed to be a judge. But either way the show will go on."

"Well, Char told me Tony never went to the B&B last night. He didn't contact my mother at all."

"Really." Jake frowned. "So where was he? They wouldn't have let him stay at his house."

"I wouldn't think so. So I have no idea where he was. Cyril's got the story on his website. Not sure how he got all these details in the middle of the night, but so much for the state police's efforts to keep this on the down-low."

"Hey, Stan!" Caitlyn yelled up the stairs. "Char's here!"

Jake grinned. "Go ahead. I'll be down in a minute."

Stan descended the steps in time to join the parade of hands helping Char bring in enough food to feed McSwigg's patrons at its peak. Char wore a sunshine-yellow dress with white platform flip-flops. She blew a kiss at Stan over an overflowing plate of beignets. "Cyril's right behind me, honey," she said, wiggling her eyebrows in warning.

She should've known. The newspaperman might be quirky beyond words, but he took his job very seriously. If he was here, he either couldn't reach Tony or Patricia and thought Stan could help, or he'd heard Caitlyn had found the body and wanted to interview her. Or possibly all of the above.

He greeted her at the front door wearing his signature black trench coat, holding the last quiche from the backseat of Char's Range Rover. "Morning," he said, climbing onto her wraparound porch. Duncan pushed past her and shoved his nose against Cyril, sniffing for quiche. Stan yanked him away.

"Morning. What brings you over so early?"

"Next time, you guys should just invite me to the party," Cyril said. "I'm surprised your mother didn't want press coverage of her big engagement event."

Stan didn't have the heart to tell him she'd invited the *New York Times.* The *Frog Ledge Holler* wasn't really high on her list of society pages. Thankfully, the *Times* social reporter hadn't been able to make it. "Sorry," Stan said. "I wasn't in charge of the guest list." She held the door open for Cyril. "Are you here to interview me about my baking prowess?"

He gave her a look. "Come on, Stan.

Much as that will make a great Sunday feature, today's all about the murder in the mayor's bathroom. Hey, that's a better title. MURDER IN THE MAYOR'S BATHROOM." He scribbled it in his notebook, then tapped his pen against his chin thoughtfully. "I should've used it today."

"I can't tell you anything, Cyril."

"They arrested someone."

"So I heard."

"Someone you know. So why'd he do it?" Cyril leaned forward suggestively.

Terrific. Stan clenched her hands into fists until she felt her nails digging into her palms. "Innocent until proven guilty, right? I'm sure they'll tell you all about motive at the press conference. And I don't recall reading a name in your article."

Cyril shrugged. "I didn't have it when I wrote the breaking news. And I can't get a straight answer on when the press conference will be. Also can't get a confirmation on the cause of death, although I've heard a few similar accounts. If you'd like to confirm for me, I can run it regardless of Trooper Pasquale's attempts to keep it quiet."

It took Stan a while to get used to Cyril when she'd moved to town. Of course, she'd been at the center of a murder investigation when she'd first made his acquaintance.

133

Now she'd grown to the point of liking him most days, this oddball, dedicated journalist with the trademark trench coat regardless of weather, curly hair that he'd never figured out how to tame, bad teeth, and intense stare. But he was sort of lovable, when he wasn't writing stories about her or her family.

"I can't comment. I wasn't the one who found her. And I don't think Trooper Pasquale is trying to keep anything quiet. I think she's trying to put facts out there instead of speculation."

"Stan, Stan." Cyril shook his head at her. "I'm disappointed. You've seen this job from both sides. Don't you remember?"

"During the five minutes I filled in for you last winter? Of course I remember." Stan had jumped in for Cyril once over the winter when he'd had a conflict of interest during a murder case.

"Then you know we have to assume the worst when people won't answer questions. And when news like this doesn't come over the scanner." He waggled unkempt, knowing eyebrows at her. "Plus, I heard your sister found her. I also heard she's staying here with you. So I'm hoping I'm invited in for quiche."

"You can come in for quiche. But I doubt

my sister will want to talk about last night, and if you press the issue I'll throw you out before you have quiche."

Cyril sighed. "Fair enough."

Another car pulled up in front of Stan's house and parked on the street. It looked like she was having a party, and it wasn't even ten yet. But this car, she didn't recognize. It was a blue Corvette, and to the best of her knowledge she didn't know anyone with a blue Corvette in town. She squinted, trying to see the driver. Cyril turned to look with her. "Who's that?"

"I have no idea," she said. "But I've never entertained so many people in my pajamas before."

They watched as a man swung the Corvette's door open and unfolded himself from the low seat. He wore a baseball cap pulled down over his forehead. Sunglasses covered his eyes. But there was something familiar about his movements. The man shut the car door and loped over to them across Stan's grass. When he got closer, he raised his hand in a wave, a sheepish smile spreading across his face.

"Hey, Stan."

Stan's mouth dropped open. Kyle Mc-Leod. Her sister's ex-boyfriend, one of the chefs from her retreat with Sheldon Allyn earlier this summer. The one for whom Caitlyn had been willing to divorce her husband, and then found out she wasn't exactly his one and only.

If Caitlyn's weekend hadn't already gone down the toilet with the Eleanor Chang fiasco, this would certainly help it along.

Chapter 17

Stan pulled her front door all the way shut behind her and held the knob, hoping to dissuade anyone from coming out and seeing their visitor. "Kyle. What — how did you even know where I lived?"

He shrugged. "It wasn't that hard. I've been following the progress on your pet patisserie. It's public news that it's in Frog Ledge. I just went to the general store and asked for you."

Public news? And darn it, Abby, don't you know better than to give out addresses to strange men? Stan made a mental note to speak to the store owner about that.

"Anyway," Kyle went on, "I heard there was a family event here this weekend and thought I could catch Caitlyn. I really need to talk to her. Looks like she's here." He inclined his chin in the direction of Caitlyn's car.

Cyril watched the exchange with interest.

Stan figured he itched to pull out his steno pad and interview Kyle, but to his credit he waited to see what would happen next.

"Um," Stan said finally. Brilliant. But what was she supposed to say? Caitlyn really cared about Kyle. She'd been devastated when she found out what he'd been up to. "Eva's here," she said.

Kyle nodded. "I don't want to intrude. But maybe you could tell her I'm here?" He looked so earnest. "I really need to talk to her, Stan. I miss her."

The doorknob twisted in Stan's hand and Jake yanked the door open from Stan's grasp. He looked surprised to see them all out on the porch, holding the door prisoner. He'd dressed in his typical McSwigg's black T-shirt with small green lettering on the sleeve. His longish hair was still damp. He had a beignet balanced on a travel mug with coffee and looked just as much like a model as he had last night in his suit. Today it could be for either hair products or pastry. "I was looking for you," he said to Stan. "Morning, Cyril," he said with a nod. Then his gaze slid to Kyle.

Stan pulled the door shut behind him again. "Jake, Kyle McLeod," she said by way of introduction. Jake looked puzzled for a second, then recognition dawned.

"How's it going," was all he said to Kyle.

Kyle nodded, went to shake his hand, realized Jake's were full, and stuffed his own hands in his pockets.

Jake looked at Stan. "Walk with me?"

"Wait here," she instructed both Kyle and Cyril, then followed him to the driveway in her bare feet. "I don't know why he's here," she said before he could speak.

"That's your sister's ex? Is he still ex?"

Stan nodded.

"Do you think she's going to want to see him?"

"I have no idea. She hasn't said much about any of that."

Jake looked back toward the house, his gaze lingering on Kyle for a second before he turned back to Stan. "Is he going to try something stupid with her kid around?"

She shrugged. "I don't really know him. He doesn't seem crazy. Aside from his relationship problems."

"Do you want me to stay?"

Stan shook her head. "It'll be okay. Go get the bar ready." She stretched up on her tiptoes and kissed him.

He touched his forehead to hers. "Call me if there are any problems. There's enough drama going on around here without this."

"You're singing to the choir. It'll be fine.

I'll call you." She watched him balancing his breakfast as he unlocked his truck, thinking how amazing that she was able to still feel so lucky despite the consistent craziness. But murder aside, she'd moved to this town more alone than she'd realized. It took this village of real people to introduce her to true friendship — and true love.

Once he'd safely deposited the beignet and coffee in his console, he turned back. "You still coming by the bar later? I'll have French fries for you." He grinned.

She laughed. "I'll be over. I'll try some of the vegetarian stew."

He cringed. "What kind of Irish girl are you, anyway?"

"One who doesn't eat meat. But you knew that when you fell in love with me." She winked.

"I certainly did." He kissed her again, hopped in his truck, and started it.

Stan waved as he pulled out of the driveway and looped around the green toward Main Street. Once his truck was out of sight, she walked back toward Kyle and Cyril, still standing on the front porch.

"Okay," she said to Kyle. "No promises. And if she asks you to leave, you're leaving. This is not the best time. Understood?"

"Got it," Kyle said. "I swear, I don't want

to upset her, Stan. But what do you mean, not the best time? Is she okay?"

"She found a murdered woman," Cyril explained helpfully.

Kyle's face paled. He looked at Stan. She knew they were both thinking about another murder victim.

"That's horrifying," he said. "She'll have a hard time with that, after . . . what happened. Please, can I see her now?"

Cyril watched the whole exchange with great interest. Stan turned on him. "This is not for prime time."

"I don't write for TV," he said innocently.

She rolled her eyes heavenward. "How is this my life? You know what I mean, Cyril." She waited until he grudgingly nodded, then turned to Kyle. "Okay. Let's do this."

She shoved the door open. "Hey, Caitlyn? Can you come here for a second?" To Cyril, she murmured, "You may want to go inside. I'll meet you in there."

Cyril didn't protest. He headed inside, nodding to Caitlyn as she passed him on her way out of the kitchen. "Hello. Cyril Pierce. Publisher, editor, and writer at the *Frog Ledge Holler.*"

Caitlyn waved her beignet at Cyril. "Nice to meet you."

Her sister was eating a beignet? The world

141

really had tilted on its axis. Stan had a moment of regret for what she was about to do, but figured if Kyle wanted to track Caitlyn down badly enough he'd do it at her house or somewhere else. Better here, where she had support. Jake could throw him out, if necessary.

"What's up?" Caitlyn asked, powdered sugar drifting gently to the floor as she bit into her treat.

Stan mouthed, *I'm sorry,* then pulled the door open wider. "You have a visitor."

Caitlyn looked expectantly at the door. Kyle stepped into view, that same sheepish smile on his face. "Hey."

Caitlyn's smiled faded. To her credit, she didn't scream or throw her beignet at him. Instead, she said flatly, "Please leave." Then turned on her heel and started back to the kitchen.

Kyle rushed past Stan before she could stop him. "Caitlyn. Wait. Please. Just hear me out, then if you still want me to go, I'll go. I just need to talk to you. Please?"

Caitlyn stopped walking, her back still to Kyle. Stan waited, holding her breath. Finally, her sister turned. "You have five minutes," she said, then flounced past him onto the porch.

Stan looked at Kyle. "I'll be inside if

anyone needs me. Remember what you promised."

CHAPTER 18

Kyle nodded and followed Caitlyn out, closing the door behind him. Stan debated listening at the door, then decided against it. Caitlyn was a grown woman who could make her own decisions. If she needed help, she'd come get her. Stan went back to the kitchen, where the mood was even more animated than when she'd left. Char's quiches warmed in the oven, strong coffee permeated the air, and Eva wore more powdered sugar than any of the beignets still on a plate. She and Brenna both alternated between eating their doughnuts and cutting Schnauzer-shaped cookies into the dough. A half-eaten piece of quiche sat next to the mixing bowl. Cyril sat at the table with Char. They both ate beignets, too. They all looked expectantly at Stan when she returned.

"What?" she asked.

"What's going on outside?" Char asked

innocently, dabbing at her mouth with a paper napkin.

Stan shrugged, looking pointedly at Eva. Her niece worked the cookie cutter in the dough while singing to Henry, who stared at her adoringly. "My sister has a visitor."

"Is it Daddy?" Eva piped up.

Brenna, Char, and Cyril all looked at Eva, then at Stan.

"No," Stan said finally. "It's not your daddy."

Eva breathed out a sigh of relief. "Good. Sometimes she throws things at Daddy."

Brenna stifled a giggle. Cyril raised an eyebrow but said nothing. Char shoved the quickly diminishing beignet plate at him. "Eat."

Cyril didn't argue. He looked like he'd gone into shock from the crazy-strong coffee, which Char topped off in his cup. Brenna loaded a sheetful of cookies into the oven, then took a bite of her quiche. "Break time!" she announced to Eva. Eva dropped her cookie cutter, then climbed on Henry's back. He blinked, then lay down.

"Eva, honey, don't sit on Henry," Stan said.

"So who's outside then?" Char asked, still trying for innocent.

Stan looked at Cyril. "Did you tell her?"

Cyril raised his hands in defense. "She threatened to withhold the beignets."

"Cyril! And Char! What's wrong with you two?"

"Hey," Char said. "I have to stay on top of what's happening in my town. So what *is* happening? Are they getting back together? Did he bring her a fancy present?"

"I have no idea," Stan said.

Char humphed. "Then why aren't you out there eavesdropping?"

Stan shot her a death glare.

"Speaking of our town," Cyril said. "We're forgetting what's really important here. Can you talk to me about last night?" He looked from Char to Stan.

Stan turned the death glare on him. "Eva, honey, why don't you take Henry into the backyard," she said. "He needs to go outside."

Eva jumped up. "Come on, Henry!" Waving a freshly baked cookie at him, she raced to the door. He trotted after her obediently.

When she heard the door bang shut, Stan turned to Cyril. "We don't know any more than you already reported," Stan said. "You should talk to the mayor."

Cyril inclined his head in agreement. "I'd love to. I saw his car at the pub, but the doors were locked."

Stan's head snapped up. She looked at Char, who looked just as surprised. "At the pub? Today?"

Cyril nodded, eyes narrowing at their reaction. "Why?"

"Just surprised," Stan said. "Jake wasn't sure he'd still be up to judging the contest."

"He's judging the Irish stew?" Char frowned. "He's not Irish!"

"So where was he last night, anyway?" Cyril asked. "When this executive got herself murdered?"

"What do I look like, an information booth? Ask him!" Stan said.

"Is your mother up to talking? I'm sure residents would like to hear from her. Given that she'll be the town's new first lady."

Stan groaned. Char wagged a finger at Cyril. "Honey," she said, "I don't think you want to go there."

Cyril considered that. He'd met Patricia. He let it go. "Then can you give me a reaction? Anything?" He ate more quiche, looking expectant.

"It was horrible," Stan said through clenched teeth. "Such a tragedy. You can quote me on that." Really, she wanted him to go. She needed to talk to Char about what she'd seen or heard and couldn't do it with him listening.

"Someone was murdered in the midst of a hundred people. So scary," Char added.

"Mmm . . ." Cyril said, trying to scribble with one hand while retaining his grip on his fork. "That's good." He sipped his coffee and consulted his notes, then looked at Stan. "What do you know about the suspect?"

Stan stood up so abruptly she almost knocked over a plate of quiche. "Cyril. I. Have. No. More. Comments. Got it?"

The front door slamming cut off any reply he had. Stan escaped into the hall and saw her sister racing up the stairs in tears.

Stan went to the front door, but Kyle and his sports car were gone. At least he'd listened to her warning. It certainly appeared he'd been asked to leave.

She went back to the kitchen in time to hear Char adding to her comments. "I hope they solve this quickly. Patricia is so upset," she said. "She was up all night. Don't quote me on that. But I heard her wandering the house. Savannah was concerned." Savannah was Char and Ray's dog who watched over the alpacas.

Stan frowned. "My mother? Wandering?" Patricia didn't wander. And nothing interfered with her beauty sleep, especially if it was already cut short.

"Yes. Well, I'm sure it must feel terrible." Char shivered. "A woman murdered in your bathroom? Heavens! It felt terrible to me and I don't live there. I can't imagine. I'd never be able to take a shower in there again." She ate more beignet.

Stan sighed. "Can you keep an eye on Eva, Char? I have to go see if Caitlyn's okay."

"Of course, honeybun," Char said, waving her off. "Give her a hug for me. No-good, rotten men."

"Hey," Cyril protested.

"You're right," Char said. "My Raymond excluded, because he knows I'd kill him and feed him to the gators if he was rotten."

Stan shook her head and took the stairs two at a time. Caitlyn's door was ajar. Stan peeked in. Her sister lay facedown on the bed. Stan knocked. "Hey. You okay?"

Caitlyn rolled over and looked at her. Her eyes were still red but her face was dry. "Fine."

"I'm sorry. He just showed up." Stan held up her hands helplessly. "I didn't know what to do."

To her surprise, her sister shook her head. "Not your fault. I'm surprised he could find the place on the map. I have no idea why he'd bother." Her voice was bitter. "Maybe his other girlfriend dumped him, too."

Stan closed the door behind her and sat on the bed. "What did he say?"

Caitlyn snorted and tossed a pillow aside. "That he loved me. And missed me. And all the other usual platitudes lying sacks of garbage say. And that he only took off with Bimbo Number Two because he was so 'terrified' " — she inserted air quotes around the word — "about his feelings for me. And he also wanted me to know he started divorce proceedings from Bimbo Number One." She flopped back on the bed and covered her face with her hands. "Loser," she mumbled.

Stan suppressed a smile. It wasn't lost on her that she and her sister had never commiserated about boys as teenagers. It felt a little weird now, but . . . kind of good. "So what did you tell him?" she asked.

Caitlyn uncovered her eyes. "I told him to get lost."

"Do you think he'll listen?"

"He better listen or I'll call the cops. Will Jake's sister escort him out of town?" Caitlyn sat up, suddenly interested. "Do you think I can ask her?"

"No! Jeez. No. She will not do that. And if you ask her she'll probably escort *me* out of town."

"How's that fair?" Caitlyn asked. "He can just go where he wants and bother people?"

Stan sat on the edge of the bed. "He's not dangerous, is he?"

Caitlyn pouted and shook her head. "All he did was cry."

"Cry? Really?" She cleared her throat when Caitlyn glared at her. "He has no right to cry. Jerk."

"You know what stinks?" Caitlyn asked.

"What?"

"I really love that jerk." Caitlyn dissolved into tears again.

Stan awkwardly put her arm around her. Caitlyn leaned her head on her shoulder. They sat like that for a while, until Eva came upstairs with Henry hot on her heels.

"Mommy, are you sad?" she asked.

Caitlyn wiped her eyes and smiled at her daughter. "A little, honey, but I'm fine."

Eva looked at her skeptically. "You don't look fine. Want me to take you shopping? That'll make you feel better."

Stan laughed. "You've taught her well." She rose. "I'm going to shower. I have to head to the pub soon."

"I'm going to hide out here," Caitlyn said.

"Good plan." Stan slipped into her room to get ready. When she emerged and went downstairs, no one was there but Brenna.

"Where'd everyone go?"

"Cyril couldn't get any good info, so he went on a hunt for more victims. I think Char's coffee was more than he bargained for. He might be working a double shift today to get all his energy out. Char went home to help Ray with some chores."

"That was a lot for first thing in the morning. Especially after a night like that."

Brenna laughed. "That's what you get when you live in Frog Ledge. It's like every day is an open house." She took a finished cookie in the shape of a bone, broke it into pieces, and handed one to Scruffy. "Is your sister okay?"

"She'll be fine." She hoped. She fished in her purse when she heard her cell ringing. It was Char.

"I wanted to tell you before you heard it somewhere else. Or saw him around town again," Char said.

Stan felt her stomach twist. "What? Saw who around town?"

"Caitlyn's chef. He rented a room at the B&B."

Just what they all needed. More drama. "With my mother staying there? Good Lord. For how long?"

"Well, that's the thing. He handed me a boatload of cash and said he would need

152

the room for as long as it takes."

"As long as it takes?" Stan repeated. "As long as what takes?"

Char hesitated. When she spoke, Stan could hear the undertone of excitement in her voice. "As long as it takes to get Caitlyn to marry him."

CHAPTER 19

Stan disconnected, wondering how to break this news to her sister. Kyle moving into Char's B&B? What would possess him to do that? And where had he gotten a "boatload of cash"? Despite herself, she wondered if Kyle'd stuck it out with Sheldon Allyn and something came from that elusive Food Channel contract after all.

She pushed the thought out of her head. She didn't care about Sheldon. Or Kyle, for that matter. She was getting her shop, and it was hers. And Jake's. They could do things on their terms. She conveniently pushed her mother's influence out of her mind.

"What's wrong?" Brenna asked.

"Nothing," Stan muttered. "Just another day in my life. When are you heading to the pub?"

"As soon as this last batch comes out of the oven. You going now?"

Stan glanced at the clock on her phone. "I

want to see if I can catch Tony before the place gets crowded."

"You should go, then," Brenna said. "People like to get an early seat for this one."

Stan drove the three minutes to the pub. Brenna wasn't kidding. The parking lot was full even though they weren't open yet. The Irish stew chefs, probably, and anyone else who could sneak in with them. Stan went around to the back and let herself into the kitchen, which bustled with activity. Pots of stew simmered on every available burner. People rushed around calling for ingredients and sampling one another's offerings. She spied Jake at the counter dicing potatoes and carrots and went up behind him.

"Hey."

He turned around, brightening when he saw her. "Hey. I didn't expect you so soon. Everything okay? How'd it go with Caitlyn and her ex?"

"She told him to leave," Stan said.

"Good. Did he?"

"No. He got a room at Char's and said he's staying until Caitlyn marries him. She doesn't know that yet. Char called me a few minutes ago, I know, I know." She held up her hand. "You don't even have to say it. I'm sorry you're stuck with someone in a

155

crazy family."

"I'm not," he said with a shrug, turning back to the cutting board and slicing neatly through the middle of a carrot. "All families are crazy, anyway. I'd be with you even if you were related to Ted Bundy."

She felt that rush of *ohmyGod* that always happened when he said things like that. "Cool. So that gives me immunity, right?"

"Immunity for what?"

"For whatever they do during the next few weeks? I'm guessing things are going to get even more interesting around here." She blew out a breath. "Anyway. Cyril said he saw Tony's car. Is he here?"

"I haven't seen him, but I was downstairs for a bit. And I hear a bunch of people out there setting up." He pointed into the main bar. "It's not really my bar right now," he said with a grin. "I'm just here to provide the potatoes. Although I am offering corned beef and cabbage and Reubens, so I have to take back my stoves at some point."

Stan snagged a carrot to offset her beignets and wandered into the main room. The mahogany bar gleamed in the sunlight streaming in the windows. One of the bartenders worked furiously cutting up limes and lemons into metal trays, the light flashing off his knife blade. All the liquor bottles sat proudly on their shelves, and above the bar hung her favorite piece of art — the carved wooden sign that read YOUR FEET WILL BRING YOU TO WHERE YOUR HEART IS in Gaelic. She loved the words because they'd been true for her. She'd been drawn to this bar from the moment she stepped into town.

They'd transformed the area reserved for live entertainment into a ministage with a long table stretched across, covered with a green tablecloth with four-leaf clovers. Irish-themed decorations were perched on both ends. There were five chairs set up with name cards in front of them for the judges. On the floor, a collection of circular tables waited for the pots of stew, today's lead act. Matching Irish decorations graced those tables as well.

"Stan! Are you cooking with us?" Betty Meany, the executive director of the Frog Ledge Library, swooped over and gave Stan a kiss on the cheek. She stood almost a full head shorter. Her short white hair stood up in youthful, carefully styled spikes. Today, the tips were a light shade of green. She'd dressed in a black pantsuit with a green silk scarf at her neck. Four-leaf clover earrings dangled from her lobes. "Is there an Irish stew for pups? How are you, sweetie? It's good to see you. I didn't even get a chance to talk to you last night, what with all the . . . disruption. My goodness, what is this world coming to?" She shook her head solemnly, then narrowed her eyes. "And what does our esteemed mayor have to do with what happened? Very suspicious, if you ask me." She tilted her head, motioning across the room. Stan saw Tony, huddled in a private conversation with Don Miller, another town council member.

Before Stan could formulate a response, Betty went on. "Anyway, we need to talk about the next art show at the library. I want you to help me with it." She wagged a finger at Stan. "And don't tell me you're too busy, either. I need your eye."

Stan couldn't help but smile. Betty's energy rivaled that of the Energizer Bunny on crack. Coupled with her fierce love of books and her town, she was a formidable part of Frog Ledge's fabric. And she knew how to run events. "I would love to help," Stan said. "We'll figure something out."

"How is the shop going? I've heard so many people talking about it. They can't wait for you to open. It's such a great idea. My Houdini already told me he wants to come for a cuppa."

Houdini, Betty's indoor cat, loved escaping into the wild. When Stan first moved to town, Houdini showed up at her door repeatedly looking for treats after word got around that her house was the place to find them. Betty took a number of precautions to keep her wayward cat from taking off for good, including window and door screens with alarms on them so she could tell when he was trying to escape.

"I hope you bring him," Stan said. "I want it to be cat- and dog-friendly. Cats are harder to travel with, so we need someone to get the trend going."

"Well, we all know I'm a trendsetter," Betty said gaily. "Count us in! Do you need help with your grand opening?"

"I'm sure I will. Since you like to plan parties and all."

"Honey, I can plan a party like you've never seen," Betty said, patting Stan's arm. "You tell me when you need me. Now, make sure you come back for our stew." She winked. "It darn well better win! Gotta go. I need some potatoes." She dashed off toward the kitchen.

Stan glanced over at Tony and Don. Still whispering to each other. She squared her shoulders and marched over to them. She realized too late she had no idea what to say until they'd seen her and let their conversation trail off.

Don Miller's eyes darted around, looking for an escape. He was less comfortable around people since his family's involvement in a scandal earlier in the year. After a long leave of absence, he'd returned to his council position, but life had clearly changed him. His big, burly, karate-schoolteacher look was gone, replaced by a gaunt, drawn, less muscular version. He rarely spent time in the public eye anymore aside from council meetings.

He nodded at her. "Hello."

"Hi, Don. Sorry to interrupt, but I need to talk to Tony for a second."

Tony pasted on his political smile. "I'll speak with you later, Don."

Don nodded and slipped away to a table of folks Stan didn't recognize.

"Little League," Tony said, by way of explanation. "His son is on the team and he's worried that the schedule could cut into council meetings. But I told him, family first. Don't you agree?"

She nodded. "I do."

"So what can I do for you, Kristan? Are you cooking this morning?"

Like nothing ever happened. What planet was this guy on? "No," Stan said. "I saw your car and stopped in to see you."

"Me?" He tried to look surprised. "To what do I owe the honor?"

"I wanted to make sure you were doing all right," Stan said, fighting to keep her tone sincere. "You know, after last night."

"Yes. My goodness. What a tragic event." He shook his head sadly. "We're doing as well as can be expected."

Who's we? According to Char, he hadn't even been back to see her mother. "Tony. Where were you all night? I heard you didn't go to Char's with my mother."

"I was with the police. They had a lot of questions, understandably, about what happened. And I didn't want to disrupt the B&B when they were done with me, so I just went to my office."

Plausible story, but why hadn't he reached out this morning? Why had he just shown up at the pub like nothing had happened? "My mother is probably frantic," she said.

Tony looked away. "I called her this morning," he said.

Stan didn't know if that was true or not. "So do the police know what happened last night? Like why they think Eleanor was killed?"

"They wouldn't share that with me even if they knew, I'm quite sure," he said. "You might know better than I what would have prompted this tragedy."

"I would? Why's that?" Her hands went to her hips.

"You're . . . acquainted with the suspect."

"So are you, apparently. He was at *your* party."

They stared at each other, a silent stand-off. Tony didn't move, but Stan could almost feel him squirm under her gaze. He didn't speak.

Which compelled her to push him. "He was at your party but you weren't," she said. "Why were you late?"

Another stare-off.

"Hey, Mayor?"

They both turned to find one of the bartenders standing there awkwardly. "Sorry to interrupt, but we're supposed to get a pre-competition photo of the judges."

Tony smiled. "Of course." He looked at Stan. "I trust we'll catch up later?"

Stan didn't return his smile. "Count on it," she said.

CHAPTER 20

The competition didn't start until one, so Stan had time to kill. She offered to help in the kitchen, but there were way too many people cooking and counter space was tight. After she almost sliced off her thumb peeling a potato, Jake took the peeler and steered her to the door.

"You need to relax today, not work," he told her. "Go grab some coffee and come back in a bit. I'll save you a seat. Okay?" He kissed her and pushed her outside before she could protest.

Jake was right. She felt useless. She got in her car and sat there for a minute, trying to figure out what to do next. Go talk to her mother? No. Then she'd have to tell her she saw Tony. Go talk to Char? No, because inevitably she'd bump into her mother. Go home? Then she'd have to tell Caitlyn that Kyle'd moved into Char's. She picked up her phone and scrolled to Jessie's number, but got her voice mail. She could talk to people who'd been at the party, find out if anyone heard or saw anything that would offer up some clue about Eleanor's death. Preferably, a clue that didn't point to Richard. Finding people who'd been there shouldn't be hard given that her mother invited half the town.

She decided to start with Izzy. That way she could refuel with coffee and whatever muffin was on special today. Sugar and caffeine seemed the best plan for getting through this day. Hopefully, by now the morning rush at the café had dispersed and she could grab her friend for a few minutes.

She drove the short distance to Izzy's and went inside, breathing in the scent of strong coffee and cinnamon. Izzy's place was her other haven in town. The coffee and chocolate component put it in the running for first, but Jake's presence at the pub won every time. Still, Izzy's place was totally trendy and cool. Completely out of touch with the farming town around her. It felt like a shop you'd find in New York or San Francisco, with its retro purple walls and framed Coco Chanel quotes.

Thankfully, it was quiet. A few people were scattered at tables around the café, alone and in pairs, but no one waited in line at the counter at this in-between time. Perfect. Izzy straightened from where she had been adding truffles to one of her shelves and waved.

"Hey, girl. I was hoping you'd be in." She leaned her elbows on the counter and waited for Stan to come over. "How're you holding up?"

"Me? How about you?" Stan asked sympathetically. Izzy opened the café at six a.m. weekdays, seven on the weekends. Which would mean she might have grabbed an hour of sleep early this morning, if she'd managed to get to sleep at all. The entire town would be cranky and sleep-deprived today.

Izzy brushed off her concern. "I'm divine. I had help this morning, so I didn't even come in until eight. What're you having?" She glanced at her watch. "I can sit with you for a bit. Jana is out back."

"I was hoping." Stan ordered a large mocha latte with a double shot of espresso and one of Izzy's caramel chip muffins, warmed. She shoved the thoughts of Char's beignets out of her mind. She'd do extra laps on the green tomorrow to make up for today's sins.

Two of Izzy's dogs poked their heads out of the back room, wagging at the sound of her voice. Elvira the poodle and Bax the boxer realized the day Stan moved in that she'd be a welcome addition to town.

"Hey, guys," Stan said, crouching to pet the dogs. Scruffy would be jealous. She loved Izzy's three dogs. "Where's Junior?" Junior was Izzy's newest addition, adopted after he'd tragically become homeless. He was an old retriever, good-natured, lazy, and happy to be part of a family ruled by food.

"He's sound asleep upstairs." Izzy sighed. "Poor guy is getting old. But he's still happy. Grab the back booth while I get your coffee." She moved to the espresso machine.

Stan took a quick look around to see who else was in the café. In the next booth over, a girl with a long, red braid giggled with her boyfriend, a bearded guy wearing a T-shirt depicting an elephant carrying a hand grenade in his trunk. College students studied in small groups scattered around the room. An older couple — definitely not locals — munched on Danish while they people-watched. Abby from the general store took an early lunch break at a window seat. No one was talking about the murder as far as she could tell.

Her cell phone rang. She pulled it out and saw Nikki Manning's name pop up. She usually talked to her best friend at least once a week. She had to tell her what happened, but didn't have time right now. She let it go to voice mail so she'd remember to call her later.

Izzy brought her coffee and muffin over, along with a latte for herself. "They were all talking about it this morning," she said, reading Stan's mind. "Despite the fact that no one in town got any sleep, this place was packed and murder was *the* hot topic." She sank into the booth facing the door. "Have you heard anything else? Did anyone find the mayor? He vanished into thin air after he went upstairs with the cops."

Boy, word did get around fast. "Yeah. He wasn't missing, turns out. He slept in his office. Now he's at the pub getting ready to judge the Irish stew cook-off."

"Huh?" Izzy cupped her hand over her ear as if she hadn't heard right. "You're kidding."

"Nope. That's what he told me. They questioned him so long he didn't want to disturb my mother and Char by going to the B&B so late." She rolled her eyes.

"You talked to him?"

Stan nodded. "I just left the pub."

"So where was he during his own party?"

"No idea. He wouldn't tell me."

"Curiouser and curiouser," Izzy said, taking a swig of coffee. "So this woman who got killed. She worked for Tony?"

"Yep. His 'executive coach.' " Stan made air quotes around the words.

"I get the sense you didn't like her."

"No comment."

"What about your ex?"

"What about him?"

"He still locked up?"

"As far as I know."

"You think he could've done it?" Izzy asked seriously.

"No! I would've known if I was dating someone who could *kill* people." Stan shuddered.

"Hey, not necessarily," Izzy said. "Look at all those serial killer wives who swear they had no idea their husbands were out at night luring unsuspecting victims to their deaths."

Stan stared at her. "So not helpful. And not the same thing, either." She sipped her latte and broke off a piece of her still-steaming muffin. "I'm serious. He didn't do it. It feels wrong. Which brings me to my visit. I need your help."

"Oooh! Sounds mysterious." Izzy leaned in. "Tell me more."

"You got to the party on time, right?"

Izzy nodded. "Six on the dot. Again, I'm

so sorry I didn't get to tell you Richard was there before you saw him."

"I don't care about that. I want to know what was going on when you arrived. Did you see Eleanor with anyone? Arguing? Talking? Heck, making out?"

Izzy laughed. "Now, see, that's the interesting part. I wouldn't have even known who she was if she hadn't been in here before. But yes, I did see her at the party. With her daughter, mostly."

"Wait. She was here in your shop?" The thought of Eleanor in her friend's place, sitting at tables she frequented, eating Izzy's treats, bothered her. But again, it was a free country. "When?"

"Last week."

"I guess that makes sense. She was working with Tony. I'm sure she came out here from time to time. I'm just glad I never bumped into her before."

But Izzy shook her head slowly. "She wasn't with Tony. She was with one of the other council members."

Stan frowned. "She was? Which one?"

"The short one who wears a bow tie to council meetings. With the annoying voice."

Stan searched her brain for his name. "Wallace. Curtis Wallace."

Izzy snapped her fingers. "That's it."

"What was she doing with him?"

"Fighting," Izzy said matter-of-factly.

Stan stared at her. *What?*

"Yup. It was Monday, I think. Yeah, because I had a hair appointment." She fingered one of her intricate braids. "They did a nice job, eh? New girl, next town over. Anyway, she came in alone — Eleanor — asked Jana if she could use my back room for an important meeting." Izzy had a small room behind the main café she usually reserved for poetry slams, painting parties, or other private events. "Jana let her, since it was empty. When I got here I came in through the back hall. Heard arguing, so I knocked on the door. Last thing I wanted was some big problem, you know what I mean?"

Stan nodded.

"She opened it, said she was sorry, they were having a business disagreement. I told her to keep it down or find a new meeting spot. Wallace left a few minutes later. Apparently, she wasn't done, because she followed him right out to the parking lot. Didn't care who saw. He looked mortified."

Stan sat back in her chair, a million questions swirling. "How does she know *Wallace?*" Was she working with the whole council? Did the others know? "Did you tell anyone this last night?" she asked Izzy.

"No. I just remembered this morning. I knew she looked familiar but I couldn't place it." She looked at Stan. "You think it means something?"

"Depends on what they were fighting about," Stan said. "And whether or not Curtis holds a grudge." She didn't say the obvious: that Curtis had been at the party last night. Had he seen Eleanor go upstairs and followed her to finish off their fight?

CHAPTER 21

Stan left her half-eaten muffin on the plate and hurried out of Izzy's. Did Jessie know about this? If not, Wallace should at least be questioned. Which might give Richard some breathing room. Stan tried her cell, her office at town hall, her cell again, and Marty's house. No one answered any of those numbers. She was probably still working. Which meant she'd be at the barracks.

She checked the clock on her phone. If she drove out there, she wouldn't make it back in time for the competition and Jake would wonder where she was. She'd better stop and let him know what was going on. As she drove over to the pub, she tried her mother's cell. Straight to voice mail, too. Where was everyone today?

Pulling back into the McSwigg's parking lot, she hurried around to the kitchen entrance for the second time. The door stood ajar as someone emptied trash into the Dumpster behind the building. Stan hurried inside, scanning the room for Jake.

"Hey, Stan!" Sean, one of Jake's bartenders, waved at her with a handful of parsley. "Looking for the big guy? He's out front."

Stan thanked him and pushed through the swinging doors into the bar area. The pace was even more frenzied now as cooks hauled batches of stew out in their warming pots and scrambled to add last-minute dashes of herbs and spices. The judges congregated in front of their table. Tony wasn't among them. She spied Jake across the room and started toward him, but out of the corner of her eye she saw a flash of red ponytail. She stopped and looked again. Jessie stood across the room near one of the Irish stewpots. Why was she here at the bar? Unless she was following up a lead. Maybe she was questioning Tony after all.

Stan made a beeline through the crowd, jostling a pot of stew in transit. She winced as she heard a splash and an indignant protest, but didn't stop. When she reached Jessie, she skidded to a stop, her mouth falling open. She was already surprised to see Jessie here dressed in jeans and a T-shirt rather than toiling away at the barracks on a murder case, and that surprise was compounded by the beer in her hand. Not to mention, it was barely afternoon. But more important, Jessie didn't drink.

"Jessie?" Stan approached her cautiously. It had to be someone else. Everyone had a doppelgänger, right? As soon as this woman turned, she'd have a totally different face. And Stan wouldn't have to feel like Alice plummeting down the rabbit hole.

But it wasn't someone else. Jessie most definitely stood in front of her, not working, not dressed in uniform, and though Stan hadn't seen her raise the glass, a real beer in her hand. She looked like she hadn't been to bed yet, either.

Jessie turned at the sound of her name. "Yeah?" Despite her obvious exhaustion, her tone held a challenge.

"What are you doing?"

Jessie glanced around. "I'm waiting for the competition to start. What are you doing?"

"Looking for you, actually."

"Well, you found me."

"Are you *drinking*?"

Jessie lifted her chin, eyes flashing. "I'm having a beer. Why? Last I checked, I was over twenty-one."

Stan glanced around, certain she was being punked. Any minute now, someone with a video camera would leap out from under one of the tables holding the stewpots. She waited, but no one did.

"Can I . . . talk to you upstairs?" Stan asked.

"Right this minute? I'm kind of busy."

Busy doing what? "Yes, right this minute. Come on." Stan grabbed the sleeve of Jessie's long-sleeved T-shirt and pulled her away.

Jessie heaved a sigh full of heavy burdens, but allowed Stan to drag her to the back of the pub. Stan pushed open the slightly hidden door leading to the upstairs apartment and used her key from when Jake lived there — thank goodness Brenna insisted she keep it — to open the apartment door at the top of the steps. Brenna took over the comfy three-room space when Jake moved in with Stan. Actually, she'd given them the nudge they needed to take the leap and move in together when she decided she wanted her own place but didn't want to give up the location. Jake'd been all about the arrangement because someone would still be right upstairs in case there was a problem at the bar. And because then he could still keep an eye on her, especially now that she had a serious boyfriend.

Stan poked her head in, called out, "Hello?" Scott sometimes stayed here and she didn't want to invade his privacy.

But no one answered, so she went in. Jessie followed, dropping onto a chair at the kitchen table. She placed her beer in front of her and stared at it. Stan closed the door behind her and surveyed the room, noticing the female touches that hadn't been here when it was Jake's bachelor pad — fresh flowers in a vase on the counter, a modern wooden bowl filled with fruit on the kitchen table. The room smelled like apple cider. She noticed a half-burned Yankee candle on a small table in the hall. It always felt homey when Jake lived here, but Brenna's touch turned it into something completely new.

She pulled out the chair opposite Jessie and sat. "What's going on?"

"With what?"

"With you! Since when do you drink beer? And why aren't you working?" If she hadn't been so puzzled, she would've seen the irony of asking this question when most of the time people asked Jessie why she was *still* working.

"It's my weekend off," Jessie said sarcastically.

"Is Marty here?"

Jessie sniffed. "No. Why? Am I not allowed out unless Marty's with me?"

"I figured you'd be working on the murder. Or sleeping."

Jessie said nothing.

Oookay. "Anyway, I need your help." Stan leaned forward across the table. "It's about Richard."

Jessie sat up abruptly, her knee banging the table and causing her beer to slosh over the edge of the mug. She cursed and rubbed her leg.

"Jeez. Are you okay?"

"I'm fine," Jessie said through gritted teeth. "But forget Richard. He's in custody. It's over." She picked up the beer and took a long swig, unable to hide the grimace as she swallowed.

Stan reached across the table and pulled the beer mug out of her reach. "Jessie. What is *wrong* with you? You haven't even heard what I have to say. Listen, Richard is a jerk. Trust me, I know this. But he's not a killer. Eleanor was . . . not the most popular person on earth. He can't be the only choice from that crowd."

"Maybe not, but I have someone on record who saw him arguing with her. 'Screaming,' was the actual quote. Then he takes off in a snit and shows up looking like he just wrestled an alligator, with some lame excuse about chasing Tony's cat."

"Tony's cat? Tony has a cat? My mother's

never mentioned that. Who heard them arguing? About what?"

"It doesn't matter," Jessie interrupted. "Forget it. Forget all of it. Last night is not your problem. It's not mine anymore, either."

"I think you need to get some sleep. You're not making any sense. Why don't you go take a nap? I'm sure Brenna won't mind if you crash here for a while. Want me to find you a blanket?" She rose to go check the living room for a blanket and pillow, but Jessie stopped her.

"Stan. Get it through your thick head." She took a deep breath. "I'm off the case."

CHAPTER 22

Stan froze, the words floating into her brain but not really sinking in. "I . . . don't understand."

"Join the club," Jessie muttered. "The official word is, 'Given the *sensitivity* and *high-profile nature* we thought it best to turn this one fully over to Major Crimes.' Which I translated to, 'We're closing this no matter what and we don't want you effing it up.' "

Stan sank back down in her chair, finally getting it. "They're protecting somebody. Not somebody," she corrected herself. "Tony. From the publicity." *Or something else.*

Jessie covered her face with her hands. "I hate hearing that out loud. I hate even thinking it. But it's the only thing I can come up with. And there's diddly-squat I can do about it."

"But listen. That's why I wanted to talk to you. I just left Izzy's." Stan recounted Izzy's story about Eleanor and Curtis Wallace. "Wallace was at the party. That's enough to at least look at him, I would think. Not to mention . . ." She hesitated. "Tony's convenient absence. It doesn't sit well."

"In any other situation, that would be enough to at least question someone," Jessie said. "But they think they have their man. Case closed. And unless I want to be totally out of a job, I can't say a word." She laughed bitterly. "Do you know how mad that makes me? I became a police officer because I believe in justice. And now the people I look up to are —" She broke off. "Maybe I'm in the wrong job after all."

"Jess. You're not. Listen to me. You can make them listen." Stan reached across the table and grabbed Jessie's arm. "You just need to figure out what really happened. You were at the party before I got there. Did you see anyone arguing with her? Did you notice her? Was she behaving oddly? You've got a sixth sense for crime. I feel like I missed whatever happened to set this off, and when I finally got there I was too busy getting yelled at by my mother and confronting the rest of my old coworkers to notice anything weird."

Jessie stared at her, then shook her head, pulling her arm away. "Honestly, for once in my life I didn't have crime on my mind. I was trying not to be miserable in that ridiculous getup while Marty ran around gawking at the house. And you're wrong, Stan. I don't usually feel like my hands are tied, but this is different. This is my captain saying, *Leave it alone.*"

"Somebody had to have heard something last night," Stan said, more to herself than Jessie. "Something other than her and Richard fighting. She fought with everyone. Jesse, I don't think Richard did it."

"Then I hope he has a good lawyer," Jessie said.

Frustrated, Stan folded her arms over her chest. "You're not a quitter. And you hate corruption. Are you really going to let them do this?"

"What can I do?" Jessie challenged. "I just told you, I have no authority to even look into this anymore. My boss made it pretty clear — he catches me going down any other avenue, I'm dead meat. I'm already in trouble because of the newspaper story. They're convinced I tipped off Cyril. Because none of the other hundred people there could've mentioned the state police presence at the party and the woman who never came out of the bathroom. And like half the town doesn't have the police scanner app." She rolled her eyes. "By the way, can you get in touch with Monica? I have her phone that I still can't get into. Left a message with the grandmother but no one's called me back."

"I'm sure I can find her. But Jess, you can't just drop this. No way." Stan rose and walked around the room. "Wait. You said if he catches *you.*"

"Me, Sturgis, Colby, any of us peons. Anyone not *authorized* to work on this. When I asked for the list of authorized people, I got one name."

"So anyone on the state police payroll can't look into it."

Warily, Jessie nodded. "Right."

Stan shrugged. "I'm not on their payroll. And you can give me advice."

Jessie's eyes almost popped out of her head. She stood up so fast her chair tipped over. "No way. You're crazy. You're not getting involved. Did you hear what I said? This one's high stakes."

"Why not? Someone has to if there's a chance an innocent person will go to jail!"

"Why *not*? I'll tell you why not." Jessie ticked points off on her fingers. "First, my brother will kill me. Second, you'll probably get yourself killed. Or else you'll get me fired. Do you really need more reasons than that? Stan, I'm telling you. Just forget about it. You don't even know for sure he's innocent."

"I can't," Stan insisted. "And I know you can't, either. But if you won't help me, I'll have to figure it out myself. And I'll start with Wallace."

Jessie grabbed her ponytail in one hand, tugging on it so hard Stan was afraid she'd yank it out of her head, and stalked around the small room. She reminded Stan of a captive zoo animal who hadn't yet gotten used to its enclosure. "You're impossible. You make my life a million times harder than it needs to be. You know that, right?"

Stan held Jessie's gaze, not giving in.

"Wallace is a moron anyway. He's about as dangerous as a ladybug. If I was still *allowed* to investigate my own case, I'd be all over Tony like flies at a picnic."

Stan raised an eyebrow. "So you didn't like his answer about where he was all day?"

"Like it? I didn't get a chance to like it or not. I never got an answer. But nobody cares about that." Disgusted, she stalked another lap around the kitchen.

"I'm fully capable of being discreet," Stan said.

"And how exactly do you plan on gathering this information?" Jessie demanded.

"You're just going to ask Wallace what he and the dead woman were fighting about and figure he'll tell you? Same with Tony about where he was all day?"

Already tried that, Stan thought, but didn't say it. "Actually, I do know what I'm going to do with Tony."

Jessie raised an eyebrow, her foot tapping a staccato beat on the floor. "I can't wait to hear."

Stan smiled. The idea came as she watched Jessie pace the floor. Divine wisdom. Or a mental illness finally showing its symptoms. "I would think," she said slowly, "given the media interest this is sure to get, that Tony would need to be well prepared in how to handle that. Given his prior track record."

Jessie looked puzzled, then it dawned on her. "Oh man. You wouldn't."

Stan spread her hands wide. "What? Clearly, he's going to have a job opening for an executive coach now." The thought made her stomach turn, but it made the most sense. An insider had the best chance of finding out what really happened last night, especially if Tony and his political cronies were involved. If she put her acting hat on and pretended to be concerned, she could be that insider with no problem. Her mother would be delighted. She wouldn't suspect a thing.

Plus, Stan owed it to her mother to find out if Tony wasn't who he appeared to be. She hoped she wouldn't find out anything, but still. And figuring out who killed Eleanor and freeing an innocent man were also good motivators.

Jessie blew out a long, resigned breath, but some of the fire had returned to her green eyes. "You're gonna do what you want anyway. I may as well make sure you don't get into too much trouble."

Stan grinned. "I appreciate it. Here." She pushed the beer at Jessie. "Finish your beer and let's go back down before someone notices we're missing."

Jessie wrinkled her nose. "You can have it. I don't even like beer."

CHAPTER 23

Jessie went downstairs first, not wanting to draw attention to their huddle. Paranoia, certainly, but Stan obliged. While she waited the instructed five minutes, she poured the remnants of Jessie's beer down the sink and rinsed out the mug, pondering these latest developments.

Tony had influence. Enough influence that the state police seemed willing to make a bad arrest to keep the heat off him. But why? She'd seen him slipping out with the captain. It hadn't looked like trouble. It looked . . . cozy. He had to have pull somewhere. Or knew someone's dirty little secret.

Stan kicked herself for not making an effort to get to know Tony, either as her mayor or her future — she gulped at the thought — stepfather. They'd gotten off on the wrong foot, and things got more awkward when her mother started dating him. Given the instability of her own relationship with her mother, she'd been content to try to ignore the whole thing. Now she realized how little she knew about this man who was dangerously close to becoming part of her family.

But someone had to have looked into him. Cyril Pierce, for one. A background check at the very least. Tony couldn't have gotten away with running the mayoral race if he had a criminal record. She racked her brain to that time nearly a year ago, trying to remember if she'd read any of the inevitable background stories done when a new candidate came to town. So much else had been going on, though, that she couldn't recall. She made a mental note to ask Cyril as soon as possible. Financial questions were at the top of her list. Even a salary of $50K was pushing it. So where'd he get the funds for his fancy house?

Another disturbing thought pushed through her subconscious. What if her mother was the one with the influence? She certainly had money. Would her mother really sink so low as to bribe the police? She was a lot of things, but dishonest had never been one of them. Unless she'd been pushed beyond her breaking point. But what was her breaking point?

187

The disturbing image of Eleanor with the diamond ring in her mouth kept flashing in front of her eyes. If that got out, people would automatically assume her mother discovered Tony and Eleanor having an affair and taken matters into her own hands.

She shivered and turned to go downstairs, then realized she wasn't alone in the kitchen. She jumped, bobbling the beer mug, gasping in surprise.

"Sorry, Stan!" Scott, Brenna's boyfriend, rushed to catch the heavy glass, dropping a pile of clothes he carried. Stan reached for it, too. Both of them missed and it fell with a thud. At least it didn't shatter.

Scott grimaced and picked it up, examining it for cracks before handing it back to her. "I didn't mean to startle you. Sorry about that."

"No, my fault. I'm sure you weren't expecting someone to be in here." Stan took a breath and willed her heart to stop pounding. *Who did you think it was, Tony coming to get you?* she chided herself.

Scott scooped up his clothes and straightened. "The door was open and I knew Brenna was downstairs. I thought some drunk person had wandered up."

"No, just me. I . . . wasn't feeling well," she lied. "I came up here to get away from the crowd for a minute."

"Don't apologize. You want to sit down?" Scott asked, concerned. "Brenna's on her way up. Here, I can make you some tea or something. Do you need food?"

Stan smiled. "No. Thank you. I'm fine, really. I feel much better now."

"You sure? Bren will be mad at me if I let you leave feeling sick."

"Yes. Honestly. It was a long night and I didn't get much sleep. I better get back downstairs. Are you coming down for the competition?"

"I am. I came up to change. I had to go in to work unexpectedly this morning." He held up the clothes as if proof of this statement.

"On Sunday?" Stan frowned, searching her memory for his profession. Something to do with social work, if she recalled correctly.

"I'm a counselor," he said, as if reading her mind. "I work with people in recovery from addiction, mostly. And since we're short-staffed, I also work with the agency that supports people with mental illness. Often the two go hand in hand." He shrugged. "Jack-of-all-trades. Plus, I need the overtime. Which sometimes means I work weekends, usually when people are in crisis."

"That must be tough," Stan said.

"Tougher for them than me. Like this client I had to see this morning. Sad." He shook his head, his face clouding over.

Stan thought he had kind eyes behind the hip black glasses he wore. They were a chocolate brown that reminded her of Scruffy's. He was cute in an outdoorsy way with sun-streaked, brownish hair and a perpetual tan. He smiled a lot, too. And anyone could tell he completely adored Brenna. "What agency do you work for?" she asked.

"Safe Harbor in Hartford. I travel around the greater Hartford area. But I'm hopefully getting a new job on this side of the state, so I don't have to travel as much. Plus, it would be a supervisor job." He tossed his clothes over the back of the chair. "That way I can be around to help Brenna, too, since she's working so many jobs."

"That's great. Good luck," Stan said.

"She's really excited about your shop," Scott said. "I told her to tell you, if you guys need anything let me know. I'm pretty handy. I can save you some money."

"Thank you," Stan said, delighted. "So sweet of you to offer. I'm sure we'll take you up on it."

"I hope so. See you downstairs."

Stan returned to the packed pub. The tantalizing smells were even more intense than before — vegetables steeping in broth, traces of garlic lingering in the air. She could almost forget the stew ingredients if she didn't actually see them. She saw Jake behind the bar. He caught her eye. She blew him a kiss, then moved into the heart of the crowd gathered near the stews.

The different groups cooking the stew chose charities to support with their entry fees and, hopefully, their winnings. The grand prize winner got two thousand dollars for their charity. Stan scanned the participating groups. Betty Meany and Lorinda, one of the librarians, stood proudly behind the Frog Ledge Library table with their stew, spooning out samples for the guests. Amara and Vincent, Stan's neighbors and the owners of the town vet clinic, were set up next to them. Amara fussed over her pot, sniffing and adding dashes of salt and pepper. Izzy Sweet's Sweets had one also, although Izzy wasn't manning the table. One of her baristas, Kayleigh, looked like she was taking stew duty seriously, making notes on a pad in front of her. The local Rotary Club, the Girl Scouts, and the senior center occupied the next tables. Stan squinted at the last sign. The state police? Jessie hadn't mentioned that.

A man stood behind the table, carefully filling a paper cup for a waiting customer. He looked vaguely familiar. As he finished spooning and handed the cup over with a smile, Stan recognized him. The new-to-town officer who'd been at her mother's last night. Colby. He looked different without his hat and police gear. Guess they were all looking for something to fill their time since their investigation had been shelved.

"Want some?" he asked, noticing Stan watching him. "Mine's got just the right amount of Guinness," he added with a wink.

Stan moved closer and peered into the pot. "Does yours have meat?"

"Of course!"

She wrinkled her nose. "Then no. I don't eat meat."

He laughed. "I hope you're not a judge. Garrett Colby." He held out his hand. "We met . . . last night. I'm new to this town, on assignment."

"Stan Connor." She sniffed the stew. It smelled delicious, anyway. She told him as much.

"Thanks." He beamed. "I hope I win. My partner — my dog, Rosie — needs a vest for work."

"A vest? Like, a bulletproof vest?"

He nodded.

Stan understood the work police dogs did, but that didn't stop her from worrying about them. She didn't like to think of dogs getting shot at. "She doesn't have one?"

"No, ma'am. Not yet." Garrett stirred his stew. "She's the newest dog on the force, and there's no budget left for this year. So I have to raise the funds, or wait for her number to come up next year."

"How much is the vest?"

"About fourteen hundred dollars. If I win, though, we can have some in the fund for the next few dogs. It's all about keeping them safe, right?"

"Okay, folks," a woman's voice boomed over the speaker system. "It's time for the judges to do their thing. If everyone could step back, they'll be making their way around the tables."

"Good luck," Stan said to Trooper Colby. He flashed her a thumbs-up.

She retreated to the corner of the room and watched the five judges. Tony led the group. She wondered if he'd recused himself from the council table. The second judge was Emmalee Hoffman, the owner of the Happy Cow Dairy Farm. The owner of

Crystal's Country Kitchen restaurant, the postmaster, and the principal of Frog Ledge Elementary rounded out the group. They ate their way through all the stations while taking notes, then sat at their judging table and compared comments.

"Did you try any?" Jake appeared seemingly out of nowhere and slipped an arm around her waist, kissing the top of her head. Even at her decent height of five foot seven, he stood a head taller than her.

"No way." She leaned into him, thinking again how nice it was to have someone to lean on. Literally. "Haven't stumbled on the vegetarian ones yet. Plus I'm holding out for the French fries."

"I have a fresh batch going as we speak."

"Sweet. Have you seen your sister?"

He shook his head slowly. "No, but someone told me they saw her with a beer. I told them they were nuts. Must be someone sleep-deprived from last night and seeing things."

Stan swallowed, but luckily was saved from answering as the microphone boomed to life again and Sean the bartender hopped onto the stage in front of the pots of stew.

"I think we're just about ready to announce our winners," he said. "Can I have the mayor come up, please?"

CHAPTER 24

All eyes turned to Tony, who emerged from the crowd and walked up the two steps to the stage. He'd changed into a suit since this morning, and he wore a solemn expression that looked like he'd practiced it in the mirror.

"Thank you," Tony said when he'd accepted the microphone. He paused for a moment, looking out over the crowd. "Welcome, everyone, to the annual charity stew cook-off. And a special thanks to Jake McGee and his staff at McSwigg's for hosting and opening up their kitchen to all the cooks." He cleared his throat as everyone clapped. "I'll announce the winners in a moment, but first I want to take a moment of silence in memory of my colleague, Eleanor Chang, who you might have heard was killed last night." He paused and bowed his head.

Smart move on his part. Stan halfway

bowed her head, glancing around to see what people were doing. Many of them were pretending to pay attention but stealing sips of their beer or sneaking a French fry. People who hadn't been at the party wouldn't have a clue anyway.

Tony lifted his head and continued. "I'd like to reassure you all that the police have this handled and have made an arrest. While this won't bring Ms. Chang back, it will give her family some peace of mind."

Stan could imagine Jessie's blood boiling at this little speech. She felt her own blood pressure rise considerably. As if he could read her mind, Jake squeezed her hand.

"Ms. Chang had three young daughters who'll now face life without their mother," Tony went on. "And while I know we can't control the vicious actions of unstable people or bring back what was taken from them, we can at least try to help in the aftermath." He nodded, as if agreeing with himself. "So I'm starting a fund for the victim's children. If anyone wishes to donate, please see me. And perhaps our stew winner will choose to donate some of their proceeds as well, although I understand each already selected a charity. In some cases, that charity is their own nonprofit, so we'll leave it up to them where they'd like to share the funds."

The crowd clapped obediently. Tony smiled and nodded. Stan felt a rush of disgust, but grudgingly acknowledged the strategy. Eleanor must've taught him well during her tenure. First he used his so-called power to thwart justice, and now he expected kudos for standing up and proclaiming his own generosity. Stan wanted to grab the mic and ask him how much he'd donated to the fund to get it started. Jake squeezed her hand again, a warning. He knew her well.

"So are you ready for the winners?" Tony asked, holding his hands wide.

The crowd cheered a loud "Yes!"

"All right! Can we have the envelopes, please!" Tony looked expectantly to the left where Sean the bartender waited. Grinning like Vanna White, he performed an exaggerated strut onto the stage to hand Tony the envelopes. He faced the crowd, took a bow, then leaped down.

Jake shook his head. "What a ham."

Tony announced the fun prizes first: most unique use of spices, most creative, best unexpected ingredient. Then it was time for the best stews. He announced the best vegetarian, then made a big deal about opening the second-place envelope and shaking out the paper. "And our second-place stew award goes to the Frog Ledge Library staff! Betty, please come up. The library will receive a donation of one hundred dollars, along with your portion of the entry fees, because of your cooking."

Cheers erupted as Betty Meany hurried to the stage to collect the certificate. Stan knew she'd be seething a bit. She did love to win. Tony looked like he wanted to ask her to donate the money to the Chang kids' fund, but changed his mind.

"And in first place" — Tony held out his hand for the next envelope as the crowd held their breath — "is . . . Amara Leonard and Vincent DiMauro of the Frog Ledge Veterinary Clinic! The proceeds from tonight's event will go to the Frog Ledge Animal Control and Shelter. And perhaps to the Chang Fund," he added with a meaningful look at Amara as she made her way to the stage. "Congratulations!"

Stan clapped along with the rest of the audience as Amara joined him at the podium, happy for her friend and the town's stray animals. Their vet clinic had a separate area for sheltering some of the town strays that the animal control officer oversaw. They'd included that in their clinic to help more animals and also draw attention to the condition of the old town pound, where the majority of the animals were housed. The original space was in dire need of upgrades, but the town hadn't been able to pass a budget allowing for substantial improvements.

She felt bad for Trooper Colby and his dog, though, out protecting and serving without a bulletproof vest. Maybe she could use her treats to fundraise for them.

"What are you in such deep thought about?" Jake asked, squeezing her around the waist.

"I'm thinking about what I can do to help Trooper Colby. He needs to raise funds to get his dog a bulletproof vest since he didn't win the competition."

"Aww. And that's why I love you." He kissed her nose. "Be right back. I have to go make an announcement." He went up to the stage, picked up the mic Tony'd abandoned, and turned it back on.

"Hey, McSwiggers! You having fun?" he asked, his voice booming off the walls.

The crowd cheered.

"Cool. So congrats to Amara and Vincent, and the Frog Ledge Library," he said, leading another round of applause. "In keeping with the spirit of fundraising, McSwigg's will donate five dollars for every Guinness

purchased tonight to one of the three charities we heard about today: the library, the
animal shelter, or the Chang Fund. So drink
up."

He left the stage to more applause. It
didn't take much for people to descend on
the bar. They were even more inclined if
they could say it helped a good cause.
Justifiable drunkenness.

Chapter 25

Drinks in hands and good deeds done, the crowd lined up once again to polish off the stews. People still streamed in the doors, a testament to the community of McSwigg's. As the only bar in town it got a lot of traffic anyway, but Jake's place was welcoming and safe. A lot of people thought of it as their home away from home. Kind of like *Cheers,* but with even quirkier characters. And after what happened last night, it made even more sense people would seek out companionship.

She made her way to the stew station where Garrett Colby frantically spooned stew into cups to keep his line moving. "I'm sorry you didn't win," she said when she reached the front.

Garrett shrugged. "Hey, it happens. We'll get the money, I'm sure of it. Rosie's worth it."

"Of course." Stan reached into her bag

and pulled out a business card. "Why don't you call me this week. I want to help you raise the money."

His eyes widened. "You do?"

"Yes."

"Wow. How come? I mean, that would be amazing, but you don't even know me."

"My work is all about taking care of animals," she said with a smile. "This is a different opportunity to help."

Garrett slipped her card into his pocket. "I like this town already," he said with a grin. "Now I just need to get my new colleague to like me."

"Jessie? I mean, Trooper Pasquale?"

"You got it."

"It takes her a while to open up, but when she does you'll have a friend for life. And last night was pretty stressful," Stan said.

Garrett suddenly became intent on stirring his stew. "Yeah," he said. "But the case went to another division. Not our problem anymore." He feigned indifference, but she saw the same look on his face she'd seen on Jessie's. A cool outrage. "Hey, at least I didn't have to work today. Otherwise I would've had no money raised. At least I got a little for being here."

"What do you mean?" Stan asked, playing dumb. "What other division?"

"It's a Major Crimes case," Garrett said. "Apparently, they're a lot smarter than us. Stew, sir?" He held out a cup to the man behind her, clearly not wanting to discuss it anymore.

"I'll let you get back to your customers," she said. "But let's plan on something at the end of the week. Would that work for you?"

He nodded, his face brightening. "I'll call you."

As she walked away, she felt a hand on her arm. "You look exhausted," a voice said next to her ear.

Stan whirled around and found Francie Tucker, smiling sympathetically at her. "Hey, Francie. Yeah, it's been a long weekend," she said wryly. "What time did you end up getting home this morning?"

"Not until nearly three. Too much for me. I can't handle late nights anymore at my age. But I couldn't sit alone in my house all day." She glanced around at the crowd. "I needed to be near people."

"I hear you," Stan said.

"I must admit, I'm breathing a bit easier to hear they've arrested someone," Francie said. "How is your mother doing? The poor dear was so distraught yesterday."

"I haven't spoken to her," Stan said. "But

I'm sure she's hoping to get back to normal."

"I can't imagine how they could ever get back to normal after a murder in their house." Francie shuddered. "I hope the stress doesn't affect their upcoming wedding. They're such a dear couple."

"Mmmm," Stan said noncommittally.

"Hello, ladies." Mona Galveston, former Frog Ledge mayor, paused on her way by and gave Stan's arm a squeeze. "How are you both doing?"

Stan didn't know Mona well, but she'd always liked her. When Stan first moved to town and was under suspicion for a murder, Mona hadn't passed judgment like some. Instead, she welcomed her as a new resident. Stan never forgot it. Tony'd interrupted Mona's eight-year stint as mayor, which was a shame. She'd worked hard to make positive changes in town.

"So nice to see you, Mona," Francie said, giving the other woman a hug.

"You too, darling." Mona air-kissed her and turned to Stan. "How are you holding up? And your poor mother? What a crazy night. Although I'm sure you're tired of people coming up to talk to you about it."

Stan smiled. "It hasn't been too bad."

"Sounds like they've found the culprit,

though," Mona said. "That was fast work."

Stan worked to keep her face neutral. "Sure was."

"Will we hear more about why he did it?" Francie chimed in.

"I have no idea," Stan said. "You'd have to ask the police."

Mona smiled. "Come now. You have to have some clout."

"Mona!"

They all turned at the loud, belligerent voice barreling toward them. Stan did a double take when she recognized Councilman Curtis Wallace III, of the prim and proper bow ties and condescending demeanor. Just who she'd been hoping to run into. But what would she say, especially with all these people standing around them?

He worked his way over to their circle, sloshing beer over the side of his mug in an equally astonishing show of sloppiness. He had the trim body of a tennis player or some other country club sport. Stan could never figure out how old he was, although she'd guess early sixties. He obviously took pride in his appearance. Even though it was Sunday, he still wore his bow tie and dress pants, though no jacket. But beer foam glistened in his short brown beard, and his eyes had the glaze of a man who'd been working on his buzz for a while. On second thought, it didn't look like the best time to talk to him.

Mona sighed, keeping her smile pasted on. "Hello, Curtis."

Wallace leaned in and gave her a loud, wet kiss on the cheek. Stan could almost see Mona fighting the urge to wipe her face with her sleeve. "Your old job might be up for grabs again," Wallace said. "Have you heard?" His voice sounded odd. Instead of the clipped tone he used at council meetings, today it was deep and full, like he'd finally learned how to use it.

"What?" Mona asked, looking confused.

Wallace snorted. "The mayor job! What else? I'm sure we can get that travesty of a mayor impeached now." He took a swig of his beer. Half of it missed his mouth and dripped down his shirt. "Although you've had your run. May be time for someone else to take the gavel."

"Impeached?" Mona repeated, glancing around to see if anyone listened. "I'm not sure that's possible. There are a limited number of towns in our state that ever successfully recalled a mayor. And for what reason would we attempt that?"

Another snort. "Come on. That woman died in his bathroom while he was conveniently *otherwise occupied.* That man they've locked up is just a scapegoat. There's something wrong with all of us if we don't get him out of office this minute." He gestured with his mug to accentuate his point. More beer sloshed over the side and dripped onto his sleeve. He muttered something that sounded like, *"Drat."*

People around them started to stare. Stan glanced around, hoping Jessie was nearby. She had no idea what Wallace was up to, but his words rang in her ears: *That poor jerk is just a scapegoat.* Basically echoing her and Jessie's thoughts from a few moments ago. Did he know something about Tony? Or was he trying to divert the blame from himself?

"Curtis, I think we'd better talk about this somewhere else," Mona said tightly, taking his arm.

"Why?" Curtis protested, yanking free. "These ladies should hear what I have to say, too. In case they voted for *Mayor Falco* last time around." He sneered the words. "Ladies, please. Who did you vote for?"

Jessie popped up over Stan's shoulder. Her sixth sense must have been hard at work. "Problems?" she asked.

"No, Trooper. No problems here," Wallace said. "I'm simply telling some of our constituents that this murder case smells funny."

Jessie's face paled, but she kept her voice stern. "This isn't the place to discuss it. It's technically closed, Councilman."

He opened his mouth to respond, but Mona grabbed his arm again. "Curtis. Your wife's looking for you." She pointed to a slight, silver-haired woman moving toward them looking like she was on the warpath.

Wallace glanced at his wife and his bravado drained away. "Fine," he muttered, then let Mona lead him away.

Mona glanced at them and shook her head. "Lovely to see you ladies," she said, and melted into the crowd.

Francie watched them go, wide-eyed. "Goodness. Curtis doesn't typically drink, so I guess this is a good example of what happens when people act out. He should be careful what he says, though. I certainly don't think what happened to that poor woman is Tony's fault." She turned to Jessie. "Especially since your colleagues found the perpetrator."

Stan and Jessie looked at each other. Jessie broke eye contact first. "I'll go talk to Curtis." She walked away.

"Anyway," Francie said brightly, turning to Stan. "I know you said to call on Monday. About the job. I hope you don't mind, but

I'm so excited I thought I'd ask you now. When can I start?"

Stan forced her brain to shift gears from murder to hiring employees. "Right. No problem. How about tomorrow? Brenna and I have a to-do list that could wrap around town twice, and it keeps growing. We would love the help." That way she could skip the baking and work on the website, the pastry cases, and proving Richard's innocence. Having staff could be a great thing.

Francie clapped her hands. "I'm so thrilled! I can't wait."

"I don't have a huge budget yet," Stan cautioned. "We'll have to figure out hours and what works for you."

"I'm not worried. Whatever we work out for hours and pay will be fine. And perhaps a small discount on treats for Cooper." She smiled shyly.

"Discounts are a given," Stan said, grinning. "And the dogs get to eat on the job. How about two days a week baking while we're prepping to open, then we can talk about a more permanent schedule after that? We can work out the details later."

"Done!" Francie reached over and took Stan by surprise by enveloping her in a big hug. "Thank you so much," she said. "You have no idea how much this means to me."

Stan patted her on the back. It felt good to know she'd made someone happy. "Welcome to the team," she said.

CHAPTER 26

Stan stayed at the bar until she could barely keep her eyes open. Exhaustion and the added stress of solving a murder had her feeling like a zombie by eight, and it wasn't like she could have private conversations with Tony or the drunken Curtis Wallace in that crowd.

She went home and found Caitlyn passed out on the couch. Eva sat on the floor, glued to *Frozen* playing in surround sound on TV, her legs perched on Henry like he was her own personal ottoman. The other dogs sprawled on the floor around her. Stan blew her a kiss and went upstairs, collapsing on her bed. She wanted to go to sleep now, but she had to call Nikki back first. Her best friend had called two more times this afternoon, but only left one short message: "Call me back, I'm home."

Nikki Manning ran a rescue organization, Pets Last Chance, and spent her days saving mostly dogs and some lucky cats from certain death down south. She operated out of her farmhouse in a rural part of Rhode Island and had volunteers from New England to Georgia doing runs to bring animals north. She ran transports at least once a week, and if she had people doing legs for her, she could do two to three. Scruffy came from one of those transports.

Nutty stalked into the room as she picked up her phone, his fluffy Maine coon tail high and proud like a peacock. He jumped up on the bed and rubbed against her arm. Stan hoped the gesture was meant to comfort, but she assumed he wanted dinner. Still, it was nice to feel his soft fur and calming presence. A minute later she felt a similar rubbing on her leg. Looking down, she saw Benedict, looking hopefully at her with adoring eyes.

"Hi, you guys." She gathered Nutty against her and slid down to the floor, snuggling Benedict with her other arm. "Benny, is Nutty teaching you to ask for dinner or did you just want to see how I was feeling?"

Benedict meowed. Definitely wanted to see how she was feeling. Nutty must've interpreted the comment the same way, because he blinked at him reproachfully. She figured if he could speak, he'd say something along the lines of *Don't be too soft, bro. Always keep the upper hand. Make sure you get food before you give too much love.* It was okay, though. Nutty had a reputation to uphold, but he was really a big softy.

"I'll get you guys dinner in a few minutes," she promised. Gaston poked his head in the room to see what was going on, his tail waving madly as he approached Stan for pets. Benedict froze, still not sure how he felt about the dogs, then dashed under the bed. He was a timid cat, having lived alone with one of Frog Ledge's elders before her tragic death last winter. He was getting used to life here, but he still preferred to keep a good distance between himself and the dogs.

"I know. You're all hungry. Give me ten minutes," she said, then made the call.

Nikki answered on the third ring. "Hey," she said. "How was the shindig? You tell your mother I'm mad she didn't invite me?" She was joking, of course. Nikki liked fancy parties about as much as she liked seeing adoptable dogs on death row.

"Count your blessings. You won't believe what I'm going to tell you. You have to swear on all your dogs' lives that you won't talk about this," she warned.

"Uh-oh. That doesn't sound good. But

213

wait, don't tell me yet. I have news for you, too. At least I think I do, but if I don't and you didn't mention it to me you know I'll be mad, right?"

Stymied, Stan said, "I have no idea what you're talking about."

"Of course you don't. You need to get out of that little town more. I'm guessing there's nowhere to pick up the latest issue of *Foodie* around there?"

Foodie was, unsurprisingly, a magazine dedicated to the world of gourmet food. "*Foodie?* Why? I don't usually buy that anyway. Nikki, I have something really important —"

"Of course you don't. Which is why you have no clue that your own cat is the cover model!"

"Huh?" Stan wasn't in the mood for jokes.

"Nutty," Nikki said, sounding exasperated. "Didn't this all happen in Rhode Island last month?"

"Didn't *what* happen? *Foodie* sent a photographer to that nightmare of a dinner. They took pictures." It was part of the lure of her ill-fated weekend with Sheldon Allyn and crew. "The story didn't run because of what happened, I thought. But she did take quite an interest in Nutty."

Nutty'd also had a little adventure that

weekend and went missing for a few harrowing hours. The photographer was onsite for his dramatic rescue, and had shot tons of photos. But nothing had come of it. Had it?

"Well, he's the cover story of this month's magazine," Nikki said. "I'm telling you. She even mentioned your shop."

"Come on, Nik." Suddenly, she remembered Kyle's odd comment about "following the progress of her patisserie," and it being public knowledge that it was in Frog Ledge.

"Come on what? I'm serious!"

"Holy crap. And you didn't send me a copy?"

"I couldn't. It was on the table with my mail and one of the cats threw up on it. I'll go buy more and ship them to you tomorrow. Nutty looks very handsome, by the way. You think they Photoshopped him?"

"He'd claw your eyes out if he heard you say that!" Stan exclaimed. "He doesn't need Photoshop. Was the story good?"

"The story rocked. Your place is going to be the talk of the town, my friend. I'm so proud of you."

"Hopefully, it will be done in time to open this year. If this weekend doesn't screw everything up."

"What do you mean? Does this have to do with your mother? Okay, tell me your story."

"Better sit down." Stan waited a beat for emphasis. "Tony's executive coach was murdered at the party. I used to work with her. She was horrible. And Richard, my ex, was there with a bunch of my old coworkers and somehow got himself arrested for the murder."

Nikki didn't say anything for a full moment, then she chuckled. "Nice try, sister. Is this some kind of engagement party game or something?"

"Nik. It's not a game. I'm dead serious." *And someone else is dead.*

Silence while Nikki tried to formulate a response. "Girlfriend," she said finally. "I hate to tell you, but I think someone put a curse on you. Your friend from down south. You sure she isn't sticking pins in some voodoo doll that looks like you? Because this stuff doesn't happen to people more than once. Usually not even once! And this is your — how many times?"

"No need to count," Stan interrupted. "I get it. I've got some kind of black death cloud hanging over me. That's not the point. The point is, my ex got arrested!"

"Why was he there?" Nikki wanted to

know. "*I* didn't even get an invite to this thing."

"I honestly don't know," Stan said.

"Did they catch him, like, standing over the body or something?"

"No. There was . . . a slight altercation with Jake and me. Richard was a little drunk and he took off outside. In the meantime, they found the body, then grabbed him and said he was trying to sneak away. I'm not sure they have a good reason for thinking it's him. It was all very convenient."

"How's your mother taking this?" Nikki asked. "And her beau?"

"That's the other thing. Her *beau* was missing for half the night. No one will say where he was."

"And no one thinks that's weird? Did he kill her?"

"I don't know what's going on. But it doesn't look like the police are open to looking at anyone else." Paranoia had her choosing her words carefully. Who knew if this was a conspiracy that warranted tapped phones? Especially given Jessie's assessment of the situation today.

" 'Night, Auntie Krissie!" Stan heard from the hallway as Eva stampeded up the steps.

" 'Night, sweetie," she called back.

"Who's that?"

"My niece. Caitlyn's here."

"Your sister? What for?"

"She's visiting for . . . a while."

"A while?" Stan could almost hear Nikki shaking her head on the other end of the line. "I'm starting to think your old life was less complicated."

"Me too," Stan said with a sigh. "At least I never found dead bodies before. But I have Jake now, so that makes up for it."

"How's that going?"

"Amazingly." She smiled in spite of herself. "It's really nice to have him here."

"Well, good. I'm happy for you. It's good that you like each other's company. Pretty soon you're gonna be the only two left in that town, given the death rate. Listen, I gotta run, my transport line's ringing. Let me know what happens with your mother. And don't get involved," she warned.

Stan crossed her fingers behind her back and promised. Like Jake, Nikki knew her too well.

CHAPTER 27

Stan didn't even hear Jake come in, but when she woke up Monday he was sound asleep next to her. He was used to this crazy schedule, but some days she had no idea how he kept it up. McSwigg's stayed open seven days a week. It had to, in order to be "that place" where the townspeople congregated.

She snuggled up to him, absorbing his warmth, not wanting to get up just yet. She could see the day dawning gray and dreary outside. The chill of the impending fall crept into the air. As much as she loved fall she didn't want to be cold and gray today. She tried to doze back off, but her mind rocketed into gear, organizing her many tasks into a mental priority list. The pastry case. The menu. The website. New recipes. Store hours. Where would she find the perfect art? And then, her new duties: ingratiating herself with Tony, figuring out a way to get her ex-boyfriend's head off the chopping block. Then she sat up straight. It was Monday. Richard would be brought for his court appearance this morning. Her gut churned at the thought.

She dropped back down and pulled her pillow over her face. Maybe she should've moved to Key West when she lost her job. The weather was better year round, the vibe was chill, and she could've been a beach bum. Probably fewer dead people, too. But then she wouldn't have met Jake, so in retrospect that would've been a horrible idea.

Downstairs, the doorbell sounded. Immediately, Scruffy and Gaston bolted from their beds, barking up a storm. Henry let out a low woof, but remained snuggled in his bed. Duncan howled from another room — probably cuddling up with Eva. Who on earth would visit at this hour? She pulled the pillow off and reached for her phone to check the time. Seven thirty. Seriously?

Miraculously, the ruckus didn't even wake Jake. She envied his ability to sleep through anything. Stan slipped out of bed and left the room, closing the door behind her. She met Caitlyn in the hallway. "I didn't think you were up yet," Caitlyn said. "At least Eva didn't wake up."

"I wasn't up yet. Not sure who thinks it's a good idea to ring my doorbell at this hour, but I'll get it."

She went downstairs, where the dogs stood howling at the front door. Caitlyn followed her and started to head into the kitchen. "I'll make coffee," she called as Stan shooed the dogs out of the way. This had to be an alternate universe. Caitlyn was up and relatively cheerful before eight *and* offering to make coffee?

Stan rubbed her eyes to make sure she wasn't still asleep, then pulled open the door. Three men in suits stood there. One held a saxophone, another a guitar. The third man stood slightly in front of the other two. His hands were empty. They all smiled at her. "Caitlyn?" the one without an instrument asked.

Stan stared at them, then shook her head to clear the fog. "No," she said. "Uh, hold on. Caitlyn," she yelled.

Her sister appeared in the hall holding the coffee carafe. "What?"

When they saw her, the man with no instrument blew her a kiss. "This is from Kyle," he announced, then counted down, "Three, two, one." They launched into a rendition of what Stan recognized after a minute as Sinatra's "Baby Won't You Please

221

Come Home."

Speechless, Stan glanced at her sister, who almost dropped the coffeepot. Her face turned beet red. The dogs even stopped barking as they listened, heads slightly tilted. Stan would wager a bet that they'd never heard a saxophone up close and personal before. She wondered if the neighbors had. If they hadn't, they were getting a taste today.

Caitlyn turned and flounced out of sight into the kitchen. The musicians looked dismayed, but they kept playing. They were actually pretty good. Stan let them finish their song, then awkwardly applauded. Scruffy raced toward them, jumping at their legs looking for attention. The sax player reached down and scratched her ears.

"Did she not like our music?" the singer asked, the corners of his mouth turning down.

"That's not it at all," Stan assured him, wondering how she'd become a therapist for a traveling musical band before she'd even had coffee. "She's just . . . not in a good place right now."

"Would another song help?" he asked hopefully.

"No," Stan said. "I don't think so. But thank you. That was lovely." She grabbed

Scruffy and went to shut the door.

The singer passed her a card. "If you ever want to serenade your sweetheart, call us," he said. "We travel all over New England and the tristate area."

"Terrific. Thanks so much." Stan waved, then slammed the door and turned the deadbolt. She let her head fall against it, then sighed and stood up. Nutty poked his head out from the living room, ears still plastered back against his head. "I know," Stan muttered. "Trust me, I know."

CHAPTER 28

The phone rang as Stan reached the kitchen. She plucked it off its stand on the counter. "Hello."

"It's Amara. What the heck is going on over there? Isn't it a little early for a concert?"

Stan cringed. "I'm so sorry. It was a . . . musical telegram," she said. Caitlyn turned from the coffeepot and shot her a lethal look.

"No way! I didn't know they still did that. From Jake?" Amara asked.

"No. Not for me. For my sister."

"Your sister? I don't think I knew you had a sister," Amara said.

"Well, I do," Stan said. "She's visiting for . . . a little bit."

"Cool. Who's serenading her?"

"It's a long story," Stan said through gritted teeth.

"Okay, well, forget it, then. I'll come meet

her later. After I get some more sleep."

"Sorry to wake you," Stan apologized again. She hung up and replaced the phone in its base. Then, unable to help it, she started to laugh. The stress of the past two days combined with the sheer ridiculousness of this morning had reached its peak. Better than crying.

Caitlyn worked hard to keep the frown on her face, then gave in and giggled. That made Stan laugh even harder, and before she knew it the two of them leaned against the counter in hysterics. Tears poured from her eyes and she held on to her stomach, which hurt from laughing so hard. And that was how Jake found them minutes later when he walked into the kitchen, still rubbing sleep from his eyes.

He stared at them for a minute, then went straight for the still-brewing coffee. "I don't think I want to know," he said.

"I can't even believe this is my life," Caitlyn said between giggles. "I mean, who does that?"

"Does what?" Jake asked, taking the cream from the fridge.

"You mean you didn't hear the concert?" Stan asked.

"Concert?" He frowned. "No. I thought I

heard a saxophone, but figured I was dreaming."

Stan and Caitlyn both dissolved into giggles again at that. Jake eyed his coffee warily. "Did you put something in the coffee?" he asked.

"No. Kyle sent a traveling jazz band to our door to serenade Caitlyn," Stan said.

Jake scratched his head. "At this hour?"

"Leave it to Kyle to be confused," Caitlyn said dryly. She turned to Stan. "Do you think this qualifies as harassment? Will the cops make him leave town now?"

"I doubt it," Stan said. "Most people wouldn't agree that sending someone over to sing a love song is harassment."

"What song?" Jake asked.

"I don't even know," Caitlyn said.

"Sinatra," Stan said. "I had to be polite and listen when Caitlyn took off."

Jake looked from one to the other, then shook his head. "Just when I think life can't get more interesting with you," he said to Stan, "I'm always proven wrong."

After she, Caitlyn, Eva, and Jake had breakfast together, Caitlyn took Eva out for a walk around the green. Jake showered. He had to go to the library and help Betty Meany bring in some new furniture for the children's area.

"I've got three bartenders tonight so I may not go to the pub," he told her before he left. "Maybe we can go out to dinner?"

"I'd love that. And now that I have another employee, I can feel less guilty about it."

"Another employee?"

"Char introduced me to Francie Tucker. She was looking for another part-time job."

"That's great. She's a nice lady. And that's one less thing to worry about for your opening." He bent down to pet Nutty and Benedict, both weaving between their legs. "You guys hungry?"

"I have to get their breakfast. Oh! I forgot to tell you!" she exclaimed. "Nutty's a magazine star!"

"Sorry?"

"Nutty," she said impatiently. "Remember the *Foodie* magazine photographer?"

"From Newport?" He nodded.

"Nikki called me yesterday to tell me Nutty's on the cover of the latest issue. I had no idea."

Jake laughed. "You're kidding. His head's going to be even bigger than it is already."

She kissed him good-bye and handed him a mug of coffee to go. As he backed out of the driveway, Brenna pulled to the curb. They conversed briefly through open windows before Jake drove off.

"Morning," Brenna sang as she came in with a pastry bag and a cardboard holder of coffees. "Jake said you guys were going to dinner tonight. I invited Scott and me. And I stopped by Izzy's for something to get us going."

"Oh, man." Stan peered inside the bag. "I need to work out for about three hours today. I've eaten nothing but sugar since yesterday."

"Stop." Brenna dismissed her protests and started down the hall, prompting Stan to follow the bag. "You're eating the pastry. It's a chocolate chip breakfast cannoli. I figured you hadn't been eating anyway. Scott said you were feeling sick yesterday when you were at the pub. Are you better now?"

Oops. Her lie about why she'd been in Brenna's apartment. She shook her head. "I was fine. Just tired. I needed to get away from the crowd." She plucked the cannoli from the bag and bit in. "This is amazing," she said through a mouthful. "And I'm glad you guys can come to dinner. How'd you get out of bartending? Your boss let you have a night off?" She winked.

"Jake hired a couple extra people to give us a break. I think he's getting ready for when your shop opens and wants to start freeing me up."

"Are you okay with that?"

"Okay with it?" Brenna laughed. "I told him to. I still want to bartend a couple nights a week, but I'm not dying to do it every night anymore. Especially since Scott works days. I said I'd be late-night backup tonight. So if they get crazy after ten or eleven I can jump in, or help with cleanup." She took a sip of her coffee and picked up her own treat, waving it around. "But let's talk about the cannoli. Amazing, right? She only makes them once a week." Brenna took a bite of hers and closed her eyes while she chewed. "Which reminds me." She swallowed, then went on. "We need to talk about that. For your shop. Having a special pup pastry once a week or once a month. Something to get people excited because you don't have it all the time."

"I love that. And we can have contests to name the special pastry after one of the local animals. I've been thinking about other cool things we can do to engage people. I want the menu items named after our pets and some special pet friends from town, too."

"Yes! People love contests. You can do costumes, taste tests, all kinds of things.

This is going to be great." Brenna rubbed her hands together gleefully. "Are you keeping a list? Actually, it should be two lists. One for everything you want to do once we get rolling, and another for everything we need to do before we start. We should work on that this week."

The doorbell rang, jolting them both out of brainstorming mode. "Now what?" Stan sighed. "I hope it's not another singing trio."

"Singing trio?" Brenna looked confused.

"I'll explain later." Stan headed for the door, where the dogs already congregated. She jockeyed past them and yanked it open. Francie Tucker waited out front, anxiously clutching her pastel blue purse. She wore neat black pants, a button-down blouse, and sandals, and carried an apron over her arm.

"Good morning," she said. "Is it time to bake?"

CHAPTER 29

Mental head slap. Stan had completely forgotten she'd told Francie to come over today. At the same time, she felt weight lifting off her shoulders.

"Good morning. Perfect timing," she said, motioning her inside. "Brenna and I were just getting to the part where we're completely overwhelmed."

Francie laughed. "Well, we can't have that, can we? Hello, babies." She knelt down to greet the dogs, who all crowded around her, sniffing and vying for pets. "You're never lacking for taste testers, I'd guess?"

"Never. And the cats are just as bad. Come on in." She led her down the hall to the kitchen.

Francie followed, admiring the house. "This place is beautiful, Stan. You've made it feel so homey. Oh, look!" she exclaimed in delight as Nutty appeared, brushing against Francie's legs. "Hello, gorgeous."

She reached down to pet him. "I adore cats. I lost my Mickey last year. He was my son's cat. They loved each other very much." Her face clouded over and she looked down at Nutty. "With them both gone, I've never been able to bring myself to get another. It's just Cooper and me now."

"I'm sorry," Stan said, not sure what else to say.

Francie remained on one knee petting Nutty for another minute, then rose. "Thank you," she said. "How many cats do you have?"

"Two," Stan said, relieved to turn the conversation back to lighter topics as she led Francie down the hall. "I moved here with one — not just one cat, one pet! — and, well, the family expanded. Hey, Bren," she said as they entered the kitchen. "I forgot to tell you." She stepped aside and presented Francie with a flourish. "We have a new employee!"

"Yay! Hi, Ms. Tucker!" Brenna came over and hugged Francie.

"Please. It's Francie," she said, but she looked delighted at the warm welcome. "I'm so pleased you girls are allowing me to join you."

"Are you kidding?" Brenna said. "I've

tasted your cookies. The furries are in for a treat."

"You're too sweet." Francie deposited her purse on the counter and tied her apron around her waist. "Where should I start?"

Brenna showed her the whiteboard with the orders, then handed her the recipe card for the Cheezy Bacon Bites. "This one's up next."

Brenna gathered ingredients and showed Francie where everything was. Nutty perched in his usual spot on the counter, eyes glued to the food-related activity. Stan watched them all with a smile. People "worked for her" in her old life, but it was different. Those were coworkers, mostly thrown together by someone else's choice. Here, she was building out a real team who shared in her mission to make people's four-legged friends healthier. People she wanted to be around. She felt truly blessed.

"While you guys bake, do you mind if we talk through some plans?" Stan asked. "I do have a couple of things to do out of the house today, but if we can keep brainstorming that would be so helpful."

"Let's do it," Brenna said. Francie nodded in agreement.

"So we have three work streams to focus on." Stan grabbed a pad of paper off her precariously high pile of mail on the end of the counter and sat at the kitchen table. "We have the café design and planning, which Char is going to help with, too. Then we have the regular treat and meal orders to fill. And our new client. How many is that?"

Brenna checked her notes. "Three dozen by Friday. They said an assortment of our top sellers is fine."

"Cool. And I can deliver those. I want to check the shop out." Stan always made it a point to visit any store than offered to sell her treats to make sure it was up to her standards. "Then finally we have the opening and ongoing stuff like menus, promotions, website, and social media."

"I think we need to hire an official Web person to do the design," Brenna said. "I have the components sketched out, but you need a professional."

"Fine with me. Do you have someone in mind?"

Brenna beamed. "I do, actually. One of my friends from school just started her own graphic design business. She's trying to build her name, too, so she won't charge a million bucks. And she's not jam-packed, schedule-wise, right now. Want me to call her?"

"Yes," Stan said. "Let's do it."

"Awesome." Brenna pulled out her phone and shot off a text, then looked expectantly at Stan. "I'm working on a social strategy, too. We have to stay more on top of Twitter and Instagram. I'm failing you. But I've got that work stream covered. All you need to do is approve stuff."

"I'm good at social media, too," Francie said.

They both looked at her.

"What?" she asked, indignant. "I use it all the time for my business. And for the church, too."

Before she could explore that any further, Stan's cell rang. She picked it up and looked at the name, cringing a little. Her mother. "Sorry, guys. Be right back." She grabbed the phone and walked into the hall before answering.

"Morning," she said, trying to sound cheery. "How are you doing today?"

"I'm fine," her mother said briskly. "I'm heading to your shop. Please meet me there. I have the contractor coming over. We need to get moving on this kitchen design."

"The contractor? You mean Frank? When did you talk to Frank?"

"I called his office. A member of his crew is meeting me. I told them I preferred Frank because we needed to make some decisions, but I'm not sure he's available. What time can you get there?"

"Mom." Stan moved away from the kitchen so Brenna and Francie couldn't hear. "Are you sure you're okay? Have you and Tony talked? I've been trying to call you. After everything that happened this weekend, you really don't need to —"

"Kristan. I'm fine, and if you want to open a quality shop on time, we can't keep procrastinating. Now, I'll see you there in fifteen minutes, or else I'm going to have to design your kitchen myself." And she disconnected, not giving Stan a chance to decline.

Stan gritted her teeth. "Why?" she demanded. "Why do I put up with this? I told Jake this is how it would be, but does he listen?" Still grumbling, she turned and found Brenna standing in front of her, eyes wide. "Hey."

"Hey." Brenna's gaze traveled over her shoulder, then back. "I was going to the bathroom. Everything okay?"

"Fine."

"Who were you talking to?"

"My darling mother. And then myself."

Brenna grinned, getting it. "Sorry. What's going on now?"

"What's going on? Let's see. My family

has completely invaded my happy place. And not only have they invaded it, but they've brought all their drama along with it. And now I have to go to my shop, because my mother has decided that, despite the fact that someone was murdered in her house this weekend, today's the day to design my kitchen." She paused for a breath. "What else did you want to know?"

"Jeez. That's enough. But don't worry. We've got stuff handled here. We'll be cranking out the treats."

"I'm jealous," Stan said. "You sure you don't want to go meet with my mother about the kitchen?"

Brenna patted her on the shoulder. "I adore you, but no."

"Thanks a bunch. I'll remember that."

CHAPTER 30

Stan slipped on a pair of sneakers and a sweatshirt and grabbed Scruffy's leash. Her schnoodle stood at attention until Stan fastened it on her collar, then led the way out to the car. The other dogs accepted staying behind, understanding their duty was to keep an eye on the kitchen goings-on.

When Scruffy was her only dog, she'd gone everywhere with Stan. While Frog Ledge was already an animal-friendly town, Scruffy completely charmed the rest of the town and became an honorary guest in most establishments. She frequently visited the library, the senior center, and Izzy's to see her friends. Plus, whenever Stan tried to leave without her, she pouted and used her saddest face to get her to reconsider.

Henry liked to go out, but he wasn't as much of a social butterfly as Scruffy. Usually he was content to go for a walk, then go home and snooze. Duncan went to the pub with Jake most days, and Gaston happily went where anyone wanted to take him. Scruffy, however, demanded to be included. Maybe today she could provide a furry diversion.

On her way to the shop Stan called Jessie in her office. "Is Richard going to court today?" she asked.

"Yep," Jessie said flatly. "Or rather, he already went. In at nine, done by nine-oh-nine. According to a source at the court."

"Done?" Stan asked. "So what happened?"

"He pled not guilty. His bail was set at two million."

"What?" Stan yelled, so loudly Scruffy jumped.

"I don't know why you're surprised," Jessie said dryly. "Given everything else."

"Still! He's got no criminal record." She stopped. "Does he?" Wouldn't that be a kicker.

"Nope. But he's being held on a murder charge. He's not technically from this community, even though he lives in the state. They're playing hardball, Stan."

"So he has to stay there?" Stan felt a heaviness in her chest thinking of Richard staring at the walls of a jail cell. He'd been a jerk, but no one deserved this. At least, no one innocent. And her gut screamed, *Wrong Guy.*

"No. Someone posted bail."

Stan almost dropped the phone. "At two million bucks? Who likes him *that* much?"

The strangled sound Jessie made might've been a cough, or a laugh. "Are you happy he's out or not?"

"I'm happy. But wow. That's a lot of money. So what's going to happen next?"

Jessie lowered her voice. "I'm working on it, okay? I'm running names from the party on the down-low, just to see if anyone has a criminal background. I managed to get pictures of the guest lists before we had to turn them over to the captain. And I've got some friends who are looking a little deeper into Tony for me. Any news on your end?"

Shoot. She'd meant to call Cyril today to see if he had intel on Tony. "I'm meeting my mother now about something else. I'll see if I can work the job into the conversation. I'll keep you posted."

She disconnected and pulled into the parking lot next to Patricia's car. Letting the engine idle for a moment, she focused on the building, envisioning how it would soon look with two- and four-legged customers spilling out the doors, sitting in the outside patio area, having impromptu playdates made better by her baking.

Her pretty little storefront on Main Street was tucked between the dry cleaner and an ice cream shop, the latter of which fit in nicely with the going-out-for-a-snack theme. Izzy's place was right around the corner, and Jake's pub and the new bookstore-to-be were two minutes down Main Street in the other direction. Main Street met the north end of the green almost in the middle of Izzy's and Jake's, and her house was at the south end of the green. Something else to love about her new town — everything she cared about was in a two-mile radius.

Holding the happy vision of the finished product in her head, she turned to Scruffy. "I'm not going to let Grammy rattle me, Scruffy. We're going to stay focused on the end goal. Having the best pet patisserie around."

Scruffy wagged her stubby tail. Satisfied they were in agreement, they went to the unlocked front door. Scruffy strained at the leash, overcome by the new smells. She heard voices from the kitchen area and headed that way.

Her mother was on the phone, alternately talking to someone and barking orders at a scraggly looking guy who furiously took notes. Not Frank. He'd been smart and sent a minion.

"I want a tile that's not going to wear in a year," her mother was saying. "An Italian marble, preferably." She nodded to Stan, then held up a finger.

Italian marble? How the heck much would that cost? Shaking her head, Stan ducked out of the kitchen and went up front to look around.

She stood in the middle of the room imagining how it would look as Scruffy did a perimeter sniff. The walls would be happy, sunny yellow or lime green. She hadn't yet decided which. A small half-wall needed to go up, separating the café area to the left from the rest of the store. She'd have a seating area with doggie beds and couches as well as human tables and chairs. She'd already ordered her café tables and convinced Jake's bartender Sean, who dabbled in woodworking, to make fancy wooden stands for dog bowls. The town lost its longtime woodworker last year, and it was a void. Maybe Sean could fill those shoes.

Outside of the café area would be the counter and two pastry cases, a large one with dog treats and a smaller one for the cat treats. If she could sort out who'd make them, but that was a problem for later. She'd already talked to Izzy about supplying coffee and some human pastries so pets and owners could enjoy their snacks together. Outdoor seating for the summer months was a must-have, too, and would likely attract people hitting up the ice cream shop next door.

She couldn't wait.

"Kristan, hello. So glad you could make it." Her mother's voice, slightly sarcastic, permeated her happy place. She concentrated hard on keeping the smile in place as she turned. The contractor stood next to her mother. He looked stressed.

"Hi. What's going on?" She stayed where she was, but Scruffy bounded over to say hello. The contractor smiled and knelt down so she could give him a kiss. Patricia didn't seem to notice her.

"I'm making sure the contractors understand what kind of kitchen we want," Patricia said in her *Isn't it obvious* voice.

Scraggly rose and shot Stan an apologetic look before refocusing on his notes.

We? Stan stepped forward and offered her hand. "Hi. Stan Connor. This is my shop," she explained.

"Kevin," he said. "I work for Frank. He had another job this morning."

"No worries," Stan said. "We didn't have an appointment."

"And good customer-oriented firms are flexible," Patricia said.

Stan clenched her teeth. She'd need dentures if her mother didn't leave town soon.

"I wanted to make sure our efforts weren't stalling out, so I asked for a walk-through," Patricia continued. "I think we're on a good track now." She nodded at Kevin. "Let's reiterate. Two commercial stoves, stainless steel. Kristan, is gas available here, or do you need electric?"

"We can do gas," Stan said.

"Excellent. And then we'll need recessed lights, plus some drop fixtures. We'll choose those later."

"Sure thing, ma'am." Kevin scribbled another note. "I'll get right on those orders."

"Wonderful," Patricia said. "Wait! The counters." She snapped her fingers. "We'll want marble counters, too. And stainless steel sinks. I think two, right, Kristan?"

"I'd actually like to sketch it out first," Stan said. "Char said she'd help. Out of all of us, she's got the best eye for what a functional kitchen needs. Kevin, thanks so much for coming out. If you want to start pricing those pieces, I think we're good for today." It felt good to exercise *some* authority, anyway.

Patricia frowned, but kept her mouth shut. Kevin nodded gratefully, mumbled something about having a nice day, and fled.

"I wasn't quite finished," Patricia said.

"It's fine, Mom. I'd prefer if you didn't order things without my sign-off, though."

Patricia seemed unfazed by Stan's directive. Either that or she hadn't even heard her. "I was up early and decided to get a head start on the day. I assumed I'd see you here anyway. You can't dillydally, the opening will be here before you know it." She picked up her Chanel purse from the hook she'd carefully hung it on to prevent dust from finding it and searched for something inside. "By the way, I called my contact about your pastry cases. You can't leave those things for the last minute, Kristan. These people are quite sought after. They aren't sitting around waiting for you to call. I gave him an overview of what you want and your number. He'll be contacting you." She pulled out a lipstick and mirror and freshened her lips.

"Mom." Stan clenched her fists at her sides and counted to ten. Scruffy came over and sat at her side, watching anxiously. She could tell whenever her mom was upset. "I told you I wanted to buy local as much as

possible. There's a guy Jake told me about —"

Patricia waved her off dismissively. "Darling. You don't want *some local guy* you've never heard of doing something so important. The cases will be the center of your shop."

"I wish you wouldn't —" Stan broke off and forced herself to take a deep breath. A woman had been murdered in her mother's bathroom. Patricia clearly wasn't processing it very well. They didn't need to argue about pastry cases. "Mom. Forget the pastry cases. What's really going on?"

CHAPTER 31

Patricia pursed her freshly painted lips. "Whatever do you mean, dear? Nothing's going on except that I want my daughter to succeed. Is there a problem with that?"

"I'm talking about what happened Saturday. That had to have *some* effect on you, no?" She couldn't seem to keep the sarcasm out of her voice when it came to her mother, and it infuriated her. She was thirty-seven years old, for goodness' sake. Her mother shouldn't be able to push her buttons so easily.

Patricia kept her eyes focused on the mirror pretending to examine her lips more closely. "What happened was horrifying. But they've closed the case. We all have to move on, sad as it is."

Stan's stomach sank. "Mom. Tell me you don't really believe Richard was responsible."

"What else should I believe? That's what

the police believe." She snapped the mirror shut and turned away.

"Come on. You've stayed in touch with Richard long after I broke up with him. Heck, you two conspired behind my back. Of all people, you should be skeptical."

Patricia didn't turn. "People do all kinds of things for all kinds of reasons, Kristan," she said, her voice heavy with regret.

"Why *were* all those people there, Mom?" Stan asked. "The people from Warner? Were they there for you or Tony?"

"They're acquaintances," Patricia said, hanging her purse on the hook again. "Tony has a large circle. Sometimes worlds collide. I'm sorry you were upset."

"Why didn't you at least give me a heads-up?"

"Because I was extremely busy," her mother said. "Do you think I had time to run every guest by you?"

"No, but maybe you could've mentioned my ex," Stan said sarcastically.

"We're all adults. I figured you could handle it."

Stan opened her mouth to fire back, then closed it. Her mother was detouring her. All their conversations seemed to go this way, like there was a chasm between them so wide that all the important words got lost in it. Maybe she was still overtired, but today it made her sad. She wished she could find the right words, words strong enough to make it all the way over. And, most important, be heard and understood.

She tried a different tactic. "Are you back in your house yet? I'm guessing they gave you the all clear."

"I'm staying at Char's a few more nights. While the . . . cleaning crews come in."

"Is Tony staying there?"

"Yes," Patricia said through gritted teeth. "Why?"

"I'm curious. If I need to reach you, I want to know where to find you. Where was Tony on Saturday, anyway? Why was he so late to the party?"

They stared at each other. Scruffy looked from one to the other, then started to bark. She had the cutest bark, a *woo-woo* sound that charmed everyone who heard it. "It's okay," Stan murmured, patting her head. "Well?"

"He had a prior commitment that ran long," Patricia said.

"That cut into your *engagement* party? Come on, Mom. I know you. You were mad at *me* for being late, and I'm not your fiancé." Stan took a step forward, holding out her hand, a peace offering. "Mom.

Please. This is me. I'm still your daughter, and I don't want to see you hurt. What's really going on? Do you know where Tony was?"

Patricia said nothing for a long time, studying her daughter. Stan held her breath, thinking for a fleeting moment that she might open up and confide in her. Together they could help Jessie and the rest of the police get to the bottom of this.

But then the corners of her mother's lips turned down and heat flashed into her eyes. Her glare could've struck down Voldemort faster than Harry Potter's wand. "It's not your concern. If you want to show some concern, you can ask your media friends to stop publicizing this story, since the culprit's been caught. Now that's the end of this conversation."

She may as well have slapped Stan right in the face. What had she been thinking? Of course her mother would never confide in her. "You never cease to amaze me," she said, hoping Patricia couldn't hear her voice shake. "Cyril's going to write whatever story he wants. And you know what? I don't blame him. This whole thing stinks to high heaven." She called Scruffy, prepared to storm out in a grand exit. Instead, a sharp rap sounded on the front door.

Their heads both swiveled in that direction. Jessie Pasquale stood on the other side, as if she'd heard the argument from across town and driven over to put in her two cents. Stan motioned for her to come in. Jessie pushed the door open, taking in the scene.

"Morning. I saw your car and thought I'd stop in," she said to Stan, with a curious look at Patricia.

Patricia inclined her chin. "Trooper."

"Ms. Connor." Jessie turned to Stan. "Got a minute?"

"Sure." Stan walked into her back room, motioning Jessie to follow. Patricia went back to her plans for the kitchen, but Stan knew she'd be trying to hear what was going on. "What's up?"

"I'm working on a new case," Jessie said with a grimace. "Your sister just called the troop and asked if we could escort someone out of town. Some guy staying at Char's. Said he was following her around. Since it's my town they called me. After they laughed at her. You know anything about this?"

Stan dropped her face into her hands and groaned. Frog Ledge was supposed to be peaceful, not full of murder and all this insanity. She hadn't had a chance to tell Jessie this drama, with all the other drama going on. "It's Kyle McLeod."

Jessie's face was blank for a minute, then recognition dawned. "The chef?"

"Yup. He tracked her down and now he's staying at Char's."

"Is he dangerous?"

"He sent someone over to serenade her this morning. She's mad. And hurt."

"Great. Unless she's in danger, I can't help her." Jessie sighed. "I can't run the guy out of town. I can't even keep him away from her unless she can prove she needs a restraining order. You know that, right?"

"Of course."

"Do I need to tell her that?"

Stan considered. "Probably. Since I already told her she couldn't call you if he hadn't done anything."

Jessie exhaled loudly. "Glad I have some important work to do today keeping the town safe. Any luck with your mother?" she asked, lowering her voice.

Stan looked away guiltily. "No. We didn't even get to that yet. We got in a fight."

"A fight," Jessie repeated.

"I know, I know. I'll try again. Just not now, okay? She makes me crazy. You might end up with another murder on your hands."

CHAPTER 32

Stan accompanied Jessie back to her house to have the conversation with Caitlyn about what the state police could and could not do. It was preferable to the conversation she needed to have with her mother. To her surprise, she found her sister in the kitchen chatting with Brenna and Francie like they'd been friends for ages. Caitlyn had Brenna's laptop open in front of her. They all looked up expectantly when Stan and Jessie trooped in.

"What's going on?" Stan asked, taking in the scene. "And where's Eva and the dogs?"

"I'm entering all your Pawsitively Organic orders into a new accounting program Brenna downloaded," Caitlyn said. "Eva's playing in the backyard with the dogs."

"I told her all about it and she wanted to give it a try," Brenna said to Stan. "Hey, Jess."

"Bren. Ms. Tucker," Jessie said with a wave.

"Please, dear. It's Francie. How long have you known me?"

"Sorry," Jessie muttered. "I never know what to call people when I'm working."

"I didn't know you knew business software," Stan said to her sister, intrigued. "Or that you were even interested in business."

"Of course I am," Caitlyn said. "I do similar work for the museum I volunteer with, and sometimes I help out on the finance committee at Eva's school." She folded her arms and leveled a stare at Stan. "What, do you think I'm stupid or something?"

Brenna and Francie got real interested in their cookie cutting.

"No! Of course not. I'm sorry. Thank you. Can Jessie and I talk to you for a second?" she asked. "Alone?"

Caitlyn rose haughtily and swept out of the room, a move she'd clearly perfected by watching their mother. Stan looked at Jessie, shrugged, then followed Caitlyn into the den. Jessie trailed behind.

Caitlyn perched on the couch, looking at them with a touch of defiance. "What's up?"

"You called the police with a complaint," Jessie said.

Caitlyn crossed her arms in front of her chest. "I did."

"Well, I'm here to take your report. What happened?"

"I'm being stalked," Caitlyn said, lifting her chin.

"Stalked. By whom?"

"Kyle McLeod. He followed me to town and won't leave."

"I see." Jessie nodded. "What's he done?"

"He came here and caused a scene, then sent other people here to cause a scene. Then I saw him driving around the green today when I was walking with my daughter. It seems," she said, shooting a look at Stan, "that he's got a room at the local B&B."

Stan felt her face turn red. She should've told her sister about that before she heard it elsewhere.

"What kind of a scene did he cause when he came here?" Jessie asked. "Were you threatened?"

Caitlyn shifted uncomfortably. "Not exactly. He said he wanted me to give him another chance."

"You said he sent other people. Did they threaten you?"

"They sang to her," Stan said.

Caitlyn shot her a nasty look. "It was intimidating."

255

Jessie waited.

"Well?" Caitlyn said.

"Well what? I'm still waiting for the threatening part," Jessie said.

Caitlyn threw up her hands. "He's following me!"

"Listen," Jessie said. "We take stalking very seriously. I'm happy to help you take action against someone acting in that manner. But I cannot simply run people out of town because you don't like them. That's what *free country* means."

Caitlyn glowered at them both. "I know that."

Stan resisted adding a childish *I told you so.*

"Then you should know there's nothing I can do unless you want to file a restraining order. And even then, Mr. McLeod would not be asked to leave town. He'd have to comply with keeping a certain distance from you. Would you like to do that?"

Caitlyn leaned back against the couch and closed her eyes. "No. I guess not," she said, sounding defeated. "I should just go home. He can stay here."

Stan and Jessie looked at each other. Jessie mouthed, *Now what?*

To Stan's dismay, she saw a tear roll down her sister's cheek. Shooting Jessie a look, she went and sat next to her. "Hey," she said. "Don't cry."

Caitlyn opened one eye and glared at her. "I don't want Kyle to bother me anymore. He broke my heart, and I don't want to see his face. But I don't want to be the one who has to leave town." She swallowed. "I kinda like it here."

"You do?" Stan asked, unable to hide her surprise.

"I do."

Stan sometimes forgot Caitlyn was a real person to whom real-life things happened. And she felt real-life feelings about those things. It made her more likable. "Okay," she said. "I get it. Do you want me to talk to him?"

Caitlyn and Jessie both stared at her. "And say what?" Caitlyn asked.

Stan sighed. "I don't know. I'm trying to be helpful. But it's none of my business, so I have no idea why I'm offering that."

But her sister smiled. "Wow. Thanks for asking. It's . . . really nice of you to offer." She leaned over and threw her arms around Stan. Stan didn't know who was more surprised, she or Caitlyn. "Even if you didn't tell me he was staying here." She squeezed, then let go. "Don't worry about it. It's my problem. I have to put my big-girl pants on and figure it out. It's all good." She swiped a lingering tear away. "But listen, about your business. If you think this software could work for you, I'm happy to stick around and get your financials up and running. You can do tons of reporting in it, share with your team, do invoices right from your phone, all kinds of things. What do you think? It will really help you when the shop gets going."

"I think . . . that sounds great," Stan said.

Caitlyn stood. "Then I need to get back to the computer. You've got a lot of work to do before you open. Sorry to bother you, Trooper. Thanks for coming out."

And she sailed out of the room, leaving Stan wondering when, exactly, her sister had been abducted by aliens.

Jessie looked at her.

"Don't look at me," Stan said. "I have no idea who that was."

CHAPTER 33

With Caitlyn focused on something constructive, Stan knew she should go back to her mother and try again. She needed her mother to back the idea of her working for Tony; otherwise, he might be suspicious by the offer.

But she didn't have the energy or the desire. She couldn't help it — she was angry at her mother. At the thoughtless way her mother treated her, at her condescending attitude, heck, at the Italian marble. Who was she to order marble tile without consulting her? Her shop wasn't a marble-tiled place!

Jake would know what to do. He always did. Plus, she hadn't had a chance to fill him in on yesterday's developments yet. So after Jessie left, she and Scruffy got back in the car and drove straight to the library. They found him in the children's section, leaning against a couch in the middle of the room while Betty and Lorinda argued over where to put it.

"I think it needs to be near the windows," Lorinda said. "People like to read by the sunlight."

"If they're looking out the window, they aren't paying attention to the programming," Betty insisted. "Besides, it's nearly out in the hallway. We want more places for people to sit, not less. Stan!" she exclaimed, noticing her in the doorway. "And Scruffy! Who's my favorite little dog?"

Scruffy bolted for Betty, who crouched down to give her a hug and be licked nearly to death in the process.

Jake and Lorinda both turned toward her. Lorinda waved a hand with long, purple nails. "Hi there!"

"Hey, babe," Jake said. "What's up?"

"This isn't going to work," she blurted out.

Betty and Lorinda froze in place. Even Scruffy sat completely still. Jake cocked his head, studying her, then chuckled. "Wow," he said, but his voice sounded off-kilter. "It hasn't even been a whole month."

Stan stared at him, confused, then burst out laughing. "Oh no, silly! Not us. I'm talking about my mother as an investor. Are you kidding? How could you think that?" She crossed the room and threw her arms around him. He hugged her back fiercely.

"You scared me for a minute," he murmured into her hair.

Behind them, Betty and Lorinda breathed a collective sigh of relief. "Thank goodness," Betty said. "You two are my favorite couple!"

Stan smiled and tipped her head back to look at Jake. "Mine too," she admitted.

"Honey, just push that couch over to the window and go help your lady," Lorinda said to Jake with a sidelong glance at Betty. "She clearly needs you right now."

Jake grinned. "Lor, you're a master. Betty, you good with that?"

Betty sighed dramatically. "Fine. But I reserve the right to ask you for help moving it again when Lorinda is on vacation."

"You got it." Jake moved the couch into position, then slung his arm around Stan. "Outside?"

She nodded and collected Scruffy from Betty's grasp. They slipped out the back door behind the nonfiction section where the library backed up to the town green, and crossed the parking lot to the walking path. Scruffy pranced along, happy to be going on a solo walk with her parents despite the cloudy, overcast day. Stan could smell rain.

"What's going on?" Jake asked.

"My mother's crazy," Stan said. "She's not even dealing with the fact that someone was murdered in her house. Instead she's having Frank's people buy equipment for the shop that I didn't even pick out and brushing me off when I tell her to stop. She wouldn't answer any of my questions, even when I told her it was because I care about her. I was going to try to bring up the whole working-for-Tony thing, but she made me so mad we just ended up getting into a fight." She hadn't realized how upset the whole conversation had gotten her until she noticed her hands were shaking.

"Whoa. Wait a minute. Working for Tony?" Jake stopped walking and turned her to face him. "I think you need to back up."

She sighed. "I do. I'm sorry. I need to fill you in on what Jessie and I talked about yesterday. But this always happens with my mother. I get so frustrated I feel like I'm sixteen. What a loser, right?" She laughed without humor. "I'm thirty-seven and I still can't figure out how to not let her get to me."

"Oh, babe." Jake pulled her against him and hugged her. "Stop. You are not a loser."

"Feels like it sometimes."

He kissed the top of her head. "You should talk to Jessie. She goes through it with our mother."

Stan tilted her head back to look at him. "Really?"

"Totally. They fight almost every time they're together. It's their thing."

"Huh. I didn't think my mother and I had a thing," Stan said thoughtfully. Scruffy tugged at her leash, impatient to keep going. Reluctantly, Stan let go of Jake and obliged. They started walking again.

He slipped his hand into hers. "Maybe you do," he said. "And maybe it's not too late to change the kind of thing you have."

They were silent for a few minutes, watching Scruffy stop and sniff every tree, different patches of grass, and rocks along the path.

"So you going to tell me the rest of it?" he asked finally.

"Yeah." She sighed. "It's kind of crazy."

"Try me."

She filled him in on everything that happened yesterday, from Izzy's story about Wallace to her subsequent conversation with Jessie. "No matter how I feel about Richard, I don't think he did this. I told you that from the beginning. And neither does your sister. But Tony's got some clout with the cops, and everyone's brushing this under the rug. My mother, too."

"Wow," he said, digesting the story. "That's a lot."

"It is. What do you think?"

Jake raked his hand through his hair and blew out a breath. "I think it sounds like a TV show. But that said" — he held up a hand when she started to protest — "that doesn't mean it can't happen."

Pacified, Stan nodded. "Right."

"So Jessie doesn't think Richard's guilty."

"She worded it a little differently. She did say people heard him fighting with Eleanor. But she's more suspicious of Tony because of his vanishing act and her superior's reactions."

"Right. Did you ask your mother about Tony?"

"I did. She basically told me it was none of my business."

Jake snorted. "I'd bet a night's worth of bar tips that whatever Tony was up to, she either didn't know or didn't approve."

"That's the feeling I got, too," Stan admitted. "And when I asked Tony, he told me the same thing."

"You asked Tony?"

"I did."

"Stan. Be careful. If he did have something

to do with it, he's not going to like it if he thinks you're stirring up trouble." He looked at her sideways. "Does this have anything to do with the working-for-Tony thing you mentioned earlier?"

"I'm going to offer to be his executive coach." She said it fast. Rip off the Band-Aid.

He was silent for a long time. Stan braced herself.

Instead of protesting and lecturing her about what could be a potentially stupid move if Tony was, in fact, guilty of something, he reinforced exactly why she loved him. "You know I'm not crazy about him anyway," Jake said. "But I would never tell you not to do something. And if my sister's hands are tied and she's looking for some help . . ." He trailed off. "Of course I would support you."

"Really?" she asked, surprised. "I mean, thank you," she added hastily.

"I wouldn't get in your way," he said. "And I don't want you to feel like you can't tell me. I don't want us to have secrets from each other."

"No," she agreed. "Neither do I. Ever."

"Ever," he said, squeezing her hand. "So you'll keep me in the loop?"

"Of course. You can't tell anyone. Jessie'll

get in trouble. You can't even tell her I told you."

He nodded. "Deal." They walked in silence a little longer. "So Richard and Eleanor had a fight."

"That's what they're saying."

"What was his relationship with Eleanor?"

"I don't know," Stan admitted. "They didn't have one when I knew them both, but that was a long time ago. Who knows. She was tough. But I still don't believe he could kill anyone. Not even her."

"The Curtis Wallace thing is interesting," Jake said. "Especially since he led the charge to get Tony elected."

Stan stopped walking and stared at him. "He did?"

"Yeah. You weren't here long enough to know all the players, but Curtis campaigned hard for Tony. I think part of it was Mona. He doesn't like strong women. Thought it was time for her to get out of office."

"Terrific. One of those." Stan made a face. "But he came up to Mona in the bar yesterday, all drunk and belligerent, telling her she may get her job back because we should impeach Tony. Then he said she'd had her time, or something like that."

"Yeah. He's a piece of work. Not sure what he thought Tony was going to do, but he was all in."

"Wow. Hey, do you know what a mayor's salary is?"

Jake shook his head. "No. But you're wondering about his house."

"I am."

He thought for a minute. "I'm going to ask my parents about the Trumbull family. They may know something about how Tony ended up there."

"Thanks. Richard's bail was set at two million bucks," Stan said.

Jake whistled. "Steep."

"Yeah. Someone posted it, though."

"Just like that?" Jake shook his head. "You're right, the pay must be pretty good over there."

"Mmmm," Stan said noncommittally. She wondered about Michelle. Would she pony up that much money to save Richard? If not her, then who?

"Well, at least he's able to go home while this plays out," Jake said. "But someone else is sitting pretty right now, thinking they've gotten away with it."

CHAPTER 34

Stan couldn't remember the last time she and Jake'd had a real date, even just dinner out. Between the pub, getting the shop ready, and keeping up with her existing customers they were both too busy to do much more than grab ready-made meals from Abby at the general store or a quick breakfast at Izzy's. So trying the new Asian fusion restaurant near Hartford — Scott's recommendation — sounded exciting.

"I think we're getting old," Stan said to Jake as they walked into the restaurant to meet Scott and Brenna. "This is my idea of a big night out."

"We could really go crazy and see a movie after," Jake said.

"The dogs and cats would miss us," Stan protested. "Well, the dogs at least. I'm not sure the cats care that much. Hey, guys."

Brenna and Scott waited just inside the door of the restaurant. "What don't the cats care about?" Brenna asked.

"If we stay out late," Stan said. "Which we probably won't do because we really aren't that exciting."

"We're not much better," Scott said. "Brenna works late most nights and I don't think I could go out after that if I wanted to. I'm usually ready to crash. Although when I visit her at the pub I feel like I'm cooler than I probably am."

Brenna laughed. "Don't worry. I still think you're pretty cool."

Scott approached the hostess and gave them his name. Stan looked around while they waited. The restaurant had a soothing feel. Soft meditation music piped through the speaker system. The cream-colored walls had a purple tinge from the dim lights. Strategically positioned screens throughout the dining area gave the tables an air of extra privacy.

"Cool place," Jake remarked, pulling out Stan's chair for her.

"I feel bad we didn't invite Caitlyn," Brenna said, sliding into her own seat. They'd left her happily working on the computer in Stan's kitchen while Eva ran around the house with the dogs. "But I'm so glad I finally get to try this place. Scott comes here for lunch all the time and keeps torturing me with images of all-you-can-eat sushi." She leaned against Scott and kissed his shoulder.

"Don't feel bad about Caitlyn," Stan said, picking up her menu. "I think she's actually enjoying the peace and quiet of our little town. And she's pretty intent on getting me up and running on this business software she was raving about. Bren, I have no idea what you did to her, but I've never known my sister to have any interest in working on anything besides her tan."

Brenna giggled. "She's not that bad. I just mentioned that you'd need all kinds of help so you didn't burn yourself out trying to do everything, and she jumped on it. Wouldn't you much rather do the fun stuff like baking and social media anyway?"

"Yeah. Once I actually have a kitchen." Stan turned to Jake. "Do you know when they're going to get started? I never got a chance to ask Frank's guy today." She grimaced, pushing away the memory of her meeting with her mother. "He was too busy writing down everything she wanted to order."

"Whenever you give them the design," Jake said with a grin.

"Ouch. I need to huddle with Char. And don't tell my mother that."

"For the record, I'm not having meetings with your mother every day."

"Thank God. Although after today, I'm not having meetings with her anymore, either, at least not without a mediator."

"I know. I'll take that role," Jake said. "Don't worry."

"When do you open?" Scott asked.

"December. Right before the holidays. As long as everything goes as planned." *And as long as I don't give my mother her money back.* "How was Francie today, Bren? I feel bad I had to leave. I hope you didn't mind teaching her."

"Mind? I think it's awesome," Brenna said. "She's a great cook. She jazzed up the blueberry bites with a touch of pear. It was amazing."

"That's great." Relieved, Stan pushed her chair back. "I have to run to the ladies' room. Be right back."

On her way to the front of the restaurant, she passed through the bar. And slowed when she saw a familiar face. Michelle Mansfield, huddled miserably over a beer bottle while a friend talked quietly to her, obviously trying to console her. Michelle's usually big hair looked as sad and dejected as she did, hanging flat against her head. She'd traded in her low-cut sweaters and

271

tight skirts for a conservative pair of jeans and a long-sleeved T-shirt. Things must be bad.

Stan instinctively started to duck her head and hurry past. Michelle probably didn't want to see her anyway. But guilt got the better of her. She backtracked and hurried over, touching Michelle on the shoulder. Michelle's companion stopped mid-sentence and looked up expectantly.

"Michelle. Hey."

Michelle turned. A host of emotions crossed her face until it settled into a mask of distrust. "What do *you* want?"

Stan took a step back, her hand falling to her side. "I wanted to see how you were doing."

"How I'm doing." Michelle laughed without humor. "I'm doing great. My boyfriend was arrested for murder. How are you doing?"

"I'm going to use the restroom," Michelle's friend said, and fled.

"Michelle. I'm so sorry this is happening. For the record, I don't think Richard could ever do anything like —"

"Save it," Michelle hissed. "It's your fault he was out there anyway."

"*My* fault?" Stan asked, stunned.

"You and your boyfriend had to get him

agitated enough that he needed to go cool off. Or do whatever he was doing out there. Which made him easy pickings when they needed someone to take the fall." Michelle shoved her stool back and stood, ready to walk away.

Stan blocked her, tamping down her temper. "Listen," she said. "That was uncalled for. I want to help Richard. I don't believe he did this. So stop attacking me and tell me what you know about Eleanor. And why someone in that house wanted her dead."

CHAPTER 35

Stan's strong words surprised Michelle enough to shut her up. Her anger visibly deflated. "Let's talk outside," she said.

Stan followed her out to the small foyer inside the main door. When they were alone, Michelle faced Stan. "What do you mean you want to help him?"

"Just what I said. But you can't tell anyone we had this conversation. It's . . . complicated."

"Why should I trust you? You're involved with all those *people.*" She spat the word like one would a bite of salad with a hair in it.

"I'm probably the least involved with *those people* out of anyone who was there," Stan said. "Aside from being a blood relation to Tony's fiancée. And that's not my fault."

Michelle looked like she didn't want to believe her but had no other choice. "So what are you going to do to help Richard?"

Stan hesitated. "First, how is he?"

"He's a mess. He spent the weekend in jail. And it's not over." There was no drama behind the words, just simple fact.

Stan knew all too well what it felt like to be accused of something she hadn't done, even though she'd never spent time in jail while it was sorted out. "I'm going to start with trying to figure out who hated Eleanor enough to kill her. If the police get real evidence about someone else, they'll have to drop the charges."

"I hope you have a lot of time," Michelle said dryly. "Someone like her has more enemies than friends. Richard was nothing compared to how the rest of us felt."

So Michelle was among Eleanor's group of haters. "Tell me why."

Michelle rubbed her neck as if trying to work out a kink. "I'm so sick of thinking about it. This woman takes up so much space in my brain it makes me sick. But she was making all our lives miserable. God rest her soul," she added with a glance toward the ceiling.

"Meaning the people who worked with her? How so?"

Michelle paced the small hallway. Her hands were shaking and she didn't seem to know what to do with them. Finally, she shoved them in her pockets. "First she took over your job. You knew that, right?"

"I heard that."

"Yeah. Well, that was the beginning. Then they 'expanded her responsibilities.' " Michelle used air quotes. "She was basically on track to take over everything. She was already impossible but it went to her head. She was so bent on all that *power* she thought she was getting. She left a ton of human wreckage in her path, too. People quitting left and right, whether they had jobs to go to or not. When they weren't being brought out on stretchers from their nervous breakdowns."

The whole concept of living that way felt alien to Stan now. It even made dealing with her mother seem more bearable. "That's terrible. What does that have to do with you and Richard, though? Aren't you guys in a totally different department?"

Michelle smiled bitterly. "My, how quickly you forgot how the power-crazy work. Like I said, she wanted it all. She was campaigning hard to merge sales, marketing, and the media team, but she wanted to run the show. Anyone who wasn't on her bus was on their way out. Which is where Richard came in."

"Wait," Stan said. She had a compelling

urge to cover her ears like she did when she was five and wanted to pretend she couldn't hear her mother ask her to finish her milk. "Are you about to tell me Richard had motive?"

"Honey," Michelle said. "We all had motive. And he did hate her. They actually did have a fight at the party. All that's true. But Richard didn't kill her. The worst he was planning was his own resignation. She drafted him to do some dirty work for her. Fudging some data. She basically threatened to get him fired if he didn't help her. She'd already made it so his own boss was on thin ice. So Richard was working fifteen-hour days producing these bogus reports and his hands were tied."

Stan processed that information as a couple walked in and Michelle stopped talking. Fudging data? Bogus reports? She couldn't even comprehend it. But that would not look good for Richard's case if it got out.

"Who knows about that?" she asked once they were alone again.

"No one but me," Michelle said with a sad smile. "I told him he should call the ethics line but he thought it was all rigged. He figured he'd be the one to go down in flames either way."

"Whatever you do, do not tell anyone this story," Stan said urgently. "It'll look really bad for him."

"Do you think I don't know that?" Michelle snapped.

"I just don't get why she was working on the side for Tony if she was so fixated on the top rung of the corporate ladder," Stan said.

"She wanted the best of both worlds. She was obsessed with politics, thought there was big money potential there. I think she was training her daughter and some other lackeys to run the business so she could reap the profits."

Big money potential with a small-town politician? It still made no sense to Stan. "I just don't get why Tony. Or why all of you were at my mother's party."

Michelle stared at her. "You really don't know?"

"Not a clue," Stan said.

"Eleanor used to work with Tony. They were both lobbyists in DC."

Stan stared at her, openmouthed. Had her mother known that? Or had her mother's story about reaching out to Eleanor been a lie?

"Oh, yeah. They both had agendas," Michelle said. "Eleanor had big plans for Tony.

Thought he'd make a great governor. She's been relentless on the guy, pushing him to commit to running. She said she'd planned this for years, that she'd done so much for him to get him here. And *we* were going to help make it happen. The corporate contingency. She wanted to show him she had support built for him before he even hit the trail."

Stan leaned against the wall, her head spinning. Tony and Eleanor had a history? Tony wanted to run for governor? He'd just been elected as mayor not even a year ago. That would really get his supporters riled up, not to mention his dissenters. How much of this did her mother know? "But Tony's platform has been about small towns and farming. Where does the corporate agenda fit into that?"

Michelle shrugged. "Who knows? In Eleanor's brain it did. That's all that counts."

"But what was in it for Eleanor?" Stan asked.

"Payback, sounded like. She did something for him, now she thought he could repay the favor. She wanted to attach herself to his rising star. I also think she wanted her kids in politics. Especially the oldest. And positioning her with Tony from day one, first as part of her company, then as maybe an intern on his staff, would've been the girl's ticket in."

Stan remembered Eleanor's introduction of Monica at the party, the special mention of her daughter's love for politics and her double major in politics and economics. That poor kid. Patricia Connor was overbearing and opinionated with definite ideas about what her girls should do, but at the end of the day they had each done exactly what they wanted anyway.

They were both silent, each lost in her own thoughts.

"So who do you think killed her?" Stan asked finally.

"Honestly?" Michelle shook her head slowly. "I have no idea. Like I said before, enough people couldn't stand her."

"But 'can't stand' is a long way from kill," Stan said.

"Yeah," Michelle said.

They stood there for a few minutes. "Listen, I need to get back," Stan said. "If you think of anything, please call me, okay? And don't mention this conversation to anyone."

Michelle nodded. "Will do."

"Please tell Richard . . . I was asking about him." Stan turned to go back inside, then looked back. "I'm glad you were able to get him released."

Michelle's eyebrows shot up. "I didn't post bail. Are you kidding me? Two million bucks?" she laughed without mirth. "I certainly don't have that to show for all the time I've wasted in that job. If I did," she said wistfully, "you think I'd be sticking around?"

CHAPTER 36

When Stan got back to the table, they all looked at her curiously. "Sorry," she said. "There was a line."

"Isn't there always?" Brenna said sympathetically.

Jake leaned over and slid his arm around the back of her chair once Scott and Brenna started talking again. "Everything okay?" he asked in a low voice.

She nodded. "Fine. I'll tell you later." She sipped the espresso martini waiting at her place, then smiled at him. "This is awesome."

"I thought you'd like it."

A waiter came by and poured water into their glasses, then looked at them expectantly. "Appetizers?" Scott asked.

"One of everything," Brenna said. "I'm starving."

They all stared at her. "Fine," she said with a sigh. "Crab Rangoon, then."

They also ordered scallion pancakes, edamame, and seaweed salad, then decided to take advantage of the never-ending sushi for their meals. While they waited for their food, Brenna said, "So what did Jess want today with Caitlyn?"

Stan smiled wryly. "Caitlyn tried to get her ex kicked out of town. Long story," she added for Scott's benefit. "So Jessie had to explain how she can't make people leave town just because someone doesn't like them."

Jake tried to hide his smile. "And did she get through?"

"We'll see," Stan said.

"Did her ex do anything?" Scott asked. "Is he bugging her?"

"He sent over a musical trio to serenade her," Stan said.

"That sounds romantic," Scott said.

"I suppose in other circumstances it would be. But they had a . . . dramatic uncoupling."

"Ah." Scott thanked the waiter as he set down the first of their plates. "Happens. At least he's trying to fix things."

"Isn't she in the middle of a divorce, too?" Brenna asked.

Stan nodded. Scott arched an eyebrow. "Sounds like she has a lot going on."

"That's an understatement," Stan said.

"Your sister must have a lot going on, too. With that murder the other night," Scott said to Brenna and Jake. "How crazy was that?"

"Pretty crazy," Jake agreed. "But Jess doesn't talk much about work." He pushed the edamame plate out of the way so the waiter could deliver the sushi.

"I do think it was nice of Tony to offer to set up the fundraiser," Brenna said.

Stan kept her mouth shut and tasted her miso soup. Brenna didn't know much about the events preceding the murder, and there was no reason to tell her.

"That was nice of him," Scott agreed, digging into his spicy tuna rolls.

"It's so sad," Brenna said. "Mom drove me crazy in high school, but I can't imagine her not being around."

"She drove you crazy? I think it was the other way around," Jake said.

"Oh please! After dealing with you and Jessie I was nothing," Brenna said.

Thankfully, the conversation turned away from Eleanor and the murder after that. Scott told them more about the new job he expected to be offered any day now. "So if that comes through, you've got yourself an extra pair of hands for the pub," he told

Jake. "Since I'll be living here."

"Oh, yeah?" Jake glanced at his sister, the question clear on his face.

"Yeah," Scott went on, oblivious to Jake's transition into protective big brother. "I'll probably get rid of my apartment since my new office will be closer to Frog Ledge."

"We're still discussing living arrangements," Brenna said defensively. "But there's no reason why Scott shouldn't move in with me. It's silly to pay for an extra place, especially if it's far away."

Scott glanced from Brenna to Jake, finally getting it. "Look, I'm totally in it for the long haul with Bren," he said. "And I'm happy to help you out any way I can. I can pay you more rent. And I can help you, too, Stan. With the shop. Like I mentioned the other day."

"I don't need more rent," Jake said. "You don't need to explain anything to me. You're both adults. I think you can figure out that if you mess with my sister, there'll be a problem." He smiled to take the sting out of the words. Brenna shot daggers at him with her eyes.

But Scott nodded emphatically. "I hear you. I get it. You won't be sorry. I have to get the job first anyway."

Brenna nudged Stan with her elbow.

"Can't you control your boyfriend?" she muttered, only half-kidding, but Stan had drifted back to Michelle's revelations.

"Sorry," she said, forcing her mind back to the table. "Jake, be nice."

But Scott took it all in stride. When they walked out of the restaurant later, the rain, which had held off all day, pounded the pavement like it had been saving up all its energy for this moment.

"Wait here," Scott said to Brenna. "I'll grab the car." He jogged off into the parking lot.

Brenna grinned. "He's sweet, right? If you don't go get your car you look like a jerk," she told her brother. "Which you already look like, by the way."

"I just wanted to make sure he was clear on how things worked with our family."

"Yeah, you were a big jerk."

Stan held the keys up and winked at Jake. Laughing, he grabbed them out of her hand. "We'll talk about this later."

"He's such a pain," Brenna said affectionately, watching her brother dodge the rain as he ran for the Audi.

"He loves you. So you're really thinking of moving in together?"

"It's been a couple of months. Just because it took you guys forever doesn't mean it has to take us that long," Brenna said. "I like having him around. Usually I don't want the guys I date around all the time." She shrugged. "That must mean something, right?"

She had a point. "You're right. I'm happy for you. You guys coming back to Frog Ledge tonight?"

Brenna nodded. "Scott's not working until tomorrow afternoon." She glanced up as a car pulled to the curb a few feet ahead of where they waited. Stan turned to see if it was Jake, but it wasn't her car. It was a red sedan that looked vaguely familiar. Then her eyes landed on a black oval sticker on the back with white writing: SOCIAL WORKERS ROCK.

Red car. Black sticker. *Something something* rock.

Stan froze. This couldn't be the car she'd seen in front of Tony's house on Saturday night picking up Monica Chang. That was crazy. Tons of people had stickers saying something rocked.

Scott leaned over and opened the passenger door from the inside.

"See you tomorrow," Brenna called, jumping into the car. Scott waved, then drove off.

"Yeah," Stan murmured, watching the car

drive away, squinting to see the license plate in the rain. This time, she could make out the whole thing: 487 BDR.

Her sushi rolled over in her stomach. The sticker could've been a coincidence. The license plate *and* the sticker? Not so much.

This was the car Monica Chang jumped into when she'd slipped out of the party.

CHAPTER 37

"What do you mean, the same car?" Jake kept his eyes on the road — the weather was horrible — but Stan could see his hands tense on the wheel. She hadn't wanted to tell him until she was certain, but figured he'd never forgive her if she kept a suspicion like that to herself.

"I can't be sure, but it looked like the car Monica got into Saturday night," Stan said. "I went out the back door to see if she was out there, after Sturgis told me she was gone. A red car pulled up. A red car with a sticker like Scott has, but I only saw the last word: 'rock.' He has a sticker that says 'Social Workers Rock.' " She hesitated. "And I only saw some of the letters on the license plate, but those letters are on Scott's, too." She grabbed the door handle as Jake hit the gas. "Hey. Slow down."

"Sorry." He eased up. "But if this guy is involved in this somehow, he's alone with my sister. And moving in with her, apparently."

"I know. But how he would be involved? That would mean Monica had something to do with it. And she didn't look like she was in good enough shape to stand up, never mind strangle her mother."

"Can you call Brenna? Make sure she's okay?" He pulled his cell out of his jacket pocket and handed it to her.

She took it from him and leaned over to kiss his cheek. "You're so sweet."

"I'm crazy and overprotective. But that's my little sister."

Stan dialed. Brenna answered on the second ring. "Hey. I'm almost there," she said, figuring it was Jake. "I told you I was going to help with the cleanup, so you don't need to come."

"It's Stan. Jake, uh, wanted me to call and make sure you were okay. You know, with the weather. The driving's kind of bad." She raised her eyebrows at Jake.

"He's too funny. We're fine, just getting back to Frog Ledge now. Tell him thanks for calling."

Stan disconnected. "She thinks you're crazy."

"You couldn't have come up with something better than that?"

"I have too much on my mind to be clever." Stan handed him back the phone and rubbed her temples. "I'll talk to Jessie. She can run the license numbers and see if there's another red car that's similar. It can happen."

"Yeah," Jake said. "But most coincidences really aren't coincidences. I'm going to have her run a background check on that guy."

Stan leaned her head back against the seat. "This whole thing is so crazy. I saw Michelle Mansfield. In the bar. That's why I was gone so long tonight." She gave him the abridged version of the conversation.

"You're kidding," Jake said.

"Wish I was. I'm trying to figure out if my mother knew they had a history. Or if my mother lied to me about how Eleanor and Tony started working together. But if they were such good friends . . ." She trailed off, leaving the thought unfinished.

"Doesn't mean there wasn't some kind of falling out," Jake said grimly. "Stan, I don't know about you being in close proximity to Tony. I don't like what I'm hearing."

But she was already shaking her head. "There's no other way. If I can get a handle on Tony, maybe this will help Jessie get the case reopened." What she didn't say: *If Cur-*

tis Wallace brawling with Eleanor can't make that happen, it could be a long shot.

CHAPTER 38

Tuesday morning Stan awoke with the roosters across the green, buoyed by the bright sunlight streaming into her window. At least the town would dry out after yesterday's rainstorm. But even during a rainstorm, most days in Frog Ledge could be considered beautiful. Instead of waking to a loudly beeping alarm, stumbling downstairs to make coffee, finding an outfit that made her look perfectly put together and locking herself away in an office all day, she kept her own time. She still rose early most days, but now she didn't rush out of the house. She worked — and lived — in yoga pants or jeans. She took her dogs walking on the green whenever the mood struck, hung out with Jake at the pub when he worked, visited her friends around town, and sat on her porch, listening to the sounds of the country instead of honking horns, traffic, or other altercations. Frog Ledge was peaceful.

Right now, though, a sense of unease hung over the community. Eleanor's death — the death of an outsider at the home of another outsider — shook everyone despite news of an arrest. Tony's position didn't help. People were left wondering if they could trust him. Even if he personally didn't have anything to do with Eleanor's death, it still called into question his choice of associates, and *their* associates.

Ugh. So much to figure out. Stan slipped out of the room and closed the door behind her, leaving Jake sleeping. She'd brew some coffee and take it to the back deck where she could sit and think.

When she went down to the kitchen, Caitlyn already had coffee going. She stood at the stove stirring oatmeal, looking . . . normal in her fuzzy slippers and pajama bottoms peppered with well-dressed ladies in various cityscapes. She even looked a little frazzled. Stan was used to seeing her wearing designer dresses and matching shoes. Never doing lowly things like making oatmeal.

"What are you doing up?" Stan asked.

"Getting Eva some breakfast before she wakes up the whole house. I put her out in the backyard with the dogs for a bit."

"Your *daughter*?"

"What?" Caitlyn asked, offended.

"You put her out in the backyard?" Stan said.

Caitlyn sniffed. "You can make fun of me all you want. The nanny helped with these things. I had to get rid of her because Michael made such a stink about everything. The nanny, not Eva."

Stan didn't have a comment for that, so she beelined for the coffeepot. "Plans for today?" she asked instead.

Eva banged through the back door, the four dogs hot on her heels. "Mommy! The dogs want oatmeal, too."

"The dogs can't have oatmeal," Caitlyn said. She glanced at Stan a little desperately. "Anyone Eva can have a playdate with around here?"

Eva pouted. "I don't *want* a playdate. I'm playing with the dogs."

Stan hid a smile. Her niece reminded her of herself as a child — animals over people. "I don't know a lot of kids, but maybe go to the library?" she suggested. "They have all kinds of kids' programs. I can let Betty know you're coming. She could find a friend there."

"I guess." Caitlyn stirred the oatmeal, then spooned it into a bowl and handed it to her daughter. "What are you doing today?"

"Work," Stan said breezily. "What else? Things are crazy, getting the shop ready and keeping up with everything else. Hey, you could also go to Izzy's. Her café is a cool place to hang out. Or — I can't believe I didn't think of it before! You could talk to our animal control officer. She has a small shelter area set up in the new vet clinic. I'm sure she'd love some new volunteers."

Caitlyn brightened. "Eva would love that. Will you show me where it is?"

Stan nodded. "It's right on Main Street. I can take you over when I leave. I'll call Amara and let her know."

Clearly cheered at the prospect of getting out for a bit, Caitlyn turned to Eva. "We're going to go meet some of the other dogs and cats in town. Does that sound fun?"

Eva squealed and clapped, forgetting her spoon was in her hand. Oatmeal splattered the table and floor. The dogs hurried to clean it up. "Oops. Sorry. Can we bring some of them home?" she asked hopefully.

Stan and Caitlyn looked at each other. "Maybe this isn't such a great idea," Caitlyn muttered.

CHAPTER 39

Brenna arrived at nine sharp with a shopping bag full of fresh ingredients, two lattes from Izzy's, and Francie on her heels. Stan and Eva had a head start — two batches of treats. Baking usually helped Stan untangle any problem, or at least calmed her down. Today her problems seemed worse than normal and she still didn't feel particularly untangled or calm, but at least she'd been productive.

"Wow, you've been busy," Brenna said, surveying the kitchen.

"We have. I've sketched out a couple new recipes, too, if you want to try them."

"Awesome. We can play around with those today, right, Francie?"

"Absolutely," Francie said. "I'm so glad I'm working with pet food and not human food. I'd be five hundred pounds!"

Stan laughed. "They're human-grade, so feel free to sample. I'm going to take Caitlyn and Eva up to the clinic. They're going to help with the animals."

"How nice!" Francie exclaimed. "The younger you teach a child to care for animals, the better. By the way, will you see your mother today? I've been trying to get ahold of her."

"I probably will," Stan said. "Why, what's up?"

"Pastor Ellis and I wanted to meet with her and Tony about the wedding ceremony. He has some questions, and I have a lot of planning to do." Francie tied her plaid apron around her waist. "I want to be sure she's happy. And with everything else going on, she doesn't need more to worry about. I also wanted to offer to do some meditations with her. Does she meditate?"

Stan almost laughed out loud, but disguised it with a cough. "I don't think so. I would love to do some meditations, though, if you want to work with me instead. Heck, I could've used one this morning."

"I would love to!" Francie exclaimed. "I'm sure you must be feeling some stress. I should've thought of that. We can do a yoga and meditation session. You can come to my studio. I have a small one in my house."

"I would love to meditate."

"Tomorrow, then!" Francie clapped her

hands. "Bring your mother, too. She's a wonderful candidate for meditation."

"I'll try," Stan lied. "I can't wait!" She grabbed her latte off the counter and went to get dressed.

Jake came down the stairs as Stan was on her way up. "Brenna here?"

"She is."

He looked relieved. "You calling Jess? About . . ."

"Yeah. I have to stop by and see her."

"Let me know what happens. I have to go to the pub for my delivery." He kissed her and took off.

Stan showered, dressed, then called Amara.

"Hey. Forgive me yet for the concert?"

Amara laughed. "What was that all about?"

"It's a long story and much better suited for a few glasses of wine," Stan said.

"I hear that. Tell me when and where."

"Soon. Meantime, can my sister and my niece come help Diane at the shelter today? They're looking for something to do."

"Absolutely," Amara said immediately. "Perfect timing. Diane's stressed out because she's full at both sites. We're actually going to have a special adoption event on Thursday, so would love the help. Tomorrow and Thursday, too, come to think of it. Vincent and I were going to jump in but we also have a full schedule."

"A special adoption event?" Stan asked, her brain kicking into gear. "Any interest in pairing that up with a fundraiser to get the new local K9 a bulletproof vest? Or would that cut into Diane's fundraising?"

"No, she would love that. She's been trying to position us as a community partner. That's perfect," Amara said. "It'll be from six to nine. He can bring the dog, they can do a demo. People love to meet K9s. This is great, Stan!"

"Sweet. I'll tell Trooper Colby. Thanks so much, Amara. And Caitlyn'll be over in a while. I'm taking her to the library first."

Two missions accomplished, she grabbed her tote bag, collected Caitlyn and Eva, and drove them to town. Then she took a deep breath and drove to the B&B. Time to tackle her mother again.

She was thankful to see Patricia's car parked in a guest slot on the side of the inn. She was less thankful to see Kyle's car there and wondered how often he and her mother crossed paths. She rang the bell, hearing strains of jazz music from inside. Char opened the door with a champagne flute in her hand and a neon green apron tied over her yellow dress.

"Sweetie!" she exclaimed, throwing her free arm around Stan. "Come in! I was introducing your mother to dirty rice." She ushered Stan inside. Patricia sat at the table, also with a champagne flute. Kyle wasn't in the kitchen.

Stan motioned to the flutes. "Are you guys celebrating something?" she asked.

Char shook her head. "Your mother needed a mimosa with her eggs today. 'Course, I had to try it out to make sure it tasted good. Hadn't made mimosas in a while. I was rusty." She winked at Stan. "Now she's learning how to make dirty rice. It's for dinner, if you're free."

"Sounds great, but being free is highly unlikely." Stan glanced at her mother. "How are you doing?" she asked stiffly. They hadn't spoken since their disagreement at her shop yesterday.

Patricia smiled, but it was more of a grimace. "Fine." She looked, by her usual standards, like something the cat dragged in. Which, to normal people, meant she'd dressed down, in linen lounge pants and a cashmere sweater. She'd pulled her hair back in a bun and wore barely any makeup. Odd for this time of day.

"Well. I thought the three of us" — she

301

nearly bit her tongue off saying the words — "could get together and sketch out the kitchen so Frank can officially get working on it." She pulled out a chair and sank into it.

Patricia looked at her. "The three of who?"

"You, me, and Char."

"If you want me to be involved, that's fine," Patricia said stiffly. "I don't want to overstep."

Stan resisted the urge to bang her head on the table.

Char poured something out of a pitcher and handed it to Stan. "Here. You need a mimosa, too."

Stan accepted the glass without argument. Char nodded approvingly and refilled her own glass. "I would love to help sketch out the kitchen. By the way, Stan, I meant to thank you for helping Francie. She's over the moon about working for you. She came over last night to tell me."

"I should be thanking you. She's lovely," Stan said.

"She's had a rough go of it," Char said. "I'm so happy to see her enjoying life a little again."

"I don't know her story," Stan said. "She did allude to losing her son."

Char nodded. "And her husband. She

doesn't talk about it much."

"You have someone working for you?" her mother asked.

"Yes, Char referred her," Stan said. "I figured you'd be happy that I did something ahead of time. Anyway, I needed to ask you something else." She took a deep breath. Better to do this while Char was in the room. She could help moderate if the conversation went sideways. "I've been thinking about you and Tony, and wanted to offer some help." The words nearly choked her on their way out of her mouth.

Her mother glanced at her, interested now. Char froze, waiting to hear where this was going. "I want to offer him some of my time. As an advisor." She couldn't bring herself to use the word "coach." "There's going to be heavy media attention on this situation, and I can help him navigate it."

Patricia remained silent for thirty seconds, then broke into a smile wider than any Stan had seen in a long time. "Why, Kristan! How thoughtful of you. I'm so proud." She leaned over in her chair and wrapped Stan in an unheard-of hug.

Stan met Char's eyes over her mother's shoulder. Char raised an eyebrow, then turned back to her dirty rice.

"I'm going to go call him now," Patricia

said. "I know he's already gotten a number of requests for interviews to which he hasn't responded. That's not good for the image. He'll be thrilled." She hurried upstairs with new pep in her step.

Stan let out her breath in a *whoosh,* picked up her mimosa, and drank. Char brought over a steaming plate of dirty rice. She figured if she was going to keep drinking mimosas, she'd better eat something. "Thanks," she said, and dug in.

Char perched on the chair Patricia had recently abandoned. "What was that about?" she asked finally.

Stan paused, her mouth full of rice. After chewing and swallowing, she dabbed at her lips with a paper napkin. "What?" she asked.

Char huffed. "You know what! Don't play dim with me, missy. I'm onto you." She shook a finger swathed in an enormous gold ring at Stan. "I wasn't born yesterday, you know."

"I don't know what you're talking about," Stan protested.

"Humph." Char crossed her arms across her bulk. "You're up to something."

Stan said nothing and focused on her rice. "I'm not. I want to help my mother. If helping him does that, then I'll do it."

Char continued to stare at her. Stan ate

more rice.

"Now what?" she asked finally.

"I'm waiting for the full story," Char said.

Stan dropped her spoon. "Fine. You're right. There's more to it."

"I knew it," Char crowed, then immediately looked at the stairs to make sure no one was listening.

"But," Stan said, "I can't tell you right now."

Char huffed. "What on earth do you mean? You tell me everything! I can keep a secret!"

Stan refrained from commenting on that. "Look, you'll have to trust me on this, okay? It's . . . complicated. But I do need to know if you saw anything weird happening at the party the other night before I got there."

"Weird like what?" Char asked.

"Anything. People arguing, or acting funny?"

Char's eyes were like two alien probes staring into her brain. Stan squirmed under the scrutiny. "So your goodwill gesture has to do with the murdered woman," Char said.

"I can't tell you."

Char dropped her voice even lower. "You need to be careful, sweetie. This isn't a joke." She wagged her finger at Stan. "I adore your mother, but there's something about that man I just don't trust."

"I hope you're not talking about me." The voice behind them made them both jump guiltily.

CHAPTER 40

Stan whirled around to find Kyle McLeod grinning at them.

"Sweetie, of course not." Char got up and went back to her food. "Come have some rice. I'm making my famous strawberry cake, too."

Great timing, Kyle. She couldn't ask Char to elaborate in front of him. "Isn't my mother coming back?" Stan asked pointedly.

"She might be," Char said. "But they're all my guests. You don't mind eating with Ms. Connor, do you?"

"No way. When she's my mother-in-law, we'll be eating together a lot." Kyle pulled out a chair and sat. "I haven't seen your mother yet, but I'd love to," he said to Stan. "I want to make everyone understand that I'm for real."

His mother-in-law? Stan rolled her eyes. "You're for real, all right," she said. "The musical trio at the crack of dawn sure sounded real."

Kyle winced. "In my defense, they weren't supposed to come at that hour. They ended up booking another job later in the day and had to travel out of state, so they asked if they could visit Caitlyn early. I said yes, but forgot to ask them to be more specific. I certainly didn't think they meant *that* early."

Stan sighed. "What are you trying to do, Kyle?"

"Prove to your sister that I love her," he said. "And convince her that I'll never, ever betray her trust again. I know I behaved like a real jerk."

"Say you do convince her. Then what?"

He smiled. "Then we live happily ever after."

"I see," she said. *Why was everyone so crazy?* Char giggled at the stove.

But Kyle seemed to think it was settled. "So how's the café planning?" he asked, like they were old pals catching up over drinks.

"Fine," Stan said. "Are you still working with Sheldon?"

Kyle hung his head. "I am," he admitted. "It's crazy, I know, after everything that happened. But not for long. I couldn't pull the plug yet. I need the money. And he needed some help, too. He lost some ground after . . . what happened."

"Really? Did he get the Food Channel contract?"

Kyle grimaced. "No. That was a debacle. Losing Pierre hurt him, and losing you was tough, too."

"Me? I'm not even anybody," Stan said.

Char gasped and wagged a finger at her. "You don't talk like that, missy!"

"Sorry," Stan muttered. "You know what I mean," she said to Kyle.

"I agree with Char," he said. "You shouldn't say that. You're on the fast track. And now that Nutty's got some recognition —"

"Nutty?" Char asked. "What do you mean?"

Kyle looked at Stan. "Don't tell me you don't know about *Foodie.*"

Char would skin her alive for not telling her. She adored Nutty. "I heard about it," Stan said with a cautious look at Char. "I haven't seen it yet. I don't suppose you have a copy. Nikki was supposed to send me some —"

"Saw *what?*" Char demanded.

"Nutty," Stan and Kyle said in unison, then looked at each other.

Kyle grinned. "He's the cover photo and

the feature article subject in the latest issue."

Char gasped and screeched at the same time. "Why did I not know this? I knew I shouldn't have let my subscription lapse. We need to get that framed. What's the matter with you, Stan? You should be up on your own PR. You're slipping, doll. I guess I need to order them, if you're not paying attention!" She bolted out of her chair and grabbed her iPad off the counter.

Stan looked at Kyle. "Do you have it with you?"

"Sorry," he said. "I got it last week, and didn't think to bring it with me. It was a fabulous story. I'm jealous."

"I can't believe the reporter didn't even let me know," Stan said.

"I'm sure she figured you'd be anxiously awaiting the issue."

"As she should have been," Char said, closing her iPad cover with a snap. "I've ordered some copies. Twenty," she added.

Twenty? "Wow. Thank you," Stan said.

"Anyway, since I'm not a big star like him — and you, by default — I'm still figuring out what to do next," Kyle went on. "A lot of it depends on Caitlyn."

"Now that sounds like a love affair to me," Char remarked, doing a drive-by fill-up of

Stan's mimosa glass.

"No more," Stan protested. "I have a lot of work to do today."

Char made a swatting motion with her hand, dismissing her protests. "Yes, you do. You have to go buy every copy of the magazine where that baby is featured. But that doesn't mean you can't have more mimosas."

"But you ordered twenty copies!"

"Not a bad idea," Kyle said, nodding at the mimosa. "Especially if you get dragged into a conversation about the dead lady like I did this morning." He made a face. "Not what I wanted to do before my coffee."

Stan stared at him.

"What? I couldn't help it. I went to the general store to get some ingredients to cook with Miss Char here" — he winked at Char, who promptly blushed — "and there was a whole lot of conversation about it. Looked like half the town was in there picking apart the details. And a pretty hot debate about who really killed her. I got pulled into it just because I was in the store. Nobody wanted to hear that I didn't know anything about anything."

"What do you mean, who really killed her?" Stan asked. Jessie would have a stroke if she heard this.

Kyle shrugged. "Some people don't think that guy did it. The one they arrested."

Stan glanced at Char, who listened with interest. "Oh, honey," Char said. "You think this is the first time I'm hearing this?"

"It's the first *I'm* hearing it," Stan said. "What were they saying? Who do they think it is?"

"I heard someone mention the mayor." Kyle glanced toward the stairs, also making sure Stan's mother wasn't listening. He shifted uncomfortably and lowered his voice. "A couple of people thought your mother caught them having an affair. Something about an engagement ring. One person said they were in on it together, the mayor and your mom. I know it's all trash talk," he added hastily.

"They mentioned a ring?" Stan asked. "What about it?"

"I didn't hear the whole thing. I was trying to find some organic mint leaves, and the selection wasn't —"

"Never mind the mint," Stan interrupted. "The ring. Focus."

"That it was with the body." He scratched his head. "Something about her getting killed over it. So anyway, what's Caitlyn up to today?" Kyle asked.

Stan gave up getting more information out

of him. "Kyle, she's angry at you. Whatever you do, do not follow her around town. She's already called the state police." Caitlyn'd said she didn't have to talk to him on her behalf, but Stan didn't want any more drama in town. If she could prevent Kyle from doing any other stupid things, maybe they could all have a day of peace.

"She did?" Kyle threw his head back and laughed. "She's such a spitfire. Are they going to arrest me?"

"No," Stan said through gritted teeth. "But you don't need to make things worse."

"I know. I'm going to do everything in my power to make it better. She just needs to give me a chance." He fixed beseeching eyes on her. "If you could put in a good word for me that might help."

"You must not know my sister well," Stan said.

He gave her a funny look. "How long is she staying with you?"

"I'm not sure. But I have a feeling she might leave sooner than planned if the serenades keep up." Stan pushed her chair back and stood. "I have to go."

Char wagged a finger at her for the second time today. "I'll be calling you, sugar."

CHAPTER 41

Stan hurried to her car, Char's warning about Tony sitting heavy in her chest. Being from the South, Char liked everyone until she had a real good reason not to. And she'd sounded adamant about Tony.

As she turned the key in the ignition she caught a glimpse of her mother hurrying down the driveway toward her. She rolled the window down.

"Where are you going?" Patricia demanded. "I thought you were going to help Tony?"

"I am, but not right this minute," Stan said. "Did you talk to him?"

"Yes. He's delighted. Do you want to call him directly to set up a schedule?"

"I will," Stan said. "Later today, okay?"

"That's wonderful." Patricia turned to walk away, then looked back at Stan. "Thank you," she said simply, leaving Stan a teeny bit speechless. Gratitude wasn't her mother's strong suit.

But before Patricia could walk away, a twenty-something man with ratty jeans, a scraggly beard, and a blazer popped out from behind one of Char's privacy shrubs. "Ms. Patricia Connor?"

Her mother frowned. "Yes?"

The man turned and waved toward the bushes. Another guy stepped into view, a camera trained on Patricia. "I'm Jeb Ryder from the *Hartford Gazette.* Can you comment on the murder at your fiancé's house Saturday night?"

Stan swore and scrambled out of the car. "No comment," she said to the man before her mother even recovered from the surprise of a reporter hiding in a bush to talk to her.

The reporter and cameraman swung toward Stan. The red light from the camera glowed, a silent target on her head. "And you are?"

"I'm her advisor," Stan said coolly. "And she has no comment. Please turn off the camera."

Neither of them moved. "You're her daughter. I did my research," the reporter said with a knowing wink.

Stan moved past them and grabbed her mother's arm, propelling her toward the house. Behind them, the reporter called out

315

again. "Is it true Mayor Falco was missing when the woman was killed? What motive do they have for the suspect?"

Stan pushed the front door open and shoved her mother inside, then stepped in behind her. Char appeared in the kitchen doorway, holding a spatula dripping with cake batter. "What on earth?"

"The media." Stan moved to the window. The reporter and cameraman huddled together, plotting their next move.

"Looking for you?" Char turned to Patricia.

Wordlessly, Patricia nodded.

"Not on my property, they're not. They are barking up the wrong tree." Spatula in hand and apron still in place, Char marched out of the house.

"Oh no," Stan murmured, peeking through the crack in the door.

"What's she doing?" Patricia joined her, trying to see over Stan's shoulder.

Kyle poked his head out of the kitchen, licking one of the beaters from the electric mixer. "What's up? She need help?"

Char's voice rose and fell as she waved the spatula around. Cake batter rained down. The cameraman wiped at a splotch that landed on his camera. The reporter tried to write notes, but the cameraman grabbed his arm and yanked him out of the line of batter fire.

"Doesn't look like it," Stan said.

Char watched until they got in a car parked in front of the next house, then turned and came back inside. "All clear," she said cheerfully.

Kyle high-fived her. Stan and Patricia looked at each other. Despite herself, Stan burst out laughing and hugged Char, trying to avoid wearing cake batter. "You are one in a million, lady," she said.

But Patricia wasn't laughing. "Is this what it's going to come down to?" she demanded. "This . . . *mess* that Tony has contributed to?"

Startled, Stan and Char stared at her. Patricia never had outbursts, especially in front of semi-strangers.

"Sweetie," Char began, but Patricia turned and fled upstairs.

They all looked at one another. "Should I go talk to her?" Char asked finally.

Stan shook her head. "I'd let her be for now. She's not usually very receptive to people trying to comfort her."

Stan put her phone on speaker and called Jessie in her office while she drove back to town.

317

"Yeah," Jessie answered absently.

"It's me. I'm going to stop by."

"News?" Jessie asked.

"Some." She didn't want to say too much about Scott over the phone. "Can I bring you coffee or anything?"

"Yeah, actually. And some kind of high-calorie bad food that'll improve my mood."

"You got it."

"Thanks. You talk to Tony?"

"I talked to my mother. She's delighted for me to help him. I'll stop by his office today. Oh, and Kyle overheard people at the general store talking about who really killed Eleanor. That's a direct quote. And they know about the ring."

Jessie swore. "How? What were they saying?"

"I'm not totally sure. Kyle's better at cooking than storytelling."

"Did he know who . . ." She trailed off, and Stan heard some noise on the other end. "I'll see you when you get here," Jessie said abruptly, and hung up.

Stan shrugged and tossed the phone onto her passenger seat. On second thought, she picked it up and called Tony. He answered on the third ring, sounding distracted.

"Kristan. Hello. Yes, your mother told me about your offer. How generous." He didn't sound as delighted as Patricia claimed.

"I have time later today," she said. "The media is in town, just so you're aware."

Silence. Then, "I'll be at my office until six."

"Great. I'll be over shortly."

CHAPTER 42

Stan pulled into Izzy's parking lot and headed inside. Caitlyn waved at her from a table near the door where she and Eva were eating . . . cinnamon buns?

"Hey, Krissie!"

"Hey. How's your day going?"

"It's great," Caitlyn said. "We spent some time at the library, and Eva went to story time. We came back for a snack before we go to the shelter."

"They read the bear book," Eva chimed in.

"The Berenstain Bears," Caitlyn clarified.

"I love those books," Stan said. "I'm glad you had fun."

"Izzy said we could go over and see her new bookstore later this afternoon. She's over there now."

Stan paused. "You like bookstores?"

Caitlyn sighed dramatically. "Here we go again. Yes, Krissie, I like bookstores. I don't sit around and watch the *Real Housewives* all day."

"I know, I know," Stan said, although she really didn't. "Sorry. I'm grabbing a coffee and then I have to go. I'll see you later on?"

"Sounds good," Caitlyn sang.

If anyone had said her sophisticated — let's be honest, snobby — sister would be this happy putzing around her tiny little town, Stan would've sent them for psychiatric help. Shaking her head, she went up to the counter, her eyes immediately falling on the pastries and chocolates in the case. Izzy's place had the best pastry cases. The one for her chocolates, imported truffles, and other candy-coated deliciousness swooped through the middle of the store, a funky swirl design with two levels. The other, smaller case held her freshly baked pastries: danish swirled with frosting, croissants with chocolate or berries oozing out of them, muffins with cream cheese frosting, cookies of all shapes and varieties. Stan hoped her own cases would make her shop look as glamorous.

She ordered a skinny vanilla latte and a cinnamon bun for herself, fully understanding the irony in that choice, and got Jessie a chocolate caramel latte and a mocha chip muffin. As she waited, she glanced around the café. And did a double take to be sure her eyes weren't playing tricks. No, it was her.

Monica Chang sat at a table in the corner, hunched over a cup of coffee. She wore all black: leggings, a long blouse, flats, and a scarf wrapped around her thin shoulders, the complete opposite of her pink ruffled self on Saturday night. She'd perched a black beret on top of her long, straight hair. Her body looked almost emaciated today, her already-thin frame enhanced by her color choice.

What was she doing in Izzy's café? Or in Frog Ledge at all?

It would be a few minutes for the lattes, so Stan detoured over and stood in front of Monica.

It took the girl a minute to register her presence. When she looked up, Stan was startled at her pale face and glazed eyes. No recognition. Still in shock, maybe?

"Hi, Monica," she said, pulling out a chair and sitting without waiting for an invitation. "I'm Stan Connor. I met you Saturday night?"

It finally dawned on her, and she squirmed in her seat. She looked toward the door, then back at Stan. "Yeah. Hello."

"What brings you back to Frog Ledge?"

Stan asked anyway.

Monica traced the edge of her coffee cup lid. "My purse," she said in a barely audible voice. "It went missing at the party. My . . . father said I should file a report that it was stolen. And my phone. The policewoman still has it."

She sure did, and she'd asked Stan to get in touch with Monica. Instead, Monica had dropped right into their laps. Maybe while she was here she'd offer up the name of her friend from Saturday night. The friend who might be Scott.

"Yes, Trooper Pasquale. She wanted me to see if I could track you down, since she wasn't having any luck reaching your grandmother."

Monica's eyes returned to the table. "My grandma's in the hospital. She didn't take the news well."

"Oh no," Stan said, dismayed. "I'm so sorry. Will she be okay?"

Monica shrugged. "I think so."

Definitely not a concise communicator. "Have you gone to see Trooper Pasquale yet?"

"No. I wanted some coffee first." She looked pitiful. And a lot younger than her age. Stan sensed that, despite the affluence and social status Eleanor held up as a badge responsible for her happiness, her daughter wasn't cut from the same cloth. She seemed lost.

"Tell you what," she said to Monica. "I can take you over to talk to her."

Now Monica looked interested. "You can?"

"Sure. She'll be happy to help." As long as it wasn't done under the guise of an interrogation. Stan stood. "Let me grab my coffee. Did you have something to eat, too?"

Monica looked wistfully at the pastry case. "I only had enough for coffee. My money was in my purse. The missing one." Jeez. All the money Eleanor had, and the poor kid had nothing but a few bills stuffed in an evening bag?

Stan took pity on her. "Come on," she said, getting up and motioning her to follow. "Let's grab you something to eat before we go."

Monica joined her, face pressed against the glass like a little kid. She chose a chocolate chip muffin. Stan paid for the food.

"Thanks," Monica said, avoiding her eyes. She tore into the muffin as soon as the countergirl handed it to her. By the time Stan had taken a sip of her coffee, the muffin was almost gone.

Monica's eyes met hers over the remains, unapologetic. "Thank you for buying me food," she said. "If I get my purse I can pay you back." Her face fell a bit. "I don't think I have a job anymore, now that my mother's gone."

"Please. Don't worry about it." Stan set Jessie's latte and her own in a tray and placed the bag of pastries on top, then led Monica outside.

"How are you doing otherwise? How are your sisters?" she asked as they climbed into her car.

"We're okay."

"Are you staying with your father now?" Stan asked.

"No. Our place is paid off and I'm old enough, even when my grandmother isn't there." There was a touch of defensiveness in her voice.

"But you're in touch with your dad."

Monica pulled her scarf tighter around her like a wrap. "We had to tell him about Mom. He's helping plan the funeral." She kept her hands clasped tightly together, knuckles turning white from the pressure. Stressed about being back in the general vicinity of her mother's death?

Stan drove the short distance to the town hall and parked. Monica looked around, wary. "This doesn't look like a police station," she said.

"It's not, technically. The resident state trooper, the one who has your phone, has an office here. The official state police barracks are about twenty minutes away. Trooper Pasquale can take care of some things here, like police reports." She turned off the car. "Ready?"

Monica met her eyes. Hers were round and almost fearful. "I guess," she said, her voice hushed. She got out of the car, and plodded along through the parking lot behind Stan.

CHAPTER 43

The gold sphere high above the town hall's clock tower gleamed in the afternoon sun. Monica pulled open the door for Stan, who balanced the coffees and pastry. Inside, the first floor of the three-story building bustled with the usual activity. Residents lined up outside the tax assessor's office, some waiting to pay a bill, others there to argue about an incorrect calculation. Around the corner, a small crowd waited for the elevators. Stan opted for the stairs instead. They climbed to the second floor, walked by the city clerk's office and stopped in front of Jessie's closed door. She could hear muted voices inside, so she knocked.

The door opened immediately. Stan jumped back, startled, and found herself face-to-face with Captain Quigley. His gaze traveled from her to Monica, then he pulled the door wider and motioned them in. "Trooper. Looks like you have some citizens to attend to," he said. Then, with a nod at Stan and Monica, he left.

Jessie sat at her desk. Her face said she was either sick or mad, but when she saw Monica behind Stan she reverted to her typical blank expression. "Hey," she said, and only Stan would've noticed the tremor in her voice.

"Hey." Stan placed the lattes and pastry bag on Jessie's desk and handed her the cup. "Chocolate caramel latte."

"Thank you." Jessie made no move to take the cup. She lifted one eyebrow to Stan, a silent question, then turned to Monica. "Hi, Monica."

"Hello," Monica said softly.

"Thanks for coming by. I have your cell phone." Her tone was icy. Stan knew Quigley had chewed her out for Monica's escape. It riled Jessie that the Major Crimes guy who'd actually let her waltz out the door had escaped unscathed.

Jessie went over to a cabinet, unlocked it, and took out a plastic bag with a label on it. She removed a piece of paper and Monica's phone in its orange case. "Can you sign this?" She handed over the paper and a pen.

With a shaky hand, Monica scrawled something that may or may not have been a random scribble.

"Great. Thanks for coming by." Dismissing her, Jessie picked up her coffee and sat back down at the desk.

Something was up. Stan was willing to bet Jessie's captain didn't often come to visit her here. "Jess. She needs something else," she said softly.

Jessie looked up expectantly. "What?"

Stan nudged Monica. "Tell her," she said.

Monica took a deep breath. "I need to file a report. I think my purse was stolen."

"Your purse," Jessie repeated flatly. "From the party?"

Monica nodded, eyes downcast. She rubbed her thumb and index finger repetitively together at her side.

Jessie clamped her lips together, reached in a drawer, and yanked out some papers. Slamming the drawer shut, she came around to the front of her desk. "I'll have you fill these out in there," she said, pointing to the small conference room attached to her office.

Monica went into the room looking like she faced her own execution. Jessie pulled the door shut behind her. "What's that about?" she asked in a low voice.

Stan shrugged. "Her purse is missing."

"You don't think she may have lost it in

her drunken stupor and no one's found it yet?"

"I don't know," Stan said. "Maybe someone can look for it, if that's the case."

"Yeah, well, don't look at me." She looked at the conference room door, then back at Stan. "I'm screwed."

"What do you mean?"

"The captain's unhappy about the 'continuing press coverage.' I don't get it. He knows the drill. He just wants to ding me 'cause I'm not buying into their open-and-shut case."

"Well, if he's mad about Cyril, things are about to get a lot more interesting," Stan muttered.

"What?" Jessie asked.

"Nothing." She'd tell her about the other reporters later.

"Plus, he heard people are talking about the 'real killer.' He's not happy with me. Thinks I'm planting the seed out there." She waved at the town beyond her window. "He's not listening to anything I say. I'm glad he didn't recognize her. He would've hit the roof." She inclined her head at the door. "What's up with her? She looks like she's on another planet."

"I don't know. But the car that she took off in the other night." She lowered her voice. "Did you ever run the partial plate?"

"Didn't seem necessary, especially given . . . everything."

"Well, maybe you should."

Jessie's eyes narrowed. "Why?"

Stan paced the small room. "This is going to sound crazy, but I swear it was Scott's car. Brenna's Scott. We went out to eat with them last night, and he has a sticker that looks like the one I saw. And this is his license plate." She pulled out her phone and showed Jessie the letters and numbers she'd taken down as he drove away. "Jake's worried."

Jessie stared at the numbers, then looked at Stan. "You told Jake?"

"I was with him. He knew something was up."

"That's worse than telling me when it comes to Brenna. He didn't even like that she was dating someone." She copied the number.

"Well, I'm sure it was worse last night because Scott started talking about moving in with Bren."

"Oh boy." Jessie finally picked up her coffee and sipped. "I'll run it, but what do you think's up?"

"I have no idea," Stan said. "But let's talk about it when she's not right there."

"Right. Plus, I'm sure my office is bugged at this point." The phone rang on Jessie's desk. She leaned over and answered. "Yeah, I'll meet you outside," she said, then hung up. "I'll be right back. I need to get Colby something from my cruiser."

"Garrett Colby?" Stan asked. "With the K9?"

"Yeah. Why?"

"Can you have him call me? We're going to do his fundraiser Thursday night at Amara's."

"Fundraiser?"

"Yeah. He didn't win the Irish stew contest, and he needs to get his dog a vest. Why?"

"No reason. That's . . . really nice of you. I'll tell him." She grabbed her keys and her coffee. "Be right back." She walked out, pulling the door halfway closed behind her.

Stan sipped her coffee and glanced at the conference-room door. Radio silence from inside. How long were these forms, anyway? Or had Monica pulled a vanishing act like she had at Tony's house, only out the window this time? Not her problem either way. It's not like the girl was under arrest or anything. Hitting the ladies' room would be a better use of her time while she waited.

As she walked down the hall, she checked

her watch. Maybe Monica would walk back to Izzy's so she could run upstairs to see Tony. The mayor's office was on the third floor, across from council chambers and the old jail cell the town kept for historical reasons. She used the bathroom, then headed back to Jessie's office. Jessie wasn't back yet, but Stan gasped when she saw Tony Falco standing at her desk, hand hovering over a pile of paperwork.

CHAPTER 44

They stared at each other for a long moment, Tony's hand poised over the stack of papers on Jessie's desk, until he finally removed it and shoved it in his pocket.

"Hello," Stan said. "I was about to come up and see you."

"Yes. Well. Good. I'm heading back up in a moment," he said.

Stan nodded. "What are you doing?" she asked casually, leaning against the door.

"I . . . was looking for a report Trooper Pasquale had for me." He smoothed his tie, quickly regaining his composure. "I didn't want to bother her with another phone call, so I came down. When she wasn't here, I thought I'd see if it was on top of her desk. Do you know where she is?"

Stan narrowed her eyes. She didn't buy his story. Before she could figure out how to react, Cyril Pierce stepped into the office, nearly walking into the wall as he finished scribbling in his notebook. When he looked up, confusion registered, then his eyes took on that reporter's gleam Stan knew all too well. "Mayor. Stan. Good to see you both."

"Hey, Cyril," Stan said.

Tony nodded curtly.

"Where's Trooper Pasquale?" Cyril asked.

"She stepped out for a moment," Stan said.

"Ah. Well, I'll wait." Cyril sat on one of the straight-backed chairs Tony once suggested Jessie provide to make her office "more welcoming." "In the meantime, Mayor, any developments?"

"Developments in what?" Tony asked coolly.

"The murder case." Cyril flipped to a blank page and looked up, expectant.

"That question would be better suited for me," Jessie's sharp tone came from the doorway. Every head swiveled. She did not look happy to see either of them. "Mayor, may I ask what you're doing behind my desk?"

Tony had the grace to look embarrassed. "I was looking for . . . that report."

"What report?"

"The one on the Pendleton hit-and-run," he said.

Jessie looked blank for a second, then laughed. "You mean the basketball hoop?"

Stan frowned. "Someone hit and ran a basketball hoop?"

"Family dispute," Jessie said. "The ticket recipient felt it was an unfair citation and asked the mayor to review it. But Mayor, I sent you that report last week."

"Hmmm," Tony said. "I don't recall seeing it. Maybe Arlene forgot to give it to me." Tony's secretary had assisted every mayor who'd served in Frog Ledge for the past century. At least, she was old enough that it seemed that way.

"Maybe," Jessie said. "But you thanked me."

Silence. "Must be old age," Tony said finally with his trademark movie-star smile, and edged past Stan. "I'll take a look and let you know if I need another copy." He strode to the door just as another person appeared in the doorway, blocking his exit.

"Mayor, hey!" Diane Kirschbaum, the town animal control officer, waved excitedly at him. She wore a uniform two sizes too big for her, and a small twig was visible in her tangled curls. Her sleeves draped over her hands as she motioned. "I have good news for you. I think I trapped your cat."

Stan and Jessie's eyes locked. *There really*

was a cat?

"I had no idea you had a cat," Stan said to Tony. "And my mother stays with you?"

Tony sent her a withering look disguised as a smile. "I have two. One of them got out Saturday night during all the . . . ruckus, and hasn't come home. I've been worried sick and out looking every day. Miles is lonely without his brother."

Diane seemed to notice Stan for the first time. "Hey, Stan! Thanks for sending your sister and niece over to help. They're great."

"I'm glad," Stan said. "They were looking for something to do. Thank you for keeping them occupied."

"Was this a dramatic cat rescue?" Cyril piped up. "Can we do a story on it?"

The inner conference room door finally opened and Monica came out, freezing in place when she saw all the people. Stan'd nearly forgotten she was in there. Monica's eyes locked with Tony's, and something crossed his face that Stan couldn't pin down. Regret? Pity?

"Ms. Chang," he said. "Good to see you again."

"You too," Monica said, looking like it was anything but.

At the name, Cyril perked up, turning his intense stare toward Monica. Stan tried to catch his eye and glare at him, but he didn't look at her.

"What brings you to be visiting with the police?" Tony asked Monica.

"I needed my phone back. And my purse is still missing," Monica said.

"Missing?" Tony repeated. "From my house?"

Monica nodded, fidgeting with her scarf.

Tony looked at Jessie. "I trust you're taking care of that?"

"She's filling out a report. Unfortunately, only certain members of the police department are allowed into your home, so we can't go look for it," Jessie said pointedly. "But maybe you can keep an eye out."

Stan held her breath. Cyril's hand hovered over his notepad. Tony's face bloomed red, but he didn't respond.

Diane Kirschbaum exhaled loudly. " 'Scuse me?" She waved her arms again to get their attention. "I have a dog in my truck so I really can't stand around all day."

Once Tony turned his attention back to her, she continued. "Anyway, you may be in luck. I had traps out two streets over from your place. Trying to catch a pregnant momma cat. I didn't get her, but a black kitty with a white spot on his chest wandered in, and he's real friendly. Want to come to the clinic with me and see?"

Tony looked at Stan. "Can we push our meeting off for an hour?"

"Sure," Stan said.

"Thank you. Yes, I'll come over now." Tony followed Diane out the door.

Jessie, Stan, and Cyril all looked at each other. "No comment," Jessie said when Cyril opened his mouth.

"Are you sure?" Cyril asked. "Because this jibes with the statement from the suspect's attorney. That he was chasing a cat through the woods during the time he'd stepped out of the house. And it's a detail that has yet to be released by the police department." He waggled bushy eyebrows at Jessie. "Any comment? Or maybe an official time of death so folks can draw their own conclusions?"

"Nope."

Cyril shrugged. "Fine. I'll move on to my supporting piece." He turned to Monica. "Are you Eleanor Chang's daughter?"

Monica's face went white, which was apparently answer enough for Cyril.

"I'm Cyril Pierce, editor and publisher of the *Frog Ledge Holler.* I'm doing a feature story on Ms. Chang . . . er, your mother. She was quite accomplished. Since she wasn't a local, I'd like to give people a chance to get to know her. And of course" — he looked at Jessie again — "I'd like to include an update on the investigation."

Panic flashed in Monica's eyes. She looked at Stan, then Jessie. "I don't want to talk to you," she said, and ducked back into the conference room, slamming the door behind her.

Jessie's face rivaled Patricia Connor's best death stare. She bared her teeth at Cyril. "What part of 'no comment' is hard for you to comprehend?"

Cyril didn't look fazed. "This is definitely one of my most sensitive cases," he said, almost to himself, then turned back to Jessie. "I'm still doing a feature on the victim. Stan, do you want to comment?"

"No," Stan said.

Cyril sighed. "The investigation can't be over," he said to Jessie. "You didn't even confirm the cause of death publicly. Did you get the autopsy report back?"

"I don't know," Jessie said. "I'm not leading this investigation. You'll have to call the barracks. And good luck getting an answer," she muttered, then pointed at him. "That's off the record."

Cyril hoisted himself out of the chair, exhaling loudly. "Fine. But you better not be giving the other reporters anything."

"What other reporters?" Jessie demanded just as someone knocked on her office door.

They all turned as the door inched open. The guy Char chased away with her spatula poked his head in. He did a double take when he saw Stan, then grinned. "I guess this is the place to be," he said, and opened the door wider to let his cameraman inside.

Chapter 45

"No. Absolutely not. No cameras," Jessie said, striding over and cutting them both off before they could enter any farther. "No interviews of any kind. Who are you, anyway?"

"Jeb," Stan muttered.

Jessie turned the glare on her. "Who?"

"Jeb Ryder," Jeb said helpfully. "I'm with the *Hartford Gazette.* I take it you're Trooper Pasquale?"

Cyril sniffed. Jeb ignored him.

"I am," Jessie said. "And I have no comment. About anything. Not even the weather. So if you don't mind —"

"We're working on a story about Eleanor Chang's death," Jeb said, as if she hadn't spoken.

"Like I said for the four hundredth and seventy-fifth time," Jessie said, "no comment."

"Can you confirm the relationship the

victim had to the suspect?"

"No," Jessie said.

"Why wasn't the mayor questioned more extensively? Is it true he wasn't on the premises at the time of the murder?"

"I. Have. No. Comment," Jessie snarled, then turned and walked back to her desk, dismissing them.

But Jeb still stood there, smiling like a crazy person. In a minute, Stan understood why. The cameraman had his camera on and aimed straight at her. He panned from Stan to Jessie, then back to Jeb. "While the police have no comment about the investigation and the mayor continues to be unreachable, the mayor's step-daughter-to-be is consulting with the resident state trooper," Jeb said. "This is Jeb Ryder, reporting from Frog Ledge."

Jessie slammed her hand down on the desk. "Out of my office now!"

The cameraman whistled. "Dude, sweet footage," he murmured, zooming in for a close up on Jessie.

"I'd listen to her," Cyril said offhandedly. "She threw me in the slammer once. I'm Cyril Pierce," he added. "*Frog Ledge Holler* publisher."

"Nice to meet you," Jeb said. He made a cutting motion across his throat to the cameraman, who reluctantly stopped filming. "Do you know where the mayor's office is?"

"Out!" Jessie yelled.

The pair scurried away, probably thinking she'd call Char if they didn't listen. Cyril, sensing now would be a good time for him to leave, too, followed suit, closing the door on his way.

Jessie dropped into her chair and covered her face with her hands. "How is this my life?" she asked.

Stan wisely assumed Jessie wasn't expecting an answer, so she stayed silent.

Finally, Jessie dropped her hands. "Who are those clowns? How did he know your relationship to Tony?"

"They were hiding in the bushes at Char's this morning. Accosted my mother for a quote. I was getting in my car, so I intervened. I didn't tell you earlier because you seemed like you were in a really bad mood."

"Great." Jessie spun her chair in a slow circle. "Thanks for thinking of me."

"I wonder how long they'll wait for Tony," Stan mused. "I should give him a heads-up."

"Don't do him any favors," Jessie said.

"You're right. Is Arlene up there?"

Jessie nodded. "She'll probably give them

Tony's cell phone. And what was he doing in here? You see him take anything off my desk?"

"No. I went to the bathroom. When I came back, he was in here."

Jessie's jaw tightened. "That story he gave me was pathetic, but if he was looking for anything about the murder he's definitely in the wrong place. Looks like the missing cat is for real."

"Yeah," Stan said. "Guess Richard was telling the truth about that."

Jessie rubbed her hands over her face, then sat up. "Want to get her out of my conference room?"

Stan knocked on the door, then stuck her head in. Monica sat with her head resting on the table. "Hey," Stan said. "All clear. Sorry about that."

Monica lifted her head like it weighed a ton. "Can I go now?"

"Of course. After you give Trooper Pasquale the report."

With a sigh, Monica walked out of the room and handed Jessie the paperwork.

Jessie scanned it. "I'll look into it, okay? I'll call you."

"Thanks," Monica said.

"Do you want me to bring you back to your car?" Stan asked.

Monica shook her head. "I think I'll walk. It's right down the street. Thanks for bringing me here." And then she was gone.

Stan looked at Jessie. "I'll be right back," she said.

Stan caught up with Monica outside and called her name.

Monica turned, shading her eyes against the sun. "Yeah?"

"Can I ask you something?"

Monica shrugged.

"The person who picked you up the other night. Who was it?"

Monica tugged her scarf tighter around her neck. "Why do you want to know?"

"Because it's important," Stan said. "Everyone who was at that house when your mother died is important."

"They caught the guy who did it. I'm not stupid. So why don't you all just leave me alone? I didn't do anything!" She turned and bolted down the stairs and out to the street, heading toward Izzy's in the first show of feisty Stan'd seen from her.

She watched her go, little alarm bells dinging in her head. Something wasn't right with this girl. Yes, she'd just lost her mother. But her gut screamed there was more to it. Monica slipping out of the party the other

346

night bothered Stan more and more, not just because of her potential partner in crime but because it was an odd way of dealing with such a shocking situation, especially one involving her own mother.

She counted to ten, giving Monica time to get far enough ahead, then followed. What were the chances she'd call the driver of the red car?

She turned the corner a minute after Monica and scanned the street ahead. She saw Monica turn into Izzy's parking lot, but she didn't go back inside. Instead, she crossed to an old-style BMW and climbed in the driver's side. She started the car but remained parked, still fiddling with her phone. Stan ducked into the entryway of the flower shop and watched until she pulled onto the street and hit the gas, heading out of town. Too bad she didn't have her car — she could tail her.

Frustrated, Stan kicked at a rock in her path and turned back to the town hall, walking with her hands jammed into the pocket of her sweatshirt. Conspiracy theories ran through her head. Monica hadn't given her the right passcode for her phone, either. At the time, Stan chalked it up to stress and drinking. It was easy to forget a number or misspeak. But now she had to wonder if she'd given her the wrong code because she didn't want anyone to get to her contact list. Whose number was in that phone?

Number. Phone. Stan suddenly stopped dead in the middle of the sidewalk, almost getting run over by a woman pushing a baby carriage behind her. "Sorry," she muttered, stepping out of the line of traffic and pulling her cell phone out of her pocket. How had it taken her three days to remember that Monica had used *her* phone to call her ride on Saturday?

She scrolled through her outgoing calls. Nothing she didn't recognize. No unidentified numbers. She scrolled again. It should have been between Jessie's call to the troop shortly after she'd found out about the situation, and the call Stan made to Jake right before she left the ill-fated party.

But it wasn't. Which meant Monica deleted the number after she'd made the call.

CHAPTER 46

Stan stood rooted, trying to tamp down the growing feeling of unease that surfaced every time she thought of Monica and this red car. Monica obviously hadn't wanted Stan to see the number. She must know Stan could easily go online to her cell phone account and find a listing of all the calls made to and from her number. But she'd gotten rid of easy access to it. Or Monica hadn't thought she'd go to that much trouble to find the number. So what was she hiding? *Whom* was she hiding?

The possible answer to the question made her palms sweat. *Stop,* she commanded herself. *You're losing your mind.*

Everyone heard stories about kids who killed their parents. More often than not boys were the culprits, but there were those truly remarkable cases where girls committed the unthinkable, or got their boyfriends to help them do the deed. Sometimes the killings were chillingly unprovoked, like the story Stan read a few months ago about a girl in Oklahoma who'd stabbed her mother to death while she slept because she'd given her a ten o'clock curfew. Other kids, after years of abuse, finally snapped.

But that ring stuffed in Eleanor's mouth seemed symbolic of something.

Stan didn't know anything about Eleanor's family but it wasn't a stretch to believe she brought her demanding, perfectionist personality home at the end of the workday. She'd seen a glimpse of how Monica and Eleanor interacted on Saturday. It hadn't reeked of love and compassion. Was Eleanor the type of mother who treated her kids the same way she treated her employees and coworkers? Did she run her house as a ruthless CEO would run a Fortune 500 company? And did that mean Stan was barking up the wrong tree focusing on Tony? Had Monica killed her own mother, drunk herself into a stupor, then called someone she trusted — a friend, or possibly a beau — to come get her? Like Scott? Or had this person been in it with her? If she worked at Tony's, she'd have a good lay of the land and could find an easy way in and out for an accomplice.

Stan took a deep breath and tried to shake

off this insane train of thought. Her imagination had completely gone off the rails. Jessie would offer some perspective.

But when she burst through the town hall entrance and yanked open the door to the stairwell, Tony Falco blocked her path. She skidded to a stop to avoid slamming into him.

"Tony. I . . . was coming up in a minute."

"We need to find somewhere else to talk. There's a reporter and a photographer camped out in my hallway." He looked a lot more frazzled than when she'd seen him an hour ago. His hair was rumpled, as if he'd run his fingers through it repeatedly, and his shirt wrinkled and wilted. He had the start of a five o'clock shadow. She could see black cat fur clinging to his clothing in clumps. She found that strangely endearing and tried to block it out.

"Did you get your cat back?" she asked.

"I did, thank goodness. Sammy isn't an outdoor cat, and three days is a long time." He glanced around. "We should get out of the stairwell. Let's go to Joe Rizzo's office. He's out of town this week." The town manager's office was at the end of the second-floor hallway.

Stan hesitated.

"If you're looking for Trooper Pasquale,

she's not there," Tony said. "I was looking for you and I tried the door. It's locked."

Locked. Great. Was Quigley in there yelling at her again? Then another thought struck her. What if Jessie ran the license plate and found out it was Scott's? She could've gone to talk to him. Stan itched to know what was going on.

But Tony waited impatiently, so she followed him. Once they reached Rizzo's office, Tony knocked and stuck his head in to make sure it was empty. He closed it firmly behind them. "So who are these reporters and why are they here?" he asked, leaning against the large wooden desk in the center of the room.

"Because someone was murdered in your house and the story's getting around," Stan said. She didn't sit, either.

"They arrested someone," Tony pointed out.

"They did," Stan said. "But that person is innocent until proven guilty, and I guess they still have questions."

They stared at each other for a few seconds, then Tony looked away. "How do I get rid of them?"

"You can't. They'll keep writing about it and saying you haven't returned calls for comment. I think it's wise to put out a statement."

"I was advised not to speak to any media," Tony said.

"Advised by whom?"

"The police," he said.

Sure. The corrupt ones. Stan shrugged. "It's your choice, Tony. But if you want my help, that's the advice I'm giving you." She played her next hand. "If they can't reach you, they're going to ramp up their efforts to get someone close to you. Like they did to my mother earlier today."

Tony's head shot up and Stan saw the first glimpse of real emotion she'd seen since this whole thing began. "They're bothering Patricia?"

Stan nodded. "Hiding in the bushes at Char's." Did he really care, or was he simply worried Patricia would say the wrong thing?

"Did they . . ."

"I was there. I got rid of them."

His breath came out in a whoosh. "Thank you. I don't want this terrible situation to reflect badly on her."

"Well," Stan said. "They're going to keep going after her. And it could get worse. I know the word's out around town about the ring. It's only a matter of time before the media hears about it. I'm sure Cyril already has, and hasn't played the card yet. Then things are really going to get ugly for her."

Every last bit of color drained from his face. "H-how? How would they know about that?" Which meant he did know. Captain Quigley must've filled him in.

"I couldn't tell you, given the amount of effort the police put into keeping this quiet. The media doesn't simply accept when you don't want to comment, especially in something high-profile like this," she said.

Tony's jaw set. "Fine," he said. "We'll put out a statement. What do we need to do?"

"First we need to get your story straight. Which means you, me, my mother, and anyone else who may be asked a question on your behalf."

"There wouldn't be anyone else," he said tightly.

"Aside from the hundred or so people at your party," she pointed out. "Who are already telling their own versions of the story. There was a whole crowd debating the real killer over fresh bread at the general store." She reached into her bag and pulled out the small notebook she'd begun carrying around to keep track of her ever-growing to-do list. She flipped through the pages with hastily scrawled lists, sketches of the café's doggie seating area, and other numerous to-dos, and found a clean sheet while she let that sink in. When she raised her head, Tony looked green.

"Listen. I told my mother I would help you, and I will. But I won't — I can't — help you if you're going to be hiding things and lying to me. Someone died, Tony. And there's still a lot of mystery around it, no matter who they have in custody." She waited a beat. "So are you going to talk to me or not?"

He sank down into the chair opposite her and nodded slowly.

Stan braced herself, then asked the question again. "Was that my mother's ring?"

"Yes. It was your mother's ring."

CHAPTER 47

Stan leaned back in her chair, her heart dropping into her stomach. Was she right about an affair? "Why?" she said finally. "Why would Mom's ring be . . ."

Tony met her eyes. "I have no idea," he said. "And your mother doesn't, either. She swears the ring was in our room. Waiting for me to present it to her."

"If Richard killed Eleanor, why on earth would he stuff another woman's diamond ring in her mouth? How would he have known where to get it?"

Tony was silent.

"Tony." Stan stepped directly in front of him. "The only way the ring makes any sense is if the rumors are true." She took a deep breath. "Were you having an affair with Eleanor?"

He looked up, real surprise on his face. "No! God, no. Is that what people think?" He barked out a laugh. "Of course it is," he said, answering his own question. "It's always about sex, isn't it? It's not true, Kristan. Eleanor and I . . . have been friends for many years. We worked together in Washington. She was just out of school, and I was mid-career. She was always quite ambitious. I left that firm a few years later, and down the road we wound up working together again. We weren't having an affair. Your mother didn't think we were, either. At least I hope not. She knew we were old friends."

Stan didn't mention that she already knew about his history with her. "So you'd still been in touch."

"On and off for years, mostly off. In recent times she'd reconnected with me. Through LinkedIn."

"When was this?"

He thought. "Around the time I started my campaign for mayor here in Frog Ledge."

That made sense, given what Michelle had told her. "So it wasn't true that my mother found her through my old connections," Stan said.

"I'm afraid not." Tony shoved off the desk and walked slowly around the room, hands buried deep in his pockets. "Your mother was adamant that I needed an executive coach. That part was true. I didn't feel as strongly. That's why she asked you for help last winter. When you weren't interested, she let it go. I thought the subject was closed. Then Eleanor contacted us."

"Why'd she lie to me about how Eleanor came to be working with you?"

"Eleanor approached me with an offer to help. She was quite motivated. Eleanor was . . . very intense."

"Tell me about it," Stan muttered.

"You can't tell your mother you know this," he said. "She's sensitive about these things. Patricia simply wasn't comfortable with Eleanor appearing at my doorstep offering to help. She wasn't sure of her motivations. And your mother likes to feel . . . in control."

"Again, tell me about it." For the first time, Stan felt a wave of compassion for Tony, caught between those two giant personalities. While he could play the role of enigmatic leader well when he wanted to, she'd gotten the sense someone else made the decisions. Not because he was stupid, but because he lacked the strong personality most successful politicians were born with. Meanwhile, Patricia and Eleanor both had those personalities, in spades. And as a woman in the cutthroat corporate world,

Eleanor's mission had been to make hers even stronger.

"So what were her motivations?" she asked casually.

"She simply wanted to help."

"What was the goal?" Stan pressed. "Why'd you need her? No offense, but being mayor in a town like this doesn't require you to be a political rock star. And you just won an election less than a year ago. No one spends three years campaigning for a small-town mayor job."

Tony looked away. "It wasn't all about campaigning. It was about me developing more polish. Having more experience with serious politics."

Still nothing about his gubernatorial ambitions. "Okay. So you guys came up with this story about how she started working with you. When did she start? How was it going?"

Tony narrowed his eyes. "Kristan. Are we writing a statement or are you interrogating me for some reason?"

Oops. She detoured smoothly back to the matter at hand. "Just making sure you have answers to the questions that will surely come your way," she said.

"I thought I was sending a statement, not taking questions," he said.

"They'll have follow-ups."

"And I won't feel compelled to answer them. Now, let's get this done." He glanced at his watch. "I have a meeting tonight about my upcoming wedding."

Stan's stomach turned at that. "Fine. Here's how I would do this. The statement should basically say how troubled you are about this situation, and how you've been trying to protect the family's privacy by staying out of the spotlight. You reiterate how sorry you are for Eleanor's family, how this sort of violence is unthinkable. You're shocked and saddened, and horrified this happened in your home during what was supposed to be a joyous occasion. You can also mention the fundraiser you started for her daughters."

Tony nodded. "That sounds reasonable. Will you write it?"

Stan nodded.

"And we'll send it to the media outlets?"

"Yes."

"Which ones?"

"To Cyril, of course. All the major outlets covering the story here in Connecticut. Your friends upstairs from the *Gazette*. We'll see from there."

"Fine. Will you send me a draft?"

"Sure. Later tonight. To your town

e-mail?"

"My personal e-mail." He recited it. "Anything else?"

She closed her notebook. "Not about this. I do have one other question."

He looked at her, wary. "Go ahead."

"Curtis Wallace," she said.

Tony rubbed the back of his neck. "What about him?"

"Why does he have it out for you?"

He paused. "I didn't realize he did."

"He sounded like it at the pub on Sunday. Talking about impeaching you."

Tony's face turned red for the second time that day, although this time it was an angry red. "Did he, now."

Stan nodded.

"Curtis called me two years ago about running for mayor here," Tony said. "He thought the leadership was stale, and that this town needed a lift. Someone who could help bring it back to its focus on farming and agriculture and its roots. So I find it hard to believe he'd change his mind so soon into my appointment."

"You said he called you?" Stan asked. "So you knew him already?"

Tony hesitated, then nodded. He didn't offer other details.

"How did you know him?" she pressed.

"I'm not sure why this is important, but through his brother. He's an old family friend. Kristan, I really have to get going. I'll look forward to reviewing the statement later tonight." He strode out of the office and shut the door behind him, leaving Stan alone.

She wasn't sure why it was important, either, but somewhere along the way something had gone wrong between Tony and Curtis. When? Why? Did it have to do with Eleanor, or did Tony really not know Curtis knew Eleanor? How *did* Curtis know Eleanor? So many questions. And since Curtis had fought with Eleanor in the weeks leading up to her death, she needed answers.

Stan made her way back to Jessie's office, but the door remained locked. Frustrated, she turned the corner and walked toward the stairwell, head bent over her phone as she texted her again. She jumped when she heard her name. Francie Tucker held the stairwell door open, smiling.

"Hey, Francie."

"What brings you to town hall?" Francie asked.

"I, uh, had to drop something off for Jessie," Stan said. "You?"

Francie wrinkled her nose. "Paying my motor vehicle taxes. You wonder how they get away with charging us taxes on something we already bought and paid taxes on, wouldn't you? I swear, these politicians are the real criminals."

"I hear you," Stan said. "Isn't that office on the first floor?"

Francie looked around, surprised. "Oh, my. You're right, of course. I'm losing it," she said with a little laugh.

"Happens to me all the time. The bakery closed for the day?"

She laughed. "Yes. Brenna had to run, so we packed it up early. We got a lot done, though. Three dozen cookies baked and boxed for the new account."

Stan wanted to kiss her. "You guys are amazing. Thanks so much again, Francie."

"You're welcome, dear. I'll see you tomorrow morning at eight for meditation? I can take you through some exercises. Tomorrow's my day at the church, but I don't have to go in until eleven."

"That sounds wonderful," Stan said. "I'll be there."

"Good! I left my address on your whiteboard. By the way, did you talk to your mother?"

"I didn't," she lied. "But I'm going to see if I can catch her tonight."

"Fantastic. I'll see you tomorrow." She

waved and dashed down the stairs.

Stan checked her phone again. Nothing from Jessie. May as well head home while she waited to hear from her. She had a million things to do anyway, and she had to figure out how she was going to run a fundraiser for Trooper Colby and his dog.

CHAPTER 48

This day had been exhausting, and it wasn't even three o'clock. Stan dialed her mother's cell once she got back in her car.

"So you're writing Tony a statement?" Patricia said by way of greeting.

"Hi to you, too. Yes, I am. But I had a quick question for you. I didn't know Tony had cats."

"Yes, there are two cats. Why?"

"Do you know where they were during the party?"

"They were supposed to be locked upstairs, but something happened. One of them even got out the front door."

"But where were they locked up?"

"Kristan, really? Why is this important? I think I closed them up in the master bedroom, if you must know."

Stan thanked her and hung up. Why had Eleanor been snooping in her mother's room?

She leaned back against her seat and closed her eyes. Every answer led to another question. All she wanted to do was go home, make herself something decent to eat that didn't involve carbs or sugar, and work on her café. Three months seemed far away now, but her grand opening hurtled toward her like a speeding meteor, and at the rate she was going, she wouldn't be ready for it.

But instead of pointing her car toward her house, she took a left out of the town hall lot and drove the short distance down Main Street to the newly renovated building that would soon be home to the town's first real bookstore. The building was the Frog Ledge Library's first home, so it was especially fitting. It might even have a ghost or two, but that hadn't been 100 percent confirmed.

The renovations took her breath away. Stan parked out front and admired Frank and team's handiwork. They'd managed to keep the look and feel of the original design while giving it a modern makeover, bringing the safety standards up to speed and ensuring it would hold up against the elements for another hundred years or more. Granted, Frank could be a pain in the patootie, but he did nice work. She could hardly wait to see what he did for her shop. Stan went in the front entrance and paused in the foyer. The door directly in front of her leading to the bookstore was still blocked off. Izzy had a ways to go, much like Stan herself, to get ready for her grand opening. Instead, Stan followed the typewriter-shaped sign on the wall pointing to the stairs heading down to the *Frog Ledge Holler* offices. Cyril might not be back from poking around town hall yet. She reached for the knob, but the door flew open. She jumped back. Tyler Hoffman looked as surprised to see her as she was to see him.

"Hey, Ms. Connor! Sorry about that." He looped his camera around his neck. "You looking for the boss?"

"Tyler, it's Stan, for the hundredth time." She gave the boy a hug. "How are you doing?" The oldest of the Hoffman children, Tyler had been the heir apparent to the Happy Cow Dairy Farm. But after his dad was killed last fall and the family did some soul-searching, Tyler turned to his real passion — photography. He'd gone out of town to school for a semester, but transferred to a local school and started working for Cyril part-time.

He smiled shyly. "I'm doing well . . . Stan. Off to shoot the new signpost on the south end of the green. Have you seen it?"

"Signpost? I haven't."

"It's pretty cool. One of those old-school posts with a bunch of little white signs shaped like arrows. It's for the historical stuff, but my mom's farm is on there since it's right near the green."

"Cool! I'll take a look later. I'm embarrassed to say I haven't even noticed it." The signs for all the town's upcoming events tended to congregate at the south end of the green, across from her house. "Is Cyril here?"

Tyler pointed over his shoulder. "He's there. Working on a story about the woman who was murdered." He dropped his voice. "Not getting very far, from the sounds of it." He slipped past Stan and out the door.

Stan walked into the office. They'd done a nice job down here, too. The last time she'd seen this basement, she'd been at the top of a staircase that crumbled literally beneath her feet moments later. But now, with all the debris hauled away, the walls Sheetrocked and painted, and a trendy metal ceiling installed, she would never have believed it was the same room. Cyril had positioned a few thrift-shop desks around the room for his operations and decorated the rest of the space with used, mismatched furniture — chairs that looked like they'd come from an estate sale, a small couch in the waiting area for people visiting or perhaps signing up for a subscription, a rickety table holding a Keurig and some coffee fixings.

He sat in the back of the room at the biggest desk, glaring at his computer. Next to him, a scanner crackled.

"Hey," Stan said.

"Hey," he said without looking up.

"No luck finding people to talk about Eleanor?" She pulled up a chair and sat in front of him.

He glanced at her, finally. "Why? You interested?"

"Not me."

Cyril shoved his keyboard away. "What's up?"

"Question for you."

"That's a switch."

Stan looked around the makeshift newsroom. "Anyone else here?"

Cyril smiled. "My advertising person works, like, three hours a week. You're safe."

"When Tony was running for mayor, did you do any stories on him?"

"Of course I did," Cyril said, offended. "Didn't you *read* them?"

"I should've expected that," Stan muttered. "I'm sorry. I didn't. But I'm trying to find out if you found anything weird about him. You know, any scandal, or any . . .

financial stuff that seemed off."

Cyril tilted his head to the side, studying her. "Why?"

"Why what?"

"Why are you worried about Tony? It couldn't possibly be because of what happened at his house, could it? I mean, that case is closed." He winked at her, a gesture that just looked creepy coming from Cyril. "Isn't it?"

Stan narrowed her eyes at him. "Can you help me or not?"

He motioned for her to stand behind him. She did. He pulled up the recently updated *Holler* website and typed Tony's name in the search bar. A bunch of hits came up, mostly from city council meetings or other town goings-on. He scrolled through the list, then pulled up a story.

"Here's one."

Stan skimmed it. Cyril's research said Tony grew up in upstate New York, spent summers with family in Connecticut, was a former high school baseball star, and went on to Yale. Always interested in politics, he went straight to Washington after college and worked on political campaigns of all levels. He went to law school but did not finish, and eventually went on to become a lobbyist, working for two different firms during his tenure. His mayoral campaign in Frog Ledge was his first foray as a candidate.

Cyril tried to get why Frog Ledge and why now, but Tony's generic quote, "Connecticut has always felt like a second home," was as far as he'd gotten.

"Family in Connecticut," Stan mused. "Did he say where? Names?"

"He wasn't very forthcoming," Cyril said. "I tried to get dirt on him but really, I couldn't come up with anything."

"Financials?" Stan asked.

Cyril shrugged. "Unfortunately, it's not like he was running for president and asked to release his tax returns. This job was small potatoes. The salary is $40K, and that's public record. He did promise this would be his full-time job so he could devote himself completely to doing whatever the town needed him to do, blah blah. I think that's in my other story." Cyril went back to scanning his archives.

"Did he have any corporate funders?"

Cyril paused. "Not that I found."

Frustrated, she walked around the newsroom. "How does he live in that house? No one wondered about that?"

"He didn't live there while he campaigned," Cyril said. "He promised everyone he'd move as soon as he won the election. Said he was taking his time looking for the right place."

Stan frowned. "And people bought that?"

"His supporters did a good job. They were passionate about him. The farmers rallied around him hard. You must remember that. The Hoffmans were all about Tony."

Stan did know that. Part of Tony's appeal in this community was the lobbying work he'd done in support of farming and agriculture. That'd been his main platform. Not corporate greed.

"Do you know anything about the Trumbull family?"

"I know a lot," Cyril said. "They're the founding fathers of this town. A Trumbull has lived here since the day they put the sign in the ground." He smiled. "I know where you're going, Stan. I've gone there a few times myself. I'm telling you, you should think about doing freelance work for the paper. You think like a reporter."

"I'm not looking for a job," Stan said impatiently. "I'm looking for some intel on Tony."

Cyril picked up a paper clip from his desk and twisted it out of shape. "I know the Trumbull kids moved away, and old man Trumbull wanted to stay there after his wife died seven or eight years ago. I did go to town hall once in hopes of finding the deed, but I couldn't find anything with his name and I never bothered to check again. Honestly never gave it much thought after that, and no one came asking about it. That's how I get a lot of my stories, you know. People around here love to give tips. I suppose I could do more digging, since you're giving me a tip."

"That would be awesome. Thanks, Cyril. Let me know what you find out. One more thing. Do you know where I can find Curtis Wallace during the day?"

"Wallace?" Now Cyril looked interested. "Why?"

"I heard he was an accountant," Stan said, the lie slipping off her tongue. "I need a new one."

Cyril looked suspicious. "The firm's Maxwell and Sampson."

"Thanks." As she was turning to leave, Cyril called her back.

"I've been meaning to give you this." He reached into his desk drawer and handed her a magazine.

Stan glanced down. Then did a double take. Nutty's face stared back at her, larger than life in vibrant color, all Maine coon poise and arrogance on the cover of *Foodie.*

Her eyes automatically slid to the accompanying text. *Rescue cat inspires new trend in pet food.* And next to that, *Meet Nutty, the genius behind Pawsitively Organic.* Despite herself, she couldn't hold back the grin when she raised her eyes to Cyril.

He flashed her a thumbs-up. "Cover models wish they had that much face time."

"I guess so. Man, they covered this page with him." And the photo was so sharp she could count his whiskers.

"You haven't seen this yet?" Cyril gaped at her. "What's wrong with you? If this murder hadn't upset my editorial calendar, I was planning my own feature on Nutty, talking about *his* feature."

"You were?"

"Of course. We like to promote our famous residents."

She scanned the piece, splashed across four pages in the center of the magazine. Lots of photos. It detailed how she and Nutty found each other, why she'd started baking, and how Pawsitively Organic came about. Sheldon must be livid. There wasn't one mention of him.

"Where did you get this?" she asked.

"My copy showed up Friday."

"Showed up? You have a subscription to *Foodie* magazine?"

Cyril's casual shrug, the skittering away of his eyes was her answer.

She sighed. "You're still looking for dirt on Sheldon and the gang? You know I'm not going to comment on any of that."

"I subscribed when you got the gig with Sheldon," he said, defensive. "I figured you'd be showing up in all kinds of magazines like that so I wanted to be prepared."

She blew out a breath. "Great. Let me know when you want to do the story on Nutty. I'll clear his calendar." She waved the magazine at him. "Do you mind if I take this?"

"Kind of," he said. "There are some recipes in there I wanted to try."

She stared at him. He sighed. "Fine. Take it. But at least take pictures of the recipes and text me," he called after her as she made a beeline for the door.

CHAPTER 49

Every time Stan stopped at a light or stop sign — only twice between Cyril's and her house — she couldn't help picking up the magazine to admire her beautiful boy's picture. Both times, someone behind her honked impatiently. She felt like getting out of the car to show them the magazine, but refrained.

At least she could show Caitlyn. But when she drove up, Caitlyn's car was gone. She and Eva were quite the social butterflies these days. Duncan and Jake were at the pub, so they couldn't even see it yet. She'd have to announce it to all the other animals and catch them up later. She hurried into her house, greeting Scruffy, Henry, and Gaston at the door, then went looking for the cats. She found them in the kitchen, lounging on the counter. Nutty napped, and Benny purred.

"Nutty, look!" She held up the magazine

excitedly. Nutty opened one eye, gave her a look, then closed it again, his tail twitching his displeasure at her interruption. Her smile faded. "Really? You're not even excited about being on the front cover of *Foodie*? What's wrong with you?"

He didn't answer. Maybe he *was* worried about a Photoshop scandal. She took a picture of the magazine and texted it to Jake, Brenna, Char, Izzy, and Jessie. Everyone *oohed* and *aahed* appropriately except Jessie, whom she still hadn't heard from. That put a damper on her excitement. The red car still hung over her head.

But, nothing she could do about it now except wait for Jessie and check her cell phone account online for the number Monica called. First, real food. She fixed a salad and green smoothie, hoping to counter the effects of all the recent sweets. While she ate, she took out a notebook and drew a table with four columns. In the first column, she wrote Richard's name. In the second, Tony's; the third, Monica's; and finally Curtis Wallace's. Under Richard's name, she wrote "Arrested" and added a sad face. Under Tony's she wrote "Disappeared, long history with Eleanor, blackmail? Finances?" Under Monica's, she wrote "Suspicious behavior, didn't get along with mom."

Finally, under Curtis she wrote "Fighting with victim."

Stan sat back and looked at her list. No great revelations popped out at her. She started to add more things to Monica's column: "Wrong phone passcode." "Red car." "Missing purse." "What is her deal??" She underlined the last question and tossed her pen in disgust.

She found her iPad in the den. Sinking onto her comfy love seat, she logged on to Verizon and pulled up her account details. After a little scrolling, she located an unfamiliar number. Holding her breath, she dialed. The phone rang four times, then voice mail.

"I'm not available. Please leave a message." A male voice, but muffled, as if there was a lot of background noise when he recorded. Plus, the greeting was so short. She wished she could say she recognized it unmistakably as Scott's, but she couldn't.

So much for that bright idea. Annoyed, she texted Jessie one more time, then curled up on her side and rested her head on her fuzzy purple pillow. Just for five minutes. She was so tired.

When she woke up, the clock on her cable box claimed it was almost eleven and she had a leg cramp from sleeping on a too-short couch. Benny was draped over her head, and Nutty's tail hung in her face. When she moved her head, a note fluttered to the floor from the pillow: "We're home and in bed — love, C."

She hadn't even heard her sister come in. And she hadn't sent Tony his statement yet. She was surprised her mother hadn't called to remind her. With a sigh, she swung her legs off the couch, wincing as they protested this new position. The dogs, all crowded on the floor underneath her, rolled over to see if they were moving somewhere else. When they realized she was settling into a different position, they all went back to sleep. Stan wrapped herself in the extra blanket she kept on the couch and picked up her phone, hoping for a response from Jessie. Nothing from her, but Jake left a message an hour ago.

"Hey, babe. Where are you? Brenna's here working with me, so I'm keeping my eye on that situation. Find out anything? Love you."

She hadn't found out anything, but at least Jake felt like it was under control for the night. Stan pulled up a fresh document and banged out a quick-and-dirty media statement for Tony. She didn't put a ton of effort into it, but still admired her ability to produce something good in under fifteen minutes. She e-mailed it off to Tony, then did something she hadn't done in weeks — flipped on the TV. Scrolling channels, she paused on the classic movie station, currently airing the cult favorite *Mommie Dearest.* Her finger on the channel button, she paused for just a minute to watch.

An hour later, she was still glued to the screen watching Faye Dunaway portray Joan Crawford's abusive treatment of her children, and she couldn't stop thinking of Monica Chang. As tears rolled down her cheeks, she convinced herself it was exhaustion and all the crazy emotions that surfaced after last weekend. The whole thing was ridiculous because she had no proof that Eleanor abused Monica. Well, maybe emotionally, just knowing Eleanor.

That made her think of her own mother — not abusive, but emotionally unavailable — and she cried even more. She couldn't think of a time growing up when she hadn't wished for some kind of common ground with Patricia, something that would bridge the gap for good. But she hadn't found it, and she had no reason to believe she ever would. Which was gut-wrenching and good for a few more sobs.

And that's how Jake found her a few

minutes later when he got home way earlier than usual, even though she tried to get herself together when she heard him come through the front door. He heard the TV and came looking for her. When he poked his head in the room, his smile faded to concern as he took in her red-rimmed eyes and the crumpled tissues next to her.

"Stan? What's going on? What happened?" He came over and sat down next to her, reaching for her hand.

"Nothing," she sniffed. "I was watching *Mommie Dearest*."

He cocked his head at her. "You were what?"

"Watching that stupid movie about Joan Crawford abusing her kids." She reached for another tissue and blew her nose. "It made me think of my mother and Monica Chang — I saw her today — and that made me sad, and now I'm concerned that maybe Eleanor was horrible to her and maybe Monica killed he because she couldn't take it anymore. Lord knows she was horrible to everyone e-else." She started to cry in earnest.

"Oh, honey." Jake hugged her to him, probably trying to follow that train of thought.

She rested her head on his shoulder and

sniffled. When she finally stopped crying, she swiped at her tear-streaked face and looked up at him. "What are you doing home so early anyway?" she asked.

He smiled. "Nice greeting."

She winced. "I didn't mean it like that."

"I know. It was slow tonight and I had enough people on that they could get a head start on cleanup. I figured I'd take advantage of it. Plus, I hadn't heard from you and I was getting worried."

"I fell asleep, and then I figured you were busy so I didn't call back. That's when I started watching the movie." She tugged her blanket tighter around her. "I still haven't heard from Jessie on the license plate. On anything, actually. She left her office today and vanished."

Now he frowned. "Vanished?"

"That might be dramatic, but I haven't heard from her since. Her office door was locked and her phone's off."

"Maybe she and Marty went out somewhere. I didn't see him at the pub tonight and he usually comes in on Tuesdays for the half-price appetizers."

"Maybe," Stan agreed, but she didn't think so. Even though it was unofficial, Jessie would be focused on this murder case, which would mean she didn't have time for things like date nights.

"You said you saw Monica Chang?"

"She came to town to file a police report about her missing purse."

"With Jessie?"

"Yup. So much happened today." She briefed him on the media, Tony's snooping around in Jessie's office, Monica's visit, and her conversation with Tony afterward. Stan pulled the ponytail holder out of her hair, letting it fall around her shoulders. "Cyril's looking into Tony's financials for me."

"Yeah?" Jake sat back, keeping his arm around her shoulders.

She snuggled against him. "Yep. I want to know how he could afford that house. I know things are cheaper over here compared to the other side of the state, but that house cost a pretty penny." She looked up at Jake. "I want to know if my mother bought it for him."

"Whoa." Jake sat back. "You think he's scamming your mother for her money?"

"I don't know!" Frustrated, she threw the blanket off and got up to pace. "That's part of the problem. I don't *know* him. I know Richard well enough to say I don't think he killed anyone. I can't say that about Tony, and it bothers me."

"How does Monica fit in?"

"I don't know that, either," she admitted. "But I do know if you push a kid too far — especially one who's fragile — they're eventually going to break. The question is, if Monica broke, would she hurt someone else?"

Jake nodded slowly. "And not knowing about Scott and this car is making it worse." He got up. "I'm going to take a ride by Jessie's house. See if she's home."

She jumped up, the unease she'd felt earlier returning doubled. "I'll go with you." Jake was clearly worried, she realized as they slipped out the front door. He wouldn't go out in the middle of the night if he wasn't. And when Jake worried, things were serious.

CHAPTER 50

They'd found Jessie's house dark and empty.
Jake let them in to look around and found
nothing out of place, but it still didn't sit
well. Especially when they drove by Marty's
and didn't see her car there, either. Marty's
car was in the driveway, but his house was
also dark.

"She could be working on another case.
Out at the barracks," Stan said into the
darkness sometime around three a.m. as
they both tossed and turned. "Maybe
they're trying to keep her out of this case
and asked her to work overtime on something else."

"Maybe," Jake agreed, but Stan knew he
wasn't convinced. For that matter, neither
was she. "I'll call Sturgis in the morning."

"Good idea." She could call Colby, too.
Maybe he could shed some light.

Stan finally fell asleep around four. When
she woke a few hours later, Scruffy and

Henry were the only ones around. Scruffy slept at her feet, Henry in his usual spot by the bed.

Scruffy rolled over and looked at her, stubby tail wagging. "Morning, sweetie," Stan said, reaching down to rub her belly. "Where's everyone?"

Scruffy didn't answer. For one blissful moment she thought about staying in bed for the day and pretending none of this drama was happening. Then she sat bolt upright, remembering she'd promised to be at Francie's for a yoga and meditation session this morning bright and early. Like, in half an hour.

"Crap," she sighed. "There's nothing relaxing about rushing to do yoga and meditate."

She rolled out of bed. Scruffy and Henry followed her into the bathroom, where she took a fast shower. They all trooped downstairs. Stan had to blink when she entered the kitchen. Caitlyn stood at the stove making scrambled eggs and talking with Jake, who sat at the table drinking coffee. Eva sat on the floor on her knees, using what looked like Caitlyn's hairbrush on Gaston, who sat patiently. Duncan watched from under the table. The cats watched from the counter, Benny curious, Nutty disdainful.

"Morning." Jake rose when he saw her and gave her a kiss, then went to get her a mug of coffee. His bloodshot eyes and tense jaw gave away his state of mind, but he put on a good show for Caitlyn and Eva. "Did you get any sleep?"

"Some." Stan glanced at her sister.

"What?" Caitlyn asked. "I know, you didn't think I could cook, either."

Stan held up her hands in defense. "I didn't say a word." She sipped the coffee Jake handed her. "I have to go in a minute. I'm going to yoga and meditation at Francie's studio this morning."

"That sounds nice," Caitlyn exclaimed. "Can I join you? Oh. Shoot." She grimaced. "I'm so used to having a nanny."

"Don't worry about it. Go do your thing. I'll stay with Eva," Jake said.

Stan and Caitlyn both stared at him. "You will?"

He nodded. "We'll have a good time. We can do yard work and play with the dogs. How's that sound, Eva?"

She continued to brush Gaston. "I can help in the yard too," she offered. "Dominique lets me rake leaves."

Caitlyn arched an eyebrow at that, but didn't comment. Instead, she looked at Jake. "You're fabulous."

He made a *no big deal* motion with his hand. "She's a lot of fun." He looked at Stan. "I have a bunch of calls to make, anyway."

Caitlyn looked at Stan. "He's fabulous."

"I know." Stan hugged him and drained her cup. "I'm a lucky girl these days, murder aside." She whispered to him so Caitlyn couldn't hear, "Text me if you hear from her."

It took Stan and Caitlyn seven minutes to get to Francie's house across town. Barely enough time to drink half her travel mug of coffee, but she pulled in at eight-oh-three. Francie lived in a neighborhood called Strawberry Hills, which didn't make sense because there was no hill Stan could see. Strawberry Hills was one long, U-shaped street and Francie lived smack in the middle of it. Her little white house looked cozy and inviting, with its picket fence and carefully planted flowers. A small sign with a yin-yang symbol in front of her garage said YOGA.

Francie opened the front door as Stan pulled in, waving. A golden retriever tried to nose his way out behind her. "No, Cooper. You have to stay in the house. Hello! I'm so glad you brought Caitlyn," she exclaimed as they got out of the car. "But where's your mother?"

Caitlyn looked at Stan and burst out laughing. "*Mom* was coming to meditate? You've got to be kidding."

Francie looked from Caitlyn to Stan. "This must be something we can work on with her."

"We could try," Stan said. "She's been busy. I never connected with her yesterday. Not about meditation, anyway."

"I'll put her on my contact list," Francie announced, opening the door leading into her garage. "I have a newsletter going out later this week about my upcoming meditation groups." She led them up a flight of stairs and opened another door, waving them in ahead of her.

Stan stepped inside and admired the studio's gleaming wooden floors and mirrors all along the back wall. A selection of yoga mats were already laid out on the floor. Yoga balls, additional mats, and yoga blocks lined one side, and a selection of weights the other. The recessed lights were dimmed and candles glowed on a small table. Soft meditation music sounded through a speaker system. The light, airy scent of incense sweetened the air.

"This is so nice," she said. Caitlyn nodded her agreement.

"Thank you." Francie beamed. "I love this room. It used to be a storage area for all kinds of junk. It's so peaceful now, isn't it? The perfect place to center yourself. Would you like some tea?"

"I would love some," Caitlyn said.

"Wonderful. Stan?" Francie walked over to a small cabinet where a teapot boiled merrily on a small burner.

"Sure," Stan said.

Francie took out three small teacups. "This is a special herbal blend. Good for de-stressing." She added water to the tea and poured into the cups. "After this week I think we all need a little de-stressing."

"Tell me about it," Caitlyn sighed, sinking down onto a mat. "Finding a dead body was no picnic. And having my ex-boyfriend come to town was quite possibly even worse!"

Stan swallowed her inappropriate giggle with a mouthful of tea. Her sister hadn't lost her flair for the dramatic, which struck her funny despite the subject matter.

But Francie looked distressed. "*You* found that poor woman? Oh, dear. How awful. I hadn't heard."

"It was pretty awful," Caitlyn agreed.

Stan added a little more tea to her cup. As she turned to walk to her own mat, she noticed a picture half hidden behind the selection of candles. She peered more closely at it. A younger Francie leaned against a handsome man who had his arm wrapped around her. In front of them, a young boy of maybe ten or eleven struck a silly pose. His sandy blond hair fell in his eyes, giving him an impish look, complemented by the contagious smile on his face. Her deceased son, most likely. Stan itched to ask what happened, but didn't want to be rude.

"Are you ready?" Francie asked, taking her elbow and steering her to the mats.

After a relaxing half hour of yoga and another half hour of guided meditation, Stan felt like a new woman. She hoped it lasted longer than her ride home.

"You try to keep that stress at bay," Francie instructed as she walked them outside. "Remember the breathing technique I taught you. If you feel tension, just find a quiet place and breathe for five minutes. It will center you."

"Thanks," Stan said.

"You're welcome. I'm working at the church today. And your mother and Tony have an appointment with Pastor Ellis tomorrow about the wedding. You're aware, right?"

Stan shook her head. "I don't keep her schedule." It came out snippy, though unintended.

Caitlyn elbowed her. "Do you need to breathe already?"

"I know she wanted you girls to be there. Didn't she invite you?" Francie asked. "It's very important they keep that meeting. Pastor Ellis is going out of town Thursday night on a retreat with his counseling group. If they can't get there, he won't be back for a week. I don't want them to miss out."

"You should try calling her," Stan said, slipping into her car. "If you can't get her on her cell, try her at Char's."

"She's still staying there?" Francie asked. "Why hasn't she moved home yet?"

"I wondered that, too," Caitlyn said. "Are they keeping it as a crime scene? Does that mean they're having second thoughts about Richard?" She brightened. "That's good, right?"

"I heard rumblings about that at the senior center when I did a yoga session there yesterday evening," Francie said. "Is that really true? Who do they think did it, then?"

"I have no idea if it's true or what anyone thinks," Stan said. "We should let you get to work. See you later, Francie!"

She hit the gas before Caitlyn closed the car door all the way. "Jeez," her sister said. "What's your problem? You just got de-stressed!"

"Right. And then you started talking about murder again. That subject is off limits," Stan said.

Caitlyn huffed. "Tell that to the rest of the town."

Stan looked at her in disbelief, almost crossing into oncoming traffic. "What do you know about this town?"

"Hey, I've been getting around," Caitlyn said, settling back in her seat. "I'm practically a native now. People are starting to recognize me and everything."

Stan didn't know if that was good or bad, so she said nothing.

CHAPTER 51

When they got home, Eva was having a blast playing in the yard with Jake and the dogs. He tossed tennis balls and all four dogs plus Eva scrambled to catch them. She sent him a questioning look. He shook his head slightly. No news.

"I'll take over," Caitlyn told him. "Thanks for watching her."

"Anytime." Jake squeezed her arm, a friendly gesture that said he meant it. Stan had to laugh. Her sister and Jake. An unlikely friendship.

"I'm going to see Marty," Jake said. "I've been trying Jessie all morning. I can't reach Sturgis, either."

Somehow that made Stan feel better. "Maybe that means I'm right. They could be on some case." She checked her phone again. No messages, but an e-mail from Tony popped up in response to her media statement. She ignored it.

"I won't feel better until I talk to her. I called Brenna but she hasn't heard from her, either. I didn't want to upset her, so I didn't say much," Jake said.

"Let me know what Marty says. I'm going to see Curtis Wallace," Stan said.

"Be careful."

Jake left, and Stan had one leg inside her car when a dark blue Jag pulled up in front of her house. She turned to look, shading her eyes from the sun. She didn't recognize the vehicle. A man wearing a Yankees cap climbed out of the driver's side. Sunglasses covered his eyes. He had a couple days' worth of beard. Stan's eyes widened when he pulled off the glasses, and she stepped back out of the car.

"Richard?"

He glanced around when she said his name as if he expected someone to swoop in, pick him up, and whisk him back to jail. "Hey. I'm sorry to show up like this, but I didn't know . . . Can I talk to you for a second?" He shifted from foot to foot, not the picture of confidence Stan remembered.

She couldn't stop staring at him. He'd lost weight since Saturday. Plus, she couldn't remember the last time she'd been face-to-face with anyone officially accused of murder. She shook it off. "Hey. Yes, of course. Do you want to come in?"

"Am I holding you up? Were you heading out?"

"I have a few minutes. Come on." She led him inside. The dogs immediately barreled over, their various sounds a cacophony of happiness.

Richard took a surprised step back. "Dogs?"

Stan nodded. "Jake had two and I had two."

"What happened to Nutty?"

"Nutty's great. We have a second cat, too."

"Impressive," he said.

"We love them. Caitlyn?" she called.

"Yeah?" Her sister appeared in the kitchen doorway, a butter knife in her hand. "I thought you were leaving? Want a sandwich? Oh, sorry. Didn't know you had company." Then she did a double take. "Richard?"

"Sorry. I didn't mean to interrupt," he said. "Although I have to say I'm surprised to find you two hanging out together." He tried for a smile but couldn't quite manage it.

"We definitely didn't see each other often enough in years past," Stan said, looking at her sister. "We're trying to do better."

Richard nodded. "That's a good thing."

They lapsed into silence.

"I'll let you guys talk," Caitlyn said finally. "I'll take the dogs. Guys, snacks!"

Obediently the dogs all raced after her to the kitchen.

"Let's go in here." Stan led him to the living room.

Richard followed her in, looking around the house. "It looks good in here," he said. "You did a nice job."

"Thanks," Stan said awkwardly. She motioned to the couch. "Sit, please."

Richard perched on the edge of the sofa, steepling his hands under his chin. "So you ended up with the pub guy," he said.

Stan smiled, despite all the questions desperate to pour out of her mouth. "I did."

"He live here now?"

"Yep."

"That's good." Richard nodded. "I'm glad you're happy, Stan."

Stan perched on the edge of the love seat facing him. If anyone had told her she'd be sitting here with Richard a year and a half after their demise talking about her new boyfriend, she'd have laughed them right out of town. A kinder, gentler Richard? Could it be? "That's nice of you, Richard. But I'm guessing you didn't come out here to talk about my love life."

His face clouded over. "No." He dropped his hands to his knees and rubbed them against his pants. "Stan, I didn't kill Eleanor."

Relief flooded through her. She knew it in her heart, but hearing him say it cleared away any remnants of doubt. Still, she wanted to know why they were so certain it was him.

"Why do the police think you did it, then? What evidence do they have?"

He took off his hat and raked his hands through his hair, clutching the clumps in his fists for a moment. Then he rose and walked slowly around the room. "I don't know. I swear, I have no idea what happened to her. Swear to *God.* I was thinking about myself, as usual. And how sick of everything I was. Sick of her, sick of everyone I worked with, sick of my job. Sick of spending every waking hour at other people's beck and call." He faced her. "I really thought you were crazy last year, you know. When you decided not to come back."

Stan nodded. "I know. A lot of people did."

"I figured you'd come to your senses eventually." He smiled a little. "I'm glad you didn't."

"But I did," Stan corrected him. "That's

why I *didn't* come back."

"Yeah. I get that. Me, I kept doing what I've always done. I found another woman to replace you, one who still lived in my world. We worked together, we traveled together for work, we talked about work." He smiled, but now it was sad. "Kind of like what you and I did for so many years."

"Yeah," Stan said. "What a colossal waste of time. No offense," she added quickly. "We were both at fault."

He nodded. "You're right. The crazy thing is, I'd just started to realize that. And then, Saturday happened." He sat back down. "I didn't want to go to the party, but we had to. It was one of those 'mandatory fun' things we used to laugh about." He faced her again. "One thing's true. I hated Eleanor. Hated her with a passion. The police asked me if we had problems and I didn't even lie about it. We did. But I didn't kill her."

Stan held her breath, not wanting to break the spell. Richard seemed to need to tell her this. Therapeutic, perhaps. And it made her feel a whole lot better hearing him so adamantly deny doing this.

"Anyway, I tried to stay away from her Saturday. Pretend she wasn't even there. So I got drunk." He shrugged. "I'm sure you heard she and I got into it."

Stan nodded. "What were you fighting about?"

He shook his head. "Work stuff. it was so unimportant and stupid. I finally walked away and got another drink. I never saw her again. Then your boyfriend — well. You know. I got mad, I went outside in my drunken stupor. And I accidentally let the black cat out. I ran after it. I remembered what you always said about Nutty. How he didn't belong outside anymore. I felt bad so I chased the cat. Into the woods. Which in hindsight was pretty stupid, given that it was getting dark and the cat was black." He laughed, but there was no humor. "I tripped over something and fell. Landed in a muddy puddle. Twisted my ankle. It's what I get for drinking, I guess. I ended up sitting outside for a while, thinking about how I could have possibly ended up in this moment. I don't even know how long I stayed out there. When I finally got my act together, it was like I'd had an epiphany. I didn't want to do this anymore. You know?"

"I sure do," Stan said.

"So I was coming inside to get Michelle. Or leave her, if she didn't want to leave. Then I was going to go home and write my resignation letter." He smiled a crooked smile. "I was never as good as you with money, but I had enough. Thought maybe I'd take a three-month sabbatical to Thailand or something. I've always wanted to travel the world." His face twisted into a grimace. "Guess that dream'll never come true now."

"Richard! Don't say that," Stan said. "They're going to figure out who did this. I know they are. Don't give up. Promise you won't give up. Listen. I'm not the only one who thinks you're innocent." She leaned forward earnestly. "Whoever posted your bail certainly thinks you are. Who posted it, anyway?" She'd intended to be more subtle with that question, but it just blurted out.

He looked at her, head tilted slightly. "I don't know," he said finally.

"You don't *know*? How could you not know?"

He shrugged. "I don't know. It was cash. They didn't tell me who it was when they let me out, just said I'd made bail."

Stan sat back, trying to process that. Richard had an anonymous donor with that much cash on hand?

He looked like he was about to say something else, but it was lost when Nutty jumped into his lap. Nutty settled in and began kneading lightly on his leg. Stan held her breath. Richard never cared much for Nutty. Or any animal, for that matter.

But today, he reached down and stroked the cat. "I take it that means you think so, too? Thanks for believing in me, Nutty." He glanced back at Stan. "I never did find Tony's cat. I feel bad about that."

"Don't. The animal control officer trapped him. He's totally fine and back home." She smiled. "I have to say, I'm impressed that you gave the cat a second thought."

"Yeah. You taught me well."

CHAPTER 52

Stan followed Richard out to the porch. She stood there for a long time after he drove away, then went back to her car with a renewed sense of purpose. Richard hadn't killed Eleanor, but he'd pay for it if they couldn't figure out who did. Caitlyn was probably dying of suspense, but she didn't have time to go fill her in. She had a murder to solve.

Her phone rang as she got back in her car. She didn't recognize the number and answered warily, figuring the media had tracked her down.

"Stan, it's Garrett Colby."

"Garrett!" she exclaimed. "I'm so glad you called." She was. Finally, someone who might know what was going on with Jessie, since she still hadn't heard from Jake.

"Not as glad as I am that you're hosting a fundraiser for me and Rosie," Colby said. "Jessie told me it's tomorrow at the vet

403

clinic. Rosie and I are so excited. Is there anything I can do to help you out?"

"No," Stan said. "Just show up with Rosie and be ready to do some demos and introduce her, talk about her training, what she does, all that good stuff."

"You got it," Colby said. "If you think of anything else, just give me a call."

"Will do. Is this the best number to reach you?"

"It is. Or try me in the town hall office."

"You're at the town hall office? Terrific. Is Jessie there? I've been trying to call her."

Silence.

"Garrett?"

"She's not."

"Do you know when she'll be back?"

He hesitated. "I'm not expecting her back."

"You mean this afternoon? Is she off?"

"Sort of," Colby said.

Stan swallowed against the bad feeling rising in her throat. "What's going on, Garrett? Where's Jessie?"

"I can't believe she hasn't told you," he muttered.

Her stomach twisted into a vicious knot. "Told me what?"

Colby sighed. When he spoke again his voice sounded funny. "Jessie's been suspended. The captain asked me to take over in town for the time being."

Stan sat in stunned silence in her car after Colby hung up. Suspended? Had someone found out they'd been looking into this further? She had to call Jake, but the phone rang in her hand first. Another unrecognizable number. "Hello."

"It's me," Jessie said.

"Jess! Thank God. Where are you? Colby said —"

"I know," she interrupted. "Don't worry about it. Can you and Jake meet me somewhere? Somewhere the whole town won't hear us."

"Izzy's back room," Stan said immediately. It wasn't lost on her that was one of Eleanor's last haunts in town. "When?"

"I can be there in ten minutes."

"I'll call Jake. He's out looking for you."

"He was never that great of a detective," Jessie said, and hung up.

Stan called Jake first and told him to meet her, fending off his million questions. Then she called Izzy and asked if they could borrow her room.

"Use it for as long as you need to," Izzy said. "I'll tell Jana. I'm heading over to the bookstore. Your sister is coming to help me."

"My sister?" Stan asked.

"Yeah. She found a playgroup for Eva and now she's looking for something to do before she goes to the clinic later. It works out perfectly because I have some shelves up and I need books stocked. And she's going to help me sketch out some displays."

Stan shook her head and hung up as Jake climbed out of his truck and walked over.

"What?"

"My sister's turning into quite the little helper. She's working at the bookstore with Izzy today."

"It's good for her. She's a good kid, Stan."

"I know. I'm just . . . not used to this Caitlyn."

"People change."

Yes, they do. She thought about Richard, his soul-searching and ultimate decision. She hoped, once this mess was over, that he stuck to it and found real happiness.

When they got inside, Jessie already waited in the back room with coffees and pastries — and Scott. He lifted his hand in a sheepish wave.

Stan looked from Scott to Jessie to Jake. "What's going on?"

"It better be good," Jake said, eyes on Scott.

Jessie shot her brother a look. "Sit and eat something," she said. "Izzy insisted they serve us." She turned to Stan. "I'm sorry I didn't get back to you yesterday. I got my behind handed to me by Captain Quigley — you heard I got suspended — but I'd already asked a friend to run that plate at the DMV. So I went over to see my friend. As a civilian, of course."

"But why are you so blasé about being suspended?" Stan demanded.

"I'm not. But I'm dealing with one thing at a time. And when my friend ran that plate and the only other possible combination in Connecticut registered to a red car like the one you described was out in Danbury, I went looking for our friend here." She indicated Scott. "And now he's going to tell you why he was at Tony Falco's house the other night."

Stan whipped her head around and eyed Scott. "It *was* you picking up Monica."

He nodded.

"Did Monica kill her mother?" Stan asked.

Scott's mouth dropped open. "*What?* Is that what you think?"

"We don't know what to think," Jake said. "But we don't want our little sister involved, whatever it is. So how do you know this girl?"

Scott toyed with his coffee cup but didn't drink. He looked troubled.

Jessie nudged him. "Go ahead. I already told you this would stay confidential." She looked at Jake and Stan. "I promised. Not a word outside of this room."

Stan had to refrain from pounding on the table in frustration. "Will someone tell us, already?"

Scott held up a hand. "I'm telling you. But this is a breach of privacy for Monica, so you can't discuss this with anyone."

"You were counseling her," Stan said, the light finally dawning.

Scott nodded slowly. "I worked with Monica in my last job. I worked solely with addicts. She'd just come out of a special rehab program and the counseling was part of her release. She'd had a really rough time and . . ." He hesitated. "Her family life wasn't helping. Her mother didn't understand her illness. She wanted Monica to pick up where she'd left off. Be sorry for all the trouble she caused and work hard to make up for it." A look of disgust crossed his face. "It caused Monica a lot of anxiety. Anyway, I worked with her until I took this new job, and it seemed like she was on the right track."

"But she had a relapse," Stan said.

"Unfortunately, yes. Her mother freaked out, Monica left home. When she turned up she was in pretty bad shape. They got her back into treatment, but she didn't hit it off with her counselor. She started calling me again. She'd kept my phone number. I never changed it, job to job, because . . . if someone needed me I always wanted to help, if I could. Anyway, she called me. I tried to convince her to give this new person a shot. It's not good to be dependent on one person. You start looking at them like a savior or something. But she wouldn't do it. Said she wouldn't do counseling at all. So I started having unofficial sessions with her once a month. Her mother found out and called me. Offered me almost another year's salary to work with her consistently, outside of my regular job." He paused. "Social workers don't make any money. I accepted the offer."

Stan poured some coffee and sat back. "So theoretically, you were working for Eleanor."

Scott set his jaw. "I did it for Monica."

"But you had to answer to her mother," Jake said.

"Yes and no. She grilled me after every session, sure. But I told her from the outset that everything Monica told me was confidential."

"Eleanor didn't like that," Stan guessed.

"No. But too bad for her."

Stan looked at Jessie, trying to read her. Jessie had her cop face on, letting Scott explain. She turned back to Scott. "Monica got very defensive with me when I asked her if she was drinking Saturday."

"She was also taking pills," Scott said grimly. "And obviously would want to deny it. Her mother would've killed her." He grimaced at his choice of words. "Sorry. When she called me to come get her, I could tell right away she was using. When she told me what happened I honestly thought she was hallucinating."

"What did she say when she called you?" Stan asked. "She used my phone, but I couldn't hear anything."

"She said someone killed her mother. That she was in Frog Ledge. I didn't know her mother worked with Tony. Monica never mentioned that, so I was really confused about why she would be there. She told me where she was. I asked her if she'd been doing drugs and she said yes, but she was very adamant about her story."

"So you came to get her," Jake said. "Funny how it didn't take you long."

Scott met his gaze, unflinching. "I was at

410

your pub. With Brenna and a hundred other people. Helping in the kitchen."

Jake looked at Jessie. She nodded. "I have witnesses. You think I wouldn't check that out?"

"Monica was back here yesterday," Stan said. "Were you meeting her?"

"No."

"She came to file a police report about her missing purse," Jessie said.

"Yeah, she did say her purse went missing. I think she was freaked out because she had a stash of pills in it." Scott hesitated. "And because of Pastor Ellis. I thought she just misplaced it, but so weird no one found it and turned it in."

"Wait. Why would she freak out because of Pastor Ellis?" Jake asked.

"Pastor Ellis does a lot of work with addicts. He volunteers tons of time up in the Hartford area. We've worked together often. We actually worked together on Monica. Pastor Ellis talked to me about the special pilot program and I suggested Monica for it."

"So he knew Eleanor, too," Stan said.

They were all quiet.

"I guess he would've met her," Scott said. "But I really don't know."

"Scott." Stan took a deep breath. "Are you

sure Monica didn't . . ."

"No." He shook his head, adamant. "Monica's a sweet kid. The only person she's ever hurt is herself."

"Did you ask her if she had any idea who did this?" Stan asked.

"I did. She said she didn't know." He met her gaze again, and his own was troubled. "But like I told Jessie, she said something like 'If my mother had just let him fire her this wouldn't have happened.' "

Jake frowned. "Let who fire her? Tony?"

Scott shrugged. "Had to be. Who else would she be working for down here?"

CHAPTER 53

Curtis Wallace did his accounting on the second floor of a dilapidated building on Main Street in Bloomingfield, one of the towns bordering Frog Ledge. Stan'd never visited, and hoped she'd never have to again. From what she could tell, Main Street was in serious need of some TLC. The burrito place on one side looked like it specialized in *E. coli,* and the storefront windows on the other side had boards across them.

She found a parking spot right away across the street and hurried into the lobby. Opting for the stairs instead of an elevator that looked like it could plummet her to her death, she hurried upstairs and into the office.

A receptionist talking on her cell phone looked up, annoyance crossing her face at the interruption. While she waited, Stan took in the dirty white walls and carpet desperately in need of an upgrade. The wall art was old and faded, all drab colors and historical depictions of the Revolutionary War, a big piece of this area's history.

The receptionist switched to Spanish, said a few more words, then put the phone down. "Can I help you?" she asked, her tone bored.

"I'm looking for Curtis Wallace," Stan said.

She picked up the phone and jabbed a couple of buttons with a long nail. "Someone to see you," she said, then hung up and began playing with her phone again.

Curtis Wallace came out a minute later, his face expectant, his bow tie askew. Must be a tough day in the office. When he saw Stan, he looked confused. "Ms. Connor," he said. "Can I help you with something?"

"Yes, please," Stan said.

When she didn't say more, he motioned her to follow him. His office was the size of a large walk-in closet, and the decor was similar to the waiting area. She pulled out a mismatched chair in front of his desk and sat.

"Are you looking for a new accountant for your business?" he asked. "Or do you have IRS issues?"

"Neither," Stan said. "I wanted to ask you

about Tony Falco and why you're so interested in removing him from office."

That wiped away the smirk. He leaned back in his chair, twirling a pen between his fingers. "Why? Did your mother send you?"

Stan leveled her best ice queen stare at him. "I'm not an errand girl. I'm here because I live in Frog Ledge and I'm interested in knowing why your position changed on the mayor."

"People change their minds. So what?" Wallace said.

"You were his strongest supporter."

Wallace shrugged. "I smartened up. I supported him because my brother asked me to. They were friends. But I soon learned he's all talk."

"Your brother?"

"Tony," Wallace said through gritted teeth. "Matthew and Tony were law school friends. Matthew said he was the real thing and asked me to help him. So I suggested he run for mayor and helped with his campaign. Live and learn."

"So what did he drop the ball on that made you so mad?"

He leaned forward, clasping his hands together on top of his desk. "Young lady. I don't understand why you came all the way out here to talk about this, but if you must know, I'm a proponent for farming. Our town has deep agricultural roots, and those shouldn't be tossed away lightly. We're getting further and further away from those roots with every trendy storefront that opens up."

Stan bristled. She hadn't been called "young lady" since she was sixteen, and she certainly wasn't going to put up with it from this presumptuous, bow-tied big mouth. And she was pretty sure those "trendy storefronts" he referred to would include her own shop. "I'm sorry you feel that way," she said, though she wasn't sorry at all. "But I think many people in town would disagree with you. Change isn't a bad thing, as long as those people who still want to farm are being supported. And a smart leader would understand that. New shops bring new people, which could benefit the farmers." She thought of Emmalee Hoffman and the milk, cheeses, and homemade candies on which she turned a profit. Her business grew when college students and families spilled into town because of Izzy's café.

But Wallace didn't want to hear it. "Well. I don't choose to support those places, Ms. Connor. And I'll continue to advocate for what's best for our fine town. I think what happened Saturday was disgraceful, and another smudge on Frog Ledge. Tony should be accountable for that. Now if there's nothing else, I have work to do." He turned back to his computer, dismissing her.

"If you're such a fan of Frog Ledge," Stan asked, "why isn't your office there?"

Wallace sent her a withering look, but didn't answer.

Stan shrugged and remained seated until Wallace turned back to her, exasperated. "What?" he demanded.

"That's a pretty big leap to accusing him of murder," Stan said.

His eyes narrowed into slits. "I did no such thing."

"Maybe you were too drunk to remember, but Sunday you were at the pub and said it was suspicious that he was missing when Ms. Chang died."

Wallace chuckled. "Therein lies the problem, Ms. Connor. Regrettably, you're correct. I'd had too much to drink and don't even remember what I said, to be honest. So I wouldn't put much stock in whatever it was. At the end of the day, it was Tony's house, so whatever happened he's not completely blameless."

"I see." Stan nodded slowly. "So why were you and Eleanor Chang fighting at Izzy's café? If you never went there," she added.

417

"Since it was so trendy."

Wallace froze, all the color draining from his face. "I have no idea what you're talking about," he said, but his voice sounded strangled.

"Come on, Curtis. Just because your pals don't frequent the place, you never know who might recognize you," Stan said. "How did you know Eleanor Chang?"

Wallace rose from his chair, his face red. He cast his gaze around the room somewhat desperately, as if looking for an exit. "That is none of your business."

Stan got to her feet, too, and leaned forward, meeting his gaze head-on. "Wrong. Someone's been accused of this murder who is very likely innocent. Fighting with her a week before she died doesn't look so good."

They watched each other for a minute, then Wallace lowered back into the chair, a look of defeat on his face. "You're way out of line, Ms. Connor. Not that it's any of your business, but I'd engaged Ms. Chang as a consultant."

Stan sat back down, too. "To do what?"

"Coach me." He shrugged. "I heard Tony was using her, so I thought I could benefit, too. I don't want to be second fiddle for the rest of my life, after all. She was open to the idea. Didn't think it was a conflict of inter-est."

That was so Eleanor. "So you want to be mayor."

"I haven't ruled it out," he said coolly.

"Did Tony know you hired her?"

He shook his head. "Not to my knowledge. She assured confidentiality." He looked embarrassed. "I didn't want my colleagues to know I needed to work on some . . . stylistic elements of my demeanor."

They probably don't need to be told. The thought flitted through Stan's head and almost exited her mouth. She clamped it shut.

"Nor did I want Tony to know he'd have competition going forward," Wallace added.

"I take it you didn't have the best working relationship with Ms. Chang," Stan said.

He snorted. "She was very demanding. She wanted to dictate, not coach. And she did want me to spar with Tony. Insisted it would be good for both of us to be on top of our games."

"She wanted you at odds," Stan said.

Wallace nodded. "That's what I felt, anyway. Like the landscape here would be more interesting if we were publicly blasting each other. Which meant she never intended to keep our work confidential. I wasn't interested in her tactics. And frankly, she wanted a bigger time commitment than I was able to give. I suppose it was good that she took her work seriously, but I only wanted to meet once a week and get tips on how to be more effective. She wanted me to proactively engage with the media, offer to do speaking engagements . . ." He waved a dismissive hand. "Who has time for all that? And that poor daughter of hers. She brought her along to every meeting, barked orders at her, talked to her as if she was stupid. It was terrible. Not an environment I wanted to be in. I wanted to terminate our relationship."

"Is that what you were fighting about? Did you fire her?"

"I tried. I asked her for a meeting. She insisted we meet at that café. I told her I didn't wish to go there. She didn't care, said if I wanted to meet, that's where it would be."

"So what happened?" Stan asked.

"I fired her," he said simply. "She didn't want to be fired and tried to talk me out of it. More aptly, bully me out of it. She got very nasty. Even said I didn't have what it took to be mayor." He snorted. "Because *that's* such a hard job."

Maybe Monica had misspoken, and it

wasn't Tony she meant when she made the remark to Scott about her mom not letting someone fire her. "Did she threaten you with anything?"

"There was nothing to threaten me with," Wallace said. "There was nothing unseemly about our collaboration. My wife knew about it. She had no leverage."

"Maybe she threatened to out you to Tony."

Wallace nodded. "Sure she did. But what difference would it have made? She'd already told me he was considering a gubernatorial run. My mayoral campaign wouldn't have made much difference to him at all. No, Ms. Connor," he said. "The only thing I'm guilty of is choosing the wrong consultant."

"But then you had to see her again on Saturday night. Did she say anything to you at the party? Cause another scene? What happened, Curtis?"

Wallace's eyes were black slits. "She paid no attention to me Saturday night. She was too busy yelling at the pastor out by the pool shed."

"The pastor?" Stan asked.

"Pastor Ellis from that Unitarian-whatever church. I have no idea what the poor man did to get on her bad side, but maybe you

421

should talk to him. She certainly let him
have it."

CHAPTER 54

"Did you know Pastor Ellis and Eleanor had a fight at the party?" Stan asked Jessie the next morning, her first opportunity to call her.

"I hadn't heard that," Jessie said. Stan could hear cartoons in the background. "It's so weird to be home at this hour," she muttered. "I'm so sick of *Dora the Explorer.* Anyway, go on. What happened?"

"I don't know if Curtis was just deflecting, but he said he heard them out by the pool shed fighting," Stan said.

"Pastor Ellis." Jessie thought about that. "I would hate for that to be true."

"Eleanor brought out the worst in people," Stan said. "I have one more stop I'm making today. Curtis Wallace's brother. Might be a dead end, but I want to see if he'll talk about his old buddy. I have to go, Brenna's here. Call me later."

She went to the front door to meet

Brenna, throwing her arms around her when she walked in. "I'm so relieved," she said, hugging her tight. The dogs, excited about their excitement, joined in by jumping all over them. Except Henry, who stood back and waited to be petted.

Brenna laughed and hugged her back, deftly juggling the lattes in her hand. "About Scott? Jeez, you guys are all too much. I could've told you there was a good explanation. But I guess every dumb woman in love with a guy says that, right? You would've insisted on going off on your own to figure it out. Here." She thrust the tray of coffees at her.

Stan took it, sighing with happiness. "You're spoiling me. Thank you, as always."

"Are you kidding? Izzy just gives it to me. She says we're her favorite business in town next to her own, and we all have to help each other. So drink up."

Stan grinned and sipped. "I have the best friends in the world."

"So you seriously thought Scott and this girl got together and hatched a plot to kill her mother?" Brenna asked as they walked into the kitchen.

It sounded absurd now that she knew it wasn't true. "I panicked when I realized Scott's car had the same sticker and license plate. Especially with Monica's actions. It's wild to think they knew each other. I hate that stupid phrase about it being a small world, but man, it's a small world."

"It is." Brenna dropped her bag on a chair and leaned against the counter. "So is my sister in trouble? She wouldn't tell me anything. I swear, they both treat me like I'm five."

"Careful, or we'll dial it back to treating you like you're three," Jake said from the doorway. They both turned, Brenna's arms crossing her chest defensively. "Kidding," he said, coming over to hug his little sister. She gave in and hugged him back.

"I guess I forgive you," she grumbled, but she smiled.

"You're pretty lucky we like you enough to care," Jake reminded her.

"I know."

"How's Scott? Does he forgive us?" Stan asked.

"Yeah. Which makes it harder for me to stay mad. He's just so darn nice!" she exclaimed. "He knows it looked bad, given the situation." She blushed a little. "And he said he loves it that my family is so protective of me."

"Aww," Stan said.

"I know! This is another reason why he

wants the supervisor job. So he's not out in the field as much. He cares a lot — like, too much — about the people he works with. It's ingrained in him," she said. "His brother had some problems when he was younger. It messed up their family, and it's why he decided to go into social work. But you didn't answer my question. Is Jessie in trouble?"

Jake and Stan looked at each other. "She got suspended," Stan said. "But I'm sure it will get resolved quickly."

"She does everything for her job. She *loves* her job. Why would they suspend her?"

"They're trying really hard to brush this case under the rug," Jake said. "Jessie doesn't believe it's been solved."

Brenna frowned. "So does she really think this girl did it?"

"I'm not sure she knows what to think yet," Stan said.

"Excuse me?"

They all whirled as a voice came from the hallway, Stan's hand flying to her chest. Not even the dogs had heard the door open.

"I'm so sorry to frighten you!" Francie exclaimed.

"Francie, hey. No worries," Stan said. She looked at Jake. "Did I leave the door open?"

"Caitlyn let me in," Francie said. "She was

on her way outside to see the banner."

Stan, Jake, and Brenna all looked at one another. "Banner?" Jake asked.

"Yes. You should go see it," Francie said. "I can't believe you didn't see it on your way in, Brenna."

"I was on the phone," Brenna said. "And drinking my coffee. It's still too early to be observant."

They all went to the door. Caitlyn stood on the porch, her mouth open. Stan followed her gaze. Across the street, a banner was strung up on two poles spanning a large portion of the green directly facing Stan's house. The banner itself was pink with purple text — in what appeared to be size 100 font — reading, I LOVE YOU CAITLYN CONNOR! PLEASE TAKE ME BACK! LOVE, KYLE.

"Oh, my," Stan said. Caitlyn buried her face in her hands.

Brenna and Jake crowded behind Stan. Brenna squealed. "How *adorable* is that?"

Jake elbowed her. Stan held her breath, waiting to see if Caitlyn would freak out. Instead, she looked hopefully at Stan.

"You think now the cops can get him for defacing public property?" she asked.

"Are you sure you don't want me to make

this delivery for you?" Francie asked later that morning. After Caitlyn went upstairs to try to find someone to remove the banner, Jake and Duncan left for the pub and Stan, Brenna, and Francie got to work, with a little help from Eva. "Aren't you going to the wedding meeting this afternoon with your mother? You may be late."

"No, I don't mind at all," Stan said. "I like to meet my new accounts and make sure the places are up to par. The meeting's at three, right?"

Francie nodded.

"I'll make it. I haven't connected with my mother about it, but I'm still planning on going. As long as you two can bake some extras for the fundraiser tonight, I'll be good. But thank you."

"Got it covered," Brenna said. "We have ten batches planned for the fundraiser, and some extras already made if we need them. I'll bring them to Amara's when we're done so they're already on-site when she goes to set up."

"Thank you, thank you," Stan said.

"I brought those carrying cases you were looking for," Francie remembered. "They're in my car."

"You're amazing." Stan'd mentioned she needed an extra pastry carrier for her new client and hadn't had time to order one. "I'll go grab it."

"You don't need to —" Francie began, but Stan waved her off.

"It's the least I can do." She headed outside with Francie still in mid-protest. Francie's Hyundai Elantra was parked at the curb. Spying bags in the backseat, Stan opened the door and peered inside. The first bag held a pile of neatly folded clothes. She moved it out of the way and pulled the next bag over. Same thing. As she went to place it on the floor and reach for the last bag, her eyes fell on the black evening bag with the rhinestone flower and Guess logo on the front, tossed haphazardly on top of some T-shirts. Curious, she lifted the flap.

There was a hole where the snap should've been. Just like the purse Monica Chang was missing.

"Find it okay?" Francie's voice just over her shoulder made her jump, and Stan whacked her head against the roof of the car.

"Ouch," she muttered, rubbing her head. She grabbed the bag with the pastry carrier and backed out of the car. "Yeah, I have it."

"I'm sorry." Francie winced. "I worried you would have to dig through all the dona-tion bags I picked up to bring to the church later, and realized I should've told you which one it was in."

"No worries." Stan shut the car door and they walked back inside together. "Those bags are donations?"

"Yes. We do weekly collections at various spots around town. All the items are distributed to an inner city homeless shelter Pastor Ellis supports."

"How nice," Stan said casually. "Where were these bags picked up, if you don't mind me asking?"

"Those were from town hall," Francie said. "We get nice donations from that spot. People are so generous. Ow! Sweetie, that hurts!" she exclaimed, looking down at Nutty, who'd tried climbing her leg to say hello but apparently deployed his claws while doing so.

"Nutty! Sorry," Stan said. "He does that sometimes. He knows you usually give him treats. Although he's been good not clawing Eva when he's asking her for things."

Francie rubbed her calf and smiled at Nutty. "It's all right. He's such a handsome fella, I could never hold it against him."

CHAPTER 55

Curtis Wallace's brother, Attorney E. Matthew Wallace, lived and worked in the shoreline town of Madison, a mere twenty minutes away from Stan's new client. So after she met and fell in love with the owners of the doggie spa, an adorable retired couple who'd waited their whole lives to open this business and spend their days with dogs, and signed a contract for monthly orders, she plugged the address into her phone and headed toward the water. If nothing else, it was a gorgeous day for a drive. Chilly enough that she needed a jacket, but still warm enough for an open sunroof.

She didn't know if Wallace's brother would even talk to her. Chances were, if he was like his brother, she was wasting her time. But she felt like time was running out. Richard would get a court date. Her mother would move forward marrying Tony. But if he'd had something to do with it . . .

Her mind drifted back to the purse in the donation bag Francie picked up from town hall. Had it been Monica's? With only the girl's description to go on, Stan couldn't be sure. But it sounded like the description she'd given. So who'd dropped it there? Eleanor's killer? The bin would be easy access for Tony Falco, who came into the office every day. Or someone who'd found the purse and tossed it in without another thought? Stan didn't like that option. The normal reaction to finding a purse would be to turn it in to the police. In this case, it would've been super easy, since Jessie's office was at town hall. So that didn't make sense, unless the person thought the bag'd been meant for the donation bin since it was broken.

The other option was Monica herself. Had she tossed the purse as part of a more elaborate scheme — namely, her mother's murder? But how did her evening bag fit into that? Only one explanation made sense. If Scott was right and she'd hoarded drugs in her bag, she could have pretended the bag was lost, sent Stan to find it, then retrieved it from another part of the house before she made her escape. Then she could've removed the drugs and, when she returned to Frog Ledge two days ago, dumped the bag to keep up the charade that it'd been stolen. If she'd killed her mother over a relapse, it made sense.

Or, she could just be crazy. She had to tell Jessie.

As she pulled up in front of the attorney's office, she wondered what the "E." in "E. Matthew Wallace" stood for. Maybe it was simply a requirement for attorneys to include in their names because it felt snooty. In any event, Wallace's office looked snooty. The lawn in front of the brick building was so green Stan had to look twice to make sure it wasn't artificial. She took some pleasure in walking across the grass. She imagined Wallace watching in horror from his office window and wondered if he wore bow ties like his twerpy brother.

The engraved wooden sign next to the door suggested he practiced alone. A small sign in the window said the office was open. She tried the knob. Unlocked. There was no reception desk when she walked in. Instead, a handsome man with good hair and a tan stuck his head out of an inner office. "Good afternoon. How can I help you?" he asked, flashing her a smile full of white teeth.

"Hello. I'm looking for Attorney Wallace."

"You've found him. One second." He

slipped back into the office, then returned a moment later with a notepad and a coffee cup. "Please. Have a seat." He motioned to some comfy-looking chairs in a waiting area. He didn't look like a twerp at all. And he didn't have an assistant? Odd. He certainly didn't look like his brother. Taller and good-looking. And pleasant.

"Coffee?" he asked. "I just made some. I need a little pickup right after lunch."

"No, thank you," Stan said.

"Let me know if you change your mind," Wallace said, taking a seat. "So, what can I do for you?"

Stan sat, too, thrown off by his easy manner. "I'm Stan Connor. I live in Frog Ledge."

He nodded, the same pleasant expression on his face.

"Our mayor is Tony Falco," she said.

Wallace nodded again.

"A woman was murdered at his house last weekend. While Tony was allegedly not there."

"I heard that. What a terrible story." He leaned forward. "Are you seeking legal counsel, Ms. Connor?"

"No! I just . . . I know your family is friendly with Tony. My mother is engaged to him," she explained.

An *aha!* look crossed Wallace's face. "I see. So you're looking for someone to vouch for him," he said with a grin.

Stan flushed. "I heard you two were friends. That you told him to run for mayor and asked your brother to help. Your brother isn't a fan of Tony's lately, it appears."

Matthew Wallace grimaced. "My brother is a horse's behind. Pardon the expression. He goes whichever way the wind blows. I suspect he anticipated Tony would catch some fallout from Saturday's events and was positioning himself accordingly."

"Oh," Stan said, not sure what to say to that.

Wallace got up and went to the window. He took the OPEN sign down and put it out of view, then returned to his chair. He sipped his coffee, his eyes on Stan over the rim of the cup. "Ms. Connor," he said. "I get the sense there's something else you want to ask me."

Stan fidgeted in her chair. "I do. I just didn't figure you'd talk to me."

He raised an eyebrow. "Why wouldn't I talk to you?"

"You're a lawyer," Stan said. "And you're friends with Tony."

He laughed. "You're right on both counts. Tony's not my client. He's my friend. I don't practice criminal law, though. I practice real estate law."

"Oh." Stan thought about that. "Here's the deal, Mr. Wallace —"

"Matthew," he said. "Mr. Wallace is my father. My real first name is Eli, which I despise. So please, call me Matthew."

Stan smiled. She liked E. Matthew Wallace. "Matthew. This woman who was killed at Tony's house. She knew him for a long time, turns out. And Tony allegedly wasn't at the party — his own engagement party — when she was killed. But no one will say where he was, and the cops . . ." She swallowed. She was still taking a chance here. "The cops arrested someone and he . . . couldn't have done it. It feels like they're protecting Tony. And I need to know if he had something to do with this."

But Matthew didn't clam up or get angry. Instead, he laced his fingers behind his head and leaned back in his chair, a troubled look on his face. "I told him this was going to happen," he said quietly. "I told Tony he should just tell people his story. Frankly, it would help in the political realm. But he's so darn stubborn."

Stan frowned, confused. "I don't understand."

"I'll tell you this in confidence, Ms. Connor, only because I've heard so much about you and I know your heart's in the right place," he said. "But you can't tell Tony you know."

"You've heard about *me*?" This was getting freaky.

"Yes. Tony's told me about you. How talented you are, and how you embraced his relationship with your mother despite your difficulties with her. How welcoming you were when he came to town."

Jeez. And here she'd thought Tony didn't like her much at all. She waited for Matthew to continue.

"Tony's been my friend since law school. He's a good man. If you're worried about your mom, don't be," he said. "I wanted to say that first. Now, I'll tell you about Tony's sister, Natalie. She was a good person, too, but she had some problems. I won't go into the details, but she went to jail five years ago, leaving two teenagers behind. The entire family was devastated. Tony took the kids to live with him in Washington. Their father was useless. It was tough but he made it work. A few years ago, he said he wanted to get out of the Washington scene, but still wanted to work in politics — as long as he could do so without his niece and nephew being dragged into any mudslinging. My

brother was on the council in Frog Ledge.
We talked about it. Curtis suggested he run
for mayor, that the incumbent needed a
challenger. Tony liked the idea, so he pursued it — if the kids were on board."

"So he stayed close to them?" Stan asked.
She wondered if her mother knew this story.
If she did, she certainly hadn't shared it.

"Oh, absolutely," Wallace said. "He took
full responsibility for them. His nephew was
in college at that point, but his niece agreed
to move with him if he came up here. Allison was seventeen then. She's going to college now, too, but she's at UConn. She
wanted to stay close to home. To her uncle,
that is."

"What did Tony's sister go to jail for?"
Stan asked.

Wallace hesitated. "A federal crime."

"Okay. So he runs for mayor. How'd this
not come up in the campaign?"

"Because he'd been working with someone
to make sure nothing connected him to his
sister's name. He wanted to protect her kids
from any dirty politics. She'd been married
so it was a bit easier name-wise, but he had
someone who was helping to erase the connections."

"Eleanor Chang," Stan said.

Wallace nodded. "She was very eager to

work on his campaign."

Sure she was. So it could benefit her. "So she pays people to get rid of this black mark, he wins, and moves here. With his niece." She hesitated. "Does he have a lot of money?"

Wallace smiled. "I'm afraid not, although he's comfortable."

"He lives in a nice house," Stan said.

"A family member's home, from what I understand," Wallace said. "On his mother's side."

Tony was related to the Trumbulls? Could also explain why the police had been so accommodating.

"The person couldn't take care of the house anymore and let Tony live there when he won the campaign," Wallace continued. "With one condition. That he take care of the man's cats."

"The cats," Stan murmured. "I wondered. Matthew, thank you for telling me this. But do you know anything about Saturday night?"

"I do," Wallace said. "Tony called and told me the whole story. He was late for the party because he was with his niece, Allison. She'd been in a car accident earlier that day and he'd rushed off to see her."

"Oh, no," Stan said, dismayed. "Is she okay?"

Wallace nodded. "She was brought to the hospital up near the college. He hated being late for the party. Hadn't even told your mother what happened, just that he had to go see Allison. Understandably, she was upset because she didn't know."

"So he really wasn't around," Stan said.

Wallace shook his head. "He doesn't lie, Ms. Connor. If he said he was with his niece, that's where he was. Whatever trouble Ms. Chang found herself, it wasn't with him."

"What about running for governor?" Stan asked.

Wallace laughed. "That was Ms. Chang's push, not his. Tony didn't want to be governor. He told her this many times. In fact, he was about to fire her. He didn't think he needed her help any longer, and she'd become quite insistent about what she thought he should do. He thought it was time for her to move on."

CHAPTER 56

Stan left Wallace's and headed back to Frog Ledge. While she drove, she used her Bluetooth to call Jessie. Who, of course, didn't pick up the phone. With a frustrated sigh, she hit the Disconnect button and drummed her fingers on the steering wheel. Tony wanted to fire Eleanor. Or maybe he'd already tried. What if, like with Curtis Wallace, she didn't want to be fired and a fight ensued? But if Tony had really been at the hospital with his niece, they couldn't have fought that night. At least not in person.

Every answer led to another question. Of course, there was still the possibility that Tony's old friend was protecting him, and the whole story about the niece had been fabricated.

She called Jessie's office. Colby answered. "Can you have someone find out if a college student named Allison got admitted to a hospital near UConn on Saturday?"

Colby hesitated. "Why?"

"Colby. Jessie would just do it."

Colby sighed. "Allison what?"

"I don't know."

"You don't *know*? Which hospital?"

"I don't know that either. But you guys are good at this detecting stuff. It's important. I swear."

She hung up while he was still protesting and called her mother. When she got her voice mail, she left a message. "Mom. It's me. Are you planning on going to the wedding meeting at the church? I'm heading over there. Francie said you wanted me and Caitlyn to go. I'm not sure if Caitlyn can make it, but I can be there. Let me know." It was one o'clock now; she'd have plenty of time. She figured Caitlyn was still dealing with Kyle and the banner. Maybe if she got there early she'd have a chance to talk to Pastor Ellis about Saturday, too, and what his alleged fight with Eleanor had been about. *If* Curtis Wallace was to be believed.

Stan walked up the front steps of the Unitarian Church and pushed the heavy door open, entering the small chapel room with its stained-glass windows, beautiful woodwork, and theater-style seats in a half circle facing the altar. Pastor Ellis sat alone in a back pew. He rose when he saw her. "Hi, Kristan," he said. "Nice to see you again."

"Hi, Pastor. Please, call me Stan," she said. "I didn't see my mother's or Tony's cars. Are they here yet?"

Pastor Ellis sighed. "No. And I can't reach your mother. Tony confirmed he was coming. They're my last meeting before I head up to Vermont for my retreat tonight, otherwise I would've left earlier. We can wait in the meeting room."

Stan followed him down the hall, past an office and another room marked DONA-TIONS. Which reminded her of Monica's bag. Maybe she could take another look at it. Or grab it and bring it to Jessie. "I saw the lovely items from the town hall dona-tion bin," she said casually. "Have you seen them yet?"

Pastor Ellis frowned. "Town hall?"

"Yes, the ones Francie picked up. They were in her car when she came over."

"That's odd," he said. "We don't have donation pickups at the town hall. Perhaps she meant from the schools. We often get items when the teachers hold clothing drives."

No pickup at the town hall? Maybe someone had organized an unofficial collection. Stan made a note to ask her. Who knew — maybe whoever took the purse in the first place, to cover their tracks.

He led her to a small sitting room. A comfy but worn-looking couch faced two chairs. A small bookcase leaned crookedly against the wall with only three books in it. "Can I get you anything?" he asked.

Stan shook her head. "No, thank you."

"I'm glad you came," he said, crossing to a small refrigerator and taking out a water bottle. "How is your mother holding up?"

"She's surviving."

Pastor Ellis nodded. "I hope so. Such a devastating end to what began as a happy night." He uncapped the water.

"It sure was. It must've been hard for you, too, since you knew Eleanor and Monica," Stan said, watching him carefully.

He slowly lowered the bottle without taking a sip. "I wondered how long it would be before that got out," he said. "I try extremely hard to keep my outside activities separate from my life here in Frog Ledge, but in this case, clearly that wasn't meant to be."

"You worked with Monica Chang," Stan said.

"I did. The poor woman had a terrible time. Her mother was desperate to get her help. And her counselor knew of our new program and thought she would be a good fit."

"Scott Grayson," Stan said.

Ellis nodded. "Small world, isn't it?" he said with a sad laugh, echoing Stan's comments from earlier today.

"What was so special about this program?" Stan asked.

"Our high success rate with young adults. That's our focus. It's a progressive facility, with very innovative leaders. And the center was piloting a new program. They'd just bought a facility down by the shore. A former convent. Quiet, removed, and combined with some cutting-edge treatments that had great outcomes with the test groups."

"Yet Monica relapsed," Stan pointed out.

"So I've heard." Ellis smiled, but there was no mirth. "We're not miracle workers. Sometimes our patients are up against insurmountable odds and their personalities . . . make it difficult for them to enjoy continued success."

"Her mother got in the way," Stan said bluntly.

"That sounds so judgmental."

"Did you know before Saturday night that Monica relapsed?" Stan asked.

Ellis nodded slowly. "Eleanor contacted me about a month ago. She had concerns but no hard proof, so she didn't contact the treatment center. She was angry about it, given the money she'd spent to get Monica into that program."

"Pastor Ellis," Stan said. "Did you and Eleanor have a fight Saturday night?"

Now the pastor's face went ashen. "How did you —"

"It doesn't matter. Someone heard you," Stan said. "What were you fighting about?"

Pastor Ellis drank some water. Wiping his mouth with the back of his hand, he carefully capped the bottle and placed it on the floor next to his chair. "I'm ashamed that I lost my temper," he said. "But I couldn't stand her using her money and imagined influence again to solve a problem without taking time to fully understand what was *driving* the problem."

Stan didn't know what he was talking about. "Pastor, it's been a long week, and Tony's going to show up any minute. Can you please not speak in riddles?"

Ellis sat up straighter. "Fine. Eleanor wanted me to pull strings and get her daughter back in the same program she'd participated in previously. She felt I *owed* it to her, since the treatment failed." He shook his head, pressing his lips so tightly together they nearly disappeared. "A ludicrous statement. But, that was her modus operandi."

"So you said you wouldn't help her."

"It's not that I didn't want to help Monica. Of course I did. I want to help all of them." He looked away, but not before Stan saw tears glinting in his eyes. He swallowed and took a minute to steady his voice. "But I wanted Eleanor to understand that she was part of the problem. At least according to her daughter. And rehab wasn't going to work if Monica was just going to be released into the same environment. You know," he said, turning back to Stan, "people think addicts only have to fear going back to their addict friends. But if they're in living situations that are inherently stressful, it's just as bad. Anyway, I wanted her to know that if she tried to pull any of the shenanigans like last time, I'd put a stop to it myself."

"A stop to it *how*?"

He grimaced. "Not like that. I meant I'd speak to the directors and let them know what she was doing. There's no reason deserving people should be denied treatment simply because she had more money to throw around."

Stan frowned. "What do you mean?"

Ellis hesitated. Stan leaned forward in her

chair. "Someone's been accused of this murder who shouldn't be. There's a chance they're going to reopen this case." She prayed it was true. "You were seen fighting with Eleanor."

"I hope you're not insinuating —"

"I'm just trying to find out what happened," Stan said. "Tell me why you were angry with her."

Ellis sank back into his chair. "I shouldn't be talking about any of this. But I'll tell you," he said as Stan opened her mouth to protest. "The first time, when she approached us about the program, it was full. The next one wasn't scheduled for six months, and she felt Monica couldn't wait. She pulled every string she could think of, but they had a strict cutoff for participants." He hesitated. "But Eleanor was very . . . resourceful. She found that one of the people on the list was not self-funding, that their participation was negotiated at a reduced rate as a gesture of goodwill. She went to the director and offered double the original fees for her daughter to attend. I'm ashamed to say the board voted to take the money. It was a new program and they were on a shoestring."

"They just tossed the other person out?" Stan asked. "They couldn't make an exception for one person?"

"They only had a certain number of counselors. Based on the structure of the program they'd built and gotten approval for, they couldn't deviate from the structure they developed. Believe me," he said. "I live with the guilt every day. They tried to find other accommodations for the person, but it didn't pan out. And a month later, the boy overdosed and died."

Stan sucked in a breath. What a tragedy. For everyone involved.

"I can see why you wouldn't want to live through that again," Stan said.

Ellis nodded. "I didn't kill that woman, Stan. God forgive me, but I was very angry with her. And it didn't help that I have to see every day what happened to that other family. I was blind with rage Saturday night, thinking of it happening to someone else. But I would never stray that far from my faith."

"What do you mean, you have to see it every day?" Stan asked.

He looked at her quizzically, then his face fell. "You don't know."

Stan shook her head. "Know what?"

"The boy who died after not getting into the program was Francie's son."

Stan felt like she'd been punched in the

gut. As she tried to process that development, a voice came from the doorway. They both jumped, startled. She spun around and saw Tony Falco hovering in the doorway.

He stared at both of them. "Sorry, I thought you heard me come in. Have you seen my fiancée?"

CHAPTER 57

Stan, Tony, and Pastor Ellis waited half an hour for Patricia. When she didn't show up, Tony wanted to look for her but Stan said she'd go. She left the church and drove to the B&B, her heart in her chest, her gut twisted into knots. Francie's son died of a drug overdose after Eleanor used her money and influence to steal his seat in a rehab program.

So what did that mean? Francie was at the party, too. But that was absurd. Francie, the sweet, sad woman who'd lost her family and worked three jobs — one of them at a church, for heaven's sake — could not be a cold-blooded killer. It was insane.

Was it? She had Monica's purse and lied about where it came from.

With shaking hands, she took out her cell phone and dialed Jessie. Voice mail. She left a hurried message for Jessie to call her — no details — as she pulled into the B&B

parking lot. Before she got out of the car she took a quick look around for any reporters or camera people hiding in the bushes, then bolted for the front door. She had an hour before the fundraiser.

She knocked. No answer, but she heard voices inside. She tried the door. Open, so she stepped in. "Char?" she called, following the noise to the kitchen. When she got there, she stopped in amazement. No Char. Instead, her mother and Kyle McLeod sat at the kitchen table together with two empty bottles of wine. Kyle held a half-full bottle mid-pour over her mother's glass.

"Mom?" she asked. "What's going on?"

They both turned in her direction. "Stan!" Kyle jumped up and gave her a sloppy hug. "So glad you came."

Stan shoved him off her and turned to her mother. "We were at the church waiting for you. What's going on?"

Her mother waved her hand, sloshing wine. "I'm not getting married," she announced.

Oh, good Lord. She did *not* have time for this. "What are you talking about? Of course you are."

"No," her mother said. "I'm not. I've decided."

Kyle nodded. "I've decided, too. I'm

gonna go home. Your sister hates my guts." He slurred the last words. "She ripped my banner down."

Stan closed her eyes and counted to ten. When she opened them, they were both still in front of her, both drunk. "You know, this is great," she said, her hands going to her hips. "Really great. You're both quitters now? Kyle," she said, turning and pointing a finger at him. "I thought you said you'd changed."

He raised his hands as if she'd pointed a gun at him. "I am. I did."

"No, you didn't. You're still running away from your problems. You told Char you'd be here as long as it took. It's been four days. If you love my sister, then act like it. Stop behaving like you're five and go convince her. And you," she said, whirling and pointing the same finger at her mother, who looked equally as startled. "If you're worried that Tony killed someone, you should ask him. Or call the cops on him. But if you really know where he was Saturday, and it's true, then you have no reason to be upset with him. Get over yourself, Mom. For once, try to see how hard other people are trying to please you. And that's all I have to say to both of you. I have bigger fish to fry tonight."

Stan stormed back down the hall to the front door, almost knocking Char off the front stoop. "They're in there getting drunk and being stupid," she said, before Char could say anything. "Can you please talk sense into them?" Without waiting for an answer, she hurried to her car and drove to the clinic and the fundraiser.

"You look frazzled," Amara said immediately when she got out of the car and joined the setup crew. "Have you gotten any rest since last weekend?"

Stan didn't want to think about it. "I'm fine."

Amara snorted. "Right. And I'm a contestant on *The Voice*. The dog cookies are awesome, though." She picked one up off the tray and admired it. "So creative."

They were. Brenna and Francie went all out with the designs. The one Amara held was shaped like a police badge. "Brenna and Francie get all the credit for those," Stan said. "What can I do? I'm sorry I'm late."

"No worries, we're almost all set up. Your trooper is here with his dog." She winked. "He's a hottie."

"I won't tell Vince you said that. Is Jessie here, too?"

Amara shook her head. "Haven't seen her."

Stan resisted the urge to curse out loud as Eva ran up to her. "Hi Auntie Krissie! I'm helping the dogs!" her niece exclaimed. "I'm gonna have a job here!"

"That's so sweet, Eva," Stan said.

Caitlyn came up behind her. "She's in love with this place. I swear, she's going to follow in one of your footsteps," she said.

"I think she's better off doing food then vet care," Amara said.

Stan walked away a few steps to call Jessie again. Voice mail, again. She felt a hand on her arm and turned. Colby, with Rosie by his side. Rosie wagged her tail.

"Hey," he said. "This is great, Stan. Thank you so much."

"You're very welcome." She crouched to say hello to Rosie. "Can I pet her?"

"Of course."

Stan crouched and rubbed Rosie's head. The dog rewarded her with a big kiss.

"And look." Colby reached into his pocket and pulled out a check.

Stan looked at it, then at him. "A thousand bucks? From Diane?"

He nodded. "Her brother is a K9 handler in the military. Said she's in awe of our dogs. This is so great. I love this town already."

"I learn something new about this place every day," Stan said. "I'm glad. Hey, have you heard from Jessie?"

He shook his head. "No."

"Trooper Colby!" Amara called from across the parking lot. "Can you bring Rosie over here?"

He looked at her, apologetic. "I have to run. Talk to you in a few."

She nodded and watched him go, then tried Marty's house again in hopes of tracking down Jessie. No answer there. Being suspended was one thing, but going dark every time Stan needed her was quite another. She didn't want to tell anyone about what she'd learned before talking to her. Jessie would probably tell her she was nuts. That everyone in town could vouch for Francie.

And yet . . .

She'd been at the party. A grieving mother with a motive. Stan kept coming back to that simple point. In that state, she imagined how easy it could be to lose sight of reality and blame someone who, granted, had acted selfishly, but couldn't be held responsible for another person's choices.

Her cell phone startled her out of her reverie. She glanced at the number. No one in her contacts list. "Hello."

"Stan. It's Scott."

"Scott," she repeated. "What's up? Is Brenna okay?"

"She's fine. But I think Monica's in trouble."

"Monica?" Stan asked, her voice sounding far away even to her own ears. "What do you mean?"

"I got a message a little while ago from Monica that she was going to be in Frog Ledge tonight. Said she got a text message from Pastor Ellis to attend a group session at the church. She must be feeling lousy because she said she wanted to go and asked if we could meet for coffee afterward. But Pastor Ellis told me — unless I've got my dates screwed up — that he was going away tonight on a retreat. The church voice mail says he's out of town," Scott said. "By the time I got the message and called both their phones, neither of them are answering."

"He is out of town," Stan said slowly. "I saw him this afternoon, right before he left. My mother and Tony were supposed to be his last meeting."

Silence. "So then, what's going on?" he asked.

"Meet me at the church in ten minutes," Stan said. "And try to call Jessie. I've been calling her all day with no luck."

Stan tried Jessie's cell once more to no avail. Frustrated, she went looking for Trooper Colby. He stood with two state police K9 officers and their dogs, a black Lab and a German shepherd. And Captain Quigley stood with them. Great. She couldn't exactly break up their little party with the revelation that she may know who'd killed Eleanor Chang with Quigley the Cover-Upper in the vicinity. She could text Colby, but he'd likely not see it. His demo was starting any minute and the crowd had multiplied, with people anxious to meet the dogs.

She and Scott would have to deal with it. She hurried to her car and hopped in, pulling out as inconspicuously as possible, and headed for the church.

CHAPTER 58

When Stan arrived, she cruised slowly though the parking lot. Parked at the very back, an old BMW that looked like the one Monica Chang was driving the other day. No other cars were present. Dread coursed through Stan's veins. Was she inside? Or had she been taken somewhere?

She drove back around and parked out front, hoping her car might serve as an SOS signal if Jessie happened by. She raced up the front steps and grabbed the door handle. Locked. She went back down the steps and circled to the back of the building. There was a basement entrance she remembered from last winter's Groundhog Day celebration that led to a meeting room, bathroom and a kitchen. She tried that door.

Also locked.

If Monica was in trouble, she couldn't get to her.

She went back around front in time to see

Scott careening into the parking lot. He was out of the car and running toward her without even shutting the door. "What's going on?" he demanded.

"The doors are locked, but her car's here. Out back. I think she's in trouble," she said flatly. "I think the woman who works here killed her mother."

Scott frowned. "What woman?"

"Francie Tucker." Stan gave him an abridged version of Pastor Ellis's story.

"You're kidding."

"I'm not. And we don't have time to talk about it. If Monica's here and Pastor Ellis didn't call her, then something's wrong."

"Is there a back door?" Scott asked.

Stan nodded and led him around back.

He pulled something out of his pocket and positioned himself so he blocked her view of the door. "Don't look."

"Really?" she muttered. "The least you could do is show me how to break in. It could come in handy."

He ignored her and went to work on the lock. It took less than a minute before it turned in his hand. "Cheesy lock," he said, then shrugged. "You pick up skills along the way." Scott shoved the door open and stepped inside.

Stan didn't ask. She followed him in, shining the flashlight app from her iPhone. The meeting room was dark. She pointed to the bathroom. They took up positions like cops in a TV show. Stan stood to the side with her phone while Scott shoved the door open. Also empty. The Keystone Kops came to mind, and Stan clenched her jaw to avoid bursting into a hysterical fit of laughter.

They moved side by side down the hall, sweeping the light in front of them, until they got to the stairs. Stan paused and dimmed the light. They both listened. Nothing.

"I'll go first," Scott whispered.

Stan protested, but he slipped in front of her, leaving no room for argument. Chivalry was still alive in Frog Ledge.

She followed him as quietly as possible to the top of the steps. He pushed the door open a crack and listened. Hearing nothing, he nudged it open enough that they could step through. They were in the hall, directly across from the meeting room where she'd met with Pastor Ellis earlier today. The door was closed. Stan pointed to the chapel and jerked her thumb at Scott, indicating he should look there. Scott nodded and slipped down the hall. Stan went to the meeting room door and nudged it open. At first glance, empty. Then she realized one of the chairs was at a different angle than it had been earlier, its back facing the door. The chair was tall, and she might have closed the door and gone on her way if she hadn't noticed what looked like black fringe dangling over the arm.

Taking a tentative step into the room, she peered over the edge of the chair. And gasped when she realized the fringe was hair. And it belonged to Monica Chang, who was slumped over in the chair.

"Oh, no," she cried, rushing to her side and dropping to her knees next to Monica, desperate to see her chest rising and falling, feel a pulse, anything. It seemed like five minutes, or an eternity, before she saw the faintest movement that said she was at least still alive.

"No, no, no," she murmured, hands shaking as she fumbled for her cell phone.

"Don't bother." The familiar voice came from the doorway, and Stan felt her own heart nearly stop when she turned and saw Francie Tucker in the doorway. Holding a pistol.

CHAPTER 59

"Francie." Stan rose slowly, holding her hands out. "What happened to her? What are you doing with a *gun*?"

Francie looked down at her hand like she hadn't even realized the weapon was there. "It's Pastor Ellis's," she said with a shrug. "He spends a lot of nights in the inner city. Have to protect yourself these days. He thought he'd hid it well, but I saw him tuck it away in a hidden compartment in his desk." She stepped forward and snatched Stan's phone out of her hand. "And don't bother looking for your friend," she said. "We've already bumped into each other."

Fear clutched Stan's chest. "Is he . . ."

"I didn't shoot him, if that's what you mean," she said. "I don't believe in killing people for the sake of it, Stan. I thought you could figure that much out. Since we've gotten so close lately." She smiled, but her eyes were flat. Dead, Stan realized with a chill. "He's indisposed, though. I had no choice. I'm leaving here tonight without interference. So you can decide how this goes."

Stan looked down at Monica, desperate to see her still breathing. "What did you do to her? Did you give her something? We need to call an ambulance, Francie. Now. Look. I'm sure whatever happened, you didn't mean it. Let's just get her some help and we can get it sorted out later, okay?"

"Do to her?" Francie sneered. "She's an addict. She loves to drink. And take whatever poison she can get her hands on. She got very upset when she realized Pastor Ellis wasn't here. So I simply gave her some liquor to calm her nerves, with some of her own pills mixed in. The ones she had in her purse Saturday night when she was throwing it in my face that she'd wasted her opportunity to get better. Wasted it while my son didn't even get a chance to get better and paid with his life!" Her voice rose to a fevered pitch, and Stan could see the glint of madness in her eyes. Despite the fear clutching her like a vise, she felt compassion for this woman. She was so broken.

"Francie," she said, taking a step forward, trying to speak calmly. "I'm so sorry about your son. I can't even imagine what you've gone through. But this is not you. You're a good person. I love working with you. You rebuilt your life after something so tragic. Don't throw it away now. Please, let me call for help."

But Francie jerked the gun up higher. "Don't move," she said, her voice choked with emotion. "You're right. You have no idea what I went through. The struggles my beautiful Andrew faced. He wasn't an addict. *They* did this to him. Those doctors. He got hurt playing sports. They gave him those terrible pills. For pain, they said. Just for a few months. But a few months later he was doing heroin."

Stan sucked in a breath. "Francie. I'm so —"

Francie cut her off. "You have *no idea,*" she said again. "My husband left me to deal with it because he couldn't do it anymore. Then one day Andrew didn't come home." Tears rolled down her face now, but she held the gun steady. "The Hartford police came to tell me they'd found him two days later, and how the drugs he bought were laced with something toxic. You have no idea. Neither does she." She jerked her head toward Monica's still form. "And that mother of hers. She deserved what she got. She had no remorse. She didn't even remember me, or my son. She didn't care that she'd used her money to toss his life aside." She shrugged. "So I didn't care that I tossed hers aside."

"You killed her," Stan said softly.

Francie's eyes narrowed into slits. "I did. I didn't intend to. I went to tell her that Monica was drinking. She didn't want to hear it. Didn't even know who I was."

"Were you trying to frame my mother? By leaving her ring . . . where you did?"

"Frame her?" Francie looked shocked, like she hadn't even thought of that. "My goodness, no. I'd gone to get your mother's ring for her when I happened upon Eleanor, upstairs where she wasn't even supposed to be. She didn't care. She didn't care about anything but herself. She told me to mind my own business. She was surprised, though. When she finally realized who I was." She smiled coldly. "At about the same time as she realized I wasn't going to let go of the scarf around her neck. Your mother's ring — I'd put it on the bathroom counter. And it seemed so fitting. Such a token of wealth and power. No offense to your mother, of course. But I wanted to silence that horrid woman with something she could relate to."

Stan's entire body went cold as ice.

Francie'd gone from sounding like a broken-hearted mother to a cold-blooded killer within seconds. And she had a very bad feeling about her chances of getting out of here to find Monica help in time.

"So what are you planning to do to us?" she asked. "Are you just going to let her die, Francie? That makes you just as bad as Eleanor."

Francie's face went blank with rage. "Shut up! You don't know anything." She motioned with the gun. Did she even know how to shoot it? Stan thought maybe she should try to grab it.

"I put enough pills in her Jack Daniel's that she should be out of her misery soon," Francie said. "Good thing the good pastor keeps a stash of booze. I didn't even have to go buy any. It took a little bit to get her to drink it all, but in the end she gave in. She wanted it." Francie shrugged. "I'm going to leave. It's up to you whether you're going to cause a problem or not. I don't want to hurt you, Stan, but I can't stay in Frog Ledge." She looked around, dropping the gun to her side. "Too many memories."

"Francie. I'll let you go. Just give me the phone so I can get help for Monica. Please," Stan begged. "Trooper Pasquale knows I'm here," she lied. "She'll figure it out soon enough. You should go. Now."

The gun was back, pointing at her again. "She doesn't need help. She needs to be put out of her misery. Like they said about my son. He's happier now," she mimicked, her voice taking on that frenzied pitch again. "He's not sick anymore. Well, what about me? What about *me*?" The last word turned into a scream of anguish, then everything happened so fast.

Scott dove through the door, throwing himself at Francie's legs in an attempt to surprise tackle her. She went down. Stan heard the gun clatter to the floor, miraculously not going off and shooting her. She dove, casting about desperately, but couldn't find it. On the edges of her vision she saw Francie reach for it, getting to her feet, everything slow motion. Scott was already up and yelling something, the syllables crashing together in an onslaught of words she couldn't grasp. And then she heard a *crack* and felt something shatter behind her as she dropped her head and heard the sound of a body thudding to the floor.

CHAPTER 60

Two weeks later

"I think the ovens should go here," Char insisted, making a note on the piece of paper she and Patricia hunched over at Stan's kitchen table. "She needs space. That way, there's room here for the refrigerator and you're not eating into counter space."

Patricia inclined her head in agreement. "Okay," she said. "I can live with that. As long as we have marble counters. When she gives tours and classes, she needs a classy kitchen."

"Tours and classes?" Brenna murmured to Stan. The two were at the counter, each with two mixing bowls going. They were down a baker, and the orders were backing up. This rainy, chilly Saturday morning was all about catching up before the day's big plans. And spending time with people they loved.

"I guess she's adding that to my offerings." Stan smiled. "It's fine. She's been much better. Actually asking me what I want. So I let her order the pastry cases from her person. Life's too short. My shop's opening. We're all still here. That's all that matters."

"Yeah." Brenna sobered.

"How's Scott doing?" Stan asked quietly. She'd relived the moment in the church every night since, knowing how close they'd both come to serious injury or death. When Francie made the split-second decision to turn the gun on herself, she could've easily shot one or both of them, too.

"He's devastated. Definitely taking it personally." Brenna dropped batter onto a cookie sheet. "I know he understands on a logical level it wasn't his fault, but he feels like he let Monica down. He's not even sure he wants to stay in that line of work."

Monica Chang hadn't survived that horrible night in the church despite the best efforts of the emergency responders. Francie thought she'd knocked Scott out with a paperweight from Pastor Ellis's office, but dazed and bleeding he'd still been able to call for help before he tried to take Francie out himself. Jessie, however, had already been en route. With Captain Quigley, who hadn't been in town to keep an eye on her, but to help figure out who really killed Eleanor. The Trumbull family, Tony's second cousins, had put the pressure on to keep things quiet while they investigated, but Jessie had been relieved to find out no one was trying to cover anything up. Quigley had publicly suspended Jessie to take the heat off all of them, but had been working with her behind the scenes.

"Scott's a hero and he should know that," Stan said.

"Hear, hear," Char called from the table. "What a brave man you have there, Brenna."

"Maybe someday he'll be ready to hear that," Brenna said. "But not now."

Patricia, uncharacteristically quiet, squeezed Char's hand across the table. "Char's right. He tried his best for that poor girl."

The front door opened and the sound of stampeding dogs and laughter filtered down the hallway. Jake entered the kitchen, followed by Caitlyn and Kyle holding hands. Eva rode on Kyle's shoulders. The dogs raced excitedly around them, dodging between legs.

"The house is adorable," Caitlyn announced. "And it's right near Izzy's. We're totally getting it. Thanks for taking us over, Jake."

"Anytime." Jake came over and wrapped Stan in a hug. "They're a lot faster than us," he joked. "Two weeks back together and they're buying a house. In Frog Ledge, no less."

Stan poked him in the chest with her spatula. "Hey, we're not in a race. I think we're doing just fine."

"You guys are our role models," Caitlyn said. "And I love it here. Especially now that I'm getting a job at Izzy's bookstore. My dream job, no less. And working for you, too, of course," she added hurriedly, looking at Stan. "And the schools are great. Eva's looking forward to making some new friends."

"And y'all need more restaurants," Kyle drawled. "Perfect place to open a vegan, organic eatery, don't you think?"

"I love restaurants," Char said.

"Especially that kind," Stan added.

"Plus, we needed the house. For the dog," Caitlyn said.

Char pressed a hand to her heart. "You're gonna make me cry. Adopting Cooper is the nicest thing you could do in Francie's memory." She blinked away tears. "I'm sorry. I know she was troubled, but I'm just so sad for her. Now, you finish those cookies," she said briskly to Stan. "We have to get to Jessie's party."

Tonight, they were celebrating Jessie's promotion to sergeant, the direct result of her hard work and dogged determination to do whatever was necessary to solve this case.

"You're right. Going back to the B&B to change." Kyle kissed Caitlyn. "Be back in an hour to pick you up."

Jake grinned. "Jessie hates us for this, you know. But the pub's all decorated and ready to go. The whole town will be there."

"Hey, you don't get promoted every day," Char said with a shrug. "She'll have to deal with it. Just like your momma over here, getting all mad at her surprise engagement party."

Patricia blushed. "I was not angry. You just didn't need to do that, is all."

They'd partied last night, too, at the B&B. A decidedly smaller, but much happier engagement party so Patricia and Tony could celebrate together. Patricia was moving back into Tony's house this weekend. With the suspicions about him cleared up, the wedding was back on. Stan thought it might be time to get to know him a little better.

Brenna stuck the last two trays into the oven and set the timer. "I'm going to get ready. I'll see you later at the pub," she told

Stan. With a wave to everyone, she slipped out the door.

Char stood. "I'm going, too. Have to pick out my outfit and make sure Raymond's dressed. See you soon!" She blew them a kiss and followed Brenna out the door.

When Stan, Jake, and her mother were the only ones left, Patricia looked at Jake. "Do you have it?"

Jake nodded.

"Have what?" Stan asked distractedly, checking the cookies through the oven door.

"This," Jake said.

She turned to find him holding a hand-carved, bone-shaped, red wooden sign with the word STAN'S carved into it in yellow.

"To match your walls," he said, referring to the sunny yellow color she'd decided on for the shop. "And to make sure everyone knows the place is yours. From your mother and me."

She felt tears well up and spill over, and all she could do was hug them both. Tight.

"I'll put it upstairs for you," Jake said, taking it from her. "Until the shop's ready for it." He kissed her cheek and left the room, then poked his head back in. "Almost forgot, this was in the mail." He handed her a postcard. "No name, though."

She took it, turning it over in her hands.

The front of the postcard was a brilliant beach scene, with a mountain she didn't recognize in the background. On the back, it said *Sunset over Ahmed beach, view of Mount Agung, Bali.*

Bali? Her gaze drifted to the four words scrawled in the white space: "You taught me well."

Richard. She broke into a grin. It felt like the last scene of *The Shawshank Redemption.*

She looked up to find her mother watching her. "Glad he didn't need to skip bail to get there," she said softly. "I really didn't want to be out two million dollars."

Stan's mouth dropped open. "You . . . *you* bailed Richard out?"

Patricia nodded. "I knew he didn't do it. Of course, I knew Tony didn't do it, either. Well, I was ninety-eight percent sure," she amended.

Stan linked arms with her mother and walked her out of the kitchen. She thought it might not be so bad having her whole family here in town.

RECIPES

BLUEBERRY BISCUITS
1 1/2 cup wheat flour
2/3 cup oatmeal
1/4 cup flaxseed meal
1 cup blueberries
1/2 cup vanilla Greek yogurt
1/2 cup water

Combine all dry ingredients in a large bowl. Add wet ingredients and mix well.

Using a cookie scoop, drop tablespoon-size amounts of mixture onto a lightly greased cookie sheet.

Bake at 350 degrees for 18 minutes.

Cookies may be dehydrated for a longer shelf life.

VEGETABLE BEEF CRACKERS
1 tablespoon chopped parsley
1/2 cup shredded carrots

2 ounces of vegetable beef (or beef only) baby food
1 egg
1 tablespoon vegetable oil
3/4 cup water
2 cups wheat flour
1 1/2 cups white flour

Combine all ingredients in bowl, adding flours last. Mix until well blended.

On a lightly floured surface, knead dough for about 3 minutes.

Roll out dough to 1/4-inch thickness and cut out shapes using mini cookie cutters of your choice.

Bake on a lightly greased cookie sheet for 25 minutes at 350 degrees.

Cookies may be left in oven after baking (while oven cools down) to harden for a crunchier bite.

Yields about 35 cracker-size cookies.

PARMESAN CHEESE BONES

2 eggs
1 tablespoon vegetable oil
1 cup water
4 cups unbleached all-purpose flour
1 tablespoon active dry yeast
1 tablespoon garlic powder
1 cup grated Parmesan cheese

Mix all wet ingredients. Add flour and remainder of dry ingredients, and mix well. (About 2 minutes in a stand mixer.)

Roll out dough to 1/8-inch–1/4-inch and cut into 2-inch or 3-inch bones.

Convection bake at 350 for 20 minutes or until golden brown.

Treats may be dehydrated for a longer shelf life.

COCONUT-CAROB COOKIES
(MAKES APPROXIMATELY 18 COOKIES)

1 cup oat flour
1/2 cup old-fashioned oats
1/2 cup shredded unsweetened coconut
1 tablespoon vegetable oil
2/3 cup water
1/4 cup carob chips

Combine all ingredients except for carob chips. Using a cookie scoop, drop batter onto a lightly greased cookie sheet. Bake at 350 degrees for 25 minutes.

While cookies are baking, slowly melt carob chips. This can be done in the microwave, heating carob in 10- to 20-second intervals or on the stovetop using a double boiler on low heat. Carob can be thinned out with a drop or two of vegetable oil to help with desired consistency.

Once cookies are done and have cooled, drizzle melted carob over the top. No pastry bag necessary; this can simply be done with a spoon and a light hand. Allow a few minutes for carob to harden and then feed to drooling doggies! Cookies can be dehydrated prior to topping with carob for a longer-lasting shelf life.

Recipes courtesy of The Big Biscuit, Franklin, Massachusetts.

ACKNOWLEDGMENTS

This is always my favorite part of writing the book — saying thank you to all the people who've helped get it to the finish line, in one form or another. So thank you to all the readers, who make this writing life possible. To my agent, John Talbot, for creating this series with me — can you believe we're on book five? John Scognamiglio, my editor, and the whole team at Kensington, thank you for making the books even better, and for the fabulous covers!

I'm lucky enough to have a neighbor in law enforcement, although he may not feel so lucky when I start asking him questions. A huge thank-you to Officer Chris Worchel for answering all my questions about how to handle murder at a dinner party without suspecting me of illicit activities.

I've made so many special friends on this writing journey, and I'm grateful for every single one of them. Most especially my besties, the Wicked Cozy Authors — Jessie Crockett / Jessica Estevao, Sherry Harris, Julie Hennrikus / Julianne Holmes, Edith Maxwell / Maddie Day, and Barbara Ross — what would I do without you on this crazy journey? I'm thankful every day for you (and all your alter egos!).

And Sherry, thank you for always being my first editor, even when I'm under the gun and you're on deadline, too. You're amazing.

My close-to-home writing and art group was instrumental in helping me hammer out the nitty-gritty details of this book during our Sunday sessions, so thanks to Kim Fleck (for that and so much more — see below!), Dacia Jackson, and Shari Randall for helping me keep my creativity going!

Of course, Vanessa Sealy from The Big Biscuit in Franklin, Massachusetts, must be thanked for always testing out thoughtful, yummy recipes for these books. The dogs and cats love them and we hope your pets will, too.

I always name a couple of animal rescue angels in these pages. This time we're giving a schnoodle shout-out in honor of Scruffy to the Miniature Schnauzers & Friends Rescue out in California. Schnauzers/ schnoodles are near and dear to my heart, and this place does great work for these guys — as well as other schnauzer mixes. Check them out at *msfr.org*. My other shout-out is to the Starfish Animal Rescue group, which is doing amazing work in rural Kentucky saving animals from the many high-kill shelters out there. They're at *starfishanimal rescue.com,* and they rock.

Thanks to my own family, furry and human — thank you for putting up with me while I wrote this book amidst two major life changes, especially Cynthia and Doug Fleck for their unwavering support.

And Kim, I know you probably won't remember this next time I'm in Book Jail and next to impossible to deal with, but I appreciate everything you do for all of us. As the backbone of Brand Fearless, you keep us alive on social channels, and at home, you make everything better. Thanks for keeping things afloat and being the best partner anyone could ask for. Love you always.

The employees of Thorndike Press hope you have enjoyed this Large Print book. All our Thorndike, Wheeler, and Kennebec Large Print titles are designed for easy reading, and all our books are made to last. Other Thorndike Press Large Print books are available at your library, through selected bookstores, or directly from us.

For information about titles, please call:
    (800) 223-1244

or visit our website at:
    gale.com/thorndike

To share your comments, please write:
    Publisher
    Thorndike Press
    10 Water St., Suite 310
    Waterville, ME 04901